Five Star Fraud

For Linda,
Thank you for
Reading my book,

Five Star Fraud

Margaret G. Cahill

Margaret G. Cahill
March 9, 2010

This story is a work of fiction. Names, characters, places, and incidents either are products of the author's imagination or are used fictitiously. Any resemblance to actual events, locations, or persons, living or dead, is entirely coincidental.

Dedication

In memory of my brother Michael who first enlightened me to a corporation's capacity for corruption.

Acknowledgments

Many people brought this project to fruition. I am blessed to be a part of a clan by blood and by choice that includes my wonderful supportive husband, Edward, my three sisters, Evelyn, Mary Ellen, and Rita, three brothers Vincent, Thomas, and Kieran, their spouses, and their children.

Along my life's journey I have had the good fortune to connect with numerous encouraging people. I am grateful and indebted to Charlotte writing instructors, Judith Simpson, Maureen Ryan Griffin, and Gilda Morina Syverson; to my critique group, Penny Lindblom, Elaine St. Anne and Joanne Williamson and especially to early readers of sections of my manuscript who offered insightful suggestions—Kathleen Cummings, Karen Early, Pam Haddock, Beverly Kibler, Sandy LeBouef, Cynthia Lynes, Todd McCuen, Priscilla Meyer, Beryl Owen, and Liddy Wilson.

Those who critically assessed the entire novel include Marilyn and Tom Cahill, Linda DeLuca, Julia Gillespie, Susan Haran, and Rita Toscano.

I also want to thank Donna Spigarolo for consistent encouragement, Jan and Joe Borden, Vonnie Hines, and Todd McCuen for their specific expertise, and Dr. Aaron Toscano for technical support.

Chapter 1

Neil grabbed the large, brass handle of the oversized, mahogany front door and stepped into the building's foyer.

"Good morning! You must be Neil," the receptionist greeted him from her desk.

A broad smile broke out on the man's face as he noticed the message stand, just inside the door, that said *Welcome Neil Landers, Director of Research*.

"Can you tell we're happy you've joined our company?" the receptionist asked.

"Very nice—thank you."

"Mr. Byrnes's secretary is expecting you." The receptionist dialed an extension. "You'll like living in the south."

"I don't need an overcoat in February. Flowers are in bloom. What's not to like?"

A woman of about forty, attractive and petite, came into the lobby, wearing a tailored, black dress, a necklace of colorful beads, and low-heeled shoes.

"Good morning, Neil," the woman said. "I'm Doris Kingston. Mr. Byrnes will be in later. We'll start with the routine paperwork for new employees."

She led him to his office in the back of the building.

The lack of a human resource department surprised Neil. This family-owned business had a national presence and to a small degree was international. Strange, that the CEO's secretary handled the personnel paperwork.

"This won't take long," Doris assured him. "I just need you to sign your name several times."

Stifling any comments as he looked at the stack of papers, Neil sat down at his desk.

"Bring the whole pile to me when you're done. I'm just down the hall on the left." Doris exited without any further chitchat.

Looking around his space, Neil noted the improvements from his no-frills office back in the lab at his New York company: a real door, bookshelves, wall space for pictures, and a full-size window overlooking a garden—luxuries in today's work world.

A mere six weeks ago, Neil had met GB Polymers's CEO, Gordon Byrnes, at a national meeting. Gordon had spared no expense in enticing Neil to move south. Neil initially hesitated at leaving in the midst of an important project, but he found Gordon's generous salary offer and apparently unlimited R&D budget irresistible. Since graduating from college thirteen years ago, Neil had worked as a research chemist for Tarrytown Chemicals. Directing research now for a CEO who believed that Neil was the best industrial research chemist in the plastics field was quite auspicious.

Neil would have preferred his office to be located in the lab, but his boss wanted Neil on the first floor, in close proximity to him, and to Elaine, the secretary Neil would be sharing with the manager of quality assurance.

The IRS's standard W4 form for federal tax topped the paperwork pile. Neil checked the boxes and signed his name. He read the health benefit description's unintelligible guidelines and signed the enrollment form. Next, he flipped through a booklet of employee rules, including a dress code that required skirt suits or dresses for women, jackets and ties for men. At the bottom of the stack, he found a large employment contract. He turned to the end. *It took nine pages to spell out the terms of employment at this company?* Neil skimmed the tedious legal language. The harshness and complexity of this document contrasted significantly with the seemingly easygoing Gordon.

Neil had no problem with the usual terms, prohibiting personal use of company resources and expecting him to promise not to e-mail smut to the White House or anywhere else. Having no interest in visiting chat rooms or shopping online, the prohibited websites presented Neil with no hardship. Company reimbursement procedures were typical. The language about trade secrets was very broad.

The aggressive noncompete agreement banned all employees from employment with a competitor for three years after leaving GB Polymers. *You're the man to solve my problems.* The thought popped into Neil's head. That's what his new boss had said when they first met. Neil had no reason to think about leaving, so this noncompete agreement was simply theoretical. He signed the document. When he returned the pen to his shirt pocket, he took out his ever-present, laminated photo of his paternal grandparents' wedding and briefly gazed at it, then tucked it back.

Eager to get to the lab, Neil returned the pile of papers to Doris Kingston.

"Let's go meet your staff," she said.

They went down to the basement level, to a door marked Storeroom Five. On the Saturday that Gordon had shown him the lab, the disingenuous sign had struck Neil as odd. When he inquired about it, Gordon explained that he worried about rival businesses learning the secrets of his company's successful products. That same day, Gordon had asked Neil if he wanted any particular equipment for his lab. Without hesitating, Neil told him that a field emission scanning electron microscope topped his wish list. Gordon's reply stunned Neil: *Tell me where to order it, and we'll get you one.* Gordon agreed to purchase the $182,000 item because Neil wanted it.

"The code to get into the lab is 0505," Doris said, as she punched the keypad and released the lock. The Storeroom Five door concealed an impressive modern research and testing laboratory. It had an array of equipment, large lab benches, state-of-the-art instruments, built-in, wooden cabinets, and an extensive, up-to-date technical library.

A technician wearing a Star Trek insignia pin on his white lab coat lapel approached Neil. "Welcome to our world. I'm Tom Jameson." He extended his hand.

"Thank you," Neil said. "What bold experiments are you working on?"

"Call me if you need anything," Doris said, as she exited.

"We're trying to improve the bond between our polymer coating and ceramics," Tom answered.

"Trying to go where no one has gone before?" Neil asked.

"You a trekkie?" Tom asked.

"I have all the original Star Trek shows," Neil replied.

"Online searches have their limits—there was nothing about you being a trekkie."

Surprised at Tom's blunt honesty, Neil asked, "What *did* you learn about me?"

"You have three patents. You gave a talk last year to the mid-Hudson section of the American Chemical Society, and you were a popular volunteer scientist at Tarrytown High School."

"Not much gets by you, Spock," Neil chuckled.

"My curiosity piqued when I heard Gordon praising your talent. He's sparse with accolades. You're not what I pictured," Tom said.

"You imagined wild, red hair topping a wiry-built nerd?"

"No, someone older. More like mid-fifties than late thirties. More like Gordon."

Neil stood five feet ten, with wide shoulders, a middle-age paunch, and a thick head of coffee brown hair topping a round, soft face.

"Disappointed?" Neil asked.

"Not at all. Let me introduce you to your illustrious crew. They're curious to know what to do with the fancy microscope."

"It's here?"

"Arrived two days ago." Tom motioned to the device. "We rearranged space to accommodate it."

"I've read about this equipment but never used it," Neil said. "I can't believe Mr. Byrnes sprung for it."

"Be careful, nothing's free with him," Tom warned. "We all know that about our boss. He'd lend his mother her own money and charge her interest. Nice, he's not."

"Give me a lab sample for a demo."

Tom selected a small, rectangular piece of concrete. "Our polymer coating usually bonds very well to concrete, but for some reason it's not adhering to this sample," Tom said. "Can the electron microscope show us why?"

"Yes." Neil turned on the monitor. He moved the electron gun to focus a beam on the concrete sample. "We'll get an interaction between this shaft of light and our sample, producing characteristic X-rays." While making adjustments, Neil noticed a man enter the lab. He was tall, with dark hair, a boyish look, and an athletic build that was evident even in his dark pinstriped suit.

"I'm Neil Landers. Can I help you?"

"Chadwick Byrnes," the man replied, with a nervous laugh. "I was on vacation when my father hired you. Is this your first director's job?"

"Yes, and I'm happy to be here."

"My father says you know chemistry. I hope he's right." Motioning to the microscope, Chadwick asked, "What's this?"

"A tool that produces images to help us understand product failures," Neil explained.

Chadwick looked unimpressed. For someone just back from a vacation, he seemed uptight, Neil thought.

"What's the price tag on that machine?" Chadwick asked.

"I haven't seen the bill," Neil hedged. "Its ability to pinpoint problems will pay for itself. Precise analysis saves considerable man-hours."

Chadwick stopped Neil from extolling the virtues of the new equipment. "Why focus on problems?"

"Best way to avoid 'em," Neil responded.

"Our last director of research left a while ago. He had a stroke. We need to pick up the pace and get back on schedule."

Somehow, Neil knew that *pick up the pace* did not include Chadwick.

"Did my father go over my tracking system for product development?" Chadwick asked, opening his thick binder of forms.

"No." Neil swallowed, feeling a sudden wave of apprehension about his new job.

"I need new formulas fast to meet our marketing priorities. Let me go over our timeline," Chadwick continued. "Revisions to eight products need to be completed in the next thirty days. Our sales staff wants to meet the specifications for the U.S. Departments of Transportation in as many states as possible. They need improvements in our existing products. Contractors pay a premium for certified material."

Neil refrained from saying that what Chadwick was asking for was not feasible in a month's time. Instead, he said, "I'll look at the existing test data and see what we can do."

"Besides these upgrades, we need to get three new products out ASAP," Chadwick insisted. "My last research director promised me a pumpable slurry that would solidify hazardous liquids, like oil or gasoline. There's considerable interest in that product. How soon can you finish it?"

"This is the first I've heard about it. I'll check with the technicians on the development status."

"Let me know by the end of the day," Chadwick said. "Oh, and I've asked Matt to install the project management software application on your computer today. It creates PERT charts, a diagram showing the step-by-step flow from start to completion of a new product. I use them to monitor our critical tasks and stay informed on our progress. Get on the slurry." Chadwick exited the lab.

"Charming fellow," Tom said. "Learned it at Harvard. He thinks you can develop a formula for a product as speedily as he adds it to his spreadsheet. He's into aggressive growth."

"Isn't that the type of thinking that destroyed the banks in this town?"

"He thinks he's invincible," Tom said.

"Doesn't seem pleased that I'm here," Neil said.

"It's not you he's unhappy with, as much as his father's making independent decisions. Chadwick thinks he's really the CEO."

"Show me the test data on that slurry."

Tom retrieved a notebook from his desk. Neil scanned the various experiments.

"Too much gasoline is leaking out," Neil said. "Let's incorporate an absorbent in the formula. Add 5 percent of a synthetic zeolyte."

"I'll move on that at warp speed," Tom said.

"Phone for you," a technician motioned to Neil.

Neil took the call, saying, "I'll be right there, Doris."

"Big guy arrived?" Tom asked with a grin.

"Yeah. I'll be back."

Neil climbed the stairs from the basement level to the first floor and appeared at Doris's desk outside Gordon's office.

Doris picked up her phone. "Mr. Byrnes, Neil Landers is here." Nodding to Neil, she said, "Go on in."

Gordon's office had the look of a penthouse living room, only with an incongruous computer on a large oak desk. Designer-fabric-upholstered, wingback chairs were positioned on either side of two facing sofas. An authentic, New England fieldstone fireplace had white birch logs stacked on a wrought iron grate. A very good reproduction of a Winslow Homer painting of a cottage by the sea hung on the wall next to a huge portrait of Gordon posed with a roll of blueprints. A glass curio cabinet displayed fancy china plates that were decorated with hand-painted, flying ducks.

Gordon was in his mid-sixties, with thin, gray hair. He stood an easy six feet four. His suit, although obviously expensive, did not fit him right. He was awkward—even clumsy—in walking up to shake hands with Neil.

"Thanks for stopping by. How's your first day?"

"Just fine. The microscope's excellent. Thanks."

"I need you to look at this." Gordon handed Neil a stack of papers fastened with a large black clip. "You'll need to work fast. I told the committee chair I'd mail the revisions tomorrow."

"Sure," Neil said. He could hardly say no. A quick glance revealed a huge, time-consuming assignment for him to do at home this evening. For the remainder of the day he needed to focus on Chadwick's requests.

At 4:20 that afternoon, Neil dialed Chadwick's extension.

"Chadwick Byrnes's office," the woman's voice said.

"This is Neil Landers. May I speak with Chadwick?"

"Mr. Landers, he's gone for the day."

Chapter 2

Bridget made her way through a maze of boxes to greet Neil that evening. "How'd it go?" she asked, hugging him.

"Very well. I got my new microscope."

"Congratulations. And did you have time to play with your new toy?"

"Briefly."

"Tell me about your staff."

"There are five technicians. All of 'em have been with the company less than a year. The chemist, Tom, has worked there for three years. He's a character. You'll like him."

"Any women?"

"Not in the lab. My boss is old-fashioned. All female employees are secretaries, and they can not wear pants."

"You're kidding!"

"Afraid not."

"Tell me about Tom."

"He's a trekkie and a fan of Turner Classic Movies."

"You have that in common."

"Would you believe his favorite movie is *The Man in the White Suit*?"

"How did that come up?"

"I was showing him how to use the new microscope, and he said it was better than the one the chemist had in *The Man in the White Suit*!"

"You two will get along just fine. How about a walk around uptown and finding a place for dinner?"

"I can't. I have a special assignment to do tonight." Neil pulled a stack of papers from his attaché case. "I have to proof these technical definitions and submit suggestions for revisions and additions."

"What? Do it tomorrow."

"Gordon volunteered weeks ago at the national meeting. He waited for my arrival. It has to go out tomorrow."

"Overhauling technical terminology in an evening, even for you, seems unreasonable."

"I don't have a choice."

"I was hoping to go out and celebrate your new job."

"Another night. I have to finish this."

"Okay. I'll unpack some more boxes. We'll do takeout."

"That'd be great! Thanks."

Neil checked the CNN highlights for five minutes and then went to his study with the seventy-six pages of technical terms. Scientific minutiae challenged Neil; in fact, he excelled at noting details and nuances. He would have liked more than fifteen hours to meet Gordon's deadline.

Two hours later, Bridget reminded him that he had not eaten. "I'll be right down," he said. He took twenty pages with him.

Bridget scooped some pasta salad onto a plate and put it on the dining room table. While he ate and continued working, Bridget picked up a sheet of Neil's typed work and read aloud, "Epoxy resin is a thermosetting synthetic polymer based on the reactivity of an organic compound containing a reactive group resulting from the union of an oxygen atom with two carbon atoms or with … this is incomprehensible. Who cares?"

Neil laughed. "Architects, contractors, chemists, lawyers, oh, plenty of people. Some will even argue about this wording and propose changes."

"Sounds like you're enjoying this."

"I'd prefer a more leisurely pace, but it's interesting."

"I hope Gordon appreciates you."

*****

"Good morning, captain, you okay?" Tom asked Neil in the lab the next day.

"Yeah, Spock. Up too late last night. I only slept four hours," Neil said.

"Working on Chadwick's projects?"

"No, a Gordon special assignment, revising technical terminology."

Tom shook his head with a sympathetic look. "First payment on the microscope, I warned you. Gordon likes to appear smart. Would you like some of my special blend of Earl Grey tea, captain?"

"Isn't it forbidden to brew tea in the lab?" Neil asked, and he laughed. "I'd love some."

"So many rules." Tom poured Neil a mug of tea. "You'll like this, captain." He picked up his notebook and showed Neil the test data. "Impressive."

Neil scanned the page. "A good start. We'll do better."

"You hit on something combining the properties of plastic with ceramics."

"It needs work," Neil said.

"Not loads of time to hit the Chadwick targets," Tom said, with a sly smile.

"Right. Thanks for the tea, Tom. I'm off to hand in my homework."

As he turned down the first floor hallway to Gordon's office, Neil heard Gordon bellow, *"God damn it!* The blue is all wrong. Doris, get Chadwick."

Neil stopped and hesitated before walking the remaining steps to Doris's desk. "I'll leave this with you," Neil said in a low voice. "Call me if he has any questions."

Gordon marched out of his office waving a glossy booklet as Chadwick appeared.

"This is not American flag blue," Gordon ranted. "It's too light."

Braced like a little boy expecting a slap, Chadwick squared his shoulders, inhaled a deep breath and said, "We printed fifty thousand booklets. Reprinting them would be very expensive."

"Damn it! The color needs to be right. I want American flag blue," Gordon yelled.

Neil slinked away. He hated conflict and detested shouting.

He heard Chadwick argue, "The decision makers who buy construction grouts and fireproofing coatings focus on the technical data, not the color of our logo."

Gordon's final bark chilled Neil. "Order more with American flag blue. And fire the person responsible for this atrocity."

"Captain on the bridge," Tom called from his bench as Neil wandered into the lab, struggling to recover from witnessing the repulsive argument between Gordon and Chadwick. He moved around and checked on each technician's project.

"What's up, captain?" Tom asked. "Your trip upstairs didn't agree with you?"

"No, it didn't."

"Big guy not happy with the color blue. Not royal enough?"

"How'd you know?"

"I may spend my day in a subterranean vault, but I'm connected." Tom smirked. Let me show you something, captain." Tom flipped to a page in his notebook. "I record all sorts of statistics, not just test results. Here are the names, titles, and exit dates of former employees. GB has oodles of casualties. Today I'll have another entry."

"You keep a list of fired employees in your lab notebook?" Neil's surprise registered in his voice.

"What better place than a bound notebook to preserve a permanent record?" Tom countered.

"Gordon told me he detests technical devices and insists on old-fashioned bound notebooks," Neil said.

"I like the no delete key feature," Tom said. "So who will Chadwick blame for the color blue crisis?"

"I don't know." Neil stared at Tom's list.

"All mistakes require a sacrifice. It's the Byrnes way. So what if a pallet of paper loaded with the wrong shade of blue is sent to the Dumpster? So what if that discarded paper equals the cost of farm equipment for the country of Chad or the annual budget for school supplies at a Charlotte elementary school? If Gordon wants American flag blue, by God he'll have it." Tom slapped his lab bench. "Gordon Byrnes, descendent of Mayflower pilgrims, will not settle for sea spray blue. I predict the fall guy will be the marketing manager, Victor."

Neil felt sick.

"Have you seen my shrine?" Tom motioned to shelves in a corner. "Things left behind by former workers."

The eclectic display included a bouquet of dried flowers in a work boot, a crushed Classic Coke can, a water bottle with the heart association logo, six or seven rolled up papers tied with ribbon, a college physics textbook, coffee cups—Bank of America, NASCAR—and a Panthers cap.

Picking up a pledge card for juvenile diabetes, Tom said, "Not a trinket here for a slacker, a thief, or an irresponsible employee—all good people."

Tom's memorabilia, a quirky tribute to fallen coworkers, saddened Neil. They involuntarily exited employment at GB Polymers because of a Byrnes whim, a perceived transgression, or a need for a scapegoat.

Turning from his memorial, Tom asked. "Have you seen the offending blue?" He held up a copy of the technical literature brochure. "Too pale," he mocked. "Bad ink day."

"You've got a copy? Gordon demanded them all destroyed."

"Right." Tom slipped the booklet into a folder.

Neil delayed returning to his office on the first floor for another hour. When he finally made his way upstairs, he immediately encountered Gordon.

"The terminology revisions look good," Gordon said, displaying no ill effects from his altercation with Chadwick. "Listen, some Chinese clients are visiting in two weeks. I'd like you to meet them."

"Chadwick mentioned a Taiwan customer. Is that who you mean?" Neil asked.

"Yeah, yeah, them. Chadwick says they're important. He wants them to sell our stuff in Red China."

"Sounds good." Neil resisted giving a geography or history lesson.

"My father did fine without going to Red China for business," Gordon said. "He founded the Byrnes Engineering Company in Greenwich, Connecticut, during World War II. You know my father graduated from Yale. He had good business sense and understood the value of selling to the United States government," Gordon gloated. "He loved to say that supplying goods to the government was great: the markup tremendous, the demand steady, and payment assured. For thirty years Byrnes Engineering furnished blueprints for government office buildings throughout the United States."

When Gordon took a breath, Neil said, "Expanding in the international market is smart."

"Chadwick says there's money to be made in China. My wife Rosemary and I will have a dinner for them at the Lake Norman Five Star Club. Invite your wife to come along."

There was a definite assumption on Gordon's part that Neil and his wife would be thrilled to make his guest list for a dinner party.

Neil returned to the lab. "Thanks for the update," Tom said into his cell phone. Turning to Neil he said, "Captain, breaking news; our marketing manager Victor and his assistant—I mean secretary—Adele are history."

Chapter 3

Two weeks later when they were preparing for Neil's company's dinner, Bridget said, "I should have sprung for a salon for this gala." She fixed her hair with a disapproving frown in the mirror.

"You look great," Neil said. He kissed her reassuringly. "I'll feed the fish, and then I'm ready. How about you?"

"Two minutes," she said, adjusting her pearls.

"Hi guys," Neil said to his prize fish. A pair of large blue discus, with three generations of offspring, swam in the comfortable, constant warm temperature of Neil's 120-gallon aquarium. "You have the life—a predictable environment with no surprises and me to attend to your needs." After shaking the prescribed food flakes into the water, he watched with admiration as the discus approached their meal, darting among the tall grasses. At age ten Neil had read about the rare, magnificent discus. Knowing they were a challenge to keep in a tank, he was determined to be a proud owner.

"I'm ready," Bridget said.

They drove north on Route 77. Crazy, impatient drivers cut in and out, gained half a car length, and then jammed on their brakes to a dead stop in front of Neil's car.

"Wouldn't uptown make more sense for out of town visitors?" Bridget asked.

"Probably," Neil replied. "But Gordon loves the Lake Norman Five Star Club. He lives a mere three minutes from it."

"Good to know this event's convenient for someone." Bridget reached to change the radio station.

"Can I listen to the end of *All Things Considered*?" Neil asked. "There's only about ten more minutes."

"Sure, I forgot it's early."

He switched to 90.7 for NPR.

"We're talking about concerns that there is tritium, a radioactive isotope, in the drinking water near the Connecticut River Nuclear Power Plant. We have with us Albert Cranston, a spokesperson for the plant," the announcer said. "Mr. Cranston, in recent months New York, New Jersey, and Illinois have reported elevated tritium levels in drinking water near nuclear power plants. Citizens Protectors, an environmental advocacy group, believes Martin Ridel's suicide was related to his bringing attention to tritium contamination in private wells near the Connecticut River Nuclear Power Plant. Any credence to that?"

"None at all. It's an outrageous allegation. The man was despondent about personal issues," Cranston said.

"How awful that someone killed himself because of a cover-up of a radioactive leak! What do you think?" Bridget asked.

"I don't know anything about it," Neil answered.

"I'd like to find out more about this story."

They were now moving along at twenty-five miles an hour on a four-lane highway.

"This traffic is miserable," Bridget said.

"We're in it because Gordon believes he's bestowing an honor on us. This is my reward for making him look good at the industry standards meeting. Please show appreciation."

"I won't say I'd rather have a bowl of cereal on a park bench," Bridget quipped. "Business dinners are drudgery, not at all enjoyable. Let's review the ground rules on what I can and cannot say. Can I mention my work in geriatrics?"

"Illness and old people are not fun conversation," Neil half joked. "Don't say you're a social worker. Gordon will think you're a communist."

"Scratch my work. I'll keep it light. I wish I had gone to a salon this afternoon. I could talk about that."

"I'm not sure that your descriptions of pampered salon clientele would be safe," Neil said, laughing. "Don't worry. Gordon will dominate all conversation. We're superfluous. If forced, go with faint praise."

"He must have grown up like a British prince," Bridget said. "Backcountry Greenwich, Connecticut, is a land of long driveways that wind up to a mansion or a castle complete with polo fields, ponds, and pastures with horses and stonewalls."

"He believes he's special. Gordon brags that his father was a Yale-educated engineer, and his mother was a talented pianist."

"We should be grateful we're deemed worthy to sit at his table," Bridget said with more than a hint of sarcasm. "He must really like you."

"I doubt it. My function is to increase his bottom line."

Finally, they came to exit twenty-eight. Bridget read the directions, and Neil turned left at the light and wound their way to the Lake Norman Five Star Club. Three flags marked the spot: the United States, North Carolina, and the Club's sailing ship pennant.

"Is there a flag with the Byrnes coat of arms somewhere?" Bridget asked.

"Maybe in the private dining room—say something complimentary if you see it." Neil nudged in the direction of the line for valet parking.

"You're not serious," Bridget said.

"Our four-year-old Saturn makes a statement," Neil chuckled and turned their car left into a self-park space. They walked to the brick circular driveway and under the covered carriageway to the club's entrance.

"We can do this," Bridget chanted like a mantra. A spectacular floral arrangement in an oriental vase dominated the foyer.

"The Byrnes party," Neil stated.

"Yes, sir. Straight ahead."

They walked down a tastefully decorated faux marble hallway that was lined with oversize chairs, mirrors, sconces, and paintings and stepped into a strikingly beautiful room. "Wow," they said together.

"Hi, Neil. Hi, Barbara." Gordon came across the room and greeted them. Neil expected Bridget to correct Gordon, but instead she forced a smile and shook his hand.

"Our international visitors are running late," Gordon said.

"What a lovely setting, Mr. Byrnes," Bridget said, with her best social skills.

"That's my wife's department." Gordon motioned to a tall, thin woman who was speaking with a handsome man in waiter attire.

Rosemary walked over and welcomed Neil and Bridget, "Thank you for coming," she said. Rosemary was at least six feet tall, thin, and dark-haired and looked as if a team of artists deserved the credit for her appearance.

"Your dress is beautiful," Bridget told her.

"A Christian Dior—my favorite designer." Rosemary's jewelry looked as if it could finance an average family home, Bridget thought. Her platinum drop 1920-ish necklace included countless diamonds surrounding a very large sapphire.

"I love what you've done with this room, Mrs. Byrnes," Bridget said. "It's simply gorgeous."

"My party planner deserves the credit, and my neighbor who recommended her. Of course, Felipe had plenty of ideas for this evening. The only thing I claim is continuing my mother's tradition of bouquets of eglantine roses. My mother had vases at all her parties. Please enjoy the music and cocktails. I have to speak with the banquet manager."

When they moved farther into the room, Bridget said, "Bunches of narcissus would be appropriate. Did you imagine this extravaganza?"

"I've had limited experience. I didn't know what to expect." They stood in awe and took in the elaborate decorations. Elegant flower bouquets placed on pedestals created an area for a trio of musicians.

"Live music. I love it!" Bridget walked over and smiled at the harpist. Enjoying the enchanting sounds, Bridget continued to take in the details of the room. A waiter set five decanters on a tray on a sideboard. Neil and Bridget watched as he opened bottles and with precision poured dark, red liquids into glass carafes.

"Let's check out the table," Bridget said. The place settings for ten were set on opulent white linen. The waiter must have followed an architect's blueprint to position the silver, crystal, flowers, and candles in their proper place, Neil thought. Rich, green brocaded fabric covered the chair backs.

"Look at the place cards," Bridget said. Gold calligraphy-lettered place cards sat on illuminated glass bases etched with the GB Polymers logo of blue bubbles floating out of a beaker.

Three people separated Bridget from Gordon. One of the Taiwanese guests was to sit at Neil's right and the international salesperson at his left.

The table paralleled a wall of glass revealing the golf course and a bit of Lake Norman. Neil looked out on the green. He loathed the tacky, characterless grass of country club grounds. "The fake, plastic green grass looks ridiculous," Neil commented. "It can't be a half-inch high and the pretend fountain in the background looks more like someone dropped a garden hose with a spray nozzle into the pond."

"No one will care. The inside is fabulous," Bridget said. "Except maybe for that." Her gaze rested on a china cabinet. Pointing to the display of hand-painted bird plates on glass shelves with a collection of carved wooden ducks on the top, she said, "What's with the duck motif?"

"Duck hunting is important to the country club set," Neil said.

"I don't get it!"

"Especially when these small creatures don't stand a chance against the technological lures and guns of today's hunters," Neil said.

"What's the thrill in killing something so small?" Bridget asked.

"Don't ask." Neil laughed.

Chadwick arrived and strode directly to Neil, "Hi. Any problems getting here?"

"No, your directions were fine. This is my wife, Bridget."

"Pleased to meet you," Chadwick said, with a silly giggle. "My wife couldn't make it." Chadwick's nervous laugh seemed louder to Neil than usual. For a senior staff person with authority over sales and marketing, Chadwick was shockingly ill at ease with people. He anticipated the profits of this business arrangement with the Taiwanese boosting next year's bottom line, yet he delegated all the face-to-face contact with the visitors to the international salesperson, Felipe Obrado. It struck Neil as strange that Chadwick was not more directly involved with clients.

"Let's get some hors d'oeuvres. My father certainly went over the top with the spread tonight," Chadwick said. They moved toward a table skirted with pleats of the green brocade fabric. A large platter of shrimp arranged in a circular pattern of four hearts dominated the artistic display. Silver tiers held plates of filled pastry. Pate´ molded in the shape of the island of Taiwan looked delicious.

"Your guests will be impressed," Neil said. He took a plate and selected three appetizers.

Felipe Obrado, the international salesman, arrived with his wife, Carmen, and the visiting executives. He greeted Mr. and Mrs. Byrnes cordially before coming over to Chadwick, Neil, and Bridget to introduce the visitors from Taiwan.

"Neil, I'd like you to meet our guests, Mr. Chang, Mr. Lin, and Mr. Hwang, and my wife, Carmen," Felipe said.

Neil nodded, shook hands, and introduced Bridget.

"Pleased to meet you," Mr. Lin said in good English. Mr. Chang and Mr. Hwang nodded. Carmen smiled.

"This is the man who comes up with the products to meet your needs," Felipe said, resting his arm on Neil's shoulder.

Felipe summarized their ride over and made small talk. Mr. Lin never took his eyes off Neil. When there was a lull in the conversation, Mr. Lin asked him, "Director of research, right?"

"Yes," Neil answered.

"Have you figured out what was wrong with our last shipment?" Mr. Lin asked.

Chadwick interrupted, "Nothing wrong on our end. Our test data revealed no problem with the quality of the product."

"The shrinkage was extreme," Mr. Lin said.

"It was installed incorrectly," Chadwick said.

"My customer complained about the gap under his machines. Could I go over the test data with you?" Mr. Lin asked Neil.

"Sure," Neil said tentatively.

"We've made some changes in our product line," Chadwick said. "You'll be impressed. I'll give you our technical brochure tomorrow."

"Listen," Felipe said.

"The Taiwanese national anthem!" Mr. Lin was definitely delighted.

They stood respectfully quiet and paid attention to each note. Chadwick slipped away. He reappeared at Neil's side when the musicians finished the piece.

"Mr. Byrnes requests you find your seat at the table now," a waiter said. Gordon and Rosemary stood at opposite ends of the table as their guests sat down. Chadwick surprised Neil by sitting next to him.

"Water, please," one of the Taiwanese visitors requested of the waiter taking the drink orders.

"Order a highball," Gordon insisted with a disapproving stare.

The man who requested water looked puzzled.

"A highball." Gordon lifted his arm in a drinking motion more appropriate for a fraternity toga party than the country club.

Surprised at Gordon's attempt to control what the guest drank, Neil's eyes met Bridget's. She rolled her eyes. He thought of the one-liners that she would like to utter. Instead, Bridget ordered a glass of wine, sat back, and enjoyed the music.

Rosemary chattered about shopping at Nordstrom and her bridge games. Carmen, Felipe's wife, let Rosemary monopolize the conversation while she appeared interested. Bridget stayed quiet.

Felipe directed the waiter pouring red wine, complimented the decanting process, and promised Gordon an exceptional after-dinner port.

The visitor, Mr. Lin, who Neil had thought would be sitting next to him, sat on the other side of Chadwick. His conversation with Chadwick consisted of serious negotiating—no inane prattle for this man, Neil noted. Neil detected that Mr. Lin wanted assurances before he finalized a contract with GB Polymers to be the local licensee in Taiwan.

Neil was surprised to hear Chadwick say, "Our construction grout and fireproofing products are now far superior to any others on the market."

In his dreams, Neil thought. He estimated nine months, maybe a year, before he had a higher strength and higher temperature-resistant formula for those products.

The salad of field greens with walnuts, mandarin orange sections, and a citrus dressing appeared. Neil did his best to enjoy the food, feign interest in the conversation, and periodically nod in the direction of Gordon or Rosemary.

Droning on about how much better Greenwich, Connecticut, and Bermuda were than Charlotte and Lake Norman, Gordon seemed to have forgotten that he had chosen to move south for more space and the cheaper labor. It must have been confusing for the guests to listen to descriptions of New England and Bermuda. Neil assumed Gordon loved being the focal point of the evening, that he believed his assembled guests respected him, and that their interests paralleled his own.

"Mr. Lin is involved with some interesting projects," Felipe said to Neil. "Tomorrow, Gordon wants to show our visitors the U.S. National Whitewater Center, but I'm hoping you can spend some time with Mr. Lin."

"Whitewater?"

"Don't ask," Felipe stopped Neil. "You know that the U.S. Olympic training center gives Gordon a platform to talk about his grandfather winning a medal in the Olympics a hundred years ago, and that today he generously sponsors young athletes' training."

"Of course, makes perfect sense," Neil said.

"Anyhow, Mr. Lin wants time with you. I'll try and make it happen. He's the top contender to supply the nonshrink grout for the new Taipei nuclear power plant project."

"I didn't know we supplied nuclear power plants," Neil said.

"We'd like you to come to Taiwan, Neil," Mr. Lin said, as soon as people were up from the table and moving to leave. Before Neil could respond, Chadwick interrupted their conversation, "Neil's too busy. I plan to visit your operations with Felipe next month."

"Tomorrow I'd like to go over some of the physical properties of the nonshrink grout," Mr. Lin said to Neil.

"I'll be happy to review it with you," Neil said.

"If there's time," Chadwick said. "We've a significant number of licensee details to finalize in order to execute the contract while you're in Charlotte."

Chapter 4

Neil stood in the check-in line at the Sheraton Hotel in Toronto, Canada. Soothing sounds of a waterfall cascading behind a glass wall contrasted with his troubled thoughts of work and the unpleasant changes in his life since he had taken the director of research position at GB Polymers. During his two years in Charlotte, Neil's uneasiness about working for Gordon and Chadwick steadily grew. He kept his head down, focused on his work and reminded himself that their relocation had come at a perfect time for Bridget's transition to a new career.

This ASTM meeting offered a welcomed break from Gordon and Chadwick's frustrating demands. Neil handed his credit card to the clerk.

"Welcome, Mr. Landers. You're here for the big meeting."

"That's right."

"There are 450 guests registered. I never heard of this company, what's the ASTM?"

"It's not a company. It's a volunteer organization with more than 30,000 members," Neil said.

"Volunteers? What do they do?"

"Create standards."

"Standards?" She looked puzzled.

Neil picked up a bottle of water from the counter. "How do you know that this is safe to drink?"

"It's sealed. No one opened it."

"How do you know there's no lead in the water?"

"It's not allowed."

"Can you be sure nothing contaminated this water?"

"I never thought about it."

"The ASTM volunteers do. They wrote up the techniques for testing the water. These members, unpaid people, set standards for water and also everyday items such as pipes for plumbing and even football helmets."

"Pipes and exercise equipment?"

"And much more," Neil said.

"What do the letters ASTM stand for?" She asked.

"American Society for Testing and Materials—that's the original name. With members from all over the world today, the name is ASTM International."

"Is it new?"

"No, it was created more than a hundred years ago. The railroad builders wanted assurances that the tracks in Illinois would support the same weight as the tracks in Pennsylvania. Professors and engineers created standardized terms and testing for iron and steel. The industries now include metals, paints, plastics, textiles, petroleum, cement, medical devices, and consumer products."

"And it's all volunteers? That's impressive. I hope you enjoy your stay with us!" She handed him a room key.

Making his way to the elevators, Neil bumped into someone who looked vaguely familiar. "Neil! Let me shake your hand, good man." The man's badge identified him as being with Ricktel Construction.

"Hi," Neil said, surprised at the enthusiastic greeting.

"Your new construction grout simplifies my life. It's excellent! There's increased demand for basic components. Great job!"

Neil hoped that he did not look clueless, but he had no idea why he deserved this man's praise.

"Have to run—maybe we can have a drink sometime this week?" The man patted Neil's shoulder and moved off into the crowd of attendees.

In his room, Neil set down his bags, soaped a washcloth, and cleaned all the doorknobs, the phone, and the TV remote. He tossed the wet rag in a corner of the bathroom. Then he moved the information binder and breakfast menu to the top of the TV cabinet and proceeded with the unpacking rituals he had developed in his years of travel. Past experiences with ants and debris from previous hotel occupants influenced his almost obsessive practices of coping with his basic assumptions about the lack of cleanliness in a hotel room.

He hung up his suits, stashed his plastic bags of socks and underwear in a dresser drawer, set his slippers by the bed, and piled his paperwork for the meetings on the desk. Fearing a three AM blast awakening him from sleep, Neil unplugged the hotel radio clock and set his own travel alarm for five-thirty AM.

Neil looked again at his agenda for the eight o'clock AM meeting he was to chair. Organized and ready for the morning, he set out for the conference registration area.

ASTM staff at the check-in desks dispensed meeting materials. Neil picked up his badge and the week's schedule and then perused the latest standards and testing publications displayed on the tables. He flipped through a heavy volume on ceramics.

Taking the escalator from the mezzanine level to the lobby coffee shop to get some dinner, Neil recognized another man as a regular at these meetings, someone who had served with him on other committees.

Neil hailed him. "Hi, Fred, nice to see you again. How's it going?"

"Fine. I'd like to talk with you."

"I'm headed for dinner. Join me, if you'd like." Neil hoped his tone did not give away his disappointment in the prospect of having to talk about work over dinner.

"Here?" the man asked, aghast. "I planned to grab a cab to a restaurant near the university."

"This works best for me. I've got an early day tomorrow," Neil replied.

"Two?" The hostess asked.

"Yes," Fred answered.

As soon as they sat down, Fred said, "I've been working on products similar to your line. Mine fall short in every way, so I did what you and anyone else in this business would do: I bought your stuff and analyzed it."

"And what did you learn?"

"Come on, Neil. Your claims for strength and temperature exceed reality. First, I thought I did the test wrong. I've done it twice with similar results. My boss is furious that we lost business to GB Polymers because of the exaggerated claims on your nonshrink construction grout."

"I'm surprised! I'll check on it."

"I'm under pressure to formulate a product that's as good as yours. I don't think that's possible," Fred said.

The Ricktel engineer Neil had met earlier clearly had believed GB Polymers had something superior. Now this technically competent chemist sitting across the table from him disagreed. Neil had to think about this. The dinner conversation turned to other, more general industry matters and family.

Having trouble staying focused during the remainder of his time in Toronto, Neil chaired two subcommittee meetings with unexpected poor performance.

Chapter 5

On his first day back from Toronto, Neil felt like driving right past GB Polymers. His muscles tightened in his shoulders as he walked into the building. In his office, he accessed his voice mail messages.

Thank you, Neil. I've exceeded my sales quota for this month.

Contractors love your new grout.

You're the best! It's so easy to sell your higher-grade fireproofing.

Neil stopped listening. This was excessive. First, the Ricktel engineer had gushed about improved product performance, now sales people praised his new products. In his time at GB Polymers, a little more than two years, no one on the sales staff had called Neil. They reported to Chadwick. They did not have offices in the Charlotte headquarters. Gordon and Chadwick kept every division detached from others.

The physical layout of the building augmented employee isolation. The lab, still labeled Storeroom Five, shared the basement with typical mechanical equipment and three other storage rooms. The lab was off-limits to everyone except Chadwick, Gordon, Neil, and his technicians. Lab staff remained at their benches during working hours or in their designated break room on the same floor. They did not generally wander around on the upper levels.

The first floor had the reception area, offices for Gordon, Neil, the manager of quality assurance, and the accounting department at the end of the building farthest from the lobby. The second floor housed the marketing department, Chadwick's office, the computer equipment, and the technical services staff, who answered customer calls.

Wanting to see the technical literature brochure, Neil went to the marketing manager's office. The door was open, but no one was in. Neil glanced around for the booklet. Not seeing it anywhere, he approached the woman who assisted in the marketing department.

"Hi. I need a copy of the technical literature. I hope you can help me out," Neil said in a no-nonsense manner.

"I have strict orders to keep them locked up, but I guess you're safe, Mr. Technical," she said, smiling. She unlocked a file cabinet, removed the glossy, six-page brochure, and handed it to Neil.

He thanked her, returned to his office, and then flipped to the data page. He shivered at what he saw. *What the hell? Fifteen hundred degrees Fahrenheit! No way!*

Why had no one caught such an error, he wondered. Remembering the color blue fiasco from his first day at this job two years ago, he dreaded telling Chadwick about another costly printing mistake. Even more, he feared wide distribution of fraudulent figures to customers. Not stopping to call, Neil went directly to the upper floor.

"I need to speak with Chadwick."

Chadwick's secretary picked up the phone and dialed an extension. "Neil Landers would like to speak with you. Go ahead," she said to Neil.

Chadwick was sitting at his desk reading a magazine. He put it down. The opened page had a large picture of a chef in a waterside restaurant.

"The information in this booklet is wrong," Neil told him.

"Where did you get that?" Chadwick got up from his chair.

"It doesn't matter. The numbers are wrong."

"You're mistaken," Chadwick blurted, with a nervous jerk of his head.

"No, I'm not mistaken." Neil struggled to remain calm. "The grout and fireproofing don't work at fifteen hundred degrees. Under ideal conditions, the best results are in the area of eight hundred degrees. That's a huge difference." With much frustration, Neil added, "We need to retract this claim."

"This is not your decision, Neil. Marketing is my area. I thought you would have a more successful formula by now. I like to be ahead of the curve. I'm confident you'll get better results soon. I've waited on widespread distribution. It'll be fine."

"You might know which restaurant has the best recipe for cordon bleu, but you are out of your element in having anything to say about a chemical formula." Neil picked up the magazine and threw it at Chadwick.

Flabbergasted at learning it was such a calculated lie rather than an honest error, Neil brusquely left and headed straight for Gordon's office.

"Ask Mr. Byrnes if I can have a word with him," Neil said to Gordon's secretary. She got the okay and motioned for Neil to proceed.

"Mr. Byrnes I thought you would want to know about an error in the product literature."

"It looks great!"

"There are inaccurate statements. The temperature range is wrong—significantly. We need to correct this."

"Chadwick's in charge of marketing. See what he thinks."

"I did. He's not interested."

"It must be fine then."

"It's not! These claims are false," Neil said.

"Our customers know we have the best products," Gordon insisted.

Neil returned to his office. Gordon did not understand the implications of inaccurate data. Most CEOs would worry about potential lawsuits but Gordon with his sense of superiority believed he was invincible.

Chadwick was over his head. Looking again at the technical literature, Neil noted the phrase 10 CFR 50 Appendix B. What does that mean? He read, *Manufactured in accordance with the most rigid quality control procedures; GB Polymer's Quality Assurance Program meets the requirements of 10 CFR 50 Appendix B.*

When Neil searched the Internet for 10 CFR 50, he found thousands of hits. Quality Assurance Criteria for Nuclear Power Plants topped the list. With a click, the U.S. Nuclear Regulatory Commission's Quality Assurance document came up on the screen. After scrolling down the eighteen sections marked with roman numerals, he bookmarked the page. Next, Neil read the NRC description of a rigorous Quality Assurance System. Recognizing much of the language, he realized Chadwick used the very wording of the NRC document in his marketing material without anything to substantiate it.

Neil sat back in his chair wondering how not-so-clever Chadwick came up with this ruse. The top left of the quality assurance page had a link to the NRC home page. There, Neil found the agency mission and more links, including one on reporting a safety concern. The hotline number stood out in bold print in the brief explanation of the process for informing nuclear regulators of potential safety problems. *Not an option,* Neil told himself. *I'm a scientist, not a police officer.*

Chapter 6

Three days later, Neil sat at his dining room table in the middle of the night.

"Something wrong?" Bridget startled Neil as she came into the room to join him.

"Couldn't sleep."

"That's not like you," she said.

"I was afraid I'd wake you, so I came downstairs." He decided not to mention his nightmare of a five-story concrete apartment building collapsing. For three consecutive nights now, he had seen this structure crumple, smothering its occupants with its fall.

"What time is it?"

"Three-thirty."

"Something's wrong," Bridget said. "You've not been yourself for days."

"I'm okay."

"Is it work?"

"No."

"Are you sick?"

"Not really. Just tired."

Bridget frowned. "I can't keep guessing. It would be easier if you would tell me what's going on."

"Nothing. Why are you badgering me?"

"You're different. You've stopped talking about your work."

"There is nothing to tell. I show up," Neil told her. "I direct some experiments. Occasionally I have a good idea for a new product. It's not the stuff of exciting conversation."

"Maybe taking this job was a mistake."

Unaccustomed to censoring his conversation with his wife, Neil found it surprisingly taxing. He never mentioned his computer browsing that brought him to the NRC Website. Chadwick's false claims were constantly on Neil's mind. He had a real appreciation of the stress of keeping a secret. He could not bring himself to tell her that he regretted taking this job.

Moving to Charlotte provided Bridget with a fresh start in a new career. She stopped teaching after fifteen years, completed a masters in social work program while assisting her parents in their final years. In addition to caregiving, Neil and Bridget contributed financially to her parents' support when medical expenses drained their resources. Neil encouraged Bridget to pursue her dream and not worry about subsidizing her parents, her graduate school costs and two years without income. Although he was sensible about managing their finances, Neil never considered unemployment in his future. Adding to his anxiety was a mortgage based on his earnings and significant losses in his retirement account with the downturn in the stock market.

As an independent contractor, Bridget had no employer-paid benefits and her income was less than what she had made as a teacher. Neil knew the loss of his income would negatively affect them.

Thoughts of looking for a new job were daunting in light of the onerous noncompete agreement he had signed when he first took the job. Noncompete clauses were standard but Gordon's history of vindictiveness scared Neil.

*****

Dreading the workday, Neil gripped the wheel as if he were driving down a curving, mountain road that was slick with ice instead of making his way a few miles on wide, level streets that were lined with century-old trees, treasured for their uniqueness. He briefly considered the idea of returning to his New York job, but he had angered that company's president when he had left without finishing a major project. The CEO expected Neil's new product to reverse shrinking sales. He had to find a way to survive here in Charlotte.

Turning left onto Fairview, the sight of the high-rise condominiums there jolted Neil's nostalgia for past morning views of the stunning Hudson River in New York. Passing the Piedmont Towne Center—*who spells town with an e on the end?*—Neil's apprehension expanded. A specialty food market, a nail salon, a spa, a café, and a yoga studio anchored this pretend village. Buildings with smooth, stone veneers provided living quarters that looked liked extensions of employees' daytime work cubicles.

Neil drove through the iron gate entrance of GB Polymers onto the main driveway of expensive bricks, suitable for a private estate. As he circled the two-tiered fountain with tumbling water at the front of the Byrnes Building, before continuing on to the parking area in back, Neil remembered his first impression of this office building, with its large, arched glass panels, ornate gas lanterns, and architectural details that were usually skipped in today's streamlined construction.

A little more than two years ago, Neil had felt proud and lucky to be at this place. Today, his workplace looked sinister. The salespeople's messages, telling him that the new products— especially the construction grout and fireproofing—were easier to sell, irritated him.

Absorbed in thinking about his meager options, Neil did not notice a woman in tears standing next to his car until he heard breaking glass. It was Vivien, from the accounting department.

Gathering the strewn contents of her dropped box, she sobbed, "I don't know what I'll do without this job."

"Vivien, let me help you." Neil picked up a few of her books. He righted the box to hold her backsaver pillow and several tiny stuffed cats. The glass that once covered her wedding photo lay in pieces between their cars.

Regaining some composure, she said, "I carry our family's health insurance. My husband is self-employed." Then her voiced cracked. She covered her face with her hands.

He placed the box in her car. Having no words of comfort or reassurance, he said, "I'll clean up the glass."

"Thanks." She stifled more tears. "My son has cancer. Even if I get another job, it may not cover his medical expenses," she blurted. "And I won't be able to afford the COBRA private insurance program."

Her words chilled him. "I'm sorry for your trouble."

She nodded to him and got into her car, crying uncontrollably.

Once Vivien drove away, Neil rummaged in his car's trunk for gloves and picked up the broken glass. Finished, he stood motionless, remembering that Tom had once told him that the list of casualties from medical insurance data was long. This encounter upset him.

GB Polymers was self-insured, allowing Gordon access to all the employees' medical claims. According to Tom's theory, Gordon routinely reviewed health insurance claims to identify diagnoses that triggered high medical usage, and then he dismissed the employee associated with the health problem for some fabricated reason.

Two people that Tom frequently had talked about were the sales clerk whose child had diabetes and the secretary with multiple sclerosis. Both of them had told Tom that their doctors had requests for specific medical information from their employer just before they were terminated. Gordon's monitoring must have flagged this woman as being too costly for the company.

Chapter 7

That evening, when Bridget walked into the living room, she took one look at the television and said, "Hideous. Don't buy that necklace for me."

"Unh. I didn't hear you." Neil looked dazed.

"Your new interest—shopping?"

"What?" Neil asked.

"Big jewelry is in, but I prefer dumbbells for weight work."

"I'm looking for the news channel."

"Yeah, right," Bridget told him. "You've got the news on automatic pilot. Sitting here with the shopping channel on for more than a nanosecond concerns me. What's up?"

"Nothing." He got up and clicked off the TV.

"Want some tea?" she asked.

"Earl Grey, hot." Neil followed Bridget to the kitchen. They never switched to the Southern iced tea, no matter how hot the temperature. Their favorite beverage was brewed in a pot and served hot.

Neil picked up the teakettle from the stove, filled it with water, and put it in the microwave. He hit digit two on the express pad.

"What are you doing?" She put the cups on the counter and intercepted the inevitable catastrophe. Opening the microwave door, Bridget shouted at him, "A metal kettle doesn't go in the microwave!"

"Sorry! I wasn't thinking."

"Ouch! The plastic handle is melting. Enough already—what's wrong?" She let go of the kettle and put her hand under cold water.

Neil's face was pale; his shoulders slumped as he leaned against the counter. Looking like a boxer punched too many times, he struggled to stay upright. "My company sells questionable material to nuclear power plants. I'm afraid there could be an accident."

"Oh, my God." Bridget looked shocked.

"Every day I get more messages from sales staff, thanking me for improving products."

"Isn't that a good thing? Would you rather they complain?"

"I wish they had accurate information not the inflated claims Chadwick invented."

Bridget placed two cups on the table and set a large coaster for the teapot. She brought cream from the refrigerator. While the tea brewed, Neil recounted his discovery of Chadwick's deceitful marketing claims and his futile attempts to reason with Chadwick and Gordon.

"So this is the not-sleeping thing. It's a relief to know! My imagination conjured up horrible explanations."

"This *is* pretty ghastly. Chadwick is so over his head. He sees dollar signs. I see another Chernobyl cloud. It's so calculated. The salespeople, believing they peddle a superior product, sell aggressively to the nuclear industry. They have no technical background. Chadwick is very excited with my improved formulas for some products because my testing data showed they beat the competition. I'm not certain that I can get better results, and Chadwick exaggerates what we have."

"The greedy bastard. Quit."

"I can't, I'd be completely out of the industry! And maybe I really *can* make the products better."

"Maybe, maybe—it's not your style. I know you don't overreact. You're even pro-nuclear. Now *I'm* worried. Aren't we near nuclear plants?"

"Thirty miles away—eighty percent of the people in the United States are near nuclear plants."

"What are you going to do?"

"There's not much I can do. Chadwick is president, and Gordon is chairman of the board. I already talked with both of them. This is a private company. There aren't many options."

"There must be something. You're worried about a disaster."

"I'm nobody in the scope of things."

"You're credible and convincing. It's hard to believe that Chadwick and Gordon ignored you. I thought they hired you for your technical expertise."

"Right," Neil said dryly. "Chadwick was furious that I had the brochure. He actually asked me where I got it. He didn't want me to see his outrageous marketing with made-up data."

"Later he'll claim you gave him the info. You have to act. You're worried sick."

"I could contact the NRC."

"What's that?" Bridget asked.

"The U.S. Nuclear Regulatory Commission, a federal government agency that oversees everything related to nuclear power plants."

"Sounds like a force able to take on your company."

"Gordon would destroy me if I reported him."

"Do you care if he invites you to the country club? Report him. He's no match for you."

"Only if you were the judge or referee would I win any round with Gordon. I don't have a chance against him."

"What alternative do you have?"

"According to their Website, the NRC accepts anonymous calls."

"Good. Call right now."

"No. I'm not calling from here," Neil said firmly. "They'd have caller ID for sure. I can't call from my office or my cell phone."

"Remember that story of the ten-year employee at a Connecticut power plant who killed himself after being fired? We first heard about it years ago on NPR on our way to that awful dinner at your boss's club."

"Yeah. I know you were following it. What's new?"

"I recently got an online alert noting that an environmental group insists Mr. Ridel, the fired employee, was unfairly terminated for speaking out about tritium in wells adjacent to the power plant. It's still quite the controversy."

"That's awful. Tritium has been in the news lately."

"You have to be careful," Bridget warned.

"I do have to do something about Chadwick's lies. Let's take a drive and find a pay phone," Neil said.

"Too bad our cell phone age has made public phones almost obsolete."

"There's still a few. Let's find one."

"The low ones you can use from your car would be the easiest and *safest*," Bridget said.

"It's unlikely we'll stumble onto one of those. Let's go. We'll locate something tonight, and then I can use it tomorrow at lunchtime. I hope this works out."

Chapter 8

Neil walked out of his office building at noon on July 18. It was hot, but that was not the reason that moisture beaded on his forehead, pooled in his palms, and made his shirt feel damp. Hoping no one noticed the change in his predictable lunchtime habit of eating a sandwich at his desk, Neil went to his car, skipping his usual reading of local, world, and business news online.

Today was different. The only information he cared about now did not exist on the Web. He felt lucky that he passed no one in the parking lot. Neil opened his car door, glanced around before he settled behind the wheel, and exited onto Fairview Road. The index card with the NRC's toll-free telephone number remained stashed in his shirt pocket. A spasm of hiccups started, with the accompanying burning high in his chest. His hands tensed on the wheel like the tightening force on his air passages. Focused on his mission, Neil drove on, looking into the rearview mirror every ten yards.

It was a short distance to the payphone at Circle K on Woodlawn Avenue that they had selected the previous evening. Neil pulled beside the pole that anchored a phone he could reach from his car. These drive-up phones, less common today, were prevalent at one time. Before omnipresent cell phones, eight or more of these phones, covered in a protective shell, squatted car height at highway rest areas, allowing drivers to keep in touch with home or office without leaving the car.

Grateful to have the privacy of his car, Neil lowered the window thinking, *I must be crazy to do this.* Reminding himself of the inherent safety risks and knowing someone needed to stop this dangerous fraud, his hiccups and labored breathing returned.

He took a deep breath to tame his rampant anxiety. Resolute, he opened the window, reached for the receiver, and pulled it to his ear. He dialed the number. "I'm calling to report a safety issue," Neil blurted out, aware of a queasy feeling in his stomach and the shaky sound of his voice.

"Are you making a formal allegation?" the person asked.

"Yes," Neil answered. *Why else would someone call this number?*

"One moment, please."

A rather strange response for the United States Nuclear Regulatory Commission Safety Hotline, Neil thought.

"Good afternoon, NRC."

"I'm calling to report…."

"Sorry, I picked up the wrong line; someone will be with you in a moment." Click.

Stunned, Neil reached to replace the phone and disconnect the call when he heard, "Good afternoon. I'm Roy Levine. How can I help you?"

"I'm reporting a safety issue," Neil repeated with a little less frustration.

"Thank you for your call. I'll need some information for our allegation coordinator. What exactly is your concern?" Roy asked.

"My employer exaggerated the working temperature for products used at nuclear power plants."

"What's the name of your company?"

"GB Polymers in Charlotte, North Carolina."

"What kind of products?"

"Structural construction grouts, fireproof coatings, and penetration sealants," Neil said.

"And you think they're used at nuclear power plants?"

"Yes. I'm sure. They are used as basic components. The grout supports critical equipment like coolant pumps and the reactor. The fireproof coatings are for pipes and cables to tolerate extremely high temperatures and contain a fire if necessary. The penetration sealant is used in the containment dome as the final barrier to prevent radiation from escaping into the atmosphere." Neil tried to shift his sense of urgency to the person on the other end of the line.

"Can you hold one moment, please?"

"Sure."

The first time Neil visited the NRC Website, he learned that *basic component* in NRC jargon meant very serious. Anyone working at the agency must know that phrase.

While on hold, Neil listened to a taped narration stating that the NRC mission is to protect public health and safety from the hazards of radiation. Shifting his left shoulder up toward his ear to hold the phone, he wiped the sweat from his left palm as the recorded message droned on about NRC vigilance in carrying out its duty.

I hope so, Neil thought, as he lowered his shoulder and resumed holding the phone in his left hand.

When the tape cut off, Roy came back on the line, "Can I take your name and number?"

Neil hesitated.

"Are you on the line, sir?"

"Yes," Neil replied. "I'm calling from a pay phone on my lunch hour. I want to remain anonymous." Neil tapped his right fingers on the shift handle as he spoke.

"That's difficult."

"Your Website states you accept anonymous calls," Neil retorted, increasing the tempo of his drumming.

"We'll keep your identity confidential, but I do need your name and a phone number for a call back. We need additional information," Roy explained. "Please let an engineer call you this afternoon."

"No," Neil insisted. "I can't talk with the NRC while I'm at work."

"It's illegal to retaliate against an employee who brings safety concerns to the NRC's attention."

Being found out by his employer meant inevitable retaliation. *I'm far from retirement,* Neil thought. *I'd like to work in my field.*

"I've no doubt that if my employer finds out I made this call, he'll fire me," Neil said in a voice barely audible. He hung up the phone.

Holding his forehead in his palms, Neil felt the blood pulsating through his veins. *What a mess.*

His head rushed with recollections of when he first saw Chadwick's outrageous claims in the company's product brochure. Neil untangled the web of a very successful and very lucrative marketing plan. He resisted driving away, telling himself that without an informant, an external agency would never uncover Chadwick's convoluted system of business practices designed to deceive.

Targeting the nuclear industry as a profit center, Chadwick placed the exact words from the NRC Code of Regulations in his marketing material, assuring consumers that they purchased high quality products that met industry standards. Some buyers even thought that the NRC endorsed these products. He started to reach for the phone just outside his car, hesitated, and pushed the lever of the car's air-conditioning fan. Although it was at maximum, the air felt warm. Continuing to search for a rationale to do nothing, Neil remained parked.

After Neil comprehended the potential danger, he could not put it out of his mind. After learning of GB Polymers' transgression, even when he had slept, he had worried. Nightmares had woken him. He was not bound to report wrongdoing, he told himself. *I am a scientist, not a police officer. I'm not any kind of enforcer, and I do not want to be one.* However, he did want the NRC to stop GB Polymers.

Who else could bring this serious crime of phony claims for strength and temperature of products used to contain radiation to the attention of an authority?

He reached for the phone and dialed the NRC number again.

"I'd like to speak with Roy Levine," Neil said.

"Levine here."

"Roy, my name is Neil Landers. I'm the director of research for GB Polymers."

"Thanks, Mr. Landers, for calling back. Can I have your number so that someone from the NRC can call you tonight?"

Neil gave his home phone number and asked, "Who'll call me?"

"I'm not sure."

Neil ignored the irony of going to great lengths to make an anonymous call and ending up identifying himself.

He placed the phone back in its cradle and shifted his car from park to drive.

While stopped at a traffic light, a blaring horn brought a green light to his attention. Traveling west on Tyvola Road, Neil saw signs for Route 77. Realizing his mistake, he turned into a barbecue restaurant and corrected his direction. Somehow, he arrived back at GB Polymers. With relief, he saw no sign of Gordon Byrnes's Cadillac.

Before Neil even put his car in park, Chadwick Byrnes pulled his navy blue Lexus SUV into his designated space. Neil's stomach lurched. Like a guilty child, he feared Chadwick somehow knew how he had spent his lunchtime. He waited until Chadwick entered the building before exiting his car. Neil punched a four-digit code into the security pad. A red light blinked. "Darn," he muttered to himself. His hand trembled. Again, he pushed four buttons. A green light flashed. He pulled open the door and hurried to his office.

Digging in his pocket for his key, Neil cursed Gordon's fanaticism about security. The locking and unlocking ritual of his office several times a day was a nuisance, especially when he kept the formulas for the products locked in a file cabinet and on a secure computer site. With difficulty, Neil worked the key into the slot and opened the door. Closing the door behind him, he collapsed into his high-back, cushioned chair.

Layers of anxiety created tension in his shoulders and throughout his body. Even his eyes hurt. With his elbows on the desk, his arms bent upward, he brought the palms of his hands against his closed eyelids. He wanted to relieve the pressure. He fought not to cry.

The phone rang. A technician in the lab asked, "How do you want me to proceed with the samples that came in this morning?"

"I'll be right there."

With regained composure, Neil got up. Maybe a distraction would settle his stomach. He walked down to the lab.

"Captain on the bridge," Tom announced.

Five technicians, all in white lab coats, were busy with various tasks in the research laboratory.

"I've got the infrared spectrums for you, Neil," Tom announced, reaching for papers covered with squiggly lines of peaks and valleys on a grid. He handed them to Neil.

"Good. I'm interested in seeing them."

Tom went on, "I'll have the thermal analysis results in about an hour."

"Fine." Neil expected that he already knew Tom's experiments would show degradation at temperatures much lower than claimed. He moved on to another technician.

"The compressive strength is low and the shrinkage high again on the grout you had me test," a technician said from his lab bench.

"That's not good. Prepare some new samples for additional testing. I want you to cycle the test temperature of the grout. In the morning, place the specimens in the oven at 350 degrees. Leave them there until four thirty and then remove them to cool on the lab bench overnight. Repeat this cycling ten times. After the tenth time and before you run the compressive strength test, we'll examine the surface under the microscope."

Neil's systematic scrutiny of his company's products would ascertain data that contradicted Chadwick's fraudulent marketing literature.

Chapter 9

Traveling home, Neil passed small, simple, mill houses and pictured generations of workers walking home after logging long hours in a textile mill, cogs in the wheel of commerce, much like workers today.

Swerving into the driveway, he crushed some white impatiens under the back wheels. Neil parked his Saturn, noting that Bridget had not yet arrived home. It would be at least an hour before she returned from her weekly tennis game. He appreciated the time alone.

What if there already were radiation leaks? His worries fluctuated between fear of a nuclear accident and fear of reprisals from his employer. Neil felt trapped.

Preoccupied, he skipped his usual stop in the living room for the evening news, going instead directly to his study. Perched precariously on the edge of his recliner, he pondered his workday and his next phone call.

"Hi guys," Neil said to his blue discus. "I'm very proud that you survived the move to Charlotte. I hope I do."

The stunningly colored fish were indifferent to their caretaker's mood as he stared trance-like at their swift movements. In the present lighting, the aquarium foliage lacked its typical range of greens. Dull olive dominated the tank background. The late afternoon shadows muted the room's true lavender hue to a grayish tinge. Three bronze plaques for U.S. patents inscribed with numbers, dates, and Neil's name filled spaces between shelves of history and science books. Framed photos of meteor showers and Haley's comet hung on a wall.

His telescope stood poised in the corner of his study. Neil stared blankly. Technical journals covered the desk, hid the tops of file cabinets, and were heaped in piles on the floor. Surrounded by the knowledge of his technical library, he struggled to make sense of his situation.

Although Bridget supported his calling the NRC, she could not fathom the potential consequences and would be appalled if she knew the extent of Gordon's cruelty to his workers. Neil knew that Gordon could ruin him.

Trying to rouse himself, he said aloud, "I guess I'll feed you royal creatures." He took the bright yellow, round container from the shelf above the aquarium. With a push of his thumb, he popped off the lid, shook multicolored flakes into the aquarium, and watched while the discus caught the floating specks.

Neil put the unopened magazine down and heard his own nervous chuckle. *He would block my attempts to get another job—no employment with a competitor for three years!* The harsh terms of Gordon's contract probably would not stand up in any court, but a lowly worker could not finance a legal battle against the mighty Gordon Byrnes. Removing his grandparents' photo from his pocket, he stared intently at it, seeking inspiration. This three-by-three picture had traveled in his grandfather's army uniform pocket throughout his time in Europe during World War II. Married in 1938, drafted in 1942, Neil's father had told him that his own father carried it close to his heart, certain he would return to his bride. Neil loved this story. Early in his working career, he smoothed over the cracks in the photo with plastic in order to continue the tradition.

"Hi there," Bridget shouted as she ran up the stairs. Bridget's voice pierced Neil's foggy state of mind.

"How'd the call go?"

"The anonymous one?"

"Yeah."

"Someone from the NRC is calling here soon."

"What?" Bridget stood in the doorway, her hair damp, with a visor ridge imprinted across the top of her head.

"I gave my name and phone number for a call back."

"Why?"

"They need more information. Everything is supposed to be confidential, so Gordon won't find out that I reported him."

"But you're worried it won't be." Tiny beads formed as cool air blew against her sweaty skin.

"It's a risk. It could be bad for me."

"For us." Bridget corrected, wiping dampness from her skin.

"A government agency can manage Gordon. He's not invincible," Neil said.

"Maybe you should get another job before Gordon finds out." Bridget rubbed her arms to stop shivering.

"I wish it were that simple." Pain welled in his eyes. "I signed an agreement that stipulated that if I leave, I won't work for a competitor for three years, and Gordon considers the universe his competition. He defends his contract. All my work has been in polymers. I'm stuck."

"That's outrageous. Sue the bastard. An employer can't hold you hostage. Slavery hasn't existed in the South for a long time."

"This has nothing to do with the South. Business law governs noncompete clauses in employment contracts. Gordon would spend more money than we can ever imagine. We can't take him on in a legal battle. I didn't really worry about the terms when I took the job. I planned on staying here—maybe even til retirement."

"Do you think the government can help?"

"They sounded like they want to. They need to—the potential for catastrophe at a power plant is enormous and escalating."

"Can you get me some water please? I need to change into dry clothes."

Neil went down to the kitchen and filled two tall glasses with water. He gulped half of his and refilled it before returning upstairs. In record time, Bridget finished a shower, dressed in shorts and a tee shirt, and rejoined Neil.

She took a sip of water.

The phone rang. "Probably the NRC." Neil got up and moved toward the phone on his desk. "Yes, this is Neil," He verified with a nod to Bridget that it was the call he expected.

"This is Dr. Trevor Williams. I'm an Agency Allegation Advisor at the NRC headquarters in White Flint, Maryland. Are you the person who had called our office earlier today to report a safety concern?"

"Yes."

"Let me introduce two other staff members on this call: Luke Johnson, also from White Flint, and Eric Turner from Region 2 in Atlanta, Georgia. We're on a secure line. We have some questions we want to ask you," Trevor began in an official tone.

"Fine." Neil leaned against his desk and stroked his chin with his free hand.

Trevor instructed the others on the line not to have sidebar discussions among themselves and then he asked, "What company do you work for Neil?"

"GB Polymers."

"How long have you worked there?"

"Two years," Neil answered.

"What exactly is your concern?"

"A radioactive leak could occur at nuclear power plants due to defective material." Neil feared he sounded unconvincing.

"You think GB Polymers supplied material to nuclear power plants."

"I know they did."

"Who purchased the product?"

"Various electrical utilities as well as some construction companies." Neil moved away from his desk and walked in circles.

"Name some of the utilities."

"Oh—Detroit Edison, Baltimore Gas & Electric, Duke Energy, New York Power Authority, Intercostal Energy, and Shoreline Utilities." Neil worried his statements sounded implausible.

"Intercostal Energy—would that be the Southport Plant in North Carolina?"

"Absolutely. We've supplied material to both Unit One and Unit Two."

"Luke, is Southport the plant that had a problem with nonshrink grout?"

"Not sure … maybe," Luke replied. For two more minutes, they continued a separate conversation, a sidebar Trevor wanted to avoid.

"Neil, what do you think is wrong?"

"Temperature claims. They're inflated seven hundred degrees."

"Did your company say its material met the requirements of 10 CFR 50?"

"Yes."

"You're sure they made that claim?"

"Positive. I saw the exact wording in our technical brochure."

"Are you sure they shipped substandard material to power plants?"

"I'm sure. Sales staff and Ricktel said it's easier to sell with the basic component certification, but our stuff doesn't warrant it."

"Who else might know this?"

"Oh, the company owner, Gordon Byrnes, for sure, and his son, Chadwick, and the manager of quality." Neil heard a "please believe me" plea tone in his own voice.

Trevor continued with his questions, "Who is the manager of quality
assurance?"

"His name is Richard Grover."

"Is he also a chemist?"

"No. He doesn't have a technical background."

"We'll want to talk with you some more. An NRC agent in the division of reactor safety will contact you and make an appointment."

"Is he on this call?" Neil asked.

"No, he's not. His name is Randolph Perry. Can he call you during the day?" Trevor asked.

"No. It's too risky. I didn't call from work because I was afraid someone would overhear me. If my company knew I was talking to you, I would lose my job," Neil said.

"I'll instruct Agent Perry to call your home," Trevor said. "Expect his call in two weeks."

Neil hung up the phone.

"Did they say they'd do something?" Bridget asked, as she walked back into the room.

"They'll call me in two weeks."

"No hurry, huh? Why not have another Chernobyl?" she said wryly.

"I should never have called," Neil said glumly.

"You can't undo the call. I'm hungry. Let's eat." Bridget started down the stairs.

Neil followed his wife into the kitchen and said, "The stuff they're selling won't withstand a real world accident."

"I'm scared that Byrnes has friends in high places," she said.

"Bridget, you know, of course, that we can't tell anyone about this," Neil warned.

"Who would believe this story? I promise I won't say a word."

Unable to sleep, Neil stayed up most of the night. *How does one become so avaricious?* Gordon's mean-spirited nature puzzled Neil.

Without help, regulators could not get close enough to examine his business.

"Now they'll have to. I handed them the case," Neil said aloud, struggling to sound reassured.

Chapter 10

Neil arrived at work fifteen minutes earlier than usual.

"Earl Grey, captain?" Tom asked.

"I'd love some."

"This could be our ticket out of here, captain." Tom showed Neil a small slip of paper. "Powerball is $165 million."

"I hope you win, Spock."

"Captain, do you mind if I leave around four-thirty today for my horticultural class?" Tom asked.

"That's fine. How's it going?"

"Very well. Gardening is the next step on my career ladder, my safety net for when Gordon boots me out the door. Do you think that goes against the noncompete agreement?"

"Probably. Aren't the water hoses made of plastic? How about the pots? Any company with plastic anything is a rival in Gordon's mind. I'm afraid, Spock, that any career in gardening will violate the terms of our employee contract."

"Damn. No exit."

"Tom you do great work."

"This shrine is dedicated to people who did great work," Tom pointed to blue paint strip samples.

"Victor?"

Tom nodded. "Heard the latest about our former marketing manager?"

"No. He's working, right?" Neil asked.

"Not likely. Chadwick got a call from someone in human resources at an adhesive company where Victor applied for a job. Chadwick gave the customary response, informing the person that Victor had signed a noncompete agreement. You know the intractable legal document that you and I freely signed on day one here."

"I remember. It was as voluntary as signing medical forms in the emergency room with a bone protruding through your skin," Neil said.

"Right. Chadwick threatened legal action against the adhesive company if they hired Victor. Crazy, to still keep the guy from working after firing him."

"Cruel. It's been two years," Neil said.

"I'll keep you posted on Victor's job search."

"I wish the poor guy well. Any new test results?" Neil asked.

"Yes, in my notebook," Tom handed it to Neil.

"Thanks." The hostile action against Victor distracted Neil.

*****

That evening, an NRC staff member called Neil. "We're having trouble understanding your company's products and how they were used at the nuclear power plants. Can you get us some literature? Copies of purchase orders would help and anything about the company's quality assurance procedures."

"Who are you?" Neil asked, incredulous that he was meeting another NRC worker via the phone.

"My name is Agent Holcombe."

"Why are you calling me?" Neil regretted that he did not have caller ID. He worried that this person was not actually with the NRC.

"I'm working from a Post-it on my calendar. It was here when I came in this morning. It's clear I'm to call you for written information— oh it's Trevor Williams, I see his name now."

Neil resisted saying, *how do I know who you are?* Instead, he said, "It's not easy for me to remove documents. Can't Trevor or someone from the NRC come to Charlotte and ask for whatever they need?"

"Well, first they have to determine if they should pursue your allegation," Holcombe said.

"What? Of course they need to pursue it," Neil shouted. "I've provided very specific information. *You* need to obtain additional documents. Isn't the NRC responsible to do something?"

"The NRC needs further clarification on the products you say are defective."

"So it's not enough that I called your agency. Now you want me to take additional risks. You expect me to make illegal copies, take papers out of my office, and get them to the NRC. Can I speak with Trevor?"

"He's not available."

"Your agency has thousands of employees. Surely someone can come to Charlotte and get any papers they need."

"Mr. Landers, I was told to contact you. I cannot answer your questions. Please cooperate."

"I don't believe this conversation. You don't get it. Tell Trevor to call me. Good-bye."

"I'll give Trevor your message, Mr. Landers."

Neil clicked off the phone and remained in his chair, staring aimlessly into his aquarium.

"What's up?" Bridget asked.

"The NRC wants copies of incriminating paperwork. I never use the copier! I'll look very suspicious."

"Just do it. They need help."

*****

Thinking about the best way to get paperwork for the NRC, Neil remembered that Gordon had boasted about writing the *Byrnes Engineering Handbook*, claiming it was the Bible for the industry. Neil doubted that Gordon wrote any of it. There was no evidence the man could compose a coherent paragraph—a book?—no way. Gordon bragged that he disseminated this manual to paper mills, petro refineries, and nuclear power plants.

Finding a copy on a shelf in his office, Neil regretted not asking for an autographed copy from the big guy. The handbook had useful, illustrated instructions guiding contractors in various industries on how to stabilize heavy equipment, protect electrical wiring from potential fire damage, and fireproof an area.

Neil went about his day preoccupied with the previous evening's phone call. The unreasonable, risky request incensed him. Telling himself he could not turn back, Neil listened to a message on his voice mail from Kevin, the marketing manager: *I received an urgent call from Home Depot. Give me a call.*

Instead of picking up the phone, Neil responded in person. Although Neil did not have restrictions on his movement in the building, as did most employees, he rarely traveled to the top floor of the building.

"Hi, Kevin," Neil said.

"You're winded. You need to visit me more often," Kevin greeted Neil.

"Or use the gym. What can I do for you?" Neil asked.

"Home Depot needs grout. They're having trouble keeping up with demand. The workers at their current supplier's manufacturing plant are on strike. They'd like us to deliver dozens of truckloads a day."

"You're serious?"

"Yes. I cannot believe my luck. This opportunity came my way."

"Well, there's a slight problem, Kevin. Home Depot wants tile grout, right?"

"I think so."

"In thirty-five colors?"

"We didn't discuss how many."

"They want customized colors, right?"

"I think so. Is color a problem?"

"We have gray grout. That's it. Not cream or vanilla or sand or ivory. Only gray. And our grout is not for setting household tile."

"You can't use it in bathrooms or kitchens?" Kevin asked.

"No. It's used under heavy equipment. Under machines that cost millions of dollars and weigh thousands of pounds. Our grout keeps massive machinery level and anchors it in place. We make construction grout. We don't make tile grout."

"Oh. I didn't realize."

Neil moved near the office window with a good view of the main entrance. He looked out at the fountain and smiled at the absurdity of this discussion. The last marketing manager, Victor, knew the company products and their applications.

Turning back toward Kevin, he said, "Anything else I can do for you?"

"No. Thanks for stopping."

Before exiting the top floor, Neil surveyed an unoccupied office for anything to help his cause. There was nothing. Scouting another office, he spied grout-packaging bags on the floor in the corner.

Neil picked one up and read to himself *this product meets the requirements of 10 CFR 50 Appendix B*. He folded the bag and slid it under his arm to carry back to his desk. It was compact enough to put into his attaché case later for carrying out of the building.

He retraced his steps to the first level. Back in his office, Neil plotted to locate correspondence with utilities, letters that certified the quality of material shipped to power plants. Neil decided to look around the quality assurance manager's office during one of Richard's frequent days at the manufacturing plant.

Back in the lab, Neil complained to Tom, "Our marketing manager, Kevin, has been talking with Home Depot about tile grout."

"Tile grout? Captain, did you formulate a new product without my help?"

"Kevin just asked me if we could respond immediately to their need for dozens of truckloads daily." Neil shook his head and laughed.

"Amazing. I missed a great opportunity. I should have studied marketing instead of chemistry. Did he think we did bathrooms?"

"Yep. And maybe craft projects," Neil said. "I'm not sure."

"He should have a real good time misusing the hazardous liquid slurry you're cooking up."

Chapter 11

"Good Morning, Neil," his secretary greeted him the next day. "Richard has appointments out of the building today. Unless you object, I'd like to attend an award's assembly at my daughter's school. Would it be all right if I'm a little late returning from lunch?"

"Not a problem. I trust she's a worthy recipient?"

"I hope so."

Assured ample time to search for incriminating documents in Richard's office that afternoon, Neil descended to the lab for the morning.

"Captain on the bridge," Tom called from his cushioned, high-back lab stool. "And not a moment too soon. I need executive input."

Various sized jars of chemicals were spread out on the bench, as well as hardened samples of concrete. Recording the weight from his digital scale in his lab book, Tom said, "Captain, this specimen from yesterday is already showing cracking. Do you want me to redo it?"

They discussed possible explanations and adjusted the formula. Neil appraised the other technicians' lab projects and provided suggestions as required.

Mid-day, after checking that his secretary had left, Neil strolled into Richard's office.

"He's at the plant." Chadwick startled Neil. He was sitting at Richard's desk.

Wondering what Chadwick was doing but not daring to ask, Neil said, "I'll catch him tomorrow."

In his office next door, Neil listened for Chadwick's exit. Before returning to search, Neil crossed the hall and from a window watched Chadwick leave the building. Back in Richard's office, Neil noted that Gordon's preference for paper copies was a lucky break. If he had to hunt electronically for evidence, it was unlikely that he would succeed.

Neil pulled a folder marked power plants from the file cabinet. Bingo. Neil found a letter addressed to Ricktel, a large construction contractor, and another to Shoreline Utilities, owner of a nuclear power plant in Connecticut. With a quick scan, Neil concluded he had incriminating evidence for the NRC. A memo from Richard to Chadwick fascinated Neil. It stated that a purchasing agent for Ricktel told Richard that Tennessee Valley Authority plants needed safety grade material for renovations at aging power plants. This man offered to help GB Polymers with language to describe their product that would appease the NRC. *So that's where Chadwick got the idea to market to the nuclear industry.* License extensions at ten plants and a resurgence of interest in building new plants must have persuaded Chadwick of the potential for significant profits.

Walking down the hall to the photocopier, Neil wished it were in a less public spot. He gazed at the machine. A new model that he had never used. Lifting the cover, he put one letter facedown on the glass and pushed the green rectangular button. His heart rate accelerated. He took a couple of deep breaths before producing a copy of half the letter. Repositioning, he pressed start again: a good, clean copy of the Ricktel letter landed in the output tray.

After repeating the process with the second letter, he collected all the papers. To assure himself that he had gathered everything, he lifted the cover twice and then retraced his way to Richard's office to return the original letters.

Next, Neil looked for shipping documents. Pulling stuffed folders from a file drawer labeled shipping, he flipped a pile of paper and scanned for product names and destinations. There was not time to copy everything. Using a child's selection process for discarding bland Halloween candy, he zeroed in on the good stuff by picking out five letters mailed to utilities that owned power plants and three sent to contractors who mentioned repair work at nuclear power plants.

Neil found the *Quality Assurance Manual* clipped into a paper folder. Bending the fasteners open, he removed the pages, including an official letter signed by President Chadwick Byrnes stating GB Polymers's commitment to implementing the procedures outlined in the manual. He returned to the copier.

Chadwick can't claim ignorance since he personally endorsed the quality program.

That evening, Neil called Trevor. He left a message on his tape, "I've got what you want. Where should I send it?"

Agent Holcombe called Neil back the next evening, "Trevor's out of town on a special assignment. I picked up the message you left. That's great that you have some additional information. Thank you. Can you mail it to us?"

"Give me an address," Neil said.

"I guess to Trevor here in White Flint, Maryland. The address is ... Rockville Pike.

Neil jotted down the address for NRC headquarters.

Then Holcombe said, "No, send it to Region II in Atlanta."

Neil crossed out the White Flint address and wrote the one for the NRC in Atlanta, Georgia.

Changing his mind again, Holcombe said, "Send it to Agent Randolph Perry, who will proceed with this investigation. I'll give you his address … please hold … I'll be right back … uh … I don't seem to have it handy. Neil, it would be best for you to send it to me in White Flint."

Not impressed with Holcombe's confusion about where to send the paperwork, Neil said, "I'm concerned this material will be lost." He marked thick lines through the Georgia address and wrote Holcombe's.

As he wrote the third address, Holcombe flippantly said, "You did make two copies didn't you… just in case."

"No, but I will--at Kinko's. The copier is in a public spot at work and I never use it to do my job," Neil said.

"We'll call you when we receive it."

*****

"Is anyone at your work suspicious?" Bridget asked, as they sat down to dinner.

"Of course not. Don't you think I'm good at undercover work?"

"You look stressed to me. I thought it might be obvious."

The phone rang. "Ignore it. You need a peaceful meal."

After their outgoing message, Neil heard, "This is Agent Perry."

Neil jumped up and grabbed the phone. "Yes, Agent Perry, Trevor told me to expect your call."

"I understand you're sending documents about your company shipping substandard material to nuclear power plants. I very much want to meet with you in person. Would next Wednesday work?"

"As long as we meet in the evening."

"I've checked that the Center City Marriott in Charlotte honors government room rates. Is that far from you?" Perry inquired.

"Not at all."

"What's the earliest time you can get there?"

"Six-thirty."

"That's fine. When you get to the Marriott, use a hotel phone and ask the operator to connect you with Randolph Perry," he instructed. "Then I'll give you my room number."

"See you Wednesday." Neil hung up the phone and returned to the dinner table.

"Government?" Bridget put down her forkful of salad.

"Yes," he responded without elaborating.

"Government agents aren't appealing dinner guests."

"Sorry." His food remained untouched. "I've got an appointment with an NRC agent at an uptown hotel next week."

"Please eat something."

"I've lost my appetite."

"This isn't worth you getting sick. Since you called the NRC, you're a zombie in the evening, and you prowl the house most of the night. I don't know how you get through your workday. You can't go on with such little sleep."

"I can't help it. I wish I could. I have to find a way to convince this agent to investigate Byrnes."

Chapter 12

Neil drove from the Byrnes Building to his uptown meeting, unaware of his surroundings. As he crossed Tryon Street, the red and white Marriott logo pierced his hazy consciousness. Feeling his chest tighten, he struggled to resume normal breathing.

Avoiding the hotel garage, he parked on Trade Street. The meter flashed free. He sat for a moment, and then with jerky, shifty motions, he looked from side to side, checking for anyone he might know. *Ridiculous—I'm nobody.*

Walking the short block to the Marriott, he felt like a criminal. A Lexus SUV slowed. *Chadwick followed me!,* Neil thought. Neil turned and walked down a side street away from the hotel. *Was that Lexus dark green? He could not be sure. Chadwick's was navy.*

Lacking the suave style of a spy, and a stranger to deception, Neil had no doubt that he looked suspicious. Resisting making a dash for the hotel, he resumed his stroll to a secret meeting with the government.

Standing on the sidewalk, he looked around again and noted with relief that he did not recognize anyone in the area. Neil continued to the hotel's glass and bronze doors, where the automatic doors parted. He made a final look around before entering the lobby and stepping onto a thickly woven gray and red carpet. At his right, a hotel phone sat on top of an ornate, well-polished reproduction of an antique chest of drawers. He picked it up and waited for the operator. Hoping he did not sound as strange as he felt, he said, "Please connect me with Randolph Perry."

"My pleasure, sir," the operator said.

"Perry here."

"It's Neil Landers."

"We're in Room 1421, come on up," Perry instructed. "The elevators are around the corner from the entrance."

Perry said we …who's we?, Neil wondered. He walked to the elevators without making eye contact with hotel staff or guests and stepped into an empty one, pressing button number fourteen.

The elevator door opened in front of an enormous mirror. Neil hurried away from it, not wanting confirmation that he looked awful. An arrow on a wall plaque indicated that even-numbered rooms were to the left. He walked to the right and found 1421 midway down the corridor.

Standing at the door, he took three deep breaths to slow his rapid breathing. Calmer, he knocked on the door. It opened immediately.

"Yes?" the man at the door asked in an unwelcome tone. He stood about five nine, was very athletic looking, and appeared to be in his late twenties.

"I'm Neil Landers." He attempted to sound nonchalant as if every day he showed up at a stranger's hotel room.

"Come on in. I'm Jake Fowler with the NRC office of criminal investigations." The man opened a black plastic case a little larger than one for eyeglasses. He moved it in Neil's direction to show his photo ID and brass badge.

Neil entered an oversized room, one with more than the usual hotel floor space. The carpet, standard hotel nondescript, had a mixture of blue with speckles of black and gray. Thick drapes with a bold, colorful, geometric-patterned fabric matched the bedspread. Over the bed hung a framed picture of a street scene: downtown Charlotte in the fifties from the look of the cars.

Two men sat at a dark red, cloth-covered table, not typical hotel room furnishing, probably one arranged for this meeting. A bucket of ice, a pitcher of water, and a tray of glasses were set at one end of the table.

Fowler continued the introductions as he took a seat. "This is Randolph Perry with the office of reactor safety." He motioned to a man seated closest to the water. "And Dr. Ma is a chemist," Fowler pointed to a slightly built Asian man. Both men shook Neil's hand without getting up from their seats.

Neil noted that Perry and Dr. Ma looked more uncomfortable than he did. Perry's thick glasses reminded Neil of a comic book depiction of a nerd. Even seated, he could tell that Perry was short. They displayed their badges for him.

Neil sat in the one remaining folding chair and placed his attaché case on the floor against a chair leg.

"Do you have some identification?" Fowler asked, leaning forward.

"Yeah, sure." Neil removed a business card from his shirt pocket and handed it to him.

Fowler looked at the card with quality grade paper, two colors, and embossed lettering. "Can I see your driver's license?"

"Oh, of course." Neil stood up and knocked over his attaché case. He dug out his wallet from his pants pocket, retrieved his license, and passed it to Fowler.

"Why do you need this?" Neil asked.

"It's required. We have to know who we're talking to," Fowler replied in an official tone.

Neil used his best poker face to conceal his surprise as Fowler wrote down his license number.

"I also need your Social Security number," Fowler said.

"It's … 05 … Neil stopped. "I'm—not sure."

"That's all right, we'll get it later."

"You look familiar," Dr. Ma said, as he shifted his small body. He nervously tapped his right thumb rapidly on his left thumbnail.

What's he worried about, Neil thought.

"Perhaps we met at a science convention. I'm involved with a number of scientific organizations." He remembered from Fowler's introduction that Dr. Ma was also a chemist.

"Not as many as I am, I'd bet. I'm a PhD." Dr. Ma's one-upmanship tone mystified Neil.

"We've more to do tonight." Randolph Perry cut off Dr. Ma from anymore sparring with Neil.

"Before we get to the specifics of your allegation, we'd like additional information on your company. Surprisingly, there is very little information on the Internet. All the search engines I've used brought up a home page with a message that the site is under construction," Perry said. "Tell us about GB Polymers."

Dr. Ma's earlier provocative tone distracted Neil. He had not heard Perry's question. "Could you please repeat what you just said?" Neil asked.

"I'm puzzled that I can't find any background information about your company on the Web," Perry stated.

"Just a phone number, right?"

"Yes. That's all." Perry balanced his elbows on the table edge and raised his hands with his palms thrown open. "If they do business with nuclear power plants, it should be easy for me to get information."

"It's a private business. The owner, Gordon Byrnes, is not keen on disseminating information to the public about his company and frequently says he'd like to return to the old-fashioned business practice of responding to customer-initiated phone calls. A telling statement about my employer is that there are no administrative assistants, only secretaries."

"How old is the company?"

"About seventy years."

"Who started it?"

"Gordon Byrnes's father. The original company was Byrnes Engineering."

"Does it still exist?"

"Oh, yes. Gordon adds companies. He doesn't eliminate them. The senior Mr. Byrnes understood the value of selling to the government."

"Are you saying this company sold primarily to the government?" Perry looked surprised.

"Gordon's father determined early on that's where he'd make the most money."

"Go on."

"Could I have some water?" Neil wanted a moment to organize his thoughts.

"Certainly." Perry poured a glass and passed it to Fowler who handed it to Neil.

"Most of what I know is from my boss, Gordon Byrnes," Neil started, after taking several sips of water. "Gordon expanded his father's business and started a new company, GB Polymers, that manufactured a hybrid of polymers and ceramics used as coatings. Like his father, Gordon found a market for his products with the government."

"Which government agency bought from GB Polymers?" Dr. Ma asked.

Turning to Dr. Ma, Neil responded, "At first, the military. GB Polymers coatings were more durable than glass, yet possessed similar barrier properties, effective for bulletproofing windows. Then Gordon moved on to additional, lucrative contracts with other government agencies. Remember the scandal of the famous $1200 toilet seats purchased by the Air Force for planes used by the generals?" Neil glanced around at each of the men, who nodded in agreement.

"Yeah," Fowler said. "That's when a government purchasing agent testified to Congress in the early seventies. He was fired for disclosing the overpayment."

"Right. He lost his job for exposing the cost overruns. Anyhow, Gordon told me that GB Polymers supplied the resin composition. They also sold $1850 dust covers for jet plane engines to the U.S. military. According to Gordon, the military sought protective covering for jet engines standing in the desert. Using a toddler's turtle-shaped swimming pool from Wal-Mart as a model for a mold, he morphed his $34 item into an $1850 barrier."

"The cold war treated GB Polymers well," Perry said matter-of-factly.

"That's right. In the seventies and eighties military contracts were the profit centers. Gordon boasted that relocating his company to Charlotte was a brilliant strategy for growing the business," Neil said. "Lower building and land costs attracted him. He complained that zoning ordinances cramped his plans for expansion in Greenwich, Connecticut. Gordon wanted an ostentatious corporate headquarters. His manufacturing plant in South Norwalk also limited the potential for growth."

"When did Gordon move south?" Fowler asked.

"About eight years ago," Neil said.

"This is interesting, but we have to stay focused," Perry said. "If I have the history correct, Gordon Byrnes's father started doing business with the government in the forties and fifties. Then in the sixties, when the Atomic Energy Commission granted licenses to build nuclear power plants, most likely contractors purchased components from the manufacturer that already had a track record with the government."

"Right," Neil said "But it took the third generation to get really greedy. Chadwick identified the nuclear industry's need for maintenance and upgrades of its aging reactors as a niche market. He saw the potential for profit in supplying material for building new nuclear plants."

"You're convinced GB Polymers pursued the nuclear industry," Perry said.

"Without a doubt. I'm currently working on grout slurry to immobilize liquid hazardous waste in storage tanks."

"To use at Hanford or the Savannah River storage sites?"

"I'm a long way from a good formula."

"What was your job title at Tarrytown Chemicals?"

"Research chemist."

"Was any of your work with polymers known to Gordon Byrnes?"

"I have a patent on a UV resistant polymer. I believe that caught his attention."

"You have the patent for Tarrytown Chemicals?" Dr. Ma blurted.

"Of course, the patent is assigned to Tarrytown Chemicals, but my name is on it as the inventor," Neil responded, surprised at Dr. Ma's apparent jealousy.

"Do you have your name on any other patents?" Dr. Ma asked.

"Yes," Neil said without elaborating.

"How many?" Dr. Ma asked.

"I've three U.S. patents."

"Let's talk about your background," Fowler interrupted. "Where did you go to college?"

"The University of Connecticut."

"What was your first job?"

"Tarrytown Chemicals."

"That was your only job before GB Polymers?"

"Yes. I was there thirteen years."

"And why did you leave Tarrytown Chemicals?"

"A question I ask myself every day," Neil responded wearily. "Gordon Byrnes approached me at an ASTM meeting in San Francisco."

"That's how I know you," Dr. Ma said. "I must have met you at an ASTM meeting. Were you at the Toronto meeting in June?"

"Yes." Cognizant that Dr. Ma did not like him, Neil added, "I co-chaired the Symposium on Petrographic Techniques."

"How long have you been active with ASTM?" Dr. Ma looked stunned at Neil's level of involvement.

"For thirteen years," Neil replied with satisfaction.

"Gentlemen, we're getting off-track here," Perry interrupted. "You say you were recruited by the owner of GB Polymers?" Perry gave Dr. Ma a disapproving glance.

"That's right. I did not plan to change jobs. Maybe occasionally I thought about looking for a more challenging opportunity, but it was unlikely, without a PhD, that I'd get a director of research position. I was comfortable and enjoyed the community of Tarrytown," Neil said. "Gordon was relentless, insisting I see his corporate office and lab and find out more about his company. For a weekend, he entertained my wife and me. Timing was good, the offer generous. We accepted."

"He approached you at a meeting that has hundreds of participants?" Fowler's voice registered astonishment.

"Right. I've attended meetings regularly for years. Gordon observed me and asked other ASTM members for a recommendation for someone technically competent in polymers. I'm sure he noted my involvement with committees that set standards for plastics. Gordon was anxious to fill his director of research position, and I think he believed that if he hired me I would get him special consideration with the ASTM. The letters missing after my name did not concern Gordon. Because he himself did not have any, he belittled graduate degrees."

The statement was out of his mouth before he remembered that Dr. Ma, sitting across the table from him, had a PhD. Dr. Ma's face registered the importance he placed on his advanced degree.

Neil shifted attention back to Gordon and reached for some sympathy. "The first day on the job, Gordon's secretary handed me a very aggressive noncompete agreement, making any future job changes near impossible for me."

"About your allegations," Perry said. "Tell us what you think your company did wrong?"

"They exaggerated performance claims for products they certified for critical applications in power plants."

"No power plant would accept a manufacturer's word. They would test the designated material," Dr. Ma insisted in a condescending tone of voice.

"Have you ever worked in the real world? My employer lied to utilities," Neil said. "They stated that they were doing the required testing. Utilities believed a lab, independent of the manufacturer, certified their purchases. I gave you the paperwork."

They went back and forth among themselves discussing NRC regulations. It appeared to Neil that the agents lacked understanding of their agency's most basic rules. Worse, he felt Dr. Ma did not believe him. Neil regretted goading the technical expert.

"It's not clear to us that GB Polymers violated any regulation," Perry said. "I contacted resident inspectors at a dozen power plants. They're confident that your company complied with procedures. Look at these documents." He handed Neil a dozen sheets with Spencer Chemical Research letterhead. "They're getting objective test data."

Neil noted the Central Avenue address and said, "I don't know any Spencer Chemical Research lab."

"No businessman would take the risks you described," Dr. Ma said.

"What can I say? You have copies of letters to utilities certifying that a product shipped to a power plant met industry standards. Have you talked with anyone at Spencer Chemical Research?" Neil asked.

"Yes, of course, and we plan to visit. We're prepared to do due diligence and verify GB's quality program. We'll show up unannounced and have a dialogue with Mr. Byrnes and audit the testing."

"I doubt they'll cooperate."

"They're required to give us access. As contractors in the nuclear industry, they are under NRC jurisdiction. They have to let us review data, talk to staff, and perform all tasks of oversight," Perry insisted.

"I wish you well," Neil responded.

"It's uncommon for our visits to be adversarial. We may need to talk with you again before we visit your company. Let's stop for now. I'm sorry we kept you so late. Do you live far from here?"

"No, five miles. Without traffic, I'll be home in minutes."

Neil walked in a daze to the elevator and descended to the lobby. The night clerk looked up and nodded at Neil as he walked to the hotel exit. He stepped outside onto a deserted block. He walked rapidly to his car, got in, and made a U-turn to head south on Trade, eager to be home.

Chapter 13

High-spirited fiddle sounds filled the house. Bridget was still up. Neil walked into the den.

She decreased the volume of her traditional Irish music and hugged him. "How did it go?"

"It was surreal." He told her about his meeting with NRC agents. "One of the agents introduced himself as being with criminal investigations and displayed his badge."

"Like on TV?"

"Yes."

"Do you think they can handle a Gordon Byrnes?"

"They'll do their best. They're diligent workers."

"That's good."

"I'm scared they're too trusting. Their PhD. expert knows nothing about the business world."

"Have you eaten?" Bridget asked.

"I'm not hungry."

"I'm worried you'll be sick."

"I'm okay," Neil said.

"You're exhausted. You don't get enough sleep."

"My mind is racing." Neil had not put together his company's long history with the nuclear industry until tonight. No wonder Chadwick expected to succeed with his bogus claims. With paperwork from an independent lab, the agents believed Neil was misinformed. He vowed to find out more about Spencer Chemical Research Lab.

*****

The next day, Neil drove to a strip mall on Central Avenue and parked his car in front of the place with the address he remembered from the letter the NRC agents had shown him. He walked inside, waited to speak to the young woman behind the counter, and overheard three different business names when she answered the phone. *The storefront created a virtual office for companies.*

"I'm interested in learning more about your services. My wife and I are setting up a consulting business. Can you help?" Neil asked.

"I'll be happy to, I'm Lynette. You're describing our typical customer. Excuse me." She took another call. "Spencer Chemical Research, can I help you? I'll be glad to put you through to voice mail."

Neil wished he could find out that caller's identity.

"I've got a brochure that describes how we can assist you." She handed one to Neil. "We answer your phone and accept your mail."

"And we would have remote access to retrieve messages?" Neil asked.

"Absolutely. We also offer customized features. If response time is important, an automatic beeper system contacts the business owner once I put a message through to voice mail. Wherever you are, you can call back promptly. That's one of our more popular services."

"That last caller left a message, and you alerted Spencer whatever you said to the call."

"Exactly. Spencer Chemical Research gets numerous calls a day. That's one of our more active businesses. Most of our clients are interested in the mail service, not wanting business mail sent to their home and preferring the professional appearance of a suite address rather than a post office box on their letterhead."

"Could I speak with a current user of your services?"

"Well, I've never been asked that question. Let me think."

Neil took in the layout. A phone system with a bank of numbers, a wall of mailboxes designated as business suites, and various mailing containers and packing materials.

"I'm sure the man from Spencer Chemical Research would talk with you," Lynette said. "Richard's a real nice guy. He always brings me a Krispy Kreme glazed doughnut. He's sweet. One week I mentioned that I liked Jimmie Johnson, and the next time he stopped by, he gave me an autographed picture of Jimmie, my favorite NASCAR driver. Give me your card. I'll ask him to call you."

Richard, of course, would do the legwork. Mr. Quality Assurance. "Thanks." Neil ignored her request for his card. "I'll show my wife the brochure. I'll be back."

As Neil retraced his route, he knew he had to obtain communications to customers on Spencer Chemical Research letterhead. That data would be interesting to review. He got out of his car and started toward the building. *What an idiot,* he thought to himself. Remembering the virtual office brochure on the front seat, Neil turned to go back as Richard pulled into the space next to his. Neil popped his trunk.

"Chadwick's in a bad mood," Richard warned. "Keep your distance."

Strange, that Richard chatted with him about Chadwick. Neil was not friendly with Richard. Neil pretended to look for something in his trunk until Richard left. Then he hid the brochure out of sight under the front seat.

Walking back to the lab, Neil overheard Chadwick talking to Richard. "They have to accept what's already been shipped."

Neil stopped and listened.

"Forty-three pallets are on a truck today going back to our plant," Richard said.

"No way—we have an agreement," Chadwick said.

"The project manager is not happy. He said there's a big variation from bag to bag. He had problems applying it. He thinks we didn't blend it properly," Richard said.

"He'll pay for what he ordered. Our product is fine."

"It might be better to lighten up and not pressure him. He told me that technically he should report this to the NRC."

"He threatened us?"

"He wants you to see it his way. Accept the returned load, don't charge him, and he'll go away quietly. The bottom line is that the White Marsh plant will no longer buy from us unless we take this material back and send him replacement product."

Chapter 14

"Is Las Vegas really too expensive?" Midori whispered into Olmsted's ear, as she massaged the back of his neck.

Olmsted's cell phone's familiar sound postponed a response. As he picked up the phone from his desk, he remained seated, to not interrupt Midori's skillful kneading.

"Attorney Olmsted here," he barked into the phone. "Of course, Doris, I'll take his call," "Mr. Byrnes, how's the sunny South? Sorry to hear that. Why did they say they came to your office?"

"To investigate my business," Gordon shouted.

"The U.S. Nuclear Regulatory Commission wants to investigate your business?" Olmsted held up his hand for Midori to stop.

"So they say. I think one of my competitors sent them to spy. Tell me how to get rid of them."

Attorney Jeremiah Olmsted grasped the significance; government agents rarely showed up unannounced. "Is Chadwick in?" Olmsted knew Chadwick was brighter than his father was, and easier to coach.

"No, he's on vacation."

"Tell the agent in charge that this is not a good time. Ask them to reschedule when your son returns. If that doesn't work, say something like—you don't have the right to disrupt my business."

"I like that. I'll go tell them to leave."

"Call me back." Olmsted clicked off his phone. Midori resumed massaging the back of his neck. Playfully, he lifted her hands and pulled her into his lap saying, "Plan a trip to Vegas, darling."

"A week?" She moved seductively and kissed him.

"Sure." He let out a satisfying sigh.

"Bellagio?" Midori asked.

"Whatever you want."

The phone rang again. Reluctantly, he untangled himself and noted the incoming North Carolina number. "Our funding source for Vegas." Olmsted's assistant moved away with an alluring glance. They both laughed.

"Olmsted." He pulled the phone six inches from his ear. When he drew the phone back he said, "Relax, Mr. Byrnes. They're only bureaucrats. It's most important to keep cool."

"They won't leave," Gordon said.

Olmsted proceeded to coach Gordon. "Designate an employee to stick with the agents. Instruct that person to write down every question they ask. Tell all employees not to volunteer information. If approached, they must redirect the NRC person to you or your secretary,"

"Are you sure I can't make them leave? How do I know they're legitimate?"

"Give me their phone number." Olmsted wrote the telephone number down. "I'll call and determine if there's any reason for concern. Stay calm. I'll get back to you."

"How soon can we go?" Midori resumed her position on his lap.

"Soon," he said in a barely audible voice, reaching under the smooth silk of her blouse.

"I better lock the door," she teased.

"Forget it."

Her long black hair cascaded around his head with an intoxicating scent that delighted him. Tilting back in the chair, he enjoyed the gyrations of her hips.

Olmsted loved Midori's lightheartedness in the office. Initially, he found her spontaneity disconcerting. Being old school, private, and rather self-conscious about his body, he was not innovative about lovemaking. Midori was adventurous, creative, and addicting. Although increasingly expensive, he gave little thought to what she cost him. With Midori, he reclaimed his youth, and under her spell, his pudgy, five foot five body morphed into an athletic, lean physique. Finally, after decades of acquiescing, he freed himself from his taskmaster father's demands of discipline, denial, and intellectualism and recovered his adolescence.

"Book first class tickets. We'll stop in Charlotte, and Mr. Byrnes will pick up the tab."

Chapter 15

The NRC's presence startled GB Polymers's workers. They were not accustomed to visitors and had never seen anyone intimidate Mr. Byrnes.

Doris arrived at the lab. "Neil, take off your lab coat. Wear your sport's jacket today. We plan to contain our government visitors to the conference room, but if you encounter them, these are your instructions: Don't talk with the agents—per Jeremiah Olmsted. Uh … Mr. Byrnes. And tell the lab staff the same."

"Why are government agents here?" Neil asked.

"Official audit. Gordon's crazed. He's not certain they're legit. He accused them of being with a competitor, but they have government badges, complete with photo IDs. I have to move on." Doris smiled. "More damage control instructions to deliver."

Neil smiled back. After telling his staff to keep their heads down, he proceeded upstairs with a request for his secretary. As he came out of the stairwell to the first floor, an employee from customer services stopped him.

"I can't believe my bad luck," she told Neil. "Doris gave me the task of monitoring the words and actions of the government visitors. I'm so nervous. I'm expected to write verbatim what they say."

"You'll do fine." Neil walked with her down the hall.

At Elaine's office, Neil stopped and asked, "Can you tell me where I can find the catalog for lab supplies? I need beakers."

"I think it's in Richard's office, but this is not a good time. Can it wait?"

"Sure." Neil went to his office adjacent to Richard's to eavesdrop. He pulled up Chadwick's famous PERT chart on his computer and perused the various boxes. Not much time passed before he heard Randolph Perry's familiar voice at the doorway of Richard's office.

"Here's a checklist of items we want to review," Perry said to Richard.

"Not all of these documents are readily available," Richard replied.

"And we need to see the independent testing lab."

"That will take time to arrange. It's not that close."

"Where is it?"

"Across town," Richard said.

"Please arrange to take us there tomorrow."

Richard's response had nothing to do with the lab. "Let me give you some purchase orders and communications with utilities that you requested."

"Thanks," Perry said. "I see from this red-stamped sentence on the bottom that GB Polymers certified the quality of this order per 10 CFR 50."

"Yes, we handle special requests."

"Tell us how you determined that the material met the requirements stated here."

"There are several steps. First, we do our routine quality control testing. Then another lab does more testing before we confirm a product meets all standards."

"Are audits conducted?" Perry asked.

"Yes, of course," Richard replied.

"Who does them?"

"I do."

"Do you also audit the independent lab?"

"Yes."

"And that lab is Spencer Chemical Research?"

"Yes," Richard replied.

"Please bring us last year's paperwork. Before you do that, tell me, who is in charge of quality control?"

"Ethan Porter, a person with years of experience in the industry, He does all of the in-house testing," Richard said.

"And you supervise Ethan?" Perry asked.

"Yes."

"Does Ethan send the communications to the utilities?"

"No. The manager of technical services, Larry Davis, handles all correspondences with our customers."

"We'd like to speak with Larry."

"I'll try to arrange some time. Larry's very busy. I'll get back with you later."

The progress of the visit pleased Neil. He would have liked to have stayed longer on the first floor, but he did not routinely spend large blocks of time out of the lab. Hoping to avoid any attention, he returned to the lab and maintained a semblance of normalcy.

Later that morning, Gordon called Neil in the lab. "Let's go to lunch. I have to get away from these pests. Meet me at my car."

Neil walked out of the building and encountered Richard with Gordon. Climbing into the backseat of Gordon's Cadillac, he left the front for Richard. Neil had no fondness for Richard, but preferred his presence to an unbearable one-on-one lunch with Gordon. Like a near miss of a number on a roulette wheel, a peaceful lunch eluded him. His turkey sandwich on rye sat in the staff refrigerator.

"How about the South Park Tavern?" *As if Gordon ever suggested another place for lunch.* This nearby restaurant catered to Gordon's ego by calling him Mr. Byrnes, acting as if they were glad to see him, and, most important, letting him run up a monthly bill, as at a private club. Mr. Byrnes loved signing a guest check as he exited. No cash. No credit cards. It was country club treatment.

"We can talk freely. Those government workers can't afford to eat here," Mr. Byrnes said.

The hostess ushered them to a table with a patio view. Mr. Byrnes particularly liked the water fountain in front of him, so Richard and Neil sat accordingly.

"Why are they here?" Mr. Byrnes asked, as he settled into his seat. Before anyone could answer, he added, "I'm sure our competitors sent them. Do you think they're with that midwestern company, Supreme Grout something or other? They're jealous of our market share, so someone must be paying for inside information on our business."

"They're with the U.S. Nuclear Regulatory Commission," Richard said in a gentle tone.

"Well, if they are, what can they find that would be a problem for us?" Mr. Byrnes sounded skeptical.

Since Richard had spent time with the agents, he did the talking while Neil sat silent. Doing a delicate dance, Richard gave minimum information about the morning events and still let Mr. Byrnes know that the NRC agents had serious concerns.

Richard summarized, "The agents pressed me about the independent testing for products sold as safety grade for nuclear power plants. They're very interested in purchase orders from commercial utilities, and they're intent on matching employees with their areas of responsibility."

Richard chose his words with care. Neil believed that Richard knew the agents were onto the Byrnes charade.

"Ethan Porter logs the quality control data for the sales to nuclear power plants." Richard looked Gordon in the eye. "Right now, he's on the Byrnes Engineering payroll."

"So?" Gordon looked puzzled. "Who cares how I pay him?"

"It would be better if GB Polymers paid him. If Ethan is doing GB's testing, that company should pay him."

"Tell Matt Hawkins to change the accounting records for Ethan Porter," Gordon directed Richard.

Although Richard looked uneasy with that order, he did not say anything.

Oblivious to Richard's hesitancy, Gordon's expression exuded confidence. "Anything else?" he asked, with an air of arrogance.

"They definitely want access to the lab." Richard moved back into the chair cushion, expanding the space between himself and Mr. Byrnes.

"No way!" Gordon's shouting startled nearby diners. He lowered his voice and went on, "I don't care who they are, under no circumstances can they be in my laboratory. They must respect the sensitivity of our product development. Use the reason of our secrecy agreements with other countries. Our competitors would love to know about our research work with Taiwan. Chadwick told me the Taiwanese market is extremely lucrative, and we have to keep our work under wraps. I spoke with him this morning, and he insisted that I not give the NRC workers access to the lab. I also have my lawyer, Jeremiah Olmsted, contacting the NRC commissioners," Gordon boasted.

"You reached Chadwick on Cape Cod?" Richard asked.

"Yes, and he's glad we have Olmsted on board." Gordon regained his composure.

"The agents want to talk with our director of research. Maybe Neil should go home until they leave."

"I could meet with them. What's the harm?" Neil asked.

"No, you can't meet with them. You know too many trade secrets. I'll not let them question you. Stay away from the first floor. We'll say you're much too busy. Don't you think that's the best response?" Gordon turned toward Neil.

Neil shrugged his shoulders.

"They want to speak with all employees who handle phone and mail orders and anyone who has knowledge of our certification letters," Richard said.

"I don't want my employees spending time away from their jobs."

"We could let them talk with Larry. He handles purchase orders from power plants and correspondence with utilities."

"Did they mention Grenada?"

"No." Richard glanced at Neil.

"That's good. These agents need to be gone at the end of business today," Gordon instructed Richard. "I'm leaving for Bermuda and will not tolerate their presence in my building during my absence. Don't tell them where I'm going. You shipped the artwork, right? Rosemary is counting on having those paintings."

"I took care of that." Richard returned to the topic of the day. "We should discontinue declaring that we adhere to 10 CFR 50. The lead agent said our assertions about that triggered this visit."

"We don't want to affect sales. Chadwick said we have a competitive edge. No other manufacturer makes the same claim."

Neil took notes mentally, planning to write down the details of this conversation on index cards when he returned to his office. Chadwick and Gordon clearly knew that invoking the NRC in the marketing literature would increase sales. *What's GB Polymers's business in Grenada?*

When Neil had copied shipping records and sent them to the NRC, he noticed numerous shipments to Grenada. The amount of radiation shielding sent there surprised Neil, because there were no nuclear power plants on that small Caribbean island.

With Gordon's confidence bolstered, they left the restaurant.

Richard's secretary met him in his office doorway. "The agents are asking for you."

"I hope you told them I left for the day," Richard said.

"No, but I did say you're very busy."

"Thanks. I'll get there eventually. Stay low," Richard said to Neil.

"Lunch with the big guy?" Tom asked, when Neil returned to the lab.

"Yeah, lucky me."

"How's he coping?"

"He's not. He's out of control."

"Ass-saver attorney Olmsted flying down?" Tom asked.

"He's directing it all from Manhattan, as best I can tell."

Considering the events on the floor above him, Neil appreciated the afternoon routine in the lab. Around three-thirty, his curiosity generated a reason to head upstairs. In his secretary's office, Neil said, "Elaine, I need your assistance." She looked up with an expression Neil could not immediately read. She appeared nervous. Then he saw Richard.

"Mr. Byrnes gave Elaine an important job. Can you wait?" Richard asked. He stepped in front of Elaine's desk and blocked Neil's view of her computer.

Chapter 16

"Why is the aquarium cloudy?" Bridget asked when Neil walked in from work.

"It needs new water and pH adjustment. I forgot to change it last week."

"That's not like you. You cater to those blue discuses."

"I'll do it later."

"How was your day?"

"Everyone buzzed about yesterday's visitors. Not much work got done."

"Did you do anything with your notes?"

"I expect Agent Fowler will call tonight—like, now." Neil reached to answer the phone.

"Yes. I have my notes right here."

Neil picked up a stack of three by five index cards and began reading them aloud. "Doris Kingston told me to take off my lab coat. Richard suggested I go home sick. Mr. Byrnes instructed me to say I was too busy to talk with visitors. During lunch, Gordon told Richard to have Matt Hawkins change payroll records for Ethan Porter."

"Can you meet with me Tuesday evening?" Fowler sounded excited.

"Sure—same time and place?"

"Yes. We went to Spencer Chemical on Central Avenue."

"Impressed with the lab?"

"Right. They're unbelievable. Oh—one more thing. Do you know how our visit ended?"

"Mr. Byrnes threw you out, so he could go to Bermuda. Doris told me the fax from your boss at the NRC infuriated him. She said that Gordon went ballistic about the word 'criminal.'"

"You know about the fax from the NRC?" Fowler asked.

"Oh yes, that traveled the company grapevine swifter than a stock market fall."

"Interesting. According to attorney Olmsted, Mr. Byrnes did not receive a fax from the NRC."

The call concluded with a commitment to meet at the uptown Marriott.

"Did you agree to meet him Tuesday evening?" Bridget asked.

"Yes. Do we have something else?"

"A lecture at Queens University that we talked about attending."

"I'm sorry, I forgot."

"I'll find someone to go with me," Bridget said. "No big deal."

Neil scrunched his face in pain. "I'm really sorry."

"It's all right. Just don't make it a habit. Tend to the aquarium. I'm fond of those fish and don't want anything to happen to 'em."

*****

Neil went to the Marriott as scheduled. After he gave Fowler and Perry his notes, they talked about what Neil saw and heard during the NRC's unannounced visit.

"What's the next step now that Mr. Byrnes threw you out?" Neil inquired.

"We're discussing that with the Office of Enforcement and NRC lawyers," Fowler explained. "Mr. Byrnes involved lawyers with unprecedented speed, and the NRC wants to proceed with caution."

"Sounds like the action of an innocent man," Neil quipped.

"Byrnes's lawyer insisted that Mr. Byrnes never received a fax from the NRC."

"You've got to be kidding. Soon after you left the building, everyone buzzed about the fax. They have the same privacy as passwords pasted on a computer monitor. So what happens now?"

"The legal department of the NRC will respond to GB Polymers's lawyer. My department will continue from the safety angle," Perry said.

"I'm confused about all the separate sections of the NRC."

"Back in July you called the Office of Allegations—the OA—in Atlanta. The NRC has four geographic regions," Perry explained. "Each region has an OA. Trevor, a senior agency allegation advisor, followed up with his team on your initial call and prioritized your complaint as one to look at more closely. He referred your complaint to the Office of Investigations—the OI. Fowler works with OI."

"So the OI determines if GB Polymers's action is criminal?" Neil asked.

"Yes and no," Perry said. "Fowler is responsible for verifying an allegation. When he completes his investigation, he forwards a report to the Office of Enforcement, the OE. Then it's up to the OE to submit a formal recommendation to the Department of Justice."

"What? Another agency—one separate from the NRC?" Neil shook his head.

"Yes. The NRC can't act on criminal charges," Perry said. "That's the domain of the U.S. Department of Justice. The NRC can only make a recommendation to the Department of Justice to take legal action."

"Gordon Byrnes excels in legal combat," Neil said in a dire tone. "He spares no expense."

"I doubt even Gordon Byrnes is a match for the NRC legal department and the U.S. Department of Justice," Perry stated with confidence. "Maybe this will reassure you." Perry pulled a paper from the bottom of his pile. "I sent this bulletin to every nuclear power plant." He handed it to Neil.

Neil scanned the notice that stated the NRC was unable to validate compliance with basic component standards and asked owners of power plants, typically commercial utilities, to contact the NRC regarding any problems with GB Polymers products.

"This looks good," Neil stated.

"We're warning the plants," Perry said. "This memo went to all resident inspectors. They will inform my department of any problems at their plant. I plan to visit five plants soon. We need to be certain that your employer is in fact a supplier to the nuclear industry."

"They're a supplier for sure," Neil said. "They'll stay under your radar, if at all possible. Don't your plants keep a paper trail of products bought?"

"Definitely. They're obligated to maintain detailed records," Perry said.

"And how do you know if they do?" Neil asked.

Perry hesitated. He then responded, "We expect plant managers to follow procedures."

"But not everyone goes by your honor system," Neil said. "In your experience, has any plant voluntarily come forward and told you they have had problems with material installed?"

"It's our policy. Nuclear power plants are required to report these situations," Perry insisted.

"Why would any plant manager bring attention to something that will only cost him?" Neil asked.

"We have stringent requirements for compliance in all matters of safety," Perry repeated.

"We're not talking about the U.S. Naval Academy at Annapolis, where a code of honor might work. Believing company officials are well intended and trustworthy enough to monitor themselves is crap! In corporate America, honesty does *not* improve the bottom line."

"Each plant assesses their particular situation and develops corrective actions if they conclude there is a problem," Perry responded.

"Not addressing the defective material already in place is scary, and so are your cumbersome procedures, but that's not going to change tonight. Let's continue."

"I'm very concerned that there has not been any independent testing of material designated for nuclear power plants. We visited Spencer Chemical," Perry said.

"The fictitious lab," Neil said.

"Yes."

"The audits you have are bogus. I believe Elaine typed them the day you visited."

"Amazing. How did Richard get his job?" Perry asked. "He has no suitable background."

"That depends. You may think he's more appropriate for an occupation on society's fringe, but Chadwick appreciates his skills and talent. He hired him. Chadwick believes that under-qualified people are grateful and loyal."

"Richard doesn't have a college degree," Perry said.

"That's not an impediment for Chadwick. Richard's proficient in improvisation, thinks on his feet, and adapts to change as a situation demands. Remember, he produced an audit when you asked for one. With street smarts, he excels in the nuances of slick. He can also relate to a broad spectrum of people, which is something Chadwick can't do. Chadwick relates to people similar to him—affluent, big homes, private school education, and country club memberships. That isolation is very limiting in today's business world."

"That's astounding. We need a federal criminal search warrant to get access to GB Polymers's computers and to seize incriminating documents."

"The computer hard drive will reveal the day Elaine typed these letters," Neil said.

"If Elaine and Richard fabricated and backdated them for the purpose of deceiving federal investigators, that's a serious crime."

"I'm pretty sure that's exactly what happened," Neil said.

"Tonight we'd like your input for a search warrant," Perry said. "We'll submit the request tomorrow to a federal judge here in Charlotte. We must convince a judge that there is definitive evidence of criminal activity in the building."

"That's the only way to proceed?"

"Yes. Tell us again about security at GB Polymers," Fowler asked.

"There's an alarm system. Police respond if it goes off after business hours," Neil explained.

"Are there any guns in the building?" Perry asked.

"I don't think so." Neil's eyes widened.

"We'll need all the access codes to locked areas. Do you have those?"

"Yeah, sure. Gordon has an intercom system connected to his office."

"What?" Fowler and Perry asked at the same time.

"Listening devices are strategically placed to feed conversation from various areas in the building to Gordon's office. Please don't say anything that reveals you've been talking to me," Neil pleaded.

Neil respected Perry and Fowler, who were eager to do a good job. He appreciated that they apparently took his input seriously and utilized his knowledge of Gordon and Chadwick's style and motivation. Believing there would be a good conclusion, Neil hoped it would be prompt. After he gave them all the requested information for the warrant, he drove home.

The question of the material in place nagged Neil. He understood the importance of substantiating his allegation and agreed the agents needed a search warrant to get pertinent documents. Perry's confidence in the bulletin addressed to all nuclear power plants baffled Neil. It was a piece of paper probably bound for the shredder. No plant would take the time and expense to determine if they used defective grout, penetration closures, and sealants— not if someone didn't make them.

Pulling into his driveway, Neil saw lights on all over the house, indicating that Bridget had waited up for him. He hoped he wouldn't have many more of these meetings that exhausted the both of them.

"Sorry I'm so late. You didn't need to wait up for me." Neil greeted Bridget warmly.

"Like I can sleep, knowing you're on a spy assignment. Tell me about it." Bridget took a glass-covered bowl from the refrigerator to the microwave.

Neil poured himself a glass of orange juice. "I learned the NRC is screwed up. They have more compartments than GB Polymers. I'm worried about how my complaint is tracked through this maze. It's not clear who ultimately makes a decision. No one, I'm afraid."

"Government at it's best! What did you expect—efficiency, competency? So they brought you uptown to talk about their inadequacies?"

"No, a search warrant." He placed a bowl for soup on the table.

"A search warrant? From a judge?" she asked.

"That's right. Tomorrow, Perry and Fowler are applying to a federal judge in Charlotte for permission to show up and seize company documents."

"Do you think that's a good idea?"

"I'm not sure they have a choice. They won't get anything voluntarily, and if much more time passes, documents may be shredded." While he ate his soup, Neil summarized his concerns about the baffling structure of the NRC.

"I hope no one in the judge's office is a member of the Lake Norman Five Star Club, or you can forget about confidentiality."

Chapter 17

Attorney Jeremiah Olmstead was an interesting variation on a rainmaker in that he was not a senior partner at a big law firm bringing in the lifeblood, billable hours for other lawyers. Instead, maintaining an independent law practice, he generated extensive work for legal specialists. Early in his career, Jeremiah Olmsted, a graduate of Yale Law School, built his practice on contacts with Yale alumnae by cultivating connections with the influential and powerful. Realizing that a wealthy client would part with millions to save his ass from jail, Olmsted developed a practice in which he brokered legal experts for his affluent clients. As the trusted entry point into the legal system for scared, guilty business executives, he provided discreet personal service.

Rarely representing clients directly, Olmsted did not write briefs. Court calendars seldom dictated his schedule. His referral system produced lucrative commissions, providing him with a comfortable lifestyle.

When an executive like Gordon Byrnes called him, Olmsted assessed the need, then located and retained an appropriate lawyer. His clients did not tell their story more than once. Olmsted's impressive record of accomplishment paid for his Park Avenue office, a Manhattan apartment for himself with concomitant comforts, including Midori, a Westchester County residence for his ex-wife and their three children, her country club membership and extravagances, his children's tuition, and all essential privileges.

Gordon Byrnes found Jeremiah Olmsted through a fellow Yale alumnus. Eight or nine times Olmsted had extricated Gordon from various legal messes—car accidents with personal injuries, zoning compliance issues, and state and federal tax audits. Olmsted's skill in steering Gordon to stellar attorneys and avoiding embarrassing publicity especially endeared him to Gordon Byrnes.

Personally, Olmsted did not like Gordon. As long as Gordon paid Olmsted, they got along very well. This transgression with the NRC created an uncommon commission extravaganza even by Jeremiah Olmsted's standards.

Thinking about the profile of an attorney most able to abort the NRC investigation, Olmsted decided on a Washington DC lawyer, ideally one with litigation experience with a private corporation pitted against a government agency. He first searched for cases involving the NRC. None grabbed him. Then he stumbled onto a case of the Environmental Protection Agency versus the NG Chem Supply. Olmsted scanned the particulars. A guilty-sounding company owner beat the rap. Washington DC attorney Vernon Casper had represented the defendant.

Olmsted found Casper's office phone number and called.

"Good afternoon. Attorney Casper's office," a pleasant-sounding woman answered.

"My name is Jeremiah Olmsted. I'm calling for a client who needs a DC lawyer. Would Mr. Casper be available to speak with me?"

"One moment please. I'll check."

"Vernon Casper here. How can I help you, Mr. Olmsted?" Casper asked as if they already knew each other.

"My client needs help with the NRC. Have you any experience with that agency?"

"Yes, Mr. Olmsted, I have," Casper said matter-of-factly.

"Please call me Jeremiah, Vernon. I understand you have considerable expertise with the EPA. I read with interest EPA versus NG Chem Supply."

"Thanks. That was a wild ride, and as you know, my client prevailed," Casper boasted.

"What knowledge do you have of the NRC?"

"Considerable. In fact, I have more connections with the NRC than with the EPA."

"Good. I'd like to meet you and formalize the terms of our working together. Any chance we could have coffee next Tuesday morning at National Airport, around nine-thirty, outside the security check-in?"

"I can make it work," Casper replied.

Olmsted gave Casper his phone numbers and his Manhattan office address. "See you at the National Airport's Starbucks. Looking forward to meeting you."

"Likewise," Casper said.

Next, Olmsted researched attorneys in Charlotte. He liked the Taylor and Taylor's Website. It listed white-collar crime as one of its areas of expertise. Scanning the firm's roster of attorneys, he found Harris Patterson's biography, which emphasized his seven years' experience at the U.S. Department of Justice before joining the firm three years ago. Olmsted understood the value of a former federal prosecutor. Bingo—this was the firm for Gordon Byrnes. Reviewing four of attorney Patterson's cases, Olmsted concluded that Patterson represented criminals who then beat the charges or received a minimum penalty.

Olmsted called Patterson. He assessed him as arrogant, unscrupulous, and perfectly qualified for the job. They agreed to meet at the Charlotte airport on Tuesday afternoon.

Chapter 18

After learning the plan of the NRC raid of GB Polymers from Perry, Neil briefly thought about being out sick that day, but he realized he was much too curious to miss seeing firsthand the government confront his employer. Perry assured Neil that the designated leader, Mario Valdez, had the best credentials to implement the search and seizure. His background included a service stint where he managed an army military police unit. In that role, and for the NRC, Mario had participated in numerous raids. He had a reputation of methodical preparedness. The players in Mario's team included NRC staff, U.S. marshals, and the Charlotte police. Although they would know that a confidential informant provided information about the building layout and access codes, they would not know Neil by name or photo.

Regardless of Perry's promises, Neil worried. He planned a light day for himself and his staff. In the lab, he appeared to be his usual relaxed self, joking with staff and paying attention to the tasks of the day.

A loud knock on the lab door startled the technicians.

"That's strange," one said. He opened the door.

Agents rushed into the room. "Stand up with your arms raised."

An agent seized a technician. "Don't touch the equipment, don't move anything. We're with the NRC executing a search warrant. Sit over there." He pointed to a cafeteria-style folding table off to the right.

Still looking around the room, an agent announced into his walkie-talkie, "Agent Valdez, we're in Storeroom Five."

"Don't delete any files. Don't move anything," an agent barked.

The shocked employees sat motionless. After a long moment, they pushed away from their benches. One technician reached to pick up a paper. An agent shoved his hand away.

"Hand it over," he demanded with an outstretched hand, palm up.

The technician, his face reddened, gave up his list of grocery items that his wife had asked him to pick up on his way home. The slip of paper also had notes from a phone call listing the required courses and total credits he needed to complete his American Chemical Society certification.

Chadwick ran into the lab and collided with an agent.

"You have no right to be here," Chadwick stammered.

"I suggest you cooperate," the agent replied. "A judge issued a search warrant for the NRC to inspect your premises."

The agents wasted no time establishing control of the lab, photographing the room from several angles, and collecting bound laboratory notebooks and testing data. On each box, they placed a two by three-inch self-stick tag with the characteristic NRC logo in the upper-left corner of the label, wrote the date, a unique number, a description of the contents, and documented that the items were seized in the lab. Working with a laptop computer, a red felt marker, and a mover's tape gun, they meticulously preserved the chain of evidence.

"Neil, come with me," Chadwick ordered.

"Ethan Porter to the first floor conference room," the receptionist announced on the building's paging system. Chadwick and Neil stopped at Storeroom Two. The open door exposed a space about the size of a walk-in closet in a modest residence. A sledgehammer rested on the floor. Papers were spread on a desk; the computer idled in standby mode, and a jacket hung on a peg.

"Box anything relevant," an agent ordered.

Chadwick started to enter Storeroom Two.

"Leave now," an agent demanded.

Chagrined, Chadwick stopped. He turned and said to Neil, "They have no right to be here."

They continued to the first floor. Agents were everywhere. At Neil's office, two agents opened his file cabinets, looked in his desk drawers, and removed papers.

"Do you know anyone here?" Chadwick asked Neil.

"No," Neil responded with coolness and a surprised look.

Next door, outside Richard's office, Chadwick and Neil watched as the agents took pictures of his office and packed files.

"Can I help you find anything?" Richard asked in a detached tone.

"No," Agent Fowler replied. "But I would like to speak with you."

Fowler removed a framed certificate from the wall behind Richard's desk and instructed the group of agents, "Pack all the files in this room." He spoke again to Richard, "Please come with me."

"Unless you need me for something, I'll go back to the lab," Neil said to Chadwick.

"Do you think someone is helping them?" Chadwick asked.

"I wouldn't know."

"I need to call my father. I wish I was in Bermuda."

Neil returned to the lower level, relieved to be away from Chadwick's scrutiny. Chadwick was suspicious but fortunately also in doubt. Neil realized the purpose of their walk was for Chadwick to see the agents interact with Neil. There was not a flicker of recognition.

*****

That evening at home, Bridget said, "I was dying to call you today but I didn't dare."

"It was wild. I'm surprised at the volume of papers they seized. I expected them to be more selective."

"Were the agents you knew there?"

"Yes, there were at least twenty agents that I didn't know and fortunately I never spoke with the ones I did. Charlotte Police were also on the scene and U.S. marshals.

"Why were marshals there?"

"They guarded all the exits."

"Were they concerned people would run out the door?"

"Worried they'd remove evidence."

"It's like movie material."

"For sure—agents questioned us under oath. They took papers off my desk and from my files. They took the entire contents of Richard's office. It was insane."

As Neil told Bridget about the raid, he remembered more details. He did not reveal to her that an agent mentioned Storeroom Five instead of the lab or that he worried about a witch-hunt.

Chapter 19

"Captain on the bridge," Tom greeted Neil. "Any excitement planned for today?"

"I wouldn't know, Spock. We may encounter mild turbulence or a galactic dust storm. Stay alert."

"Did you see the photo in the paper?" Tom picked up the *Charlotte Observer*'s local section, showing a clear shot of a sledgehammer and large lock cutter on the back seat of a black Honda parked in front of GB Polymers.

"Careful, Spock, the paper is probably classified as an enemy publication. Don't leave it around."

"Right. The police used the sledgehammer to break down the Storeroom Two door."

"I saw it. I heard that agents took everything in the room."

"That upset Ethan," Tom said.

"It upset Chadwick more. I was with him. Mr. Cool looked ashen."

"Phone, captain," one of the technicians said to Neil.

Neil took the call. After a moment, he said, "Okay." He walked back to Tom. "Turbulence ahead, Spock. That was Chadwick's secretary—he's debriefing everyone about yesterday."

"I think I'll practice the GB salute in case I need it." Tom demonstrated by raising both his arms above his head with fingers widespread. "My wife didn't believe me when I told her that agents entered the lab and told us to raise our arms."

"Didn't she understand they feared you'd reach for your phaser?"

"I should have brought in the family Bible. Do you think we're still under oath from yesterday or will we swear to tell the truth again today?" Tom asked.

"Hard to know. Chadwick expects us in the conference room in half an hour." Neil gave the same message to the other technicians.

Neil and his staff assembled around the conference table as instructed. Chadwick called each lab technician individually into a nearby office to ask about the worker's contact with NRC staff on the previous day. He asked for the agent's name, a summary of the questions asked, the technician's responses, and the agent's business card. He entered information in his Blackberry and pocketed the cards.

Chadwick's confiscation of the agents' cards stunned Neil. They were specifically for the employee to have access to the agents.

Chadwick questioned Neil last. "What agent talked with you?"

"This one." He handed Chadwick a business card.

"Did you ever see him before?" Chadwick asked.

"Never," Neil said, thankful it was an honest statement. He thought Chadwick also looked relieved.

"What questions did he ask?"

"My job title, how long I worked here, my salary."

"He asked what you made. Did you tell him?"

"Of course I did. I was under oath."

"You know an NRC agent asked for directions to Storeroom Five?"

Neil remained silent. Chadwick continued, "Do you think one of the lab technicians mentioned Storeroom Five?"

"I doubt it."

In turn, Chadwick named each of Neil's staff and asked if he thought that person had communicated with the NRC. Chadwick paid close attention to Neil's responses. Speaking calmly, he said that he did not suspect anyone on his staff had contacted the NRC.

"How about at the ASTM International meeting? Did anyone there seem out to get us?" Chadwick asked.

"Not that I noticed."

"Let me know immediately if you learn anything. I'm following some leads on competitors. If someone is giving information to the NRC, I'll find him."

Chapter 20

The shuttle from LaGuardia had landed at National Airport in Washington DC five minutes early. Attorney Olmsted made his way from the gate area to the Starbucks on the ticketing level. A young man in lawyer attire, a dark conservative suit, polished expensive-looking shoes, and a clean-cut hairstyle sat alone at a table making notes on a lengthy document.

"Mr. Casper?"

"Mr. Olmsted, nice to meet you," Casper stood to shake his hand. "You made excellent time."

"Sometimes I get lucky. I'll grab a coffee." He went to the counter and ordered a tall blend of the day's coffee. Casper packed up his papers.

Olmsted returned and got right to the point. "My client is the owner of a private company in Charlotte. I've known him for years. He lived in Connecticut until about eight years ago when he relocated his business. NRC agents did an unannounced visit last month and then returned with a search warrant. They seized boxes of documents."

"A search warrant in weeks—that's remarkably swift."

"Yes, it is. And that concerns me. My client says he has done nothing wrong. He believes one of his employees is working with the NRC. You know the type—someone who doesn't want to work for a living and is jealous of my client's affluence."

"I've encountered a handful of whistleblowers. They are the lowest form of life," Casper said.

"We need to assess the risk. Can you find out how serious the NRC takes these false accusations?"

"That won't be difficult for me, as I have well-placed contacts inside the NRC," Casper replied with confidence. "I'll get a status report on this investigation by the end of the week."

"Excellent," Olmsted said.

"The NRC is known for inefficiency. Strategic obstacles can guarantee your client significant spinning time, maybe even beyond the statute of limitations. Better yet, I'll get the case dropped," Casper bragged.

"Let me outline our financial terms. As legal counsel for GB Polymers, you bill the company directly for your time and expenses. As a consultant, I get 15 percent of all your billable hours, and you copy me on everything for this case."

"Sounds like a relationship I can live with. Thanks for the referral."

"Here is some information to get you started." Olmsted handed Casper a file. "Mr. Byrnes will send a retainer to your office. I appreciate your accommodating my schedule by coming here to the airport."

"My pleasure," Casper said.

Olmsted congratulated himself on another good find as he made his way to the gate for his flight to Charlotte. Casper will rack up billable hours, Olmsted thought. Gordon would pay dearly for his transgressions with the NRC, and Olmsted would net considerable cash. Olmstead hoped his Charlotte stop would be as productive.

*****

At Charlotte Douglas Airport, Olmsted and Midori walked toward the baggage claim. They stopped at the rocking chairs between Concourse B and C.

"Let's meet here in about an hour," Olmsted proposed. "Pretend you're a Southern lady on your porch."

"First some shopping—there's a shoe store here I want to explore," Midori said.

While on the escalator to the lower level, Olmsted spotted a fiftyish overweight man talking on a cell phone at a coffee shop near Area C baggage claim. He correctly guessed the man was attorney Harris Patterson. His expensive suit looked disheveled and his eyes cold.

Olmsted introduced himself, "Jeremiah Olmsted. Thanks for coming to the airport."

"Harris Patterson, pleased to meet you. We can take coffee from here down to Area D. It's less crowded. Watch your time. I came in on the upper level, and the security line was pretty long."

"My flight doesn't leave for two hours. I'll be okay," Olmsted replied. "I'll get right to the point, Harris. My client needs a powerful defense attorney. The U.S. government can be a formidable opponent."

"How strong is the case?" Patterson asked.

"I'm not sure. The NRC took boxes of documents in a raid, and my client is very distressed. It's a private company. Mr. Byrnes is not accustomed to answering to any outside authority. I've got someone in DC looking into the NRC investigation."

"Most of my clients are guilty. It's better when they are also wealthy. There are no limits on legal expenditures when the alternative is jail."

"This one has millions in cash. He'll part with a huge chunk to save his ass," Olmsted said. "There is one worker that may present a problem. He fabricated documents and lied to the agents."

"Do the feds know that?" Patterson asked.

"Absolutely," Olmsted said.

"His boss told him to do that?" Patterson asked.

"Probably, but, of course, we don't want him to say that," Olmsted said.

"That will take some creativity. The government lawyers lack originality as well as experience, so it is not impossible. We'll work them over."

"I like your confidence." Olmsted repeated the terms of his financial agreement, 15 percent of all Patterson's billing.

Patterson agreed.

"The first thing we need to do is find out what the government took and the basis of the search warrant," Olmsted instructed.

"I'll file the necessary motions," Patterson said.

"Here is the information you'll need." Olmsted handed him a folder.

Maneuvering his way through security for the third time that day, he looked forward to getting to Las Vegas. From the gate, he called GB Polymers and spoke with Gordon's secretary. Gordon was in Bermuda for another week. He told Doris that he had secured two law firms for Mr. Byrnes and promised to be in touch.

*****

Five hours later, Olmsted and Midori landed at the Las Vegas airport.

"Slot machines in the airport," Midori squealed.

"In this town, they're everywhere."

"I have to play." Midori stopped at a machine. She rummaged in her purse for money.

"We have days to play. Let's get our luggage."

"I might not see another Five Star one—that's a lucky image for me. I'm playing this one." She put a bill in and pulled the handle.

"I'll be damned." Olmsted realized the ding and clamor registered winning stars aligned on Midori's machine.

"What's it worth?"

"About fifty bucks. Not a bad start."

They proceeded to baggage claim. As they passed the drivers holding signs, Olmsted saw one with his name.

"Did you reserve a limo?"

"Of course. The taxi line is tedious. Too much walking."

"I'm the man you want," Olmsted said to the limo driver.

"Great. Hope you had a pleasant flight."

"Glad to finally get here. It seems like we left New York days ago."

"Let's collect your bags. First time in Vegas?"

"Yes."

"You won't be disappointed."

"Lived here long?" Olmsted asked.

"Born here—lived here all my life."

"I didn't know anyone was actually from here."

"There're more of us than you think. It's an exciting place—especially now that it's a destination for tourists from all over the world. Used to be it was Disney or Hawaii. Now it's Vegas."

Settled in the back seat, Olmsted put his arm around Midori.

"What's your game?" the driver asked.

"I don't have one. I'm thinking I'll try roulette."

"You'll enjoy the roulette tables at Bellagio. They're the best."

Looking out the window, Olmsted commented, "What's with all the building?"

"There are more construction cranes than cactus in this desert," the driver said.

"I see that."

"We've had a real boom in condos for frequent visitors and, believe it or not, Vegas attracts retirees. They love the weather and easy access to entertainment."

As they drove the short distance from the airport to the strip, the driver told stories of Mafia days with cheap meals and low hotel room rates. "Now that corporations rule, there are no two-dollar dinner buffets or forty-nine cent breakfasts. In 1958, the Starburst Casino, one of our oldie but goodies, boasted the biggest pool in Nevada. Today hot tubs are larger. One night at around two A.M. they blew that casino up—quite the sky show. Reminded me of when we went on rooftops to watch the atomic blasts. I saw at least four of those explosions from my home when I was a kid."

In a short time, Italian architecture came into view and transported them to Italy. Door attendants at the Bellagio welcomed their arrival as if they had been waiting all day, exclusively for them.

A greeter escorted them through the attractive lobby. Midori loved the glamour that assailed her senses: a musician played at a baby grand piano and spectacular floral arrangements sweetened the air. It was impossible to take in everything. Midori gazed upwards. "Look!" She pointed to the Chihuly glass flowers in the ceiling. "Just beautiful."

When they reached the front desk, Midori asked, "Does Bellagio sell any Chihuly artwork?"

"Yes, at the Via Fiore Shops. I'll show you where it is on our map."

"If you'd like, Mr. Olmsted, I can upgrade you to a suite on a higher floor," the clerk said.

"That would be wonderful." He smiled at Midori. When making the reservations, she had said if they arrived on a Tuesday and let staff know they were big spenders, they had a good chance of an upgrade.

"Overlooking our pristine lake or a stunning mountain view?" the clerk asked.

He deferred to Midori. "The lake, please," she said and added, "Can you make dinner reservations for us at Shintaro?"

"Our concierge will be happy to take care of reservations and tickets."

"Tickets for Cirque du Soleil?" Midori asked.

"Certainly. Right over there." She pointed to a desk in front of the conservatory.

The clerk clicked to another computer screen and scanned the room availability.

"One of our Salone suites on floor thirty-four is available." She handed them key cards. "Enjoy your Bellagio experience."

They navigated through the casino to the guest elevators. Passing the Baccarat Bar, Olmsted said, "I'll be back to these tables."

Olmsted opened the door to their home for the next week. The marble entrance sparkled; an oversized painting of an Italian village scene hung above a stone pedestal table adorned with a vase of flowering lilies. Midori pressed wall buttons, opening the drapes across the vast and elegantly appointed living room.

Crossing to the windows, Olmsted looked out. "Not Lake Como but pretty nice," he said.

"The fountains at night are supposed to be spectacular," Midori said.

Exploring the rest of the suite, Olmsted commented, "This room has more square footage than most Manhattan apartments. Roulette in an hour?"

"I'd like to do some shopping first. I'll meet you downstairs."

*****

Settled into his game, Olmsted enjoyed a cigar and the martini an attentive server placed next to his stacks of playing chips.

Midori stopped by wearing a gorgeous Hermes scarf. "Like my purchase?"

He did not answer.

"Ready for dinner?"

"I'm ready for thirty-four red. It hasn't come up yet. I need to keep playing."

"I'm hungry, love." Midori kissed him.

As the spinning wheel slowed, the silver ball bounced into twenty-two black, out again, and made a final landing at fifteen black. She kissed him again. "Better luck later. I have your favorite toys in my little silk bag. And you'll love this scarf as my after-dinner dress."

"Cash me out," Olmsted directed the dealer.

*****

The next morning, while Midori was at the spa, Olmsted started to make a business call from the room, changed his mind, and put his phone in his pocket, enticed outside by the desert warmth. Midori had taught him to welcome temptation, and he was a willing student. Remembering his reluctance to take Midori to Las Vegas, he laughed aloud. Olmsted negotiated his way to the Bellagio pool, settled into a lounge chair, and dialed the number for the NRC headquarters.

"Director of Investigations Fred Snyder, please," Olmsted asked, when he reached the operator.

"How can I help you?" Snyder said.

"I'm attorney Jeremiah Olmsted. I represent GB Polymers. The NRC was way out of line raiding my client's office."

"We legally obtained a search warrant and our agents acted well within the law," Snyder said.

"There was no need for search and seizure. Mr. Byrnes complied voluntarily. Your agents had free access to the building, staff, and documents. Mr. Byrnes simply asked your staff to suspend their visit until a later date after his vacation."

"That's not true. Gordon Byrnes obstructed an investigation. He threw NRC agents out of his building."

"I'll pursue this," Olmsted threatened.

"Three of our agents aren't confused."

"There's no need for us to squabble about this. It's now a legal argument that a federal judge will decide. Attorney Patterson, who also represents Mr. Byrnes, is filing a motion in Charlotte federal court. We assert the NRC search warrant was manifestly faulty."

"Faulty?"

"Yes, faulty." Olmsted repeated. "We're asking for all supporting documentation."

"You can't do that."

"We can and we will," Olmsted said. "This call is to tell you that my client needs all original documents returned ASAP. No business can function with boxes of missing files."

"We'll have to copy everything before anything can be returned. I'm sure, Mr. Olmsted, you realize that will take time."

"Every day you delay, disrupts my client's operations. The NRC's misuse of power is particularly abhorrent in this case. GB Polymers is not a contractor in the nuclear industry. The NRC has no authority over my client. That's another motion I've filed," Olmsted said.

"We are well within the scope of our authority," Snyder insisted.

"That's still to be determined. Your malicious communication to all plants about the quality of my client's products crossed the line. We demand a list of all NRC employees that were involved in the decision, all written drafts, and any related meeting notes showing the evolution of that bulletin."

"I'll speak with the appropriate people here about returning the documents."

"Can you be certain that one of your staff did not accept a bribe from my client's competitor to smear his good name?" Olmsted asked.

"That's outrageous. We're finished. Anything else please put in writing to our legal department."

Chapter 21

At work, Neil dreaded that someone would discover his informant role, and he found it hard to stay sharp. As he made his rounds and reviewed his staff's work, a technician answered a call and handed the phone to Neil.

"I'll be right there," Neil said and hung up the phone. *A summon to Chadwick's office could not be good.*

"What do you know about this?" Chadwick handed Neil a paper.

At the sight of the NRC logo, Neil felt a chill across his shoulders and his legs trembled. Worried that his assumed poker face failed to hide his concern, Neil read the memo that the NRC had sent to the government of Taiwan and the accompanying fax to Chadwick from the Taiwan dealer.

"First I've seen of it," Neil replied in a calm voice.

The dealer informed Chadwick that his government ordered Taiwan National Power to stop all business with GB Polymers and asked Chadwick to resolve the matter with the NRC expeditiously.

"I projected significant profits from Taiwan sales. This is a tremendous loss. Who works on the fireproofing product for Taiwan?" Chadwick asked.

"All the techs," Neil replied.

"We need to find out who is talking to the NRC. Maybe we need a clean sweep in the lab."

"Meaning?"

"Get rid of 'em all."

"That would delay your timeline on all projects. You don't want to do that."

"We need to press harder to make up for these lost sales. There's an additional bonus for you if you figure out who is working with the NRC."

Neil realized Chadwick desperately hoped Neil was not involved. He headed back to the lab. *Couldn't the NRC first take care of problems in the United States? Why involve Taiwan?*

The NRC notice to Taiwan shrunk the circle of possible informants and increased the likelihood that he would be identified. Fewer than fifteen people knew his company sold to the nuclear industry in Taiwan, and he was one of them. Chadwick had to suspect him.

Chapter 22

Attorney Patterson called Olmsted. "I have an important envelope from the Charlotte court."

"The judge unsealed the warrant," Olmsted said.

"Yes."

"Congratulations."

"He certainly took his time. I've scanned the twenty-three pages."

"The government isn't known for brevity. Tell me what the NRC submitted to get the search warrant."

Patterson read, "Imperative that we have access to documents before they are destroyed … reason to believe … our confidential informant is knowledgeable."

"So who is it?" Olmsted asked.

"I have no clue."

"This person won't be unknown for long. Chadwick and Gordon will see through the sloppy disguise and figure out the government's source."

"I'll bring it to them," Patterson said, thrilled with his breakthrough.

"I'll call Gordon. We'll have a conference call when you get there."

Patterson drove to GB Polymers. Chadwick and Gordon Byrnes were expecting him.

"You've ratted out the snitch!" Gordon got up from his desk, shook Patterson's hand, and said, "Great, it's a competitor, isn't it?"

"We're hoping you'll know," Patterson answered.

With Olmsted on speakerphone, Patterson read excerpts from the government affidavit: "Our confidential informant has inside information because he's an employee and is very familiar with the applicable national specifications and ASTM International testing requirements."

"Shit, no." Chadwick's face paled. He fell into a wingback chair in his father's office.

"Who is it?" Olmsted asked.

"Neil Landers!" Gordon banged his fists on the desk. "Damn it, that man will pay for all the trouble he has caused me!"

"Please wait, Mr. Byrnes. We can't act hastily. It will backfire," Olmsted cautioned.

"I want him out of the building *now*!" Gordon screamed.

"Hurriedly firing Landers will jeopardize your case with the NRC. We can handle him without being reckless."

"I want him fired," Gordon ranted. "I want him to pay. I want him ruined." He jumped up and stomped his feet. The redness in his face grew brighter.

"Dad," Chadwick interrupted. "We gave him a $10,000 raise and a $25,000 bonus. His chemical research work and new products will generate most of our profits going forward."

"Calm down. We can develop grounds for firing him, but not today," Olmsted said.

"I want him out of my building," Gordon raved. His face contorted.

"Mr. Byrnes, please. We don't want to give him a wrongful termination case. We'll work something out."

"Chadwick, give Patterson his resume and everything in his personnel file," Olmsted instructed.

"I leave for Bermuda tomorrow for two weeks. I can't have him here unsupervised." Gordon's growing agitation was unmistakable in his voice.

"Tell him to stay home for two weeks—an end of the year present," Patterson suggested.

"I'm not paying him another penny. In fact, I want to sue him for compensation."

"Dad," Chadwick pleaded. "The attorneys are correct. We need to be careful."

"I'll draft a letter asking Landers to take time off with pay until early January," Olmsted said. "I'll fax it to you. That will buy us some time to strategize a credible reason to dismiss him. Get it in his hands today."

"That's a good idea," Chadwick said.

"Give Patterson what you have and I'll be back to you," Olmsted said. He hung up the phone. He dictated innocuous sentences to Midori to fax to GB Polymers.

The phone rang. It was Patterson. Before he could talk, Olmsted said, "So what do we have? Some sorry ass do-gooder messing with Gordon Byrnes?"

"I don't care if it's freezing in Manhattan, I wish I was there." Patterson said.

"Good job getting the government paperwork unsealed."

"Thanks. The next steps will be more challenging."

"Did Gordon say Landers is a no-good troublemaker?" Olmsted smoothed his tie and shifted in his chair.

"Quite the opposite—Gordon recruited him and has been known to brag that he has the best formulation chemist in the business!"

"Great. At least we know what we're dealing with."

"There's nothing in his personnel file," Patterson added.

"What?" Olmsted shouted.

"Right. No application to check for lies. No resume with the usual embellishments. According to Chadwick, his father hired Landers while he was on vacation, and Chadwick met Landers after he was already working as their director of research. Gordon met him at some trade conference and wooed him from a New York company because Landers maintained a high profile in the industry, an officer in something called ASTM International. I guess it's an organization important to the Byrnes business, and Gordon believed employing Neil would be advantageous. You heard Chadwick say he's made them considerable money."

"And he'll make us plenty." Olmsted laughed. "So we'll need to be more creative. While he's on forced vacation, I'll have Chadwick review all his expense accounts, inspect his hard drive, e-mails, address book, and favorite sites. We'll print a log of all phone calls from Lander's extension."

"That should give us something."

"How was Gordon when you left?" Olmsted asked.

"Unglued. Do you think he's a mental case?"

"Without a doubt. He becomes a lunatic when he thinks someone has done him wrong. His threshold for transgression is lower than Death Valley. Billable hours, Patterson. We can tolerate the idiot. Stay focused on the billable hours."

"I will. I'm two years from my kids' college tuition bills," Patterson said. "I can put up with Gordon."

"Let me know when you have something on Landers."

Chapter 23

Neil left work early for an eye doctor appointment. He drove by South Park Mall, which was packed with last-minute shoppers, relieved that he did not need to stop for anything. When he spoke with Bridget earlier in the day, he heard a choir singing a traditional Christmas carol in the background.

"All the nativity scene pieces are sitting on the mantel, waiting for your finishing touch," she said.

"I look forward to it," Neil said. Arranging the delicate, white porcelain figurines was his contribution to their holiday decorating. He planned to spend the evening at home relaxing in the glow of the tiny lights of their Christmas village.

She described her day as delightful, setting the buildings of the Christmas village on a makeshift table dotted with drilled holes and padded with soft, white fabric to conceal the wiring of the myriad pieces.

Neil fondly recalled the Dickens houses his parents had given them. He and his wife liked the lights of the village scene better than a tree. He anticipated his evening with Bridget, enjoying music and their way of decorating for Christmas.

*****

"I thought you'd never get here," Bridget sobbed when Neil walked into the house. "I've been calling your cell phone."

"I forgot to turn it back on after the doctor's, sorry. What's the matter?" He held her and she continued to sob, her body shaking in spite of his arms around her.

"What's wrong?" he repeated.

"I thought something awful happened to you," Bridget said hugging Neil. "A man from your office was here."

"What?" Neil asked.

"I had the music on and almost didn't hear the knock on the door. When I went to the door, I noticed an unfamiliar car parked in the driveway. I opened the front door and screamed. I recognized him as someone from your company."

"Who was it?" Neil asked.

"Matt Hawkins."

"Gordon's son-in-law?"

"Personal message delivery means bad news."

"I'm sorry. What did he want?" Neil continued holding her and stroked her hair.

"To give you a letter from Mr. Byrnes—he started to read it to me. I told him to leave. He said something like, we're concerned about Neil and we want him to take off some extra time. Mr. Byrnes doesn't want you to return to work until January eighth."

"Where is it?"

"On the dining room table."

Neil read, "You are to take vacation until January eighth. We will pay your regular salary during this time. Do not come to the Byrnes Building for any reason before January eighth. On that day, bring with you any company property in your possession...." He looked up and repeated, "Do not come into the office during this time. ... They must have found out that I contacted the NRC!" His heart rate accelerated. The blood drained from his face.

"Thank God you're not hurt!"

"I'm sorry you were scared. It's an outrage that he came to our home."

"It's a great Christmas present."

"We'll be all right. I'll find another job, but I'll need a lawyer to get out of the noncompete agreement."

The phone rang. Neil and Bridget sat motionless. Their taped answering message played. Then they heard, "Borg alert, captain. Call me. Spock."

Neil picked up the phone. "What's up, Spock?"

"You're under attack, captain. Chadwick posted a memo stating you're working with the feds and no employee is to talk with you."

"Do you have a copy?"

"Of course."

"Read it to me."

Tom read, "We've just learned that Neil Landers is cooperating with the NRC. No GB employee is to talk with Neil. Captain, did you keep one of those agents' business cards after the raid?"

"The raid happened because I called the NRC."

"Holy shit! You turned Gordon into the feds?"

"I'm afraid you'll add something of mine to your shrine, Spock. Gordon sent Matt to my house this afternoon. He doesn't want me back at work until after his Christmas vacation."

"The son-in-law gets the plum assignments. I'm sorry, captain."

"Spock, I appreciate your call. You need to be careful. Never call—I'm serious—you can't call me from your work extension. Use your cell."

"Good thinking, captain. See you in January. I wish you and Bridget a merry Christmas."

"Thanks, same to you." He clicked the phone off and turned to Bridget. "Chadwick posted a memo banning all employees from talking with me."

"Tom is so obedient. I like him. You were right to warn him about calling you from work. I wish you had a lawyer that you could talk to right now."

"Me too, and I've been thinking about that. A classmate of mine at the University of Connecticut went to law school. He married someone from North Carolina, and I think they settled in this area."

"What's his name?"

"Walter Butler. We lost touch over the years but I did know him well enough at one time. He was smart and sensible. I'd trust him. You heard my stories about my dorm, 'the jungle.' Walter followed my poker escapades, shocked at how much money I made. He insinuated I cheated. I'll find his phone number online and call him tomorrow for a labor lawyer recommendation."

Chapter 24

Attorney Walter Butler, having no plans to be out of town for the Christmas holiday, agreed to meet with Neil on December twenty-seventh at his office in the college town of Davidson, just north of the city. Not knowing the area, Neil allowed extra time to get to his scheduled appointment. He located Walter's office in a building that looked like a former private residence, found a parking space on the street, and walked to the office.

Entering the law office, he said to the receptionist, "I'm Neil Landers. I have an appointment with attorney Butler."

"Please be seated. He'll be right with you." She dialed a few numbers and said, "Your appointment is here."

Walter came out and greeted Neil. "Come on in. Any trouble finding the office?"

"No, your directions were perfect."

Walter looked more like a professor than a lawyer: not quite six feet tall, with premature graying around his temples, and thin hair across the top of his head. He wore a conservative business suit.

"Do you like this hamlet?" Neil asked.

"I do. I like the small town college community. It reminds me of the area around UConn. My kids ride their bikes freely. Occasionally they ride here after school." He opened the door to his office and motioned for Neil to enter.

"Didn't you work for a New York company after graduation? How did you end up in Charlotte?" Walter asked.

"Good memory. I was in Tarrytown until a little over two years ago. At a national meeting in San Francisco, Gordon Byrnes approached me and insisted I have dinner with him. He seemed to know all about me, but I had never heard of his company. We talked a bit, and he offered me a job."

"Just like that he offered you his director of research position?"

"Yes, it was bizarre. I didn't intend to accept, and I told him I would discuss it with my wife. When I returned to Tarrytown, Byrnes called numerous times, insisting that Bridget and I visit his corporate headquarters. He flew us first class to Charlotte, put us up for a weekend in a suite at a luxurious hotel, and hired a private tour guide to show us the city. It was a whirlwind of entertainment. The timing was right, so we came south."

"He aggressively recruited you."

"The company lab is state of the art. He offered an attractive package."

"Did you have any misgivings?" Walter asked.

"Not until my first day, when I learned about the three-year noncompete agreement. I didn't like that, but I thought I'd stay until retirement. Now it's a real problem for me to get another job."

"It could cost $25,000 in legal fees to get out of the agreement if your employer puts up little opposition."

"That's a lot of money. Mr. Byrnes defends the agreement aggressively."

"It will not play well to a jury that he frightened your wife."

"What are your fees?"

"Let's take care of that now. I'll need a check for $2,000 as a retainer to represent you. My usual rate is $225 an hour. As a courtesy, I'll charge you $150.00."

"Thanks." Neil wrote a check to Walter's firm.

"On the phone you told me that you're on forced vacation and you expect to be fired."

"Right, here's the letter my boss's son-in-law delivered to my home." He took a paper from a file and placed it in front of Walter.

"Most unusual—I'm sorry we didn't talk before you called the NRC. I would have advised you not to call and to change jobs instead."

Neil did not like that Walter thought him foolish. "His shortcuts in quality risked lives. We're not talking cosmetic details. He fooled with key components at nuclear power plants. I couldn't pretend I didn't understand."

"If I didn't know you, I'd throw you out of my office and never take this case. And I certainly would never recommend another attorney. It takes convincing evidence to develop a case. You have nothing."

"I thought I could be anonymous."

"These are outrageous accusations. There are some whistleblower laws that might apply."

"I hate that label."

"Who can I talk with at the NRC?"

"The lead investigator is agent Randolph Perry. Here's his card."

With Neil present, Walter called the NRC and spoke with Randolph Perry. Walter introduced himself as Neil's attorney and told Perry about the hand-delivered letter and Neil's forced vacation.

While they continued talking, Neil gazed at Walter's framed photo of Maine's Mount Katahdin, then signaled to Walter and softly said, "Ask him about Taiwan?"

Walter nodded. "Agent Perry, please tell me the NRC's thinking about involving Taiwan." He listened to the response.

"That's reassuring. Thanks. I'll be back to you," Walter said.

"What's reassuring?" Neil leaned forward in his chair.

"The NRC believes you. The State Department involvement is standard protocol when a U.S. supplier sells questionable basic components to a foreign company. More heat on your employer should help us, and they've given your allegation a high priority."

"You mean it would be slower if it were rated lower?"

"Absolutely. It's clear that Mr. Byrnes will fire you. Let's discuss the best way to proceed." They reviewed recent events and agreed that Neil would return to work on January eighth.

"Remember the Jackie Robinson story. He was the good guy. In the face of abuse he remained calm and polite," Walter reminded Neil. "You need to be the rational one in response to any mistreatment and craziness. January eighth could be a very difficult day for you."

"I feel more like Roger Boisjoly than Jackie Robinson." Neil sounded as downtrodden as he felt.

"Who's he?"

"The NASA engineer who protested the Challenger launch in cold weather. Boisjoly said no one had tested the O-rings in extreme cold temperatures and that it was dangerous to proceed. The executives ignored his objections."

"Unfortunately for the seven astronauts, Boisjoly was right," Walter said. "Back to this letter—it says your time off will not count as vacation time. Call Chadwick to confirm that." He handed Neil the phone.

Neil dialed the number and asked for Chadwick. The receptionist connected him promptly. When Neil identified himself, Chadwick put him on hold.

"I'm on hold." Neil mouthed to Walter and pantomimed taping.

With Chadwick back on the line, Neil said, "I'm concerned about being off so many days. My wife and I have planned a summer vacation and I don't want to disappoint her."

"As stated in the letter, this is not regular time off," Chadwick said.

"So they count as work days?"

"So to speak," Chadwick responded, with his signature nervous giggle.

"I'm surprised you never mentioned this reward of extra time during my review the other day."

"Enjoy your time. I'll see you on January eighth." Chadwick ended the call.

Neil hung up the phone. "Weird. He insists this time off is bonus days for good work. He's such a liar. I suspect Chadwick taped that conversation."

"Of course! He hoped you'd say something slanderous or threaten him. We both know he's plotting to fire you. He just has not figured out a reason yet. This is a messy situation. Your employer is very mad that the government is on to them."

"So far, the NRC has not done a great job."

"The government will prevail over Gordon and Chadwick Byrnes. On our own, we would have very little chance of winning."

"Byrnes has three or four law firms. I know of a Charlotte firm, a DC firm, and a Manhattan firm. There may be more."

"The NRC has a large legal staff and a direct link with the Department of Justice. Think about this, there are government lawyers in every state. That's sufficient resources. Agent Perry told me that the NRC receives about seven hundred calls regarding safety problems a year. Last year they prioritized three as code red. Your call is one. We should wrap this up quickly. Forget about the hourly rate. I'll take this on contingency."

"You'll be paid when Byrnes settles with me. Is that how this works?" Neil asked.

"Yes. I'll take a third for my time from whatever amount you receive. You're still responsible for any direct costs like phone, postage, copies, etc."

Neil drove home from Davidson against the rush hour traffic of workers leaving uptown and South Charlotte for homes at Lake Norman and towns north. Finding it strange not to be on vacation or at work, Neil wondered how he would cope with the remaining ten days of limbo.

Chapter 25

On January eighth, Neil returned to work. He punched in the code. A red light blinked. *I don't have access! They have changed the security code.*

Walking around to the front of the Byrnes Building, he entered as a visitor.

"Please go directly to Chadwick's office," the receptionist stated as she reached to answer another call.

Wondering what was up with Chadwick, Neil made his way to the upper floor.

In the hall, Chadwick waited for him. "How was your Christmas, Neil?"

"Fine."

"I want to go over your concerns with our products. Come with me." While walking back to the main floor Chadwick asked, "Are you aware of a government regulation that requires updated Material Safety Data Sheets every two years?"

"Never heard of it. Why do you ask?"

Chadwick did not answer. They continued a short distance in silence to a large conference room. Three people Neil had never seen before sat around the table. Chadwick introduced Neil to attorney Vernon Casper from Washington DC, attorney Harris Patterson from Charlotte, and a court reporter.

"We'd like to have a conversation with you," attorney Patterson began. "We're here to investigate why you think there's a problem with GB Polymers products. You've a right to have your own attorney. Do you want to make a call?"

"No. I don't need an attorney to do a day's work." Neil looked at Chadwick across the table, who kept his head down, avoiding eye contact with Neil.

Attorney Patterson began the questioning, "When did you start talking to the NRC?"

"Last July."

"Why didn't you express your concerns with Mr. Byrnes or Chadwick?" Patterson asked.

"I did. They dismissed my concerns."

"What were you worried about?" Patterson probed.

"False statements about temperature, lack of independent testing, and testing nonrepresentative samples."

"That's your opinion, isn't it?" Patterson suggested.

"It's a fact," Neil said defiantly.

"Did you discuss specific nuclear plants with the NRC?" Casper asked.

"I told them GB Polymers sells to the majority of nuclear power plants in the United States."

"Did they ask about product failures?" Patterson asked.

"Yes."

"Did you talk to the NRC about Pilgrim Nuclear?" Casper asked.

"Not that I can recall."

"What do you know about White Marsh?" Patterson asked.

"I know it's a nuclear power plant in Maryland."

"What did you tell the NRC about White Marsh?" Casper asked.

"I don't recall discussing White Marsh."

"Do you know about any difficulty pumping construction grout a long distance at White Marsh?" Casper asked.

"No," Neil answered, surprised that he had to respond to two attorneys.

"What do you know about the renovations at the White Marsh plant?" Patterson asked.

"Nothing."

"Did you discuss the construction of a new turbine building at White Marsh?" Casper asked.

"No."

"Did you discuss that GB Polymers construction grout is under the reactor core at White Marsh?" Patterson asked.

"I didn't know that. I only knew the plant used GB fireproofing barrier material. That's a product I believe doesn't meet the temperature claims stated in the literature."

"Product claims are not your area of expertise, right?" Casper asked antagonistically. Without giving Neil time to respond, he continued, "Isn't that a function of quality control and isn't it a fact that neither Gordon Byrnes nor Chadwick Byrnes is involved in quality control?"

"Chadwick signed the manual that asserts GB Polymers meets stringent quality requirements. He mailed it to every power plant," Neil stated.

The court reporter took down every word. They did not stop for lunch. Instead, Chadwick ordered his secretary to bring sandwiches to the conference room.

Determined to endure the questioning no matter how long it went on, Neil kept his image of Jackie Robinson in his mind, grateful for his attorney's suggestion. With the wits to survive two attorneys taking turns at him, he enjoyed some moments of the skirmish. Gordon and Chadwick thought Neil knew more than he did. The attorneys revealed problems with GB Polymers products at nuclear power plants.

"Do you know about any product failures at the Clinton nuclear power plant in Illinois?" Casper continued.

"Nothing specific," Neil responded.

"Do you know about any product failures at the Fitzpatrick nuclear power plant in New York?" Patterson asked.

"That plant is in the news often."

"Did you give confidential information about GB Polymers sales in Taiwan to the NRC?" Casper asked.

"No."

"Did you identify GB's international licensees to the government?" Patterson asked.

"No."

"What did you tell them about sales in Grenada?" Casper asked.

"Nothing." It was obvious that his answers puzzled the attorneys. From their line of questioning, Neil realized the problems at power plants predated his time at GB.

Patterson removed six pictures from the middle of a pad of paper. He placed them in front of Neil. "Take a look at these pictures. Do you recognize anything?"

"My office."

"You acknowledge these are pictures of your office?" Patterson said.

"Yes. I'm surprised my desk merits such attention. These are high quality prints. What camera did you use? Could I get an eight by ten glossy?" Neil relished having fun at their expense.

"Would you describe this desk as untidy?" Patterson asked.

"Yes."

"Aren't there company rules on housekeeping?" Casper asked.

"Probably."

"Don't these photos show a clear violation of company housekeeping policies?" Patterson asked.

"My office has always looked like this. No one ever complained to me about untidiness."

"That's all," Patterson said.

Chadwick escorted Neil out of the conference room. "Did you bring the company cell phone and laptop?" Chadwick asked.

Neil handed Chadwick the phone. "The laptop is in my office."

Chadwick followed Neil. Piles of unopened mail cluttered Neil's desk. Strategically placed on top, Neil immediately saw a paper with the GB Polymers distinctive logo. He picked it up and scanned the document, a copy of a memo Chadwick wrote for Neil's personnel file.

"A reprimand for not following a federal regulation for Material Safety Data Sheets? When was that my job?"

"Your negligence cost significant sales," Chadwick said. "That's unacceptable."

"This is a setup! It's harassment! I'm not putting up with this," Neil shouted. He waved the memo at Chadwick. He walked down the hallway to Matt Hawkins's office. All the restraint and coolness of his earlier decorum with the attorneys disappeared when he reached Matt's doorway. At that moment, he ignored his attorney's advice to remember Jackie Robinson. In a loud voice, Neil berated Gordon's son-in-law Matt. "You upset my wife coming to our home. She thought I was dead, you callous creep. Stay away from my home!" Neil spewed at Matt.

He returned to his disorderly office. Although he could not focus, he did not dare leave. For the remaining minutes of the workday, Chadwick hovered. At five o'clock, Neil left the building.

When Neil arrived home, he called his lawyer, Walter, about his day at work. While on the phone, the doorbell rang. "Walter, please hang on, someone's at the door." With the phone in hand, Neil opened the front door. A messenger handed him a packet with the familiar Fairview Road return address.

"I've got something from Byrnes," Neil explained, opening the envelope. He pulled out the letter. "I'm back on forced vacation for two more weeks."

"Who delivered the letter?" Walter asked.

"A courier service."

"Why'd they extend the time?"

"Bad behavior—the letter says I shouted at an employee."

"What?"

"When I saw Matt, the guy who came to my home and scared my wife, I lost it. I yelled at him. I'll be fired. It's a matter of time."

"Hang tight. I'll draft a letter stating that you're a willing worker but that you'll not tolerate harassment. You can bring it with you when you return in two weeks."

Neil hung up the phone and it rang immediately.

"Hi Neil," Perry said. "How did your day at work go?"

Neil again told the story of his interrogation by two attorneys and Chadwick's reprimand in his file. Perry wanted the names of the lawyers. Neil could not remember them.

"I'm glad you have your own attorney, Neil. I'm sorry for your trouble."

"Are you aware of problems at the White Marsh plant?" Neil asked.

"No, why?" Perry asked.

"The lawyers asked me if I knew that GB's construction grout was under the reactor. I don't know anything about the White Marsh plant. From the questions put to me, I'd guess Gordon and Chadwick are worried that the NRC knows about problems with their material at White Marsh."

"That's interesting. I've been in regular communication with the resident inspector at that plant. He never indicated GB Polymers's products were used there."

"The lawyers asked about plants in Illinois and New York. My gut feeling is problems have been ignored or covered up."

"That's not good. Can I get a transcript of your questioning?"

"When my lawyer gets his copy, I'll have him send you one."

"Thanks. Good luck."

Chapter 26

Olmsted called Patterson for a report on Neil's interrogation. "We failed," Patterson said.

"Gordon insisted the guy's a wimp." Olmsted was surprised that the bully scheme did not succeed.

"Not so. He's tough," Patterson insisted. He repeated the comic remark about the photographs of Neil's cluttered desk.

"With two attorneys questioning him, he joked about pictures of his office?" Olmsted asked.

"Right," Patterson responded.

"What about his phone records and expense accounts, anything useful?"

"Squeaky clean."

"We go to plan B. Get a private detective on Landers."

"C.V. Collins & Associates is a private investigation firm I know well. I've worked with them on numerous cases. They'll find something on this guy."

"We need something shameful on Landers," Olmsted said. "We need him to go away."

"Most people who live past age thirty have indiscretions. Collins will go back as far as it takes. His firm has a good record of digging up embarrassing minutiae," Patterson assured Olmsted.

"Find out everything. His education, former employers, and previous addresses and associates," Olmsted instructed. "Spare no expense. Get something on him."

"I'm on it. Collins will recreate Neil's life. Few can remain standing with that kind of intense scrutiny."

"Give me an update as soon as possible."

"Chadwick expressed concern about the Richard guy," Patterson said. "We have to work something out with him. Actually, his words were--We can't have him making trouble. He's someone we can work with so do whatever is necessary."

"I'll talk with Chadwick about Richard," Olmsted said.

Chapter 27

Neil sat at his dining room table with a cup of tea reading the copy of his interrogation for the umpteenth time. *Why all the questions about the White Marsh plant?* Perry called, interrupting Neil's speculating.

"I visited the White Marsh plant. A worker said there have been problems with material used for penetration closures," Perry said.

"GB Polymers's stuff?"

"I couldn't verify the manufacturer."

"I thought you required a paper trail, documentation for all purchases."

"We do, but the resident inspector can't locate anything. I've requested a report on all products used at the plant."

"It's hard to believe you're having trouble finding out exactly what products were used at the plant, given you have a specific procurement process. If workers and documentation onsite aren't helpful, what about the paperwork from the raid? You must have dates of shipments, quantities of each product used, and where it was installed at the Maryland plant," Neil insisted.

"I hate to tell you this, but Gordon's lawyers slowed the analysis process when they insisted they needed all originals. Our copies are scattered in boxes, and no one has a handle on what's where. It's totally unmanageable. I had hoped to get some useful evidence from the power plant. Agents involved in the raid are now on other assignments. No one is examining the material we took from GB Polymers."

"Great. Now what?"

"I'll check with my supervisor."

*****

Sitting in his study, Neil talked to his blue discus. "You guys are lucky I'm looking out for you. I feel like you would if I took you from this cozy tank and dropped you into the Amazon River. I wish I had a protector."

Scheduled to return to work on Monday, Neil found it difficult to imagine what awaited him. He had worked one day since Gordon put him on forced vacation. On that day, two attorneys interrogated him for seven hours. For someone who loved leisure, it surprised Neil that he found these days of limbo painful. He obsessed over the language of the hand-delivered memos. The first one had put him on forced vacation. The second one put him back on forced vacation. He read them numerous times, trying to anticipate the next hit. He could think about nothing else.

For a distraction, Neil went to the main library in uptown Charlotte. He could look at the NRC Code of Federal Regulations online, but he wanted a change of scenery. The library had a hard copy.

Late that afternoon Neil returned home and found a familiar looking packet propped at his front door. Shaking, he picked it up and went inside. Another message could only be one thing. The beat of his heart quickened. His mouth had no saliva. He needed water. Still holding the envelope, he went to the kitchen for cold water and drank a tall glass in big gulps. He felt weak, even dizzy. Staring at the envelope in his left hand, he stumbled to a chair in the living room. He felt a chill. Shivering, he crossed the room and adjusted the thermostat. He remained motionless for four or five minutes, then opened the envelope. Chadwick had signed the letter: *Dear Neil... terminated ... effective immediately ... violated a federal regulation that required updated MSDS for all products ... Material Safety Data Sheets (MSDS) ... your negligence cost us business ...*

No check. No mention of personal belongings. Neil sat stunned. *This is outrageous.* He called Perry. "I'm fired. Another message was delivered to my home."

"I'm so sorry, Neil. You do understand I'm with the Office of Reactor Safety. I can't help you with a labor issue. You need to contact the Department of Labor."

"You're not serious," Neil said in total disbelief. "Another government agency?"

"That's the law. The NRC doesn't oversee workplace complaints. The Department of Labor handles wrongful termination cases."

"This is double talk. I should never have called the NRC." Neil slammed the phone down. He felt abandoned and confused. After bringing serious safety concerns to the NRC, they blew his cover, and now he had to ask the Department of Labor for help. The NRC knew Gordon fired him for talking with the NRC and all they could say was *this is a labor issue.* Incredible!

Neil called his attorney. "I'm fired."

"Good."

"Good?" Neil was aghast.

"Legally, things are clearer. Now we can respond. What reason did they give?" Walter asked.

"The letter states I violated a federal regulation."

"Read it to me."

Neil read Walter his termination letter.

"This came in today's mail?" Walter asked.

"Delivered by messenger," Neil said.

"With the NRC's backing, we should resolve this wrongful termination issue quickly," Walter said.

"I wish it were so. I've already spoken with Perry. He told me wrongful termination is a matter for the Labor Department, not the NRC. I've always had a job. This is dreadful!"

"Can you meet on Monday to prepare paperwork for the Department of Labor?" Walter asked.

"Name a time. I'm unemployed."

*****

Neil drove the fifteen miles north of Charlotte to Walter's office in a daze. Once there, he said, "I'm glad you've had experience filing complaints with the Department of Labor."

"The DOL policy is to act within thirty days of receiving a complaint," Walter reassured Neil.

"A prompt government agency—that's an oxymoron."

"I've written a draft. I need your input for some particulars."

Neil and Walter finalized a well-written formal complaint to the Department of Labor.

"It'll go out this afternoon," Walter said. "Meanwhile, you need to be very careful. You cannot discuss this situation with anyone except Bridget. Don't risk a slander accusation from your employer. Don't give any interviews. It's customary to think you can go public to get justice. Trust me, it's dangerous for you to speak out about Gordon or your company. Please convey the seriousness to Bridget."

"Sounds like I'm the criminal," Neil grumbled.

"Remember Jackie Robinson," Walter reminded Neil.

"I don't know how he did it."

"Focus on the fact that he won. He was the good guy."

"Okay." Walter had a point.

"Be careful. No venting in a diary or a journal," Walter warned. "You can't keep one. Period."

"Bridget writes in a journal daily. She helps elderly people write their life stories. Writing is important to her."

"Tell her to stop keeping a journal."

"You're serious?"

"It could be subpoenaed," Walter cautioned. "Senator Packwood's personal diaries ended up in court."

"This won't be easy. I'm not accustomed to telling my wife what to do."

"You can't afford to have your employer sue you personally."

"What about the things I left in my office. I want them back. I had gifts from my nieces, some photos, a mug...."

Walter cut him off, "Consider them gone."

"No way! They're mine. Have I got any rights?"

"Focus on the big picture, ignore petty details."

Neil left thinking about boxes of evidence piled somewhere in NRC land. What a waste.

Chapter 28

In his Manhattan office, attorney Olmsted read Patterson's fax on detective Collins's research to re-create Neil Landers's life, uncovering names and addresses of current and past buddies, childhood friends, and classmates from high school and college—even elementary school, prom dates, and former girlfriends.

Collins had sent a detective to Tarrytown, who interviewed numerous former coworkers and neighbors. In Charlotte, Collins dispatched an investigator to canvass Neil's Dilworth neighborhood and track his day-to-day activities.

Olmsted read the details of Neil's finances: monthly mortgage payments, payroll direct deposits, and quarterly investment dividends that showed up in his bank account. Gordon's theory that a competitor paid Neil did not prove to be true. Neil donated to the United Way each pay period and regularly contributed to his church.

His prior employer had wished Neil had finished a product they were counting on to improve sales. His immediate boss resented having to complete Neil's work.

Neil had no speeding tickets in any state, no record of any prior lawsuits, and his movie rentals and borrowed library books revealed nothing scandalous. Olmsted reread the section on Neil's gambling. A classmate presumed Neil cheated in college poker games. He organized games in the dorm and won considerable cash.

Collins called the University of Connecticut, hoping Neil never finished his degree. Olmsted laughed when he read that Collins identified himself as a Charlotte executive on a committee that selected Neil for a prestigious community award. As the person to introduce Neil, Collins wondered if Neil's college file had anything remarkable to include in his talk.

The person in the registrar office confirmed that Neil had earned a degree in chemistry. She read from notes in his file that the university had pursued him, and gave him a complete scholarship. In his junior year of high school, Neil placed in the top twenty in the national Westinghouse Science Test. The registrar requested that Collins forward any local article on Neil for the university alumnae news.

It was clear to Olmsted that Collins's team amassed a large amount of information, but, regrettably, no reprehensible behavior.

What a boring nerd. Olmsted called Patterson. "I've reviewed Collins's comprehensive report."

"He's pretty frustrated," Patterson said. "Phone taps produced nothing damaging. Neither he nor his wife is long-winded over the wires. She had a variety of work calls, something with old folks, sad stories— couldn't stand to listen. She made tennis dates and exchanged reading lists with her friends—nothing valuable. Neil's calls were all job related— headhunters, contacts in the ASTM, and colleagues around the country. He's looking for a job."

"We'll invoke Gordon's noncompete agreement if he gets one. We need him to go away and drop his suit. Maybe Collins can see if the person at his former company, the one Landers left holding the bag on some project, would work with us. And revisit the college classmate that said Neil fleeced them at poker. It may be a long shot but worth a try. Ask Collins for some innovative suggestions," Olmsted said.

Chapter 29

The sun glistened off the towers of the Connecticut River Nuclear Power Plant as Susan Ridel drove to her job at the library, aware of an uneasiness that the spectacle triggered in her.

She barely arrived at her desk when the phone rang. "Reference desk, may I help you?" Susan asked. "Yes, the library has a large town history collection. I'll be glad to assist you. I'm here until three o'clock." Susan replaced the phone, thinking how much she enjoyed her new responsibilities and more contact with the public.

During the previous eighteen months, Susan had worked at the circulation desk performing various clerical tasks. Her supervisor praised her people skills, telling her she had a natural customer service personality, and rewarded Susan with the reference assistant position. Retrieving requested information and guiding individuals through the library resources pleased Susan.

After being home for nine years with her sons, returning to work challenged Susan. Her husband had had a decent maintenance job at the power plant, and with good financial management, they lived on his income. His death two years ago devastated her. She could not imagine coping as a single parent, never mind finding a satisfying job that fit her schedule. Her neighbors provided considerable support; one suggested she apply at the local library.

Susan was continuing with her tasks when a tall, well-dressed man appeared at her desk, "I called earlier," he said.

"Days of ferry travel from New York City to East Haddam, right?" Susan asked.

"Yes, I'm interested in the time when East Haddam was an active stop between New York City and northern spots on the Connecticut River. My great-grandfather lived here as a boy. I'm filling in some gaps in my family history," he said, with a smile.

"Early maps reveal a snapshot in time. Let's start there." Susan led the man to the map area. As he asked more questions, Susan directed him to possible resources. "I hope you have time."

"More than before I retired," he answered. "Thanks for your assistance."

Susan returned to a ringing phone on her desk. The caller, Andrew Gibbons, the director of Citizens Protectors, a local environmental group, spoke in an excited tone. "Call me when you're free to talk. It's very important."

"On my way home," Susan assured him. The library was strict about nonwork-related phone calls. He understood. Something in his tone, the code-like quality of his brevity, told her this was more than a reminder of a meeting time.

Susan volunteered about fifteen hours a month for the group. When Andrew Gibbons approached her to help the organization, Susan could not imagine what she could contribute without an advanced degree in science or business experience. He assured her that volunteers' backgrounds were diverse and that many were homemakers. The fact that the group monitored the local power plant persuaded Susan.

Initially she agreed to attend meetings and provide administrative support services, feeling most comfortable behind the scene. She did various tasks for the group at home after her boys were in bed. Susan gathered data for reports, filed information, and kept track of important developments. She honored her husband's memory with this commitment.

On the way to meet the school bus, Susan returned Andrew's call.

"How would you like to be on TV?" he asked.

"I wouldn't. I hate to have my picture taken," Susan responded without hesitation. "Pick another volunteer. Or you do it."

"The New Haven TV news station is interested in a comprehensive story on tritium in East Haddam's drinking water. Apparently a reporter got a hold of some incriminating data."

Susan pulled her car into a gas station and put the car in park. Once her hands were free of the steering wheel they shook wildly. "I can't," she said after a long pause.

"Please think about it. Don't give me an answer right now. I'll see you at tomorrow's meeting."

Susan checked her watch. She needed to keep moving to meet her boys. Memories flooded her mind. She felt the tears starting. Not now. "Stop it!" she shouted. Consciously on her in breath, she said "*Not*"; on the out breath, she said "*Now!*" Repeatedly, she kept up the repetitive pattern and drove the country roads to her children's bus stop.

The evening hours evaporated. Martin Jr. and William played catch outside. During dinner, they told her about their day in bits and pieces … a good play in gym, some praise from their teacher, and interesting tidbits related to a science class or a story they read.

After homework, baths, and bedtime rituals, Susan moved on to other household chores. At first, Susan had found evenings as a single parent the hardest time of day. Countless nights after her husband died, she sat and cried when the boys went to sleep. She could not mark exactly when, but gradually she had found the late evening quiet of the house to be peaceful.

Tonight, as always, she had things to do, but she procrastinated. In the living room, Susan took a framed photo from the mantel and sat on the couch. She gazed intently at the picture of their last family vacation. Her husband Martin looked so happy, fishing with his sons from the rocks at Hammonasset State Park. Susan had picked up her camera to compose a picture of her boys and their dad when another angler volunteered to take the picture of all of them. Susan regretted that he would never know the significance of his kindness. The fisherman captured the essence of her family. This smiling group enjoyed being with each other, their strong bond so evident.

"How could you do this to us?" Susan asked for the millionth time. "Why didn't we just move away? We could have started over in a new state. It's a big country." How many times did she have this conversation with her dead husband? There was no going back. It was fruitless to play the "what if?" game. Anger with her husband for taking his own life had consumed Susan for a long time. Over and over again, she relived the horror of the police phone call … *a car parked behind St. John's Church registered to your husband … a good-bye note … he jumped from the Portland Bridge….*

If it were not for her boys, she may never have let go of her rage. Intellectually, she understood her husband's devastation. He believed no one would hire a man fired for theft. The written note he left said she was better off without him and asked her to forgive him for failing as a husband and father.

Emotionally, Susan moved on as best as anyone could by creating a normal life for herself and her boys. Not wanting to relive the past, her answer to the reporter's request for an interview was *no*. She put the photo back on the fireplace.

*****

The next evening, Susan drove to the monthly meeting for Citizens Protectors. Often Susan arrived after the meeting had begun so that she had as much evening time as possible with her boys. Tonight she asked the babysitter to come earlier. Susan wanted Andrew to understand that she could not go back and experience again the time leading up to and immediately after her husband's death. She could not share his story with a TV audience.

"I can't go on TV," Susan blurted as soon as she saw Andrew. "It's too painful."

"I should have thought more before asking you," he said. "I'm sorry. I got excited when the reporter said that tritium could be a serious problem in town."

"What are you saying? Plant officials said test results showed harmless trace elements of tritium." Susan gave him a questioning look.

"This reporter has information that indicates otherwise. She showed me copies of notes from an employee at the lab that tests water from the plant wells. Apparently, there is a very cozy relationship between the lab and the plant management. The reporter believes the letterhead with the signature color logo for the lab and the business envelope are authentic. According to the note, a designated technician did all testing for the plant. When preliminary test results indicated high tritium levels, the technician stopped and tested another sample without recording the first findings. Nothing about elevated levels of tritium was ever logged."

Susan was quiet. *If this were true....* She could not finish her thought.

Others drifted in, ending their conversation. The meeting discussion went from personal catch-up with each other to a serious discussion of agenda items. One man reported on problems at the Connecticut River Nuclear Power Plant. "My friend who works there said they had a big scare the other day. Workers in the containment area followed precautions indicative of exposure to radiation. Nothing was in the news, of course."

Another person voiced frustration, "Our government regulator is no help. The Nuclear Regulatory Commission practices oversight from DC. That agency is clueless and useless. The local NRC resident inspector is a joke. His information is from the plant's public relations department. Quality has nothing to do with reality, just pieces of paper in a file."

Susan remembered her husband saying that the government regulators were ineffective. Plant officials deliberately deceiving town residents dominated her thoughts.

Chapter 30

The next day when Susan returned home with her sons, she noted the flashing message light on her phone. She hit play.

"Hi Susan. I'm Leslie. My son is in second grade with your son. It's important that I speak with you when you have a free minute. Please call."

Susan jotted down the number. Later that evening she returned the call. As soon as Leslie began, Susan heard soft sobs.

"This is so hard on the phone," Leslie said. "Could I please stop by and talk with you?"

"Now?"

"Yes, please. I'm five minutes away."

"Do you know how to get here?"

"Yes."

"Come on over."

Susan flipped on the outside lights, turned on extra lamps on the first floor, and set up the coffeepot to make four cups. She poured herself a glass of water from the cooler. Before she finished with the boys' lunches for the next day, headlights flickered in the driveway.

Opening her front door as the woman walked from her car, she recognized Leslie from the school but did not know anything specific about her, including which boy was her second grader.

"Thank you for letting me stop by," Leslie said, and she immediately burst into tears.

"Please sit down." Susan motioned to a comfortable chair. "I've certainly had moments when I've been too upset to speak. Take your time."

"I'm sorry to impose."

"You're not. Can I get you some coffee?"

"No, thank you." Leslie pulled a Kleenex from her pocket and dabbed at her eyes.

Susan placed a box of tissues on the table next to the woman. Leslie reached for some and blew her nose. "My daughter has leukemia." Leslie moaned loudly. Tears streamed down her cheeks.

"I'm so sorry." Susan's eyes welled as she placed a consoling hand on Leslie's arm. Neither woman spoke.

"I thought she had the flu," Leslie whispered. She wiped her eyes and struggled to regain some semblance of composure.

Susan's hand remained on the woman's arm.

"I shouldn't have come. I'd better leave."

"No. It's okay."

"I'm sorry. I'm such a mess."

"Please don't apologize for caring about your child," Susan insisted.

"She's only ten!" Leslie stuffed the wads of wet tissue in her pocket and took two deep gulps of air.

Susan brought a glass of water to her guest.

"Thank you." Leslie took a sip. "Our doctor was puzzled by my daughter's symptoms and ordered blood work. I got the bad news this afternoon."

"I'm so sorry," Susan said, feeling at a loss for words.

"Something else he said was very upsetting," Leslie added.

"What?"

"He's treating four other children."

"From town?"

"Yes. He actually said all of us live near the nuclear power plant."

"And he thinks there's a connection," Susan said.

With her voice cracking, Leslie managed to say, "Sounds like it."

"What does he think is the problem?"

"Our drinking water."

"Your water! Have you tested it?" Susan asked.

"Yes. I didn't know your husband, but I heard that he told my neighbor that wells near the plant could be contaminated," Leslie said.

"Yes, Martin alerted a guy he knew from high school that something seemed to be wrong with the water on the plant property."

"A group of our neighbors got together and met with officials from the plant. They insisted that we had inaccurate information. To calm us, the plant offered to pay a lab to test our water and send us the results. So we did, and all reports came back that the water was fine. My husband and I were so relieved."

"But now you're wondering if tritium is in your well."

"Yes. Maybe your husband was right. I've researched tritium on the Internet. Drinking it zaps your insides with radiation."

"Tell me the name of the lab."

"I don't remember. Do you think the plant officials lied to us?" Leslie asked.

"I don't know."

"We kept the lab report on the water. I'll get you a copy."

"A second and even a third opinion can't hurt," Susan suggested. "Maybe the lab the plant used isn't the best resource."

"Can that group, Citizens Protectors, help? My husband said you're a volunteer."

"Yes, I am. I'll speak with the director about your daughter and see what we can do to get some answers."

"I'm sorry to burden you."

"Please. I'm happy to help if I can."

*****

Susan woke the next morning with a headache. She had scarcely slept. Somehow, she got the boys off to school and went to the library. After about an hour at work, she told her supervisor she was ill and asked if another staff member could cover the reference desk.

Susan drove straight to the Citizens Protectors's office.

"Are you all right?" Andrew asked when she appeared in the doorway of his office.

"No. Tell me more about this interview."

"The WTNH TV station called me and proposed putting a face on the problem of tritium in town wells.

"I've had the face of a ten-year-old and her distraught mother in front of me all night." Susan quickly recounted her visit from Leslie.

"The reporter believes tritium is a serious problem. And that plant officials deceived the public."

"Trace elements of tritium were harmless, that was the message— liars. Tell that reporter I'll talk with her."

Chapter 31

Susan put on three different outfits before she settled on a simple olive green suit. From her jewelry box, she took the first bracelet her husband had given her, a series of topaz stones. As she snapped the clasp, she felt connected with him and confident she was doing the right thing by talking with the reporter.

The setting for the taping session was nearby in Middletown. Grateful she did not have to drive to New Haven, Susan drove north on Route 9 and exited at Washington Street. Following the reporter's direction to a tall building on Broad Street, she parked her car and made her way inside. A young man escorted her to the space created for the interview, a homey den like room with vases of fresh flowers and soothing shades of green upholstered furniture.

"Great, you're early," the reporter greeted Susan. "We've got time to go over things before we start."

The reporter reviewed the format and encouraged Susan to forget about the camera and simply act natural.

Sure, Susan thought, *I do this all the time*. "I've never done any public speaking. I hate to have my picture taken," Susan said.

"You'll do fine," the reporter reassured her.

Once they began their conversation, Susan did stop thinking about the camera.

"What was your husband's job at the Connecticut River Nuclear Power Plant?" the reporter began.

"My husband was a maintenance worker at the plant for years. He had various tasks, including working on the pumps in the test wells."

"Test wells?"

"Yes there are sixteen wells on the grounds of the power plant. Staff routinely monitors the ground water. My husband learned from coworkers that something was not right with the water. Repeated tests showed elevated levels of tritium."

"How did management react?" the reporter asked.

"They kept the testing information quiet, and that really upset my husband."

"Your husband thought wells on adjacent property might be contaminated?"

"Yes."

"What did he do?"

"He recommended to one homeowner, a man he had gone to school with, that he test his water and pass this suggestion on to his neighbors."

"How did plant management learn that your husband told people to test their wells?" the reporter asked.

"I don't know. A woman told me that homeowners in the neighborhood met with plant officials and asked about tritium. Someone obviously figured out that my husband had alerted them."

"Did his supervisor or anyone at the plant ask him if he had talked with the neighbors?"

"Not that I know."

"Did he think his bosses were mad at him?"

"He knew the neighbors expressing concern angered the plant management. Everyone knew that."

"So plant managers fired your husband for warning others of possible danger. Is that what happened?"

"That's not the reason management gave." Susan's voice cracked. "They accused him of theft."

"Theft? What do you mean?"

Susan took a deep breath. "His boss called seven workers to the locker room. Three supervisors met them to inspect all lockers for missing small hand tools." Susan fought back tears. "The missing tools were in my husband's locker."

"Clear grounds for immediate dismissal."

"Right. Anyone that knew my husband knew it was an obvious set-up."

"You think management fabricated the theft?"

"My husband didn't steal anything." Her voice quivered.

"Why didn't he fight it?"

"How?"

"Couldn't he have contacted the NRC for assistance?"

"He was fired for theft. They humiliated him in front of coworkers and escorted him off the premises."

"He could have sued."

"David beats Goliath in fairy tales, not in the real world. He believed he had no chance of winning against a big corporation."

"What happened next?"

"He came home shattered. After working for twelve years with excellent reviews, they threw him out like trash. He wouldn't talk about it. He ignored the boys and me and stayed in bed. After a week, he got up and said he was going to see someone about a job. That's the last time we spoke. When the police called I figured they had made a mistake."

"What did they say to you?"

"They had found a car registered to my husband behind St. John Church at the end of Main Street in Middletown. They believed he jumped from the Portland Bridge."

"Did you ever imagine that he'd take his own life?"

"Never. He loved his family. The fear of not supporting his family destroyed him." Susan choked back tears. Being fired for theft he never expected to get another job. He had always worked. He was so proud we could afford for me to stay home and be a full time mother."

The reporter signaled the camera operator to stop.

When Susan composed herself, she noted the time. "I'm late. I need to leave." She gathered her things.

"Of course. I'll let you know when the interview will air. Thanks. You did great."

The traffic on Route Nine South moved at a snail pace. Susan arrived at school twenty minutes late and hurried to the field behind the school where the younger grades played soccer. As soon as she caught William's eye, his disappointment pierced her heart. The coach of the little ones was very good about letting everyone play. She instinctively knew he already had his time in the game. She had missed it.

Chapter 32

Two days later, the interview aired. The six o'clock evening news hyped the story: "A twelve-year veteran at Connecticut River Nuclear Power Plant jumped from the Portland Bridge two years ago after being fired. He had alerted townspeople to check for possible elevated levels of tritium in their wells ... tune in later for an exclusive interview with the widow of the deceased."

Susan found seeing herself on the late news surreal. *This will set the record straight.* Her husband had acted naïvely and paid dearly. Recognizing his courage in letting people know about contaminated water in their homes filled her with pride.

The next morning as Susan watched her sons scamper up the bus steps, she resolved that they would grow up knowing that their father was a good man. When the bus drove off, Susan continued to the library. She parked and waved to another staff member who had just arrived. Before Susan locked her car, the person disappeared into the library. Not waiting to walk in with her struck Susan as odd. As usual, Susan reported to the reference desk. Her supervisor sat there and said, "Rita would like to speak with you. I'll cover."

Susan went down the hall to the library branch manager's office, surprised at the formality of the direction. As she walked in, Rita said, "Please close the door."

Before Susan sat down Rita continued, "I'm sorry to have this conversation, but effective immediately, you no longer work at the reference desk."

"What?"

"I wish you had mentioned your TV interview to me," Rita stated sternly.

Nothing could have prepared Susan for this conversation. Her hesitancy about speaking out on TV was all about reliving painful memories, not affecting her job.

"I had four calls at home last night and three this morning. This town doesn't want to be Wiscasset, Maine," Rita said.

"Wiscassett? What's that?"

"A town with a power plant offline. A town with drastically reduced property values. A town with diminished funds for town services," Rita said.

"People are sick! We have no idea how many people are unknowingly drinking contaminated water. Ignoring a health problem doesn't make it disappear."

"I'm very sorry about your husband but we have to stick with the facts. Trace elements do not make a health problem. The plant pays millions of dollars in taxes to our town. The library benefits from town taxes and so do the schools."

Susan wanted to defend her position but instead she said, "Where shall I report for work?"

"Data entry."

*****

Susan met her sons' school bus and looked forward to showing them some books and magazines relevant to their class science work. She planned to immerse herself in activity with them to forget her ugly encounter with the library manager. Susan looked at Martin and William with admiration as they jumped from the bus. *Resilient little guys for sure.*

When they got in the car William said, "Mom, Ian said you're a puppet."

"What?"

"Other kids said so too," Martin said. "And they said we shouldn't play soccer."

"What about soccer?" Susan gathered her things from the car to bring in the house.

"I don't know … something about uniforms."

Susan felt the rage of her morning meeting with her boss return. Her heart beat rapidly, and she felt heat in her neck and face. The Connecticut River Plant supplied the boys' soccer uniforms, the company logo embroidered on the shirt pocket.

"Some of your classmates' mom and dads may be mad at me, but no one will keep you from playing soccer, I promise. Look at the books I borrowed from the library," Susan said in as upbeat a tone as possible. She spread the books and magazines on the kitchen table. "Check out these pictures."

"Cool," William said, eyeing a spider midway through spinning a web.

Susan loved this time with her boys. While they looked at the books, she took some milk from the refrigerator and saw the message light blinking on her answering machine. She hit play. A garbled voice came on ... safety was one word she recognized and plant was another. The rest of the words were unintelligible.

Susan hit stop before a second message started. Later that night, she played her messages.

As best she could determine, the first message said there was a safety problem at the plant. She could not make out anything specific. Three messages denounced her interview.

Exhausted, Susan still had chores to do before she could go to bed. She put clothes in the dryer that she had washed that morning, packed lunches for the boys, and scanned the pile of mail. Most she left unopened on her desk. Then she remembered the envelope in the newspaper metal cylinder on the same post as her mailbox. Some law-abiding citizen did not want to misuse the mailbox. Susan picked up the unstamped envelope with no return address. Her instincts alerted her to be cautious. She rummaged under the kitchen sink for a pair of heavy plastic gloves, put them on and opened the envelope. She pulled out the folded page of nondescript copier paper with a message constructed from cut out magazine letters. It chilled her: *Stop worrying about tritium. Worry about your boys' safety.*

Susan jumped when the phone rang.

"Want to know how the plant gets good results on its water tests?" the caller asked. Before Susan answered, he added. "They switch vials of bottled water with the real sample. The substitution guarantees a good report."

"How do you know?" Susan asked, relieved that the caller was not the author of the threatening note.

"I saw a guy take test tube samples and replace them. Your husband was right to alert people. Management refuses to face the problem."

"Did you report this?"

"That's what I'm doing now. I'm telling you. No one in authority at the plant will take this seriously. You can understand that better than most."

"What can I do?"

"Your interview shook up the plant management. Figure out a way to get independent testing data."

"Meet with me," Susan begged.

"I'll call you again." Click. The dial tone hummed.

Ten-twenty was a little late to make a phone call. She picked up the phone anyway and dialed the home number of the director of Citizens Protectors.

"Susan? Is everything all right?"

"I just hung up from a call with a worker at the power plant. He said management falsifies water samples. The test results are fraudulent."

"Will he speak out?"

"I doubt it. Is there some way we can get independent testing? Technicians not connected with this town need to obtain samples, and the tests must be run at a lab outside of Connecticut."

"*Time* magazine called me. They'd like a follow-up story to your interview. A current worker would be ideal."

"This guy spoke with me anonymously. I doubt he'll speak with a national magazine. Think about the testing."

"He said he'd call again?"

"Yes."

"Keep him talking. Maybe he'll change his mind."

"I got a threatening note." Susan picked up the folder with the collage message on plain paper.

"Read it to me."

"Stop worrying about tritium. Worry about your boys' safety."

"You need to tell the police."

"I don't think so. The town budget pays police. I'm afraid I'm seen as a destroyer of overtime and a deficit maker. I'm sorry I called so late. I'll talk with you tomorrow."

"Be careful."

The phone rang again.

"I need your help," the caller said in a voice that sounded filtered through fabric. "There are cracks in the containment dome."

"Cracks?"

"Yeah, and some are pretty deep. I've got some pictures you can give to your TV reporter friend. We need the media. These clowns are doing cosmetic repairs to cracked concrete."

"Cracks?"

"Rusted rebar inside the concrete. It's impossible to know how severely the corrosion compromised the containment dome structure."

"Can we meet?"

"No, I'll get you some pictures. I'll call again."

"Please call the NRC. Someone in that agency—" The dial tone cut her off in mid-sentence.

Chapter 33

Hoping to avoid applying for unemployment benefits, Neil dialed the direct number for the director of research of his former employer in Tarrytown.

"Stanley, it's Neil."

"I've wanted to talk with you," Stanley said. "How's it going?"

"This move turned out to be a disaster. I need a job. Any chance I can come back?" Neil asked.

"Haven't you heard? A German company bought us. All manufacturing is moving to Torreon, Mexico. Two months from now we'll all be out of here."

"You're kidding!"

"I wish. Anything available in Charlotte for me?"

"Nothing you'd want."

As Stanley described the painful takeover process, the high number of terminations, and the agonizing day-to-day discouragement with fears for the future, Neil empathized and then gave only an abbreviated version of his situation. The men expressed their opinions on the state of manufacturing in the United States, reminisced with a few tales from their time working together, and agreed to keep in touch.

Now Neil had to ignore his pride and file a claim for unemployment. He drove uptown and parked in a garage near the federal building, Feeling nauseated, he made his way through security, followed the signs to the unemployment office, and waited in line for a clerk, who gave him paperwork. After filling out forms, he waited some more. An hour passed. Calculating his unemployment compensation, Neil was stunned to realize it was about 20 percent of his regular paycheck. When he completed the maze of lines and submitted his application, Neil rushed to the building exit.

He returned to his car, paid the attendant, and drove out of the parking garage. His car sputtered, and in the first block, on a diagonal across Fourth Street, it stopped. "*Now what!*" he yelled. Horns blared. Drivers gestured at him as if he had parked in their way on purpose. A few more times Neil failed to start the car. He got out. Two men who looked liked they lived in the parking garage approached Neil. One directed traffic while the other helped Neil push the car to the side of the street. He searched his pockets for his cell phone. *I left it at home. Guess I can't call AAA.*

Neil popped the hood, stared at the engine, and struggled to assess why the car stopped running.

"Could you be out of gas?" one of the men asked.

Neil turned the key and checked the fuel gauge. Buried beneath the empty mark, the needle did not budge. "That's it. I'm out of gas."

"My buddy and I can get a can at the BP Station."

Seeing the station four blocks away, Neil agreed. He handed the men a twenty-dollar bill. Watching them walk up the street, Neil wondered if he was about to be a victim of a con job. *How could I forget to get gas?*

They walked back with a bounce in their step and were all smiles. "We'll get you going, sir," one man said. His partner poured the gas into the tank.

He replaced the cap. "Try starting it now."

Neil got behind the wheel and turned the key. The engine sputtered and then hummed.

"You're good to go," the rescuers shouted, pleased with themselves.

Neil put the car in park and got out to shake their hands. He opened his wallet and gave them the five and three singles he had left. "I wish I had more, guys. Thanks."

*****

At home, Neil tossed the unemployment papers on the kitchen table, went upstairs, and threw himself on his bed. Whimpers grew into gut-wrenching sobs as he relived the humiliation of his day. *I ran out of gas. How stupid.*

By the time Bridget came home that evening, Neil had regained his composure but remained preoccupied with the day's events. "I never thought that I'd see the inside of the unemployment office. It was awful."

"I'm sorry." Bridget hugged him.

"Unemployment is only a fraction of my former salary. It will be hard to keep up with our bills. I need a job."

"You'll get one. Meanwhile we'll manage between my income and our savings. It could be worse." Bridget tried to cheer him up.

"Yeah, how?"

"You could have cancer. Alternatively, I could. Or we could both be ill, or both unemployed. And it's just the two of us. Before long, you'll hear from the Department of Labor. I can't imagine that the decision will not be in your favor. This will soon be over. Gordon will reinstate you in your job or pay you. At the very least he'll release you from your noncompete agreement."

"That's logical, but I can't conceive of him doing that."

"Better yet, you'll find a new job," Bridget said.

"I ran out of gas on the way home! Stupid, and to add to it, I forgot my cell phone."

The ringing of the house phone interrupted.

"Neil, I'd like to help you," the soft-spoken voice said. "It's Ethan."

"Ethan Porter?"

"Yes."

"Should you be calling me?" Neil asked his former coworker.

"Don't worry about me," Ethan reassured Neil. "I think I can help you. I've been in contact with an NRC agent. I'm meeting him next week."

"That could be dangerous for you."

"I'm not worried if my action hastens retirement. I'll manage."

"Thank you," Neil said, his voice cracking. "Good to know I have a friend."

"Chadwick's memo made me mad, ordering everyone not to talk with you. That's just wrong."

"Intimidation works for Chadwick and Gordon. They excel at it."

"Bringing in lawyers to gang up on you was despicable. Everyone here agrees it was outrageous."

"It sure wasn't pleasant."

"Both Chadwick and Gordon act guilty. Let me tell you about my paychecks. For the last six years, my check was from Byrnes Engineering. Now all of a sudden GB Polymers pays me—very strange."

Neil remembered that Richard had pointed out the discrepancy at the famous lunch when the NRC first arrived.

Ethan continued, "At first I didn't understand your concerns. I've since done some checking and I've figured out a few things. Prior to the NRC investigation and answering questions under oath, I had not thought much about my work environment. I liked the solitary work and the quiet of my small area marked Storeroom Two in the basement. I've got a radio if I want company. After years of working in a physically demanding, noisy manufacturing plant, Storeroom Two is a dream office. When the agent questioned me the day of the raid, he asked who instructed me to leave my work area."

"Why did they think someone told you?" Neil asked.

"They knew I left in a hurry. I left a full cup of warm coffee at my desk."

"Clever."

"I told 'em Chadwick had called my extension and ordered me to lock the door and leave. The police broke the lock to get into the room. I couldn't help wondering why Chadwick worried about the paperwork in Storeroom Two."

"What did you have in your office that made Chadwick so anxious?"

"Test data. The basis of the letters Larry Davis sends to utilities."

"The heart of the basic component certification process—that would definitely raise Chadwick's anxiety level," Neil said.

"The agents asked me if I thought the samples were representative, if we had a system for tracing back to a specific manufacturing batch, if I used special testing equipment, and in what temperature range I ran the tests. They wanted to know if I ever saw letters that certified material as a basic component at a nuclear power plant," Ethan said.

"Standard quality assurance."

"I've no experience in quality assurance and didn't know how to answer them. Now I realize the weirdness of my job. Richard gave me product samples to test. When I finished the testing I recorded the results in a log."

"Did they take your testing logs?"

"Yes, but when they returned all the boxes, I examined a dozen logs of technical data. Batch numbers were not available for every sample. I now suspect that some samples were bogus."

"It would help to have proof."

"After speaking with Larry Davis, I believe scores of shipments sent to power plants were never tested. He sent more than twenty certification letters a week for months. I never tested more than five samples a week. Larry tracked all his communications. After the NRC returned the records taken in the raid, I told Larry that I wanted to straighten out my files and his log would help me. Attempting to match my test data records with his, I discovered numerous discrepancies showing that shipments labeled certified as basic components were never tested."

"I'd love to see that paperwork."

"I made a copy for you and the agent. And I know about GB Polymers's business in Grenada."

"I've wondered about that."

"It's mysterious, that's for sure. I saw Richard's notes on shipments of penetration closure material to a cement contractor in Grenada. There were also deliveries of radiation shielding," Ethan said.

"It's puzzling why a Grenada company would buy material for power plants," Neil said.

"There's a link with Cuba. I'll give you the details when we meet."

"Name a place and I'll be there," Neil said.

"I can't make it tomorrow night. How about the next?" They agreed to meet at the Joseph Beth Bookstore's café in South Park.

Chapter 34

GB Polymers's business in Grenada intrigued Neil. However, Ethan's paperwork showing deliberate deceit and explaining the connection with the tiny island excited him. Looking forward to meeting with Ethan raised Neil's spirits to the point that his walk in the park that morning was enjoyable, not the forced march that he timed, endured, and then checked off his to-do list.

Energized, he worked on his job search, drafting an e-mail asking for leads from his colleagues in the ASTM, answering employment ads in trade journals, and identifying businesses in his field on the Internet. Following up on his application for temporary work in a lab, Neil learned of a couple likely assignments in coming weeks. His recruiter, who specialized in placing scientists in industrial positions, repeated that his legal entanglements impeded his prospects for employment.

Thinking about the inevitable job interview question—*why did you leave your last job?*— Neil resented having to answer "my employer terminated me." There would be no discussion of his talent or past accomplishments, just his failure as assessed by a fraudulent Mr. Byrnes. His lawyer, Walter Butler, insisted Neil be no more anonymous than a registered pedophile moving into a new neighborhood. He had to inform future employers that he was fired and had an open case with the Department of Labor. If Neil said he left of his own accord to pursue other positions, Gordon would succeed in the wrongful dismissal case. Any alternative explanations for being out of work risked forfeiture of his complaint.

Job possibilities scrolled in his head. *Maybe I'll write a science book for children or young adults. Ethan's evidence will free me from the shackles of a long legal case and unemployment.*

A knock on the door roused Neil. Peering through the lookout glass, he recognized his neighbor and opened the door.

"I know you'll want this." The neighbor handed Neil an envelope with Sweepstake written on it in red letters. "This arrived at my house by mistake."

"My lucky day! Maybe I'll win ten million dollars."

"Did your friend Randy find you?"

"Who?"

"He stopped by my house the other day, your friend from New York."

"What are you talking about?"

"Monday afternoon, I think … maybe Tuesday. He had my street number on a piece of paper and thought it was your address."

"That's strange. Did you tell him where I lived?"

"Yes. I pointed to your house. Didn't he come over?"

"No one knocked on my door this week except you."

"Sorry if I spoke out of line. He was very friendly, mentioned Tarrytown, New York, said he worked with you. We chatted for a while. He was a very sociable person."

"What did he look like?"

"About thirty-five years old, white male, slight build, maybe five feet eight, and he had dark hair and a dark mustache. I'm sorry. You look shaken. I don't want to intrude but—"

Neil interrupted. "I don't know what to make of it, other than strange. I don't know anyone by that name. What else did he say?"

"Like I said, he was chatty. Commented on your hobbies—gardening, photography, astronomy, and exotic fish."

"He mentioned my fish?"

"Yes, and he asked if I found you eccentric." The neighbor struggled to remember the details of the casual encounter days earlier.

"Strange," Neil said again.

"He also said something about drinking in New York bars with you. Told me you had quite the temper and the two of you were in barroom fights."

"Fights?" Neil shook his head. "Not me."

"I told him that you must have gotten that out of your system. You're so easy going. I wouldn't describe you as a hot head."

"Thanks."

"I'm sorry."

"I'll cut you in if I win this ten million dollar sweepstake."

Chapter 35

Mid-morning, after only sleeping between five and nine o'clock, Neil walked into his kitchen. Picking up a note on the table, he smiled at the stargazer on Bridget's stationery that triggered pleasant memories of happier days. It was thanks to his amateur astronomy skills that he first met Bridget. Always knowing where to look and the exact time for the best view of a celestial event, Neil attracted friends and neighbors around his telescope. An outcome of these informal observations of planets, eclipses, and meteor showers was an invitation to be a guest presenter in a science class at the local high school. Neil's science lessons began showing up in student writing assignments for an English class that Bridget taught at the same high school. Intrigued by the students' evident enthusiasm for astronomy in their essays, Bridget devised a way to meet Neil by attending one of his presentations. Although he volunteered his time, Neil loved to tell anyone that would listen that it was his unpaid teaching activities that paid the biggest premiums—years with Bridget.

Neil read the note on the table: "Good morning, my favorite stargazer. I've got some requests." She listed household chores and grocery items. "Please change the oil in my car and pick up prescription refills." It was a good thing she had left this message to remind him. Last evening she had asked him about the oil change, but this morning he would have wondered why she had taken his car. Neil knew that Bridget was worried about him being alone all day and did her best to structure his day by requiring him to leave the house.

Around one o'clock, he started on Bridget's list, going first to get the oil changed in her car. When he pulled into the Jiffy Lube on Monroe Road, he noticed a small, tan car pulled into a space in front of the Circle K convenience store in the adjacent parking lot. Neil sat in line for service, repeatedly glancing at the tan vehicle. *Was it behind me soon after I left home? Was he on my street?* The driver never got out of the tan car.

I wish I could see the driver's face. The sun hit the window at an angle, creating a glare. The car looked empty, but Neil knew that no one had gotten out. *I'm sure it followed me from home. I don't recognize the car. Why would someone follow me? I'm talking to myself. I'm losing it.*

The crew member came to the window with his clipboard.

"Hello, sir. Welcome to Jiffy Lube. Ever been here before?"

"Yes," Neil replied.

"Let me note your mileage." Leaning into the car, the man looked at the dash and jotted down the numbers. "Sir, you're welcome to use our waiting area."

"I'd like to stay in the car."

"Suit yourself."

While the crew completed the oil change, Neil kept his eye on the tan car, wanting to see the driver's face, but he could not see anything inside the car.

The mechanic showed Neil the vehicle report.

"We've put in four quarts of W30 grade oil recommended for your car, a new oil filter, and we've topped off all fluid levels. Your tire pressure is fine."

"Thanks." Neil handed the man a credit card.

The man processed the payment and returned the card and paperwork. Neil drove off to his next stop—a prescription refill at Walgreen Pharmacy—with the tan car tailing behind three car lengths.

Neil considered confronting the driver. After parking at the drugstore, Neil got out of his car, and without looking in the direction of the tan vehicle, he went inside. He walked halfway down the first aisle and then crossed four aisles, following the sign for housewares. No customers were in this area. He took out his cell phone, dialed nine and then cleared the number. *911 can't help me—what am I thinking?*

A long line wound from the pharmacy counter. Without picking up his prescriptions, Neil turned and headed to the front of the store. Three customers waited for the cashier. He stayed in line, plotting his response to his stalker while keeping the parked tan car outside in view. After two more minutes, he left.

As expected, the tan car followed Neil. He drove two miles before turning into a McDonalds' drive-through lane. Keeping watch on the tan car two vehicles behind him, Neil inched his way to the spot to place his order. He asked for a Coke. As soon as he moved forward three car lengths, he placed the car in park and pressed the camera button of his cell phone. Exiting his car, he walked straight toward the tan car, clicking pictures.

"Hey buddy, move your car," a person in line shouted. Horns blared. Neil ignored the chorus of disapproval and kept snapping with the determination of tabloid paparazzi. He aimed at the license plate and the driver. The man in the tan car accelerated, drove over the curb that segregated the drive-through lane, and tore out of the parking lot at a high speed. Neil picked up his Coke and drove home.

In the blurry first photo, Neil made out an outline of the driver's face. The next photo of the license plate showed a beat-up grill and a plastic frame of haze caused by a protective shield. There were no distinguishable letters or numbers. He flipped through his photos three more times. One clear photo showed the driver.

He was still looking at the photos when Bridget came home. As he got up to greet her, he lost his balance and steadied himself by grabbing the table and chair.

"Are you all right?" Bridget asked.

"I feel weak."

"And your color is gray. Any pain?" she asked.

"A headache." Neil rubbed his forehead. "I feel a little dizzy."

"Sit in the recliner and put your feet up," she suggested.

Before Neil moved from the dining room table into the living room he gagged and indicated he was about to be sick. Bridget ran for a bowl in the kitchen, returning too late. Vomit hit the table and the front of his shirt.

"I'm sorry," he struggled to say continuing to retch in the container Bridget handed him.

"You're sweating." She touched his forehead.

He threw up some more. When his gagging subsided, Bridget placed a cool cloth on his head and wiped the front of his shirt.

"Sit a few minutes. Has this happened before?"

"No, and I rarely have a headache."

"That concerns me."

"I'll be fine. I'm going to walk to the recliner. I'll feel better if I rest," Neil said.

With Bridget at his elbow, he slowly rose. With the gait of an elderly man, he tottered the dozen steps to the chair.

"Your pulse is racing," Bridget said, holding his wrist. "I'm calling the doctor."

"Please, I just need to—" Neil stopped, knowing it was useless to argue with her determined tone.

With Bridget's description, the doctor's nurse suggested taking Neil to urgent care.

At a facility less than five miles from their home, Neil's blood pressure registered 194 over 125.

"What's typical for you?" the nurse asked Neil.

"Much lower. Something like 130 over 90."

"Are you under a lot of stress?"

"Yes."

"You need to manage it differently. Lie back and close your eyes. I'll give you something to bring it down." The nurse opened a cabinet and pulled out a syringe with a premeasured dose. She wiped his left arm with alcohol and administered the medication. "In thirty minutes, I will take your pressure again."

Once his blood pressure dropped to 170 over 105, the nurse released Neil to return home with the promise of seeing his primary care physician the next day.

"We'll call at eight o'clock when the office opens, and someone will see you tomorrow," Bridget said.

"I'm happy the room has stopped spinning."

Chapter 36

As rain slowed traffic in midtown Manhattan, Olmsted watched the stalled vehicles from his thirty-fourth-floor office thinking that he needed a well-connected labor lawyer to handle Neil Landers's wrongful termination grievance against GB Polymers. In the past, Olmsted excelled at causing fired employees to drop complaints and disappear. GB presented numerous occasions for Olmsted to hone his skills. A letter saved on his word processor accomplished the mission. Landers presented a unique challenge with his strong case and willingness to battle Gordon.

Searching the Internet, Olmsted stumbled on a Washington news article. The Labor Department had started formal proceedings to remove its chief administrative law judge for abusing the powers of his office over a period of four years. Attorney Glen Fuller, legal counsel for Judge Steven Littleton, worked out a contract for the chief judge to remain employed with full pay and full authority while he litigated the case.

Olmsted smiled at the ease of finding the right attorney. What a break! The Department of Labor's chief judge had his own personal legal troubles. A former staff member alleged that Littleton had used government funds and his staff for personal business.

The worker also asserted that the judge billed the Department of Labor for vacation expenses including accommodations in Hawaii, a helicopter ride to view a volcano, and a fishing trip with an expert guide.

Littleton epitomized the kind of civil servant Olmsted required. As the chief administrative law judge, he made important decisions for the U.S. Department of Labor. Needing preferential treatment for Landers's wrongful termination case against Gordon, Olmsted decided to find out more about Judge Littleton's personal counsel, Glen Fuller.

From a biography posted on the DC law firm Website, Olmsted learned that Fuller graduated from Harvard Law School and was married to the daughter of a prominent Washington politician. Fuller's political connections and contacts with people in high places appealed to Olmsted.

Gathering background on Fuller, Olmsted learned that his clients included individuals in the military, corporations in various entanglements with government agencies, and high-profile Washingtonians.

Olmsted called DC lawyer Vernon Casper on the chance that he knew Glen Fuller.

"I know him well. Our children attend the same schools," Casper said.

"Vernon, you understand that my client needs an exceptional labor lawyer to respond to Landers's wrongful termination complaint," Olmsted said.

"Fuller is outstanding. If you'd like, I'll facilitate an introduction," Casper said.

"Please do. I look forward to hearing from him."

*****

"Attorney Fuller from DC is on the line." Midori handed the phone to Olmsted.

"My good friend, Vernon Casper, tells me I may be of some assistance in a labor case of yours," Fuller said.

"I hope so. When can you come to New York City?"

"My Friday court appointment was cancelled. Would Friday work for you?"

"I'll make it work. This is a very important case. Get a first class ticket. Let me know your arrival time, and I'll arrange for a car to bring you to my office."

Olmsted believed that the VIP treatment would impress Fuller.

*****

Fuller caught an early shuttle from DC to New York and arrived at Olmsted's Manhattan office at nine-thirty AM.

"A pleasure to meet you," Olmsted greeted Fuller. "Did you have a good flight?"

"Cramped, with the usual indignities of today's air travel. The smaller planes have no first class. Fortunately it was on time."

"Air travel has certainly deteriorated. Thanks for coming," Olmsted said.

Looking at a photo of a young man with children beside a river, Fuller asked, "Is this you?"

"Yes, a lifetime ago. When I was just out of college, I traveled with a volunteer group to Costa Rica, working to improve their drinking water. It was a great experience. The people, especially the children, were so appreciative. I continue to support projects in that community today."

"That's great. Sorry to digress. Tell me how I can help you," Fuller asked.

"I loved your article on military uniform buttons." Olmsted decided flattery was the best approach with attorney Glen Fuller.

"You read it!" Fuller beamed.

Olmsted gave Fuller the necessary information on Neil Landers and GB Polymers. Like letting out extra fishing line before a big catch, Olmsted conveyed an understanding of the complexities and challenges of Fuller's high-profile case with the Department of Labor judge and worked references to Fuller's experience into the conversation.

"Your client could be an asset to mine."

"How so?"

"My client has a Labor Department case that someone needs to bury or dismiss," Olmsted said.

"With the NRC hovering in the background, I doubt the judge could dismiss it."

"I'm sure there is a creative way to snarl this case in his agency. Ask him. And tell him that my client would like to help the good judge."

"I'll get right on it," Fuller said.

"Fuller, this case has potential for you. My client doesn't like to lose. He'll go for broke, including the Supreme Court, if necessary."

"We've got a deal, Mr. Olmsted," Fuller said, extending his hand. "I accept your offer, and I'm sure my client will be happy to assist."

"You understand that I'll serve as a consultant to you as this case goes forward. My fee is 15 percent of all your billable hours."

"Agreed."

Chapter 37

Neil returned from his follow-up appointment with his doctor, disappointed that his blood pressure was still too high.

He hit the play button on his answering machine.

"You and your wife are fish out of water," screeched an altered taping of someone's voice.

"Sad news, captain. Call me, Spock."

He figured that Tom had a report on another person's firing. Neil called his attorney.

"Fish out of water … what do you think that means?" Walter asked.

"I don't know. Nothing good, I'm afraid." Neil told Walter about the neighbor's visit and the man in the tan car.

"So what? It's not a crime to be behind you in a fast food take-out lane."

"What about following me around town?"

"Hard to prove—he'll say it's a coincidence. Besides, following someone is not a crime."

"This is the same guy that asked my neighbor about me. He's obviously stalking me."

"Maybe the photo will be useful," Walter said.

Neil spread the photos he had printed out onto the table. Examining the ones of the license plate with a magnifying glass, he could not decipher any letters or numbers.

Later Neil called Tom at home.

"Hi Spock. I got your message."

"Ethan Porter dropped dead!"

"What?" Neil sank into a chair.

"Around eleven o'clock this morning I walked into the men's room. I found Ethan dead on the floor." Tom's voice cracked.

"Ethan's dead?"

"I think he had a heart attack."

"You found him—how horrible! I'm sorry."

"I'm sorry for his wife and family," Tom said.

"Ethan was a good man. Let me know the funeral plans. I'd like to go."

*****

Neil arrived early for the funeral and waited in his car until the family and coffin were inside the church before he took a seat in a back pew. The sons and grandchildren Ethan had spoken about with pride were all there. The enormity of their loss was obvious.

After the service, Neil joined Tom at a coffee shop on East Boulevard as planned.

"Did you hear that Ethan's death triggered an OSHA investigation?" Tom asked.

"No," Neil said, more than a little surprise.

"An OSHA official showed up to have a conversation with Gordon. I heard Gordon went ballistic when they told him that a government official was in the lobby asking to speak with the CEO. Gordon's secretary tracked Chadwick down to join the conversation. Apparently, neither Gordon nor Chadwick could comprehend that the agency responsible for worker safety routinely examined the circumstances of a worksite death," Tom said.

"I thought Ethan died of a heart attack."

"That's what I was told."

"Ethan called me last week. We were supposed to meet the day after he died."

"What about?" Tom asked.

"He had paperwork that showed most shipments to nuclear power plants were never tested. GB Polymers often sent a letter certifying that a product met the requirements for a basic component."

"Sounds like our company."

"And he had information on Grenada," Neil said.

"Grenada?"

"GB Polymers has quite the business with unfinished penetration closure material and products for nuclear power plants to Grenada. Ethan saw Richard's paperwork."

"I didn't know there were nuclear power plants on the tiny island of Grenada," Tom said.

"There aren't. On the phone, Ethan told me GB worked with a local supplier in Grenada. He was going to tell me more when we met. And he mentioned Cuba."

"Cuba, really? Do you think his death is suspicious?"

"Hard to know," Neil said.

"I'll get more on the Grenada story," Tom said. "Without you in the lab I've got time for extracurricular activities."

*****

Although Neil had not known Ethan well, the memory of his family at the funeral saddened him. Thinking about the data that Ethan had planned to give him, Neil wondered how he could obtain Larry Davis's logs of communications with power plants that showed his company had knowingly deceived the power plants. The ringing phone interrupted his thoughts.

"Captain, the government launched a missile attack today," Tom said. "Department of Labor investigator invaded GB territory."

"Give me the details."

"Gordon ranted that the government was out of control and on a campaign to smear his good name."

"Mr. Innocent. I know the drill. That's good news, Spock, that the Department of Labor showed up in Gordon's face."

"I loved it. Picture yet another government agency questioning Gordon. It made my day. I didn't have the pleasure of meeting the investigator, but I know he spoke with more than ten workers."

"That's remarkable! Thanks."

"Glad to oblige, captain. Live long and prosper. That's the best revenge. I'm on the Grenada story. I expect to know more in a few weeks."

*****

The next day the Department of Labor investigator called Neil. "Your claim of wrongful termination is justified. Mr. Byrnes confirmed that he fired you for raising safety concerns."

"He said that?" Neil asked, taken aback.

"Essentially," the investigator said. "Mr. Byrnes is most unusual. I'm not sure he realized the seriousness of his admissions. He acknowledged firing you for contacting the NRC and admitted canceling your security access prior to placing you on forced vacation. There are none of the usual shades of gray in this case."

"His lawyers let him talk?"

"There was only one present during my interview, Vernon Casper from DC. He wasn't sharp at all. I expected a legal team to surround Mr. Byrnes espousing the usual pretense of ignorance and creative tactics to minimize responsibility. Casper sat there while Gordon incriminated himself. Attorney Patterson was late and didn't say anything."

"That's very strange."

"The strangest thing was that Mr. Byrnes threatened to get me fired."

"That's classic Byrnes bullying. He'll probably contact your supervisor," Neil said.

"I wish I recorded my conversation. I'd have material for *Saturday Night Live*. Mr. Byrnes babbled, implicated himself, and confirmed the validity of your complaint. His lawyers failed him."

"What now?"

"I'll write up my report and get it to my supervisor this week. You'll get a formal response from the department. And I'll attach Chadwick's incriminating memo."

"You've got a copy?" Neil asked.

"An astonishing, extraordinary smoking gun, an investigator's dream. And if that's not enough, the federal regulation regarding Material Safety Data Sheets Chadwick cited as his basis for firing you doesn't exist."

"Doesn't exist?"

"No such regulation," the investigator said.

"That's good."

"Very good. Mr. Byrnes fired you for talking with the NRC. It's cut and dry."

"I know that, and I'm glad you agree."

"Each worker I spoke with asked for a copy of my notes."

"They follow instructions. They don't want to be unemployed like I am," Neil said.

"It's odd that all of them complied. Everything should be fine for you soon. Lucky for you, this case wasn't with the last administration. My reports never saw the light of day under President Bush."

"Thanks." Neil hung up the phone.

Bridget walked into the house, set her briefcase on the floor and tossed car keys on the table.

Before he could update her on the Department of Labor news, he recognized a look of distress. "What's wrong?"

"This was on my car windshield." She handed him a newspaper folded to reveal an article on a missing woman believed to have been murdered in a Charlotte park. *Who's next?* was written with a red marker across the bottom of the page.

"I met Donna after my last appointment, and we took a walk in Freedom Park. When I got back to the car, I found the paper."

"Did you notice anyone nearby?"

"No. I don't know how I managed to drive home. Someone is watching us all the time. Can't Walter or the police do something?"

Shaking his head in disgust, Neil replied, "Not without evidence of a crime." His delight in hearing good news from the labor investigator was short-lived. Neil worried that Gordon's stooping to follow Bridget showed the extent he would go to force Neil to withdraw his complaint.

Chapter 38

The steady harassment of hang-up calls worried Neil. Some came during the day, others in the middle of the night; all were personally intimidating. The last phone message was a repeat of an earlier one: *you and your wife are fish out of water.*

After the first few hostile messages, Neil changed their phone number and paid for it to be unpublished. Targeting Bridget in the park bothered him the most.

Knowing there was nothing he could do, Neil still called his attorney and told him about the antagonistic message on Bridget's car. "Someone is watching my wife's movements and tracked her to Freedom Park."

"It's intimidation, scare tactics. I doubt she's in real danger," Walter said.

"Very antagonistic."

"I agree. Tell her to pay attention and be careful. I'm glad you called. I've got good news."

"I could use some," Neil said.

"We've received an excellent report from the Department of Labor."

"Read it to me."

"I'll give you the highlights." Walter read that the Department of Labor found GB Polymers guilty of wrongful termination of Neil Landers and ordered GB Polymers to pay double back wages and to reinstate Neil in his position.

"What happens now?"

"It will be an extremely unpleasant work environment. I'm sure they'll try to get you to quit. The DOL report is very bad for your former employer. Saying they fired you for reporting safety concerns, The DOL establishes discrimination and that gets them in big trouble with the NRC. Gordon and Chadwick could face prison time."

"When do I return to work?"

"Not before the check for back wages clears. I'll call Patterson."

*****

Neil sat upright in bed, trying to figure out what woke him. Bridget asked in a terrified tone, "What was that noise?"

"Something crashed." Neil listened for additional sounds in the house. Getting to a standing position, he added, "Stay here. I'll check it out."

"I'm calling 911." Bridget reached for her cell phone on the night table. "Someone's in the house."

"Wait. Let me check. Maybe a picture fell." His voice was not convincing.

In silence, he edged his way in the direction of the noise: the study. Thoughts of an intruder on the second floor of his home in the middle of the night scared him. He felt for the light switch and flipped it on.

"It's the aquarium," he gasped. His feet felt the dampness of the carpet when he crossed the threshold into the study.

Bridget followed, clutching the phone.

"Get a kitchen pot or a plastic wastebasket."

"A great time for the glass to give way from the frame!" Bridget tossed the phone on a chair and ran for her huge stockpot.

Neil hoped he could improvise a holding tank for his favorite blue discus fish with salvaged water in a container providing temporary quarters. It would take a minimum of twelve hours before bath water would be hospitable.

Water sloshed out through a myriad of openings in the large glass panels of the front and back of the aquarium. The biggest cracks were near the top, leaving three inches of glass intact at the bottom. He calculated that he had time to bail out the remaining four fish and enough water for them to manage for about a day.

Then Neil noticed a hole, about one-half inch in diameter, in the wall behind the aquarium. On the opposite side of the room, the front window blind bulged. He inspected further. A pile of glass fragments gathered on the windowsill, slivers of glass from a broken windowpane stuck to the blind. His eyes followed the projectile's path from the front window through the aquarium to the back wall. *A deliberate attack to scare him.*

The largest of the discus fluttered frenetically on the floor. Crimson was mixed with the trademark horizontal blue lines. Neil sprinted into the bathroom, turned on the faucets in the tub, adjusted the water temperature and set the stopper to collect water.

Bridget rushed in carrying a large stockpot, a wastebasket, and an empty, quart-size, vanilla yogurt container.

"Oh, my God," Bridget moaned looking at a bloodstained fish on the floor. She stared with disbelief at the shattered glass and red-streaked water sloshing out of the fish tank. She walked over to the window and raised the blind. "The window's broken," Bridget screamed. "Someone intentionally threw something."

"Close the blind." Neil pointed to the small, dark break in the wall behind the aquarium. "That's a bullet hole."

"And you're worried about the fish! I'm calling the police." She picked up the phone from the chair where she had flung it earlier.

"I want to try and save 'em. Help me," Neil pleaded.

"You're nuts! Someone's out to kill us and you're fretting about fish."

"If they wanted to kill us they could've. There are trees outside our bedroom that would give a clear shot at us. Help me. These fish don't have much time."

"There's been a shooting on Berkeley Avenue," Bridget shouted to the 911 dispatcher. "Number 813. Inside our house. Send someone, please. No, we don't need an ambulance. Two of us are here, my husband and I. Yes, we're okay, but there's a bullet in our wall."

Neil removed the aquarium cover and scooped the remaining water at the bottom of the tank into a plastic storage container.

"We'll keep 'em here until I can get the temperature right in the tub." Neil continued transferring water into the designated holding tank.

"The police are on the way." Bridget put the phone down.

They watched in horror as a sizeable blue discus hurled itself from the aquarium and landed three inches from Neil's left foot. There were no safe waters for this fish to swim.

Placing the edge of the bailing container near the fish, Neil pressed it into the carpet and gently slid the fish inside for a speedy transfer to its new habitat.

"I know you don't like surprises," Neil remarked ruefully.

A siren sound pierced the night.

"They're here. I'll let them in." Leaving Neil to his recovery operation, she ran down the stairs to the front door and opened it as the two police officers climbed the steps of the front porch.

"Mrs. Landers, did you call 911?" the officer asked as routinely as if she had ordered pizza delivery.

"Upstairs, officer." Bridget held the door open and nodded in the direction of the stairs. "My husband's there."

The police arrived in the study and witnessed the fish that had impaled itself on a broken edge of glass, in a bloody pool on the carpet.

"I'm hoping to save some of them," Neil explained, as he rigged the filter and thermostat for his improvised tank.

"That one's a goner" The officer looked at the slashed, bloody skin.

"Wow, those are beautiful," the other officer said. "What are they?"

"Blue discus—third-generation descendents of wild Amazon blue discus."

"Any idea why you'd be the target of a drive-by shooting?" The officer asked.

"This isn't a drive-by. Whoever shot at my fish was not in a car or on the street. He was level with this room." Neil raised the blind and pointed to a tree in the front yard. "He used a branch of that oak for his perch."

"A straight shot into the aquarium." The officer eyed the entry of the bullet.

"Exactly. The bullet hole in the window glass aligns with the hole in the back wall. If he shot from the street, the bullet would have traveled in at an upward angle."

"That's correct. Rather aggressive, wouldn't you say?"

"Neil, tell them what's been going on," Bridget urged.

"I've got some enemies." Neil told the officer about the strange man in the neighborhood that had followed him.

"Tell him about the hang-up calls."

"It would be better if they were just hang-up calls. There is always a cryptic message."

"Such as?"

"We're watching you."

"The last one said, *'you and your wife are fish out of water.'*" Neil looked forlornly at his fish.

"We'll check around outside. If there's anyone you want us to question, we'd need evidence."

"We need protection, officer," Neil said.

Chapter 39

The mail carrier's familiar steps approaching the front door triggered a daily ritual for Neil. Replete with trepidation, he listened for the thud of mail landing on the floor and the carrier's retreat. He waited three minutes before retrieving the mail.

Today in the pile, he found ads from grocery stores, a postcard with pictures of missing people, glossy fliers from pizza establishments, and a packet from a Washington DC law office. Neil dumped all the other mail on the table and examined the large envelope with an unrecognizable law firm's return address. His hand trembled. He pulled the tab and took out a pile of pages. He read *GB Polymers appeals the DOL conclusion of wrongful termination.* Right away, he called Walter.

"Damn," Walter said. "This is bad news. My copy isn't here yet. A DC law firm …how many does that make?"

"Too many," Neil said.

"Let's get Perry on the phone." Walter made the third-party connection with Perry's office. "Perry, Neil and I both are on the line. We just learned that GB Polymers filed a formal appeal of the Department of Labor decision."

"Appeals take a long time, years. I'm sorry."

"Please enlighten us on the next steps for Neil."

"The NRC planned on using the DOL report. I'm not sure how the NRC will proceed. Without a final decision from DOL, we've no evidence for enforcement," Perry said.

"What about your own case?" Walter asked.

"The NRC tabled all work on Neil's allegation when GB Polymers's legal tactics prevented us from developing a case. Remember, the attorneys blocked us from speaking with Neil's coworkers. The evidence we seized was before Neil was fired. Without proof, the NRC can't make a formal request to the Department of Justice."

"That's not acceptable," Walter said.

"I understand you're frustrated…."

"Perry, I don't think you realize how ludicrous it is that the NRC's staff of three thousand can't complete a simple investigation in a timely manner," Neil said. "You guys aren't even bothered about the slow pace. The way the NRC works is totally ineffective. Pressure Richard! You have plenty on him. Indict him, and you'll get whatever you want on Gordon and Chadwick."

"Neil's right. Richard's your leverage," Walter said. "Please do what you can, Perry. I'll be in contact with your legal department."

Neil hung up. He was doubtful that Walter would have any influence with the NRC lawyers, but Neil appreciated his trying. *I'll have to put this case together for them. They are hopelessly lost.*

*****

Bridget left for three days to attend a geriatric conference, and Neil found his days alone bizarre, eating at crazy times and hardly sleeping. At night, he kept the lights on in all the rooms of the house—as if that would protect him from a sniper. He checked the locks on the front and back doors several times. *I'll get the bastards*, echoed in his head. The first two *"I'll get the bastards?"* scared him. *I need to calm down....* He flipped the TV on and scanned channels.

Shot into my house. I'll get 'em. They think I'm nobody. I'll show 'em. The NRC needs proof to prosecute. It's not clear that Gordon and Chadwick knowingly sold defective material to the nuclear industry. Bullshit. As if an embezzler doesn't know the money isn't his. Gordon and Chadwick were crooks. They calculated and deceived their customers. I'll get the evidence.

An old movie showed Sandra Bullock playing a character who was tapping away at a keyboard. With the sound muted, Neil watched her easily move in and out of databases with a string of typed letters and numbers.

Neil clicked the TV off and walked upstairs. He pulled the drape away from the window and stared at the tape covering the hole in the glass. Looking at the empty aquarium stand, Neil found it a painful reminder that his extraordinary blue discuses were dead. The memory of the bloody disaster enraged him. *I'll get the bastards.* At his computer, he clicked the AOL icon and signed on.

At the Yahoo site, he set up a profile for Gordon Byrnes. Neil selected CEO for the job title. In the spot for business description, Neil typed in FRAUD, Inc. Then he created a password for Gordon. Prompted to select a question in case he forgot the password, Neil chose favorite sport. For the answer, he typed croquet. To finish the profile, Neil typed in a date for Gordon's birthday, April 1, 1943.

With the Gordon Byrnes screen name up and running at Yahoo, Neil had an ideal disguise. He typed in the string of letters and numbers for remote access to his former employer's computer system. The one-code access for all workers was shoddy gatekeeping but easier for GB Polymers's one-man Information Technology Department. Gordon, obsessed about security, was too paranoid to do it right, insisting that a family member manage the sensitive data in his corporation's computer network. Although outside consultants upgraded the technology, Gordon's son-in-law, with a couple of computer classes to his credit, directed the day-to-day operations. Neil was confident that Gordon's insistence on family-only control of his information system protected him from detection.

Knowing Gordon terminated his personal access on the day he fired him, Neil's old login was useless. At the sign-in box, Neil typed Gordon.Byrnes and began the tough part of finding Gordon's password. He typed the company name in the password box. A message popped up: User ID and password combination did not exist. Neil tried again with Gordon. An access denied message came back. For the third attempt, Neil typed Rosemary. The screen again showed access denied and no future attempts were permitted.

Neil closed the site. Three failed attempts caused a lockout. When Neil worked there, the lockout period lasted four hours, shorter than at most businesses. Employees messed up remembering and changing their password so often that the four-hour lockout was standard with an automatic reset. Neil noted the time. The next eight hours presented two more opportunities for passwords attempts.

Neil struggled to think of Gordon's dog's name, something "original," like Rover or Lassie. Sitting at the dining room table, Neil wrote down possible passwords on a pad of paper. After that, he examined the list and highlighted a dozen. With two hours to wait, he went back to the TV and mindlessly surfed channels.

At eleven-thirty-five, Neil returned to the GB Polymers sign-in page. He tried three passwords and each time he saw an access denied response. He set an alarm for three-forty AM and again his three attempts failed. Not risking a lockout during business hours, he stopped before four o'clock. Not wanting Bridget to know what he was doing, Neil hoped he would succeed before she returned home later that evening, It would be easy enough for him to take another crack at it around six o'clock that night and again at ten o'clock. In the middle of the night, it would be difficult to hide his lawbreaker behavior from his wife, but he had no plan to stop.

Bridget returned much later. "It's good to be here," she said, kissing Neil.

"Missed you." He stood and hugged his wife. "This house is strange without you."

"How've you been?" Bridget asked.

"Busy. My back is bothering me. I must have sat at the computer too long." Neil looked away.

"A pillow will help. I'll get it." She put a firm, cylinder-shaped cushion at his back.

"That feels better. Thanks."

"I'm exhausted. I didn't need a two-hour flight delay," Bridget said. "I wish I didn't have a full schedule tomorrow."

"Sorry. Get some sleep. You can tell me about the conference tomorrow."

"Okay." She yawned and headed off to bed.

Neil continued to enter three possible passwords at four-hour intervals that evening and the next two nights. At the end of the week, Neil still had no success. He knew breaking into his former company's computer system was illegal, but he could not stop. He felt awful lying about why he slept in the guestroom all week. Bridget would be suspicious of an alarm going off at three-forty AM. She believed his excuse that he did not want to disturb her sleep when back spasms woke him. Rationalizing his unlawful actions, he prepared for a marathon of attempts over the weekend with possible passwords consuming his waking hours. The list included product names, Gordon's boat, and places and things Gordon bragged about, his ancestors on the Mayflower, the name of his house in Bermuda.

At close of business on Friday, Neil logged into Gordon's sign-on page for remote access. As he finished yet another unsuccessful attempt, Bridget arrived home from work.

"If we leave at seven we'll have plenty of time to park and get to our seats."

"What are you talking about?" Neil asked. The disgusted look she gave him told him he had forgotten something important.

"The symphony is at eight o'clock tonight. I've been talking about the guest violinist for weeks. Don't you listen to anything I say anymore?"

"My back bothers me. I can't sit for a concert tonight. Can someone use my ticket?"

"Unlikely. It starts in three hours. We've got aisle seats. You could get up and walk around," Bridget suggested.

"That wouldn't work," he said a little too fast.

"I'll go myself. You'll be all right tomorrow for dinner I hope," Bridget said.

Neil knew the look on his face read clueless. He did not remember their dinner plans.

"You forgot that too?"

"I'm sorry. Maybe I'll feel better tomorrow."

"I'm worried you're becoming a recluse," Bridget said.

"Tomorrow will be better."

Chapter 40

All Saturday Neil complained of various symptoms of back pain. Every four hours he attempted to log on to GB Polymers's database.

"Do you want me to cancel tonight?" Bridget asked.

"I'd like you to go and have a good time. I'm not great company. You deserve an evening out," Neil answered.

"If we were going to a restaurant it would be easier to not go. I know Donna planned this some time ago, and when she entertains she goes all out."

"Please go."

"I'll be home early."

When he heard her car exit the driveway, Neil returned to Gordon's sign-in page and entered three more passwords. Entry denied. His failed attempts surprised Neil. How difficult was it to think like Gordon? Scrutinizing his remaining possibilities, Neil prioritized choices for his next attempt. To pass the time, Neil selected an old WWII movie on TV. Seeing soldiers in foxholes in Europe helped him feel less sorry for himself.

From his shirt pocket, he pulled out his grandparents' wedding photo. "Grampa, how'd you do it—sacrifice so much to stop the Nazis ... how'd you know it was right? Please help me."

The timer beeps woke Neil. He had missed most of the movie. Rocking himself out of his recliner, he rose with effort to a standing position. If he did not have a back problem now, he would develop one folded in a chair for hours. The outside light illuminated the back entrance to the house. Bridget had not returned. Neil tapped his computer for another round at Gordon's password. *Perseverance won WW II.* He resolved to press on with another password, eliciting another rejection response. Next Neil typed Yale1965. He stared as the computer loaded Gordon's page. "I'm in," he shouted. "Gotcha bastard," he yelled. "Look out. Your defenses are useless."

So many choices! Neil started with the icon for Gordon's mail. Numerous messages from his attorney Olmsted listed background report as the subject. Opening one, he found several paragraphs summarizing the life of NRC agent Randolph Perry, a graduate of Pennsylvania State

University with a BS degree in Mechanical Engineering and MS degree in Acoustical Engineering, single, and a twenty-one-year career navy man, including long stints on nuclear submarines. For two years, Perry had been with the Office of Reactor Safety at NRC headquarters. Neil hit the print button. "This will motivate Perry," he shouted.

"Who are you talking to?" Bridget asked as she entered his office.

Neil looked at her, fearing that his guilt was obvious.

"Talking full volume to no one?" Bridget said.

"I hope you had a good time."

"I did. You were missed."

"I just got into Gordon's e-mails," Neil blurted.

"You ... a hacker?"

"I'm desperate to get the NRC to do something."

"You broke into GB Polymers's computer system?" Bridget walked over to Neil.

"Gordon's lawyer researched Agent Perry's life. Look at this." He handed her his printout of Perry's background. "Unbelievable."

"You're unbelievable. Aren't you worried they'll find out?"

"Not really. The company is slack about it's computer system."

"That makes no sense in today's world," Bridget said.

"I know, but it is true. There is no IT Department. No one will notice this outside access or try to track it. AND I won't brag in public. I've got dirt the NRC can't ignore." He scanned the subject list of Gordon's messages. He clicked on one. "Darling, they have your speeding ticket."

"That's worthless. What nerve!"

Neil continued with his mission, opening and printing the background information on three more agents that included details of their car loans, mortgages, and a divorce settlement. Neil wanted to read everything but had to print and move on. Scanning a report on himself, he yelled, "My god, they recreated my life. I won first prize in an eighth grade science fair. Who cares?"

"Speaking of the science fair, Donna's husband asked tonight if you would judge the contest at his middle school next month," Bridget said.

"I guess I could," Neil said without stopping his searching. He scrolled through a comprehensive background on his attorney, Walter Butler. "I definitely can't tell Walter about this."

"Let me see." Bridget looked over his shoulder. "They've got his tax return."

"They call his deductions aggressive but legal," Neil said. "Interesting."

"Did you know he took the bar exam twice? And what's this about a dispute with a neighbor?" Bridget asked.

"I'll print it," Neil said, putting more paper in the printer. He checked that he had each file on paper and on a flash drive.

Bridget started reading. "There are pages on my teaching career. I haven't taught in years. Why would he bother with my employment history? And why would Gordon Byrnes care where I went to school for a masters in social work?"

"He's desperate."

"I can't believe you broke into his computer. This has to move your case."

"It better. Look at this." *Inside the NRC* subject line caught Neil's attention. Together they scanned a memo from attorney Olmsted in which he assured Gordon that he had NRC contacts that would protect Gordon.

"Too bad there aren't names," Bridget said. "Perry would be very interested in knowing which of his coworkers assisted Gordon's thug lawyers."

"I know it's late but I may not have another chance to look at the sales information," Neil said.

"Go for it. This woke me up. I'm going to change. I'll be back. My stargazer turned hacker," she chuckled as she left the room.

Bridget returned and placed a heated pad at the small of Neil's back.

"Thanks. That feels great."

As Neil continued looking through his former employer's databases, Bridget read pages Neil had piled on a chair.

"It's absurd that he dug up all this on us, the NRC agents, and Walter. What a maniac."

Neil opened Axapta. This business software held a mother lode of data. Personnel information, sales, formulas, and everything anyone wanted to know about GB Polymers were at his fingertips. Gordon agreed to modernize his business because of the promise of cost savings and because the customized Axapta program allowed limited employee access. It suited his compartment philosophy and his need for control. A salesperson could only review his accounts. A manager's access was restricted to sales staff he supervised. R&D could see formulas for products. Employees' limited access gave them what they needed to do their job, nothing more. Neil gambled that Gordon had unrestricted access.

"Wish me luck with the sales stuff."

Bridget did not respond. He looked across the room. Pages lay scattered on the floor. Asleep, Bridget's head flopped to one side in a painful-looking position. Neil took the paper still in her hand and repositioned her more comfortably. From years of experience, he knew it was impossible to wake or move her.

Only Bridget could sleep through this drama. Neil laughed as he returned to his sleuthing. He clicked the link for sales data. No problem. He was free to browse. When he queried for sales to nuclear power plants, a table listed specific products, the date sold, and to which plant. He skimmed the report.

An interesting entry indicated a contractor returned 686 bags of nonshrink grout from an 840-bag order. Neil jotted down the batch number, the vendor, and sale date. On another line, he found the replacement order with the notation *reworked—no cost.*

Only one reason warranted reworking returned grout. It had failed. It took 154 bags before the defect showed up! Neil checked the buyer: Ricktel. Perry needed to find out exactly what plants installed this grout. Neil highlighted a large section of the table and printed it. He also copied it to a flash drive.

At two o'clock in the morning, he was still reading data, noting a decrease in sales to Taiwan, a steady flow of products to power plants, and frequent travels by Gordon to Bermuda.

Shifting to his Word program, Neil typed the words Deep Throat, highlighted them, selected a font he never used, increased the letter size to about an inch and printed out the page. Next, he typed a return address: McGuire, 12700 Hagers Ferry Road, Huntersville, NC and the address for Agent Perry at NRC headquarters and printed that page.

Neil removed the flash drive. He believed that it was unlikely that Perry would insert an unknown external drive into his government laptop or his home computer. He needed copies.

Neil headed to a nearby Kinko's print store to copy his cover page and the address and to print all the files on the flash drive. With bandages covering his fingers, he removed the copies from the tray. He purchased a mailing envelope. Back home he assembled the package using gloves. Placing the page with the words DEEP THROAT on the stack of documents, he inserted everything in the envelope. Pouring a little water on a paper towel, he sealed the envelope. After gluing the addresses in place, he calculated the first class postage—using his triple beam balance scale for weighing chemicals from his high school science project days—attached the postage, drove to a post office with a twenty-four-hour lobby, and put the package in a bin.

Chapter 41

Neil's job search lagged. He spoke with numerous ASTM colleagues about possible jobs but encouraging tips did not produce interviews. A lead would shortly lift his spirits, only to be followed by a rejection or the silent treatment. He found the "no" response most maddening.

In a trade journal, Neil came across an ad for a research chemist at a New Jersey Plastic Company. *This has my name on it. Maybe I'll get lucky.* He called and spoke with a person there in human resources.

"Do you have experience testing the chemical resistance of plastics?" she asked.

"Yes, many years. In fact, I chair the ASTM International committee for the standards on chemical and physical testing of thermoplastics."

"Are you available to come to New Jersey this week?" the woman asked.

"I can arrange that."

"How about Thursday?"

"That's fine."

"I'll make the flight arrangements and call you back," she said.

Neil hung up the phone. He checked for a dial tone before yelling, "I've got an interview!" Then he picked up the phone and dialed Bridget's cell phone, leaving a message.

Five minutes later, the phone rang. It was the human resource person from New Jersey, startling Neil. He had expected Bridget. "I've arranged an electronic ticket for you on an eight o'clock US Airways flight to Newark on Thursday morning. There will be a driver to meet you at the airport and bring you to our corporate office. I've booked a return flight for Thursday evening."

"Thank you. I look forward to meeting with you."

Bridget called as soon as he hung up the phone. "I've a job interview," he told her in an ecstatic voice.

"Congratulations! That's wonderful."

"I've such good feelings about this interview. They practically hired me over the phone. They never asked about a noncompete agreement." He filled her in on the particulars.

"It sounds great! They'd be crazy not to hire you."

"Would you mind living in Jersey?"

"We'll figure it out. Not to worry."

"Love you."

"Love you too. Have to run. See you tonight."

*****

Neil had an uneventful flight to New Jersey. Needing to believe this company would hire him, Neil convinced himself the meeting was a mere formality. His R&D skills perfectly matched what this company wanted. If the Labor Department took forever to resolve his complaint, at least he would be on someone's payroll.

Neil's connections were flawless—the plane landed on time in Newark. He easily found his driver holding a sign with his name on it, and for New Jersey, the traffic was not too congested. Once at his destination, the receptionist ushered Neil into an office with plush furnishings.

"I'll let them know you're here," she said. "Please sit down."

A human resource person came in and asked, "Do you have a noncompete agreement with your prior employer?"

"Yes."

"For how long?"

"Three years."

"That may be a problem. I'll get back to you."

After ten minutes, she returned to explain that the senior technical person, who had planned to interview Neil, had a last-minute conflict. She would call next week to reschedule. The driver would take him back to the airport.

"My lawyer assures me that the noncompete agreement is illegal."

"I'll get back to you," she repeated.

In the next three issues of the monthly polymer journal, Neil saw the same ad for a chemist at the New Jersey company. Looking at his grandparents' photo he said, "This is a very different war, Grampa. I wish I knew how you'd fight it."

Chapter 42

The middle school science fair that Neil had agreed to judge, provided a welcome distraction from job searching and legal minutiae. Reviewing the judges' packet that the school had sent last week, he was impressed with the comprehensive guidelines and evaluation criteria. After checking in at the Charlotte Middle School office on the day of the fair, he followed a student escort to a science classroom, the gathering place for the judges.

"Thanks for helping out," the teacher in charge of the fair, Beverly Lewis, said.

"I'm a big fan of future scientists," Neil said.

"The others will be here soon. Here's a list of our participants and their projects."

Neil scanned the pages. "Great variety. It looks like you have a remarkable science program. Congratulations."

"Thanks. We're proud of our students."

A student ushered two men into the room.

"This is Neil Landers," Lewis said.

"A new victim," one man said.

"Don't ruin his enthusiasm," Lewis joked. "Meet Professor Jake Kaiser from the chemistry department at the University of North Carolina here in Charlotte."

"Nice to meet you," Neil said.

"And Gregory Horton, president of the local chapter of the American Chemical Society," Lewis said.

"Nice to see you again. We've been at some of the same meetings." Neil shook his hand.

"Neil's a research chemist," Lewis said, without mentioning his unemployment status. "Here's the plan for the afternoon. Things are informal. Walk around the exhibits, meet the students, talk with them about their work, and ask questions. Use the checklist to rate the projects. We'll meet back here in an hour."

Lewis walked the men to the cafeteria where the students displayed their projects. Neil meandered around the entire room without stopping to chat. Surprised at the level of sophistication, Neil guessed this student work had considerable adult input. Starting in the middle of the room,

Neil approached an elaborate model of the solar system set in a shadow box with the planets and moons rotating.

"Nice looking." Neil admired the wood grain, touched the smooth surface, and thought it looked like the work of a professional carpenter. "Tell me what I'm looking at."

"The planets—I'm showing their size and place in relation to the Earth," the boy said.

"Where'd you get the motors?"

"An electrician who works for my dad put the gears together."

"Which one is Jupiter?"

The boy proudly pointed to Saturn.

Neil did not correct him, and he hoped he concealed his disenchantment.

He moved on to a set of well-drawn diagrams on poster board illustrating the life cycle of a butterfly. The student had an album of her photos showing each stage. They chatted about how she decided on this project and the fun she had timing her photography. The fact that she did her own work restored his enthusiasm.

A display showing global warming next caught Neil's attention. This student produced two different environments, each in a ten-gallon aquarium. The atmosphere of one was a typical air mixture of nitrogen, oxygen, and carbon dioxide. The second had an enriched quantity of carbon dioxide simulating releases from fossil fuels. The student positioned identical floodlights to shine into the tanks. The thermometer in the aquarium with more carbon dioxide registered a higher temperature.

"Well done," Neil said to the boy. "This simple illustration of global warming is good enough to teach our Congress about carbon dioxide levels."

Near the end of his roaming, Neil approached a presentation on chlorophyll. This youngster gave a convincing report of his study that combined principles of biology, physics, and chemistry. There was no doubt that he actually did the experiments and learned from his work. *This one deserves the top prize.* Neil finished marking the scores on the checklist before he reconvened with the other judges and the science teacher in charge.

As he walked into the judges' meeting room, Neil heard the teacher Lewis and the other two judges discussing the kid with the planets. "His father is very generous," Lewis said. "He's a successful builder here in town who has made significant contributions to school programs. Recently he donated a new scoreboard."

Neil wished he had not heard this.

"The solar system gets my vote for number one," Kaiser said. "I liked the gear box and the way he concealed it."

"He didn't build it," Neil said. "A professional electrician deserves all the credit. And I wasn't impressed that he gave me wrong answers."

"What did you ask—the exact weight of each planet in grams?" Horton joked.

"I asked him which planet was Jupiter," Neil responded. "He pointed to Saturn."

"I'm sure he knows the planets." Lewis eyed Neil critically.

Undeterred, Neil lobbied for another project. "One student did an excellent job of connecting a number of disciplines in science, the one on electrons and photosynthesis. He actually isolated chlorophyll from spinach and then showed how the chlorophyll molecule emits electrons when illuminated by light. I was impressed with the originality and complexity of his work as well as his understanding."

The other judges pressed their case for the solar system. Neil was outnumbered. The preferred choice for the science fair winner was the son of the scoreboard supplier. Neil left disheartened with the pervasive tolerance for deception.

Chapter 43

For days after the science fair, Neil's productivity deteriorated. He barely got out of his own way and did not complete goals he had set. When Bridget came home, he struggled to recount his day.

Concerned about his growing melancholy, Bridget started calling five or six times a day to check on him and encourage him. Leaving detailed notes, she essentially directed his time with lists of errands, household chores, and yard projects for him to do in her absence.

Before setting out to tackle the overgrown hedge that Bridget asked him to trim, Neil took a call from the director of human resources at an Arizona company that had nothing to do with plastics. Neil's optimism returned. Taking this job risked no retaliation from Mr. Byrnes. The company mined, processed, and marketed calcium carbonate and related compounds. After a brief phone discussion, the director invited Neil to fly to Phoenix the next week for a meeting with the company's vice president. Neil could scarcely contain his excitement.

When he checked his emails Neil smiled as he read one from Perry that informed him of a breakthrough in the NRC's case against his former employer.

During the days after scheduling the Arizona interview, Neil spent most of his time researching the chemistry of calcium, a very new area for him.

At five in the morning, Charlotte Douglas Airport looked like rush hour. Following dozens of travelers to the self-service check-in kiosk, wishing to change his middle seat, Neil saw that all the window and aisle seats were occupied on the computer plane diagram. Resigned to confinement in a small space for hours, he focused on the employment prospect. This could be the break he needed. This time, he hoped, nothing would prevent him from actually meeting the interviewer.

In Arizona, the vice president of sales, Floyd Pittmann, met Neil at the Phoenix airport. He liked the man straight away. During the drive to the corporate office in Scottsdale, they discussed details of the position, including Neil representing the company at ASTM meetings. Answering the standard question about his current work, Neil acknowledged that he was unemployed. As instructed by his lawyer, he declared that he had a complaint with the Department of Labor against his former employer.

Feeling like a felon, Neil reported his past. Either this man excelled at acting or he believed Neil had done the right thing. Instead of the interview ending abruptly, Floyd introduced him to technical service personnel. Walking down a hallway, Floyd explained that his company sought expansion into new markets. Neil mentioned a possible coating application for steel that could inhibit corrosion.

"Anything that reduces rusting, our marketing department will love," Floyd said.

"I'm sure I could experiment with your calcium compounds and develop a formula to coat steel." Neil resisted blurting out his other ideas to avoid sounding like a game show contestant.

As they came to the executive suite of the building, Floyd showed Neil his future office, next to his and on the same floor as the company president. The day passed quickly. A gracious host, Floyd talked about desirable places to live and offered to connect Neil with a realtor.

On the second day in Arizona, Floyd and Neil traveled on a company plane to a mine in the Nevada desert. They touched down at the Las Vegas airport and drove northwest. The glitzy skyline of the strip quickly disappeared, as wide expanses of dry, dusty dirt comprised the view from the car for the next two and half hours. Floyd explained that the company located their quality control equipment onsite at the mine. Although Neil would work closely with the person responsible for quality control, Floyd explained that Neil could easily manage this aspect of his responsibilities from Scottsdale. The marketing department needed Neil's expertise to increase sales.

In addition to the rust-inhibiting coating, Neil told him that calcium compounds could enhance some construction products and that he believed there was potential for their product as an additive. Neil's suggestions clearly excited Floyd.

Mid-day, they arrived at a remote, desolate site. In contrast to the attractive corporate office, trailers served as the center of operations for about fifty mineworkers. Drilling rigs dotted the landscape; heavy equipment moved the earth, and a huge hole in the ground fascinated Neil. Millions of years ago, water submerged this land. When the water evaporated, it left a large calcium deposit. After scientists had found that this mineral helped purify drinking water, retrieving it from the ground proved a profitable venture.

Donning hard hats and earplugs, they walked into a large processing plant where conveyor belts transported piles of rock through the extraction process. Workers monitored the automated machinery as the calcium carbonate made its way through the heating unit.

Neil loved this field trip. Sample cores of the mine area showed a significant amount of calcium that would take years to extract. Finally, he had a real prospect. *No company spent this kind of time and shared this much information with a potential employee and then did not make an offer.*

The men arrived back in Scottsdale late. Floyd agreed to meet Neil for breakfast and to take him to the airport for his return flight to Charlotte. Thinking of additional ways to develop new products kept Neil awake.

The next morning Floyd and Neil met in the hotel lobby. He told Neil that Kurt Dawson, the company president, was back from his out-of-town trip and asked to meet Neil. Instead of a leisurely breakfast, they returned to the company corporate office.

Floyd walked Neil to Kurt Dawson's office.

"Please stop by the human resource department's planning meeting while I speak with Neil," Dawson said to Floyd.

Kurt Dawson, about fifty years old, struck Neil as looking slick with his fancy clothes, athletic physique, and his salon-styled blonde hair. His toys—a putting green, several golf clubs, and expensive models of planes—seemed silly. Neil wanted the job. He could endure this man.

Standing at his big window with the expansive mountain view, Kurt asked, "Is it true you turned your former CEO in to federal regulators?"

"Yes," Neil answered, aware of a sudden dryness in his mouth.

Turning around Kurt said, "You realize this position is located at the mine in Nevada?"

"I'm very interested in working for your company."

"We'll get back to you. My assistant will arrange for a cab to take you to the airport."

Chapter 44

For the next two weeks, Neil hoped Floyd would call with a job offer.

One evening Bridget walked in the house from work and began recounting to Neil the details of an appointment that particularly troubled her. "This poor man is terminal, has only days left, and his health insurance sent him a harassing letter about not covering some expenses. He actually said to me, 'kick me to the curb, it's over.'" She stopped. "You aren't even listening to me."

Neil sat in a fog-like state looking at nothing in particular.

Bridget raised the window shades in the room. "When did you last move from this chair?"

"Ooh … What did you say?"

"Get up."

"I can't," Neil moaned, pain obvious in his face.

"Yes, you can." She stood in front of Neil and placed his hand in hers. "Get up."

"I can't, I'm tired." Neil yawned and pulled his hand away.

"Get up right now," Bridget ordered, her voice trembling. With each "I can't," Bridget responded like a relentless broken record. "You have to move. Your sitting here in a stupor scares me."

"Please stop. I'm exhausted."

"Listen—when I pulled into the driveway, I felt my throat close up. I sat for about five minutes, dreading coming into this house, not knowing what I'd find."

She had shaken his lethargy. Neil stood. Every movement he made, his muscles screamed in reluctance.

"Let's walk."

Out the back door, they went in silence, down the driveway, along the sidewalk to the park. On a path that alternated between wood chips and concrete, tall, one hundred-year-old trees stood on either side of the stream and shaded the area. Neil loved creeks, and the water stumbling over scattered stones and tree branches interrupted his gloom.

"How was your day?" He took her hand.

"I already told you about one appointment … insurance threatening a dying patient … just awful," Bridget said. "He has no family. I called the insurance contact number and spoke with some nitwit. After I explained his diagnosis and his limited time left to live, she repeated that he had exceeded the coverage limits."

"By comparison, I have no real problems," Neil said.

"Exactly."

"Tell me about the rest of your day."

"Oh, the usual encounters, some entertaining and some sad. I was all over the place, in court, the hospital, a nursing home, and two home visits."

"Your elder care consulting is full of surprises, isn't it?"

"I especially like the amusing moments that help me forget the horrible ones. Today I met a client who's having a hard time with a walker. She's a petite lightweight, and the walker is heavy. Her doctor recommended a different one that Medicare does not completely cover. She'd have to pay twenty-five dollars out of her own pocket."

"Can she afford that?"

"Oh yes, but she wants to save her money for a rainy day."

"And you handed her an umbrella and gave her a weather report … rain ending sometime tomorrow." Neil laughed.

"Of course … and added that it was seeping into her home and rising fast. No, I wore my professional hat and resisted screaming. I helped her as best I could. In fact I think she'll soon decide to spring for the twenty-five dollars. That piece of equipment would be her constant companion and literal lifeline."

"Good for you. And how close to one hundred is she?" Neil joked.

"Four or five years. She's funny. We'll probably be worse."

They passed a number of joggers and walkers completing the loop around the park.

"You need to do this every day. You have too much unstructured time. You worry me."

"I'm sorry. I know you're right. I have to get out of the house. But it's *so* hard alone. Walking down the street in the middle of a normal workday, I feel like a freak. What could I possibly say if I bump into anyone?"

"Check out other places. There're some books on hikes in the Charlotte area. Pick a different area to explore. Do the greenway in sections, and then when I have time we can go together on trails you especially liked," Bridget proposed.

"I'll try. I'll have to head out before the mail arrives. Waiting for it is torture. Each day I expect something conclusive in a Department of Labor envelope that will free me from this nightmare. You know what I got today?"

"More bad news? I should have known as soon as I saw you slumped in the chair. What now?"

"The Arizona company hired someone who was a better match for their needs. The letter came today," Neil explained his despondency.

"There is no better match than you."

"Someone without baggage. No one will hire me."

"The bastards—I hate them." Rage quickened her pace. She stomped off, no longer the rational, clear-thinking social worker. She marched ahead of Neil. After about six yards she turned and said, "I'd like to punch Gordon's lights out—throw acid in his eyes—what kind should I use? Where do I get it?"

"Please stop," he pleaded. "It would only make things worse."

"Tell me what would work. I can't stand doing nothing. This is wretched. I want to harm your former boss, Gordon Byrnes, and his weasel son Chadwick."

"You'd be arrested. Calm down."

"Can we pump poisonous gas into the air circulating system in his home? How about rigging his boat motor so it ignites when he's far from shore?" Bridget asked sarcastically.

"What Gordon most dreads is disapproval."

"You've got to be kidding. He's as likeable as Hannibal Lecter. He treats people like trash, ruining lives without a qualm, which is hardly a description of someone concerned about his image."

"He thinks he's a pillar of the community," Neil insisted.

"What's the NRC doing?" Bridget asked, loud enough to cause other walkers to look. "Is anyone in charge?"

"Please lower your voice," Neil pleaded.

"An enormous government agency can't take on a bully like Gordon! How inept are they?" Bridget raged. "It's downright scary to think the NRC is supposed to protect the public. They're a bunch of jokers—useless paper pushers, parasites."

"Now *you* scare me." Neil looked around. "We must be careful. We never know when we're watched or overheard."

"This is horrible treatment—being stifled. It's hard and unfair. I can't use any normal outlets to vent. Verbalizing negative feelings is basic. I can't keep a journal. I can't shout on my own street. I can't write a letter to the editor. I can't call a radio talk show. I can't give the facts of your case to a reporter. I can't even tell my friends the whole story. What craziness!" Bridget's voice broke, and her eyes filled with tears.

"I know this is dreadful, and I'm so sorry." Putting his arm around her, he said, "Gordon would love to sue me. We can't give him any grounds for a slander or libel suit," Neil warned.

"Slander or libel? What I want to broadcast is the truth." Bridget stepped away and faced him.

"It doesn't matter. We'd have to pay huge legal fees to prove we're right. The idea of publicizing our story appeals to you, but even if you got a reporter interested, it would cease to be news in days. For that, we'd be in court for years. We'd gain nothing by speaking out," Neil insisted with a pleading look.

"I can't stand what's happened to us. We have no control. We're held hostage to a legal process."

"I'm working to defend myself."

"You're depressed. That worries me and it brings me down," Bridget said.

"I'm sorry. I wish it were over."

"If only you'd get a job."

"I'm trying."

"I know. I also wish you'd do something fun once in a while. You've stopped all your hobbies and interests. You only work on your case."

"It's always on my mind. I can't help it."

"Expecting you to do otherwise is like expecting my Alzheimer's patients to know what day it is. I don't know how much more we can endure. Find a place to view the stars this weekend. We'll take your telescope. It will be fun," Bridget suggested.

"I can't even think about it."

Chapter 45

Like so many Charlotte summer days, the intense mid-day heat was the kind that cleared tennis courts, playgrounds, and swimming pools. Neil headed for the mall to meet Tom for lunch. He liked the easy access to the food court from the parking lot. Neil arrived first. With his usual black olive pizza, he selected a table near the window.

"Good to see you, captain," Tom said.

"Thanks, Spock, likewise."

"Pizza for a change?" Tom laughed.

"A creature of habit," Neil replied. "It's comforting."

"I'll get my food." Tom returned with hibachi rice and shrimp tempura. He sat down, lifted his iced tea, and recited his usual toast for Neil, "May you have an end to your NRC saga with justice for Gordon and Chadwick and gainful employment for you. Live long and prosper."

"Thanks, Spock. I look forward to your toasting my new position with some company."

"What's new?" Tom asked.

"Not much. I'm still job hunting. It's a drag."

"If it's any consolation, Gordon and Chadwick are feeling the heat. My sources tell me the government subpoenaed Chadwick. That unglued him big time!"

"That weasel is counting on his father's legal ammo to save his ass," Neil said.

"There is mega friction between those two. Chadwick complains about exorbitant legal bills and wants this chaos to go away. He knows the government can make a case against him."

"I hope they can. They're so inept."

Neil told Tom about his two disastrous job interviews and that his prospects were dismal. Recruiters continued to send his resume to companies that needed his exact skills but the companies never offered an interview.

"You're too good for some company to not snap you up. It makes no sense."

"Nonsense fills my days. How's the mug?" Neil referred to his Starship Enterprise coffee cup that Tom had added to his shrine to mark Neil's exit.

"In a place of honor, captain," Tom answered. "This might boost your spirits. Want to hear about the business in Grenada?"

"Absolutely."

"You won't be surprised that a key player is Richard."

"Richard, of course—Chadwick's favorite."

"Once I learned that, I knew I'd hit pay dirt. I've pieced together an incredible tale—my sources are confidential, of course."

"Information just comes your way, Tom." Neil laughed. "So what's the story?"

"Richard travels to Grenada six to eight times a year to carry out a classic Chadwick business assignment," Tom started. "Richard identified a local sand supplier willing to work with GB Polymers, someone without scruples and a willingness to ignore laws. Chadwick devised a profitable scheme but Richard implemented the details."

"On his own, Chadwick could never execute an agreement with anyone in Grenada," Neil said. "Richard fills the gaps in Chadwick's Harvard business education by adapting to the environment and opening doors with his cockiness."

"Exactly," Tom said. "Richard requires no education on esoteric business law or accounting practices governing import and export taxes. Chadwick's grandiose plan includes selling to oil refineries a sealant for concrete structures and penetration closures for pipes."

"That's why the local supplier," Neil said. "Sand is a key ingredient in penetration closures. Grenada's close proximity to Caribbean oil refineries opens an untapped market. Direct sales of pipe penetration closures from North Carolina to the Caribbean would incur hefty import tariffs. Capitalizing on the island's strategic location, Chadwick circumvents extra taxes."

"Do we ship the closure product premixed in North Carolina with all ingredients except sand?" Tom asked.

"That's the way to do it," Neil said. "When the Grenada company adds the local raw material to the sealant, it creates a local product subject only to local taxes. Gaining a huge edge over competition motivates Chadwick. What's the Cuba story?"

"The Grenada company also buys the radiation-shielding product and resells it to Cuba. There are no restrictions on trade between Grenada and Cuba," Tom said.

"Radiation shielding must generate generous profits for that company and, by association, significant cash for GB Polymers," Neil said.

"Chadwick utilizes the banking opportunities outside U.S. boundaries," Tom said.

"Funds funneled to Grenada avoided U.S. taxes. That saves considerable cash," Neil said.

"Like a homemaker from Lake Norman Peninsula Estates shopping at a consignment shop, Chadwick loves paying less," Tom said.

"This banking scheme is so Chadwick," Neil said. "He is obviously confident that the IRS will remain ignorant."

*****

Later that day, Neil completed the paperwork to make another withdrawal from his 401k account. His unemployment compensation had ended months ago. Bridget's income did not cover all their expenses. Dwindling funds and a fruitless job search depressed him. There must be an employer he did not intimidate. He picked up the phone and called Perry. "For all the time I've spent on this investigation, I should be on the NRC payroll," Neil asserted.

"Why not apply? I'd certainly be a reference for you. The agency posts job openings on our Website, and all application material is available online. Let me know if I can help."

"Thanks, I will."

Neil submitted an application to the NRC. All his work experience was in private business, but he pictured himself in the role of a government employee. He could adapt. At least this potential employer would not penalize him for helping regulators.

Reading an online technical newsletter, Neil followed an employment link. A prominent ad for a patent office job fair to recruit scientists popped up. *I could work there*, Neil thought. *Albert Einstein worked in a patent office and did some of his best work there. Maybe that would be more suitable than the NRC.*

He called the patent office and spoke with someone in human resources. Neil explained that he could not attend the job fair but that he wanted to apply. The woman responded with obvious enthusiasm after he mentioned his background in chemistry. Pumped up from this positive interaction, Neil forwarded his resume to the patent office. Hearing Bridget's car in the driveway, he came downstairs to meet her and to tell her his good news.

Bridget walked in the house talking on her cell phone. "I don't think we can make it, maybe next time."

When Bridget clicked off her phone Neil asked, "What can't we make?"

"Donna's having a barbecue this weekend."

"You go if you want to," Neil said.

"I'd rather go to a movie by myself than explain why I'm solo again with some lame excuse about your back, or flu symptoms, or an abscess tooth or whatever the ailment of the day is."

"I'm sorry. I'm not much fun these days," Neil said.

"Canceling four social engagements in the last six weeks is a bit much to take. I'm not accepting invites anymore."

"It won't always be this way. My case will end and things will be better."

"Because of a tedious legal process my life is on hold … that makes me angry."

*****

Two weeks later an official letter from the U.S. Patent Office came in the mail. Neil's hands trembled as he clutched the envelope. He walked over to a cylinder of pens and pencils and from the middle of this container retrieved a letter opener. He slit the envelope open, unfolded the ivory paper with an embossed seal, and read *because you are named as the inventor on three patents there is a potential conflict of interest.* The patent office, in desperate need for scientists, had sent a rejection letter, denying him an entry-level government job. He reread the letter and stumbled to a chair.

When Bridget returned home, she immediately knew he had bad news.

"What's wrong?"

He showed her the letter.

"The bastards—what a knee jerk reaction … conflict of interest … since when did that bother the government … ludicrous."

"They're worried I might not approve something in competition with my inventions," Neil said.

"You have no control over your inventions."

"They don't know that."

"Write the commissioner and request an exception to the policy."

"It's hopeless."

"Don't say that. What's the commissioner's name?"

"It's on the letterhead."

"I'll draft a letter. What's the status of your application with the NRC? That's more realistic," Bridget said.

"I haven't heard anything. I'm thinking about going to DC and speaking directly with someone in human resources."

"Good idea."

"I'd also like to visit the NRC's Public Document Room."

"What's that?"

"It's a repository of all communication with the commissioners—things like press releases and other correspondences on cases similar to mine."

"There's no comparable case. Most have shades of gray. Yours is black and white. Anyway, how'd that help?"

"Very little information gets to my attorney or to me. I'm eager to learn firsthand the status of the NRC case against GB Polymers. We're copied on some things, but there must be other motions and letters that we never see. I'm also interested in how other cases were handled."

"Then go."

"I'll go tomorrow and be back late the next night," Neil proposed.

"Please stay two nights. I don't like you driving tired in the dark. It won't cost that much to stay outside the city and take the Metro."

"You're right. That's what I'll do."

"Let's have some words with the patent office commissioner. Help me write a letter."

Chapter 46

After a night at a hotel in Virginia, Neil went directly to the subway. Springfield was the end of the Blue Line, so he could not go the wrong way. At Metro Center in downtown DC, he switched lines to continue to the Rockville stop. Once on the street, he got his bearings and walked the short distance to the NRC headquarters.

From the Internet, Neil knew about the monumental two-tower NRC headquarters complex. Prior to occupancy, the NRC totally renovated the older building on the left, then built a second twelve-story structure to provide office space for an additional thousand employees. While most businesses steadily shrunk office space and downsized staff, this one government agency defied the trend by expanding in a high-price real estate area. The frame of a third building, fourteen stories for more than a thousand employees, stood nearby with construction workers laboring to finish on schedule.

In addition to offices, a library, cafeteria, kiosks with newspapers, comfortable meeting rooms with state of the art technology, and suites for each of the five commissioners made up NRC headquarters. A quirky amenity included in the building was the televisions tuned to CNN near the elevators on each floor.

Crumbling concrete marred the appearance of the patio-like, front entrance to the building. It took every bit of strength for Neil to walk into the NRC headquarters. He made a startlingly noisy entrance on the polished marble floor. Once he signed in, the receptionist gave him a visitor's badge. Hoping that talking with someone at the human resources department would get him an interview, he asked for directions to that office.

"It's in the other tower. Follow this corridor to your right, pass by the café area and you'll come to the lobby of Tower Two. You'll have to sign in again and ask the security officer," the receptionist said.

Neil easily navigated his way, signed in, and asked for HR.

"You'll need an escort. I'll call for you," the guard said.

Twenty minutes later a woman arrived.

"May I help you?" she asked pleasantly.

"I'd like to check on the status of my application," Neil replied.

"I'll take you to someone who can help." They took the elevator to the second floor.

A clerk sat at a desk just inside the office door. "She'll look that up for you," the woman said. "Have a good day."

"Thank you," Neil said.

"Your name?" the clerk asked.

"Landers."

She tapped at her keyboard and looked at her computer screen. "L A N D E R S," she asked.

"Yes, that's right."

"There's no record of your application here. Are you sure you sent it?"

"Yes, I submitted it online, but I've a copy. Let me give it to you." He opened his attaché case and pulled out a blue folder. He handed the staff member the application.

"You need to complete a background history also," the clerk informed Neil.

"The seven-page form?"

"Yes."

"I have that also." Neil took out more papers. "I want to be considered for any position at any location," he stressed.

"Are your references complete?"

"What do you mean?" Neil asked.

"You need to submit three references. One must be from your most recent employer. Once we receive everything, you can be considered for a job," the clerk explained.

"Are there reference forms?"

"Yes. They're also online." She removed pages from a file drawer in her desk and handed them to Neil. "Complete these and send them to the address on the letterhead. Expect a response in four to six weeks."

"Thanks." Neil retraced his way back to Tower One and asked for directions to the Public Document Room. Natural light flooded the glass-enclosed room, revealing shelves of bound volumes, loose-leaf notebooks, and magazine-type holders filled with press releases. With a deep breath and a sigh, Neil walked under the gigantic official NRC seal, an eagle with a wide wingspan and five stars in a curve beneath the bird. He hoped it was securely fastened.

Rows of empty, highly polished, wooden conference tables filled the middle of the space. Neil walked in and put his attaché case on one. Computers blinked idle and copiers waited in energy save mode.

"May I help you?" a librarian greeted Neil, sounding enthused to have a visitor.

Wanting to see every document that had his name on it or the name of his former employer, he said, "I'd like to review all correspondence on this matter." Neil showed her a paper with his NRC case number.

"Gladly," the librarian responded.

At her computer, she produced a printout of relevant documents. She explained the layout and the filing system and brought Neil a pile of papers. He began reading. There were at least ten letters to the commissioners from Mr. Byrnes's lawyers. Neil noted with relief that the commissioners' responses did not show intimidation.

Neil read an official notice of nonconformance citing Ricktel, an original builder of many nuclear power plants, for failing to assess properly the quality of materials purchased for sensitive applications at nuclear power plants. Three NRC agents visited Ricktel's corporate headquarters in Washington DC to examine its method of qualifying GB Polymers Products for nuclear power plants. When agents Fowler and Perry questioned the quality assurance manager, during the NRC visits in Charlotte, they asked many questions about Ricktel. The agents wanted to know exactly how the company determined that GB Polymers met safety-related standards specified in 10 CFR 50. This inspection encouraged Neil.

In their investigation, agents scrutinized procedures, reviewed records, and interviewed staff. They were meticulous. By questioning the Ricktel auditor assigned to visit the Charlotte corporate headquarters and the manufacturing plant, they learned that this man never stepped inside any building belonging to GB Polymers. Instead, he met with the quality assurance manager, Richard Grover, reviewed his paperwork, and accepted his word on independent testing, maintenance of batch control, lot homogeneity, and traceability of material designated for nuclear power plants. Without objective evidence of quality, Ricktel failed the NRC requirements.

What did this mean? This contractor, a big player in the nuclear business, understood that safety required rigorous scrutiny. Sloppily, they never directly examined GB Polymers's quality control data. Numerous purchase orders showed that Ricktel bought huge quantities of construction grout, penetration closures, and sealant to install at nuclear power plants throughout the United States.

Expecting severe repercussions, Neil continued reading. He came across a letter stating that the NRC found Ricktel remiss. A slapped hand for shoddy oversight! *What about material in place at nuclear power plants?*

Neil needed a break. His head was spinning. There was no end in sight to this snarled government process. Numb, he traipsed into a coffee shop down the hall. With the lunch rush over, he had a choice of tables. He ordered a soda and a slice of apple pie while still thinking about the incredulous letter in the Ricktel file that no one would read.

Back in the Public Document Room, he looked at the shelves of files and waded through more correspondence. *There is so much paper that Gordon Byrnes lawyers have a good chance of spinning out the statute of limitations.* He read until closing. On his way back to the hotel, Neil bought a sandwich—dinner—and a newspaper.

Chapter 47

When he returned home, Neil continued his daily ritual of waiting for the mail that arrived around eleven-thirty. Positioning himself within hearing of the front door, he listened for the mail carrier's push against the flap, followed by the sound of paper slapping the floor, which raised his blood pressure and his hopes. Today he had a letter from the patent office.

The commissioner responded positively to Neil's request for a waiver of policy. He copied the human resource department and placed Neil's application in active status. *That's reassuring*, he thought.

The next envelope he opened had a rejection letter from the NRC … *he was not suitable*. This communication incensed Neil. The rapid response told him that they did not seriously consider him. He was still holding the envelope when Bridget walked into the room.

"Hi there. I recognize the return address. Anything worth reading?" She hugged him.

"I'm not appropriate for an entry-level position at the NRC."

"You've got to be kidding! You've been doing quite a few jobs for that agency for some time now."

"I know."

"Call Perry."

"He has nothing to do with HR."

"That's irrelevant. He owes you."

Neil called.

"Perry here."

"Does the name Paul Cardinal mean anything to you?" Neil asked.

"No. Should it?"

"He's in HR at the NRC. He sent me a letter stating that I'm not qualified for any NRC job. Do you agree?"

"Well…."

Before he could finish, Neil said, "I want you to personally pay Mr. Cardinal a visit. Tell him who I am and ask him to reconsider."

"I have no influence with human resources. I'm with reactor safety."

"Yeah, I know. Remember, I'm not a watchdog for the nuclear industry either. I've paid a very high price for bringing safety issues to your attention. This is a gross injustice. Next week I want an update on your face-to-face conversation with Mr. HR. I'll call." Neil hung up the phone.

Chapter 48

Susan settled her boys in bed and mentally reviewed her evening to-do list. She started some laundry, paid bills, and checked her e-mails. Andrew Gibbons of Citizens Protectors forwarded a message from a *Time Magazine* reporter: *We're working with homeowners adjacent to the Connecticut River Power Plant.* Time *will finance independent testing of their water.*

Wonderful! Susan thought. She wished she could call her engineer source. Knowing he had good reason to fear reprisal, she stopped pressing him to go public. As if willing his call, her phone rang.

He got right to the point. "Vibrations near the turbine are increasing in frequency and intensity … true to form, management minimizes it with some dubious explanation."

"I've some good news. *Time Magazine* contacted homeowners and arranged for independent testing of their water," Susan said.

"That's great! If management can't control the samples, we may actually find out what's in the water."

"The article on East Haddam water is slated to be in the next issue of *Time*," Susan said.

"That's what we need. The plant is a disaster waiting to happen."

*****

I did not expect a feature article, Susan thought.

Time Magazine's cover photo showed a tranquil river scene with a concrete containment dome towering behind a bank of trees with the words "Contaminated drinking water in Connecticut" superimposed on the picture.

Susan read the article's severe criticisms of the Connecticut River Nuclear Power Plant's culture of intimidation and the management's recklessness with public safety. Independent lab tests revealed outrageous levels of tritium in wells in a wide area around the plant.

Chapter 49

Bemoaning what had happened to his life, Neil felt demoralized. His workdays had shrunk to occasional stints as a lab temp. He used their retirement savings to pay current expenses while the wrongful termination case kept him unemployed. The NRC did nothing about the safety issues he raised. His former employer's legal tactics intimidated and immobilized the NRC, preventing any action against Gordon and Chadwick for their blatant violations. Perry's e-mail about following up on incriminating information regarding his former employer heartened Neil. Perry was less fortunate with Cardinal in HR who insisted Neil was overqualified for an entry-level position with the NRC and that there were no current openings with the agency for a person with his background.

The appeal of the Labor Department's favorable decision effectively stalled a final decision, holding Neil hostage. He turned on the evening news.

"The NRC commissioners placed Connecticut power plants on the NRC watch list," the reporter said.

Neil listened to an incredulous account of troubles at a Connecticut plant.

"What's this about power plants?" Bridget asked, coming into the room.

"Problems in Connecticut—the NRC chairman shut down the Connecticut River Nuclear Power Plant."

The news showed protestors assembled holding placards that read: "TIME Regulates NRC," "Listen to the workers on the front line," and "Bureaucrats compromised public safety." The newscaster continued. "Senior staff at a Connecticut nuclear power plant ignored workers warnings of safety concerns over the past four years. According to a recent *Time* article, the problems include tritium in water and increased vibration in the area of the main turbine."

"Did I hear that right? The announcer said that *Time Magazine* triggered the NRC action against the plants."

"Yes."

"Contact that reporter."

"On advice of counsel I must remain silent," Neil mocked.

"It's maddening that anyone has such power."

"I agree, but I can't risk Gordon and Chadwick suing me personally for public statements about them or their company," Neil said. "Walter is explicit and he's right. I have to remain silent."

"Listen to this." Bridget tapped the TV's volume higher. The newscaster said, "The spokesperson from the NRC insists that all other U.S. plants are secure. We go now to a report from a Fairfield University chemistry professor."

The professor then reported that a dangerous plume of radioactive steam had escaped from the Connecticut plant. He reminded viewers that the Chernobyl accident had poisoned an area the size of Illinois.

The news cut back to protestors outside the plant.

"I'm with Susan Ridel, a member of the local environmental group, Citizens Protectors," a reporter said, holding a microphone for her to speak.

"The NRC is unfit to regulate," Susan said.

"That's the woman whose husband committed suicide," Bridget shouted.

"You think so?" Neil asked.

"Definitely—his name was Ridel."

Susan continued, "The NRC holds tenaciously to an outdated, unrealistic, honor system philosophy. They expect greedy utility owners to report themselves."

"She's got that right," Bridget said. "Good for her."

The woman activist continued, "Apparently the NRC chairman learned from the magazine article about the problems at the plant."

The spokesperson for the NRC stated that the utility would take every precaution to safeguard the public, including conducting a comprehensive investigation.

Following the Connecticut news on the Internet and on CNN, Neil saw no mention of GB Polymers's defective products. *That's strange,* Neil thought. The NRC information bulletin stated agents were unable to inspect GB Polymers, and the agency questioned the quality of its products.

Chapter 50

To calm citizens living near the plant, the NRC scheduled public meetings. Susan Ridel arrived early for the first one, held at the local high school. A former coworker of her husband approached her. "Thank you," he said. "Your husband was a good man. I'm sorry for your loss."

The NRC officials sat at a long table facing the audience with a large screen behind them. Each wore a dark suit and had the familiar haircut of a navy man. Susan noted each name and title on the folded card placed in front of them. On an index card, she wrote Director of Special Projects and listed her impressions. *A mirror is his best friend.* She looked the plant's resident inspector in the eye, enjoying that he seemed uneasy. She jotted *sleaze* and etched him in her memory.

At the end of the table sat Randolph Perry, safety operations. This guy had the body type that could actually be comfortable in a submarine, Susan thought.

Looking again at the resident inspector, she seemed to increase his discomfort. Her research revealed that the NRC had a track record of collaborating with utilities, forming alliances that resulted in superficial inspections. In time, the industry gained confidence that oversight would be nominal. With no real risk of significant penalties, they took chances. Token fines, that they easily handled, were just the cost of doing business. *What would be different, now that the public knew about the history of shoddy oversight?*

The meeting presenters droned on about corrective actions delivering assurances that all would be well. *Start-up will not resume until our independent consultants are totally satisfied.* The meeting leader flashed his PowerPoint presentation from his laptop. Each slide had a diagram, a bulleted list, or a flow-chart of boxes. He read each one.

People went to the microphone and asked questions that the director of special projects answered. He was well dressed, polished, and comfortable in front of an audience. Susan decided the NRC had sent him to Connecticut for damage control. Taking her turn at the microphone, she asked, "What exactly does special projects mean?"

His three-minute answer screamed ambiguity. Detecting a break in his smugness, Susan pressed to hear more about how the NRC regulated the local plant. He eloquently espoused his agency's competency.

"Do I have this correct—under your capable oversight this plant deteriorated to a shut down?" Susan asked.

"The plant shutdown is a courtesy to Connecticut citizens. There is no evidence of negligence or any real danger for town residents. The commissioner wants to assure the public that generating electricity at the Connecticut River Power Plant is safe," he responded.

"It would help to have a directory for your alphabet soup. It's difficult to navigate the series of letters in one box to the next in your flow-charts," Susan said.

"We'll be happy to provide you with a glossary," he said.

Susan persisted with confrontational questions. The meeting ended much later than she liked to keep a teenage babysitter on a school night. As she gathered her notes into her briefcase, an agent appeared at her side.

"Alphabet soup, I like that." He smiled.

"Agent Perry, OSO—office of safety operations, right?" Susan asked.

"You're a quick learner."

"I'm Susan Ridel, pleased to meet you," she said, extending her hand.

"I enjoyed your comments about our acronyms. I never realized how confusing our jargon is to someone outside the NRC."

"Are you sure those inside aren't baffled also?" Susan teased.

"Good point," he said.

His laugh surprised Susan. He made no move to leave. "Tell me where you fit in with this corrective action process?"

"My department monitors reactor safety at nuclear plants," Perry said.

"How often have you been to the Connecticut River Plant?"

"This is my first trip."

"You rely on the resident inspector to alert you to problems?"

"That's right."

"Big mistake—he may be paid by your agency but he works for the plant management."

"You sound certain. Is this from an inside source?"

"My husband worked for the plant. He often said management ignored problems."

"Did your husband work with the inspector or anyone in the NRC?" Perry asked.

"He tried to stay under the radar, but he did alert a friend to elevated levels of tritium in groundwater. Unfortunately, the plant management found out and fabricated a reason to fire him by planting company tools in his locker. After an excellent twelve-year work record, management set him up as a thief. The deceit devastated him. He killed himself."

"I'm so sorry."

"Plant officials silenced him. I've become his voice."

"And the voice of others. Tonight you reported that workers call you with concerns," Perry said.

"That's right. I frequently get anonymous calls from engineers and plant workers."

"Have any of them called the NRC?" Perry asked.

"No. They want to remain employed."

"It's wrong to fire someone for speaking out on safety," he said.

"Not if you call it stealing. The workers that call me are too scared to call the NRC."

"I'm sorry to hear that."

"The NRC response to a complaint is slow and ultimately ineffective. Look at your diagrams illustrating how your agency works. There are countless snags and bottlenecks."

"We need to do better. Let me give you my card. Please e-mail me any information that you have on safety issues. I'd like to help."

Susan took his card.

"Good night," he said. "It's nice to meet you. See you at the next meeting."

Driving home, Susan wondered if Perry was married. The thought startled her. Since her husband's death, she had no interest in dating. When friends suggested she meet someone, she always rejected the offer. So why was she thinking about an NRC agent's marital status? Perry's friendliness struck Susan as sincere. She decided to ask in an e-mail how long he worked for the NRC, apparently not long enough to be jaded.

Susan returned home to a babysitter asleep on the couch.

"Your mother will hate me. I'm sorry I'm so late," Susan said.

"It's okay. Both my parents admire you," the babysitter said. "The boys were great. We had fun."

Chapter 51

The NRC continued to minimize the seriousness of tritium levels in water and to convince people in Connecticut that the NRC now provided oversight to compel the plant to comply with long-standing regulations. The news frequently quoted Susan Ridel. National TV news highlighted the downside of the plant shutdown with utilities threatening significant rate hikes and residents worried about the town budget.

Perry and Susan exchanged frequent e-mails. When the NRC scheduled a final meeting for the public, everyone expected an announcement of a restart date for the power plant.

Although exhausted, Susan would not miss this critical meeting. Many nights, actually early mornings, she picked her head up from a pile of papers on her dining room table where she had fallen asleep. Usually her back and neck screamed in pain as she crawled into bed.

Her library hours of tedious data entry dragged without the people contact she had enjoyed in the past. Somehow, she would do one more NRC public meeting. At the end of her workday, Susan's energy level returned. She walked to her car and found her vehicle looking like it had sunk into the asphalt. Inspecting the tires, she noticed a gash in each one.

Having town numbers in her purse, Susan pulled the card of local services from a small zipper compartment. She dialed the police station on her cell phone.

"Four flat tires?" the dispatcher asked. "Are you sure this is a police matter?"

"Slashed," Susan said.

"We'll send a police officer."

Planning to have dinner with her sons before the meeting, Susan scheduled the babysitter for six-thirty. Susan called a neighbor while waiting for the police to arrive.

"I need a favor. Can you meet the boys at the bus and bring them to your house until I can get there? I have flat tires."

"Of course. Did you say you've a flat?" the neighbor asked.

"Not one, four! I'm afraid I've made some enemies."

"It's that activism. Of course I'll meet their bus and bring them here."

"Thanks, I owe you," Susan said.

The police car pulled into the library parking lot and Susan waved.

"What's the problem, Mrs. Ridel?" the officer asked.

"Have we met?" Susan asked.

"Everyone in this town knows you! What happened?"

"Cut." Susan pointed to the gash in the front passenger tire.

"All four?"

"Yes."

"We can fill out a report, but unless someone saw the slashing it's unlikely we can find the culprit," the police officer said.

They completed the paper work. The police officer told her how to obtain a report for her insurance.

"Can you give me a ride?" Susan asked.

"No." Without another word, he got back into his vehicle and drove away.

Stunned, Susan stood and watched the cruiser disappear. She went back into the library to ask for a ride. The responses alternated between "I can't leave now" and "No." Susan thought about the marriage benefit of emergency backup transportation.

She looked up the phone number for a local tire company and a cab company, noted them, and went back outside. First, she called the babysitter and arranged for her to pick up her sons at the neighbor's house and bring them home. Then she called the neighbor and explained the change in plans. Next, she called the tire company. They had a tow truck and could replace the tires as a rush for an extra fee. If she gave a credit card for payment, they would leave the car outside their garage for her to pick up after the meeting.

Cabs in rural Connecticut towns were rare and involved a long wait, but Susan called the cab company's number.

Susan walked into the meeting late and maneuvered her way through the packed room to a chair with the Citizen's group. She scanned the head table, noting that special projects agent looked his usual arrogant self. Agent Perry smiled a greeting that she returned. The resident inspector respectfully nodded to acknowledge her presence. She laughed to herself, as she looked over the NRC officials. *So full of themselves*, she thought.

The Citizen's activist group argued that not all the words on pieces of paper resulted in real change in culture or safety. They questioned the rationale for extending the original licenses for the Connecticut plants and many throughout the country. With the design forty years old and materials intended to be functional for that time period, it seemed dangerous to simply lengthen the life of nuclear power plants for another twenty or forty years.

At a break, Perry came over. "I was afraid you were going to skip this meeting."

"Not everyone agrees with Citizen's candid criticism of plant safety. I had four slashed tires tonight. That's why I was late."

"That's terrible!"

Susan recognized sincerity in his eyes. Knowing that she had a sympathetic ear, she moved off the tires topic abruptly. "Agent Perry, the NRC needs to do a better job. I have some questions for you, but I see Mr. Special Projects is calling everyone to order. Ambitious, isn't he?"

Perry laughed. "Glad you got here." He returned to his seat.

At the end of the meeting, the director of special projects announced that the NRC would extended the plant shutdown, citing that management needed more time to implement all the recommended changes. Numerous corrective actions were cited in PowerPoint presentations, vertical slices of data, bar graphs, and in hours of discussion at meetings.

With the NRC decision to restart the plant postponed for another month, the meeting ended.

"Can I help you with your car?" Perry asked.

"My car! I almost forgot. It's across town. I have to go."

"Let me give you a ride," Perry insisted.

"Aren't you traveling with the boys in suits?" Susan asked.

"I flew from DC today and have a rental. The others traveled from our Region One office in Pennsylvania."

"You're at headquarters and they're in Region One—got it. It's a challenge to keep it all straight."

"But you will." He laughed.

Susan directed him to the tire place. As promised, her car sat on four inflated wheels.

"Thanks for the background on the onsite inspector. I'm beginning to agree with you that he has contributed to the problem here," Perry said.

"I've no doubt. The NRC believes he assures compliance. His loyalty is to the plant management."

"I expected your state's Senator Armstrong at the meeting," Perry said.

"He hasn't been at any," Susan said.

"He chairs the congressional committee that oversees the NRC. His absence makes no sense."

"I want to know more, but I have to get home. My babysitter is a high school student and it's late."

"How old are your children?"

"Nine and seven, two boys."

"I'm sorry about your husband. It has to be tough."

"We're doing all right."

"Senator Armstrong has a powerful role. You might want to get to him."

"Thanks for the tip."

"This may be presumptuous but could I take you and your sons out for an early evening meal tomorrow?" Perry asked. "I have meetings at the CT plant until late afternoon."

Susan hesitated, feeling more than a little stunned.

"Please excuse my arrogance. I'd just like to have a chance to talk with you other than at a formal meeting and I'd enjoy meeting your boys."

"It's okay," Susan said. "We'd like that. The only place in town is the diner a mile down the road from here. How about if I meet you there as close to five o'clock as I can?"

"That would be great."

"I'll wait here to be sure you car starts," Perry said.

"Thanks. See you tomorrow."

Chapter 52

When Neil returned home, he had a message from Perry. Neil detected discouragement in Perry's voice. He returned the call.

"The Connecticut plants have taken much of my time recently. I've not forgotten about you. I'm working on convincing my boss that Gordon and Chadwick are criminals that the NRC must reprimand."

"You were lucky Connecticut wasn't worse. Maybe we'll get some straight answers now."

"My boss thinks the damn antinuke groups are blowing this whole thing out of proportion. Nuclear power is incredibly safe," Perry said.

"With every precaution taken, I agree. The Connecticut plant cut corners. You and I both know that GB Polymers's material is in place there."

"You really think GB's products played a part?"

"Yes, I do. I think it is likely that some of the penetration closures are defective. If that's the case, radioactive liquid could seep from the plant into the ground water. And I'm worried about plants in other states. The NRC needs to do something," Neil said.

"Endless meetings in Connecticut to appease the public take up staff time. My boss said we'll have to ride this out before we start anything new."

"If your boss is smart and wants to look good, he'll go after Richard. Put his feet to the fire and he'll hand over Gordon and Chadwick. It's a clear case," Neil said.

"I'll see what I can do," Perry said.

Neil went to his computer. He typed "nuclear regulatory commission" into a news search as he had so many other times. Scanning numerous statements related to Connecticut, his searching led him to Connecticut Republican Senator Armstrong, chair of the Senate Subcommittee responsible for oversight of the NRC.

Congress needs to understand the seriousness of the NRC covering up problems at power plants and that it is easy to sell poor quality in the nuclear industry.

"I'll beg the good senator," Neil vowed as he put Senator Armstrong's name into a search engine. The senator's home page, complete with picture and background information, detailed his three terms in office. He had a law degree from an Ivy League university, and nothing flashy or controversial surfaced in his lengthy Senate record. Neil respected the unremarkable description. Hardworking, good people sometimes stayed out of the limelight. He noted the mailing address.

Drafting a communication to Senator Armstrong, Neil began with an appropriate reference to a recent good deed of the senator. After indicating that he held the senator in high regard, he moved on to a supplicant plea for a congressional hearing on the NRC. He did his best to interest the clerk who would first read the letter. Eager to get the senator's attention and a positive response, he went straight to the post office and mailed his letter.

Returning home, Bridget greeted him warmly. "I just heard on the radio that next Tuesday will be ideal for viewing three planets rarely in alignment."

"Not with the cloud cover in the forecast," Neil responded.

"Come on, figure out the best place for us to go."

"I can't even think about it."

Chapter 53

Agent Perry popped into Susan's thoughts frequently. When she had introduced him to her boys, they asked if he was with the FBI and they wanted to see his gun. He laughed at the boys TV associations. They did not seem to mind that his role was less exhilarating than a gun-toting agent. Perry clearly enjoyed talking with Martin and William and they loved that he knew all about rockets. She smiled remembering their pleasant time at the diner. Perry spoke lovingly of his brother's children and of some regrets that he did not have his own family. Susan found his interest in her flattering.

Susan followed up on Perry's suggestion to learn more about Republican Senator Armstrong. From various websites, she concluded that his colleagues respected and liked him. Negative comments were actually nonexistent. *So where was he?* Trouble at power plants in Connecticut grabbed headlines. His silence on this critical issue did not give Connecticut citizens good representation.

Stumbling onto a contributor list to Armstrong's campaign, Susan discovered big businesses in every state in the union supported him. His donors made up the who's who in American energy corporations. Searching for news articles that mentioned Armstrong, Susan generated photos of him at fundraisers. *This senator had friends in high positions.*

After assembling her research on Senator Armstrong in a binder for Andrew Gibbons, Susan brought it to his office and said, "We need to get his attention."

"Give me your take on him," the director said.

"Senator Armstrong could help us if he wanted to. I'm not sure why he has such a low profile on the Connecticut plants, but I have a theory. His supporters are the very businesses he's suppose to regulate. One of the NRC agents told me he has the authority to convene congressional hearings on the NRC. Connecticut needs that to happen."

Andrew Gibbons picked up his phone and dialed the senator's office. He identified himself, summarized the concerns about the Connecticut plant, and asked, "When can we expect to hear from the senator?" The staff person gave a noncommittal response typical of a politician.

"Thank you. I'll call next week for an update," he said to the Senator's staff member.

"He forgot who pays his salary?" Susan said.

"We'll stay on him. I'll review this." Andrew pointed to Susan's binder. "We'll figure out some way to get the good senator on our side."

Over the next few weeks, Susan and Andrew Gibbons made numerous calls to Senator Armstrong. Each time his staff responded with a promise of an appointment with a member of the senator's staff, but never the senator.

Susan had wanted to take her boys to the nation's capital for some time. They were at the right age to appreciate the museums. The spring school break presented the best time to go, and once in Washington she could easily stop at the senator's office.

The national news continued reporting the problems at Connecticut River Nuclear Power Plant. Once shut down, citizens across the country expressed dissatisfaction with the Nuclear Regulatory Commission at other locations. Antinuke groups spoke out on plant problems covered up in other states and cited concerns about structural integrity at plants in Maryland, Illinois, and Pennsylvania.

The Connecticut senator's absence from any meeting and his silence on the issue angered Susan. Citizens Protectors sent faxes, e-mails, and letters requesting his position on the Connecticut plant. The senator gave no response.

In e-mails, Susan updated Perry on her research and attempts to communicate with Senator Armstrong's office. Her most recent message told him about her DC travel plans.

Perry responded promptly. He was not scheduled out of town during the dates Susan and the boys expected to be in DC. He offered to take a vacation day and show them around, suggesting that he explore the Smithsonian with her boys while she visited the senator. "Hanging out in that stuffy office won't be fun for them," Perry said.

From the library, Susan checked out a children's book on Washington DC for her boys to create their own itinerary. She looked on the Internet for a place to stay and decided on a hotel in DuPont Circle near a Metro stop.

Over the next month, Susan and her boys looked at photos and descriptions of numerous attractions in DC. They listed their choices. Susan decided the train would be more convenient and more fun for all of them. The Boston to Washington Amtrak train stopped at several Connecticut towns along Long Island Sound. Old Saybrook, a fifteen-minute drive from her home, was closest.

*****

When the Northeast Corridor Amtrak arrived in Washington's Union Station, Perry waited at the gate.

"What a surprise!" Susan exclaimed. Turning to Susan he said, "I thought I could help you get to where you're staying. I hope you don't mind."

"This is great, thanks!"

With Perry leading, they found their way to the escalator for the Metro. Its steep descent had no end in sight. "Wow," the boys exclaimed.

Perry handed each boy a Metro card. "Lead the way, Martin," he said pointing to the slot at the turnstile. Martin inserted the paper card, the barrier parted and the card popped up on the top of the turnstile. Taking the card, he walked through the gate looking forward to his first subway experience. William repeated the process.

"We'll keep these safe because we need them to exit." Perry put the cards in his pocket.

As they walked along the platform, lights on the floor blinked, announcing the arrival of the Metro train. The boys peppered Perry with questions. Susan had forgotten that she liked someone helping her. Easing into her seat, she watched and listened while her sons told Perry of their list of things to see in DC. From the DuPont Circle Metro stop, they walked the four blocks to their hotel.

*****

Neil drove northeast from Charlotte to Springfield, Virginia, in seven hours. He checked into the same hotel that he had found on his previous trip. It felt strange to be in a hotel room waiting for the next day. Hating to eat dinner in a restaurant alone, he bought a sandwich and a soda at the last rest area and stayed put for the night.

The next morning he walked to the Metro with DC-bound workers, happy to have a mission and a destination, Senator Armstrong's Capitol Hill office.

Neil arrived to a buzz of activity in the senator's office: staff talking on phones, people waiting in the visitors' area of the office suite. The scene resembled a Fortune 500 company with callers speaking only with workers many levels below the CEO in the decision-making hierarchy.

Neil overheard staff members talking: "No, the senator's not available; he's in meetings all morning." On another line a staff member said, "Yes, I assure you, Senator Armstrong is monitoring the situation."

"The senator sent a letter on your behalf," a third staff member said.

"Senator Armstrong worked with others to get that bill through Congress this session," another staff member insisted.

They sounded convincing. Neil could not help wondering if any of what he heard was true.

"Will we meet the senator today?" asked a representative with a school group.

"Oh yes, Senator Armstrong promised to make time in his schedule for the New Canaan, Connecticut, high school students. He's your senator."

Neil took in the characteristic symbols of government. Flags flanked the room's doorway bearing the seals of the Senate, the U.S. Stars and Stripes, and the state of Connecticut seal. Official photographs adorned the walls. Through the large windows, he saw the Capitol Building and surrounding grounds. With its granite office buildings, monuments to American heroes, and park-like lawns and fountains, DC had a special glamour. Neil thought it would motivate one to do good, but he feared all noble inspiration was lost on this senator.

Chapter 54

The next morning Perry met Susan and her boys in front of the Capital Building. He gave Susan directions to the Senate office building, and they agreed to meet later at the mall carousel at one o'clock.

"We'll start at the American Indian museum," Perry said, knowing the boys' must-see list included a pair of beaded sneakers. "It's right over there." He pointed to a beige, curvy structure not far from the Capital. "Then the Air and Space Museum. Call my cell phone if you're running late."

Susan hugged her sons. "Have fun. See you for lunch." And they were off. Perry could not be more different from her husband. It pleased her to see that the boys took to him so easily. Susan watched the three of them until they were out of sight and then headed for the Hart office building.

From a safe distance, Susan lingered in the hallway and watched the activity of Senator Armstrong's office. Since he had ignored phone messages and letters regarding the Connecticut River Nuclear Power Plant, walking into his office and announcing her presence would ensure rejection.

With her handout, Susan stood between the senator's office suite and the conference room. Anticipating a brief encounter, she rehearsed her greeting silently: *Senator, I'm Susan Ridel with the Citizens Protectors group in Connecticut. Surely, you know from the news or from your staff that your constituents are upset with the NRC's negligence and disregard for safety at Connecticut River Nuclear Power Plant. As chair of the congressional subcommittee on nuclear safety, what are you doing?*

Susan thought she would be lucky if she got farther than saying her name and that she welcomed this opportunity to bring to the senator's attention the concerns of the people of Connecticut before he dismissed her.

First on her list of requests was the senator's presence at the next meeting in Connecticut. She hoped to hand him her one-page collage created from newspaper headlines about the plant shutdown with the official description of the committee he chaired. Around the border, Susan added key quotes from the senator's campaign speeches that pledged his commitment to the people of Connecticut.

Like a Broadway actor exiting his dressing room, the senator hurried toward the conference room surrounded by several staff. Looking like a harmless homemaker or at least an admirer, Susan made eye contact with the senator. He gave her a courteous nod. As she started to speak, the word nuclear tipped him that she was not a fan. He picked up the pace. A staff member instructed Susan on the procedure for appointments.

He granted time to those who held him in esteem. Senator Armstrong would not tolerate an agitator telling him his job responsibilities and demanding accountability.

Rejected, Susan remained in the hallway, unsure what to do next.

"Pretty slick, isn't he?" a man said, coming up to Susan. "I've been here less than an hour and I feel I know him. He's a charade."

"Susan Ridel." She extended her hand.

"I recognize you from the news. I'm Neil Landers."

"So you know I'm upset about the Connecticut River Nuclear Power Plant. I had hoped the good senator might want to help the citizens who elected him. What brings you knocking on the senator's door?"

"I'm from North Carolina, so I can't expect help. I lost my job for informing the NRC of defective material being used at power plants. My former employer's legal arsenal snarled the investigation, and I'm left swinging in the wind."

"And you thought the good senator might help?" Susan asked.

"Exactly." Neil said.

"Do you have time for coffee? My boys are with a friend. I have about an hour free before I have to meet them. I have some information you might find interesting."

"Sure."

They asked a security guard for a nearby coffee place and were directed to a cafeteria in the lower level. As soon as they sat at a table, Susan pulled out her list of the senator's campaign contributors.

"These are big players in the energy business," Neil commented.

"Which explains his absence and his silence. Tell me more about the defective material."

Neil gave the short version of his company's greed, his contact with the NRC, the raid of his company, and his current debacle with ineffective government agencies.

"Meanwhile, shabby building materials are in Connecticut power plants," Susan said.

"All over the United States and beyond," Neil added.

"Remember, *Time Magazine*, not regulators, shut the Connecticut plants down. You need to get your story out to the public."

"My lawyer ordered me to stay silent. My former boss would sue me for slander. I can't take him on," Neil said.

"There must be something in the public arena that an environmental group could use to your advantage against your former boss. You need the media."

"I've got a long ride ahead to consider your suggestions," Neil said.

"Before you go, I want to tell you why I got involved with the Citizens environmental group."

Susan told Neil the story of her husband's suicide.

"I'm sorry for your loss. My wife and I first heard the story on NPR and we were horrified. She'll be happy to know that you and your boys are all right. So, management framed him."

"The plant did not want people to know that their wells might be contaminated," Susan said.

"Water migrates. People probably drank poison from taps in their own homes."

"My husband was naïve. He thought business executives cared. Get the media on your case," she insisted. "Here's my e-mail. Keep me posted, please."

"I had better start driving. Thanks, I'll be in touch."

Susan walked out of the Senate office building and headed for the mall, a park in the nation's capital bordered by Smithsonian museums. Tired, overworked patches of grass separated beige, gravel pathways. Languages from all around the globe floated to Susan's ears. School groups in matching tee shirts gathered under a tree for an impromptu picnic. Police officers on horseback and on bicycles meandered among joggers and walkers. A father and son kicked a soccer ball. Susan stopped and watched. She thought about her husband. *What determined one's coping style in the face of adversity?* Neil impressed her as a fighter; he did not concede defeat easily, yet Susan worried that the passage of time would crush him. She resolved to ask Perry to help him.

Passing another father and son duet, Susan spotted Perry and the boys on the carousel. Perched on a blue winged dragon sliding up and down a pole, Perry looked like a kid. The trip to the senator had proved useless, but Susan felt like a winner watching her sons and Perry.

"Mom, we saw the beaded sneakers. The designs are much better than in the picture."

"The Indian Museum had a cool video."

"We were inside the Sky Lab Space Station, Mom."

As the boys continued to recount their fantastic morning, Perry looked pleased. After lunch, they returned to the Space Museum for an Imax Show and later that afternoon, they toured DC by trolley.

Chapter 55

The tired group trouped back to their hotel for some downtime before dinner.

"Mom, can we use Agent Perry's Playstation?" Martin asked.

"Sure, for a little while," Susan said.

The boys emptied the backpack Perry brought for them.

"*Need for Speed Underground*," shouted William, looking at the game title. "I've wanted to try this racing game."

"When did you become an expert on toys for little boys?" Susan asked.

"My brother has young boys. I asked him to suggest some entertainment for your sons," Perry answered. "I thought board games and puzzles. He recommended I borrow these gadgets."

"Do you know anything about them?" Susan chuckled.

"Of course not. He assured me I didn't need to know how they worked. I owe him big time."

"What did you like to do at their age?" Susan asked.

"Fish. I grew up in rural Pennsylvania, near a river. My friends and I used tree branches, string, and night crawlers, old-fashion equipment. I loved being outside. Fishing suited me. How about you?"

"Rollerblading, ice skating, berry picking," Susan answered without hesitation. "In berry season I'd head out early on my bike to pick enough for a pie and plenty more for cereal and snacking."

As they traded background stories, the boys tested their ability with one amazing virtual adventure following another, annihilating opponents with their cunning and driving skills.

"We need to get some supper. It's late," Susan said.

"There's a pizza place nearby," Perry said.

"Yeah, pizza," the boys said. "Pepperoni."

"You can get whatever you want," Perry said.

They walked out of the hotel and down P Street. The aroma of garlic, tomato sauce, and Italian herbs permeated the air as they climbed the stairs to the second floor restaurant Perry had recommended. Seated in the middle of the room, one boy asked, "Are those real pizzas?" He pointed to colorful, painted pies on thin, wooden circles lining the walls just below the ceiling. While they ate, they planned the next day.

Back at the hotel, the full and worn-out boys got ready for bed without protest. Silence quickly overcame their whispering.

"I had a lot of fun with your boys today. They're great little guys," Perry said.

"Thanks. I'm so glad we came to DC." Susan smiled.

"Have you dated since your husband died?" Perry asked. "I don't mean to pry," he quickly added.

"I've not had time," Susan answered.

"Would you take two or three minutes right now and consider dating me?"

"We live 350 miles apart."

"I can take a train or catch a flight. Connecticut's not that far. You and the boys can show me around. It will be fun."

"They've talked about you often since the night they met you. They have really taken to you, and I've enjoyed your company."

"I'll take that as a yes," Perry said.

Shifting the topic, she said, "I met a guy today that needs your help. He lost his job."

"What can I do?" Perry asked.

"He told me he called the NRC safety hotline. His name is Neil Landers."

"You met Landers?"

"You already know him?" Susan noted the change in Perry.

"I can't discuss agency business."

"You don't have to tell me anything. He told me his story. He never mentioned you. I had no idea. I'm worried about him."

The sounds of the boys' deep sleep interrupted their conversation. Susan closed the bedroom door.

"There's not much more I can do for Landers. The allegations department handles his case, not mine. He seems to be a good guy, maybe a bit overzealous. I have tried to have my superiors at the NRC make a case against his company and his former boss. They are proud of ordering plants to stop using his company as a supplier. Unfortunately, his CEO launched an aggressive legal attack and the NRC management does not want an ugly public battle. The Connecticut situation has further diverted staff from handling the Landers case."

"Not having a final decision from the NRC regarding his termination is cruel." Susan asked. "And you wonder why workers that call me do not call the NRC?"

"I get your point," Perry said.

"What has the NRC done about material already in place?" Susan asked.

"Landers got to you. That's his persistent question," Perry said.

"It's a good one."

"How long did you talk to him?"

"Long enough to worry—a man without a job scares me."

"I'll do what I can," he promised.

"There is a limit to what one can endure. I would not want him to…."

"Please don't worry. I'll figure out how to help him," Perry said.

"Thanks."

Touching her hand, "I really enjoyed today and want to spend more time with you," Perry said.

"It amazes me how easy it is being with you, more like an old friend instead of a new acquaintance," Susan said.

Perry pulled her close to him on the couch, gazed lovingly and stroked her cheek. "You're lovely."

Susan giggled. "It has been a long time since I've done this getting-to-know-you routine. I'm more than a little ill at ease and definitely feeling old."

"I feel like I'm sixteen again. It's scary that I'm so smitten with you."

She put a hand over his heart and felt the pounding. They both smiled.

"When I drove you to your car after the last meeting in Connecticut, I knew I wanted to spend more time with you. Once I met your sons, I've been looking forward seeing you again and wondering how to make that happen. How lucky for me that you decided to come to DC."

"You impressed me as different from the rest of the NRC boys, not uptight, and someone with a heart."

"One beating strongly at the moment." He laughed.

"Have your boys ever gone fishing?"

"Yes. But it's been a while."

"Maybe we could all go some weekend and take a picnic," Perry suggested.

"We'd like that."

"About Neil Landers, I know you're worried he might kill himself. It never occurred to me. He's up against a bully. The NRC should have recommended the Department of Justice prosecute his employer long ago. His lawyers intimidated the NRC, that's a fact. It's been nasty.

Landers's boss accused agents of all kinds of corruption. They even scrutinized my background."

"Classic wag the dog. I told him his story needs to get to the media," Susan said.

"Maybe I can help with that," Perry said.

"Wonderful! Thanks," Susan said.

"You're an inspiration. What can I say." Perry winked.

*****

The Amtrak train pulled into the Old Saybrook train station with Susan and the boys lamenting how quickly their time passed in DC.

"That was the best vacation, Mom," Martin said.

"Do you think Agent Perry will really come to visit us?" William asked.

"He said he would," Susan replied.

It pleased Susan that the boys wanted to see Perry again. She certainly did.

Voice mail messages awaited their return. Susan deleted one from a satellite TV distributor and another from a gutter sales representative. One from the local cemetery bothered her. No details, just *please call*. She smiled and listened to the last message from Perry: *thank you and miss you.* After they unpacked and settled in for the night, Susan called Perry. They discussed potential weekends for him to visit. Looking at their calendars, the first opportunity was in three weeks. She could not imagine waiting that long.

The next day Susan spoke with the caretaker at the cemetery. "Mrs. Ridel, I'm sorry to tell you that someone vandalized your husband's tombstone."

She gasped and winced with pain. "How many others?"

"Only his," the caretaker responded.

"How badly?"

"The piece with his name is missing. It looks like a sledgehammer smashed it.

Susan's throat tightened. Her eyes filled with tears.

"I'm sorry," the man said again. "Let me know if you want to repair or replace it."

"I can't talk now." Sobbing, she hung up the phone.

Chapter 56

Reflecting on his visit to Senator Armstrong's office, Neil realized that meeting Susan Ridel disturbed him. She was no longer just a news story, but a real person. He felt he understood her husband's action; if Neil had two sons to support, he could not have faced them either. The poor man believed he had failed as a father. Prior to his experience, Neil did not realize how demoralizing job loss with little likelihood of finding new employment was for someone. Neil thought about Susan's suggestion of getting his story to the public, and wished someone could speak out on his behalf.

Sipping his tea and reading *The New York Times* online as he did most mornings, Neil noted a front-page article: "Justices, in a Unanimous Decision, Make It Easier to Sue for Discrimination on the Job." Neil quickly read the reporter's summary of the facts in a labor case and the court's comments. The gist of this Supreme Court ruling offered hope that a worker could prevail against an employer in a job discrimination suit if the worker showed that the explanation given for termination was false. Fast-forwarding in his mind, Neil reviewed the many times his employer lied. Prior to reading this article, Neil did not believe he would win a civil suit. The precedent overwhelmingly favored the employer. With a high price tag for Neil, Walter had advised against it, stating his only recourse was filing a complaint with the Department of Labor. This new decision improved Neil's chances to win a civil proceeding against his former employer. Wanting to intimidate Gordon and Chadwick and end the labor case, Neil called Walter.

Surprisingly, Walter objected. "A civil case is time consuming and expensive."

"We'll have more control," Neil said. "The current situation has agencies in each other's way with nobody in charge. I can claim that I was fired for acting in the public good. It also happens to be true."

"You might be right. Discovery is broad in civil cases." Walter warmed to the idea. "We can request all kinds of documentation from Gordon and Chadwick. They would have a difficult time keeping information from us."

"That'll scare 'em," Neil said.

"It'll cost at least $50,000 to do what you're proposing. Depositions are expensive. To do this right we'd have to depose current and former workers."

"I'll get the money somehow. I hate this holding pattern. My employer gave a bogus reason for firing me and I have to do something. The article specified that even in the absence of a smoking gun, a worker can win."

"And there are four or five smoking guns in your case," Walter said. "A posted memo, cancelled access to your office, nonpayment for unused vacation time, terminating your health insurance in violation of employment law … did I miss anything?"

"Keeping my personal possessions! They're all listed in the Department of Labor report," Neil added.

"A civil case has potential," Walter said. "I'll file the necessary paperwork. You do know this action will infuriate your former employer. Retaliation is likely. Remember when the Department of Labor decided in your favor, your fish were goners."

"It is hard to imagine how my situation could be worse."

Neil e-mailed Susan in Connecticut to tell her that he had started a civil case against his former employer.

Susan replied promptly. "Good move. More information will become public."

Chapter 57

Neil woke to the sound of his wife screaming his name in terror. Taking seconds to clear his grogginess, he shuddered instinctively. Bridget's hysterical shrieks persisted. He tore down the stairs.

"I've been bitten," she managed to say, cowering in the hallway outside the kitchen.

"What?"

"A big snake." Bridget shook with fright.

Neil noted marks just above her ankle. "Sit down." He walked her to a dining room chair. "I'll be right back."

"Be careful," Bridget warned.

He walked toward the kitchen and spotted the chunky head with the flickering fangs aggressively protruding from the narrow space between the refrigerator and cabinet. Neil's presence produced a chilling rattle. It was hard to tell how many more feet of reptile were connected to that snakehead. The distinctive reddish-brown, diamond-patterned skin revealed the unmistakable trademark design of a dangerous rattlesnake.

"I feel weak and dizzy," Bridget moaned.

Neil lifted the phone from its cradle on the wall and punched 911. "My wife's been bitten by a big snake," Neil said to the person. "She feels faint."

"Stay on the line. We'll send an ambulance," the dispatcher said. "Have your wife remain calm."

Neil observed the swelling. "Help is on the way, Bridget," Neil said in an even tone. "I'm going to move you to the couch so you'll be more comfortable." With the phone between his ear and shoulder, he picked her up and carefully placed her on the sofa.

"Police," Neil heard, accompanied by knocking on the door.

He opened it. "Where's the ambulance?" Neil asked.

"It's on the way," the police officer said walking over to Bridget. "What happened?"

"A snake bit me."

"A pet?"

"No, of course not."

"Did you see the snake?"

"Yes, it's huge."

The medics arrived. "Snake bite for sure," the medic assessed the marks on Bridget's leg. "Both fangs got you."

"Take off her jewelry," one ordered. He cleaned the wound and tied a cloth strip above and below the bite. "Evidence of edema. How are vitals?" he asked a second medic.

"Good," he replied.

Neil placed her rings on a bookshelf.

"That's strange for Charlotte," the police officer said after looking at the snake.

"Let's roll. She needs treatment," a medic said. They placed her on the stretcher. "Call a professional to remove the snake," the police officer said to Neil. "Don't try to capture it yourself."

"Later. I'm going with my wife." Neil grabbed his keys.

"Hope she'll be okay," the police officer said, walking out of the house with Neil.

Neil followed the ambulance to the hospital. A guard directed him to a parking space. He followed the signs to the emergency room. No medics were in sight.

"I'm Neil Landers can you tell me where my wife Bridget is?" he asked an emergency room nurse.

"The doctor will speak with you soon," the nurse said. "Have you given your wife's information to our registrar?"

"No."

"Please go over there." The nurse pointed to a woman at a desk near the door.

"How dangerous is a snake bite?" Neil asked.

"Depends," the nurse said. "The doctor will have an update on your wife soon. Please go and check in."

"I need to see my wife first."

The nurse again pointed to the registrar. Neil ignored her and pushed his way farther into the emergency room. A security guard stopped Neil.

"Don't manhandle me," Neil shouted.

"Sir, we need your cooperation. Please give your information to the registrar and wait in the visitors' area."

"I want to see my wife."

The guard escorted Neil to the designated desk. When the check-in person looked up, she asked his name. He gave it. Struggling to answer her series of questions, he acknowledged that he did not know his wife's Social Security number or the group number for their insurance or any details of her medical benefits. In fact, he did not know the exact name of the insurer.

"We're self-employed," Neil said. "The carrier's name keeps changing. I don't know."

"Do you have your insurance card with you?" she asked.

I'm lucky I'm even dressed. "No, I don't." He walked away and approached a different nurse. "Can you please tell me how my wife, Bridget Landers, is doing?"

"A staff member will call you soon. Please stay in the visitor waiting area." She pointed to a section beyond the doorway to the ER where several people sat on plastic chairs.

Neil took a seat as far away from anyone as possible. The mounted TV blared a game show. A young man sat holding bloody gauze to his hand. Someone in housekeeping mopped the floor.

"Atchoooow, atchoooow, atchoooow," a woman sneezed in rapid succession, each one accompanied by a large volume of spray she made no effort to contain. Neil gagged. He closed his eyes, attempting to block the sickening conditions around him. Another person's loud cough joined the unpleasant sound of the woman still sneezing. This man's coughing grew in volume and harshness. Neil calculated the liquid in his chest would fill a gallon jug. He wished someone would put a suction hose to the guy's throat and end the gross sounds.

I've got to get out of here.

Neil went back into the ER. Before anyone stopped him, he passed several patients on stretchers. A young man in a white lab coat approached. "Can I help you?"

"I need to find my wife. She was bitten by a snake."

"Mr. Landers, I'm Dr. Patel. Your wife's condition is grave, with her pain exceeding the normal range for snakebite. She has significant swelling around the wound and her blood pressure is low. I've administered antivenin to treat aggressively this venomous snakebite. I'm moving your wife to the Intensive Care Unit for close monitoring, and I'll evaluate her condition at regular intervals."

Before Neil could ask to see Bridget, a loud voice blared over the hospital address system, "Code blue in emergency room." Dr. Patel ran from Neil's side. He and numerous hospital staff rushed to a patient. Neil followed. In shock, he saw a nurse pushing on Bridget's chest in classic CPR rhythm. Bridget's face appeared ashen and contorted.

From the cryptic conversation of medical jargon, Neil understood that Bridget had had an allergic reaction. The staff attached her to a respirator and hung a bag of fluids to drip into her arm.

Please God save her, he prayed. Dr. Patel approached Neil, "This type of reaction is rare. The ventilator takes pressure off her respiratory system, and I added medication intravenously."

"Will she be all right?" Neil asked.

"The next twenty-four hours are critical," the doctor said. "Her blood pressure is still fluctuating. The most helpful thing you can do is get me more information on this snake."

"I saw it in our kitchen before we came to the hospital," Neil said.

"Call a pro to capture the snake," the doctor insisted. "Your wife's in good hands. Get back to me as soon as you can." Neil wrote down the doctor's name and number.

As medical staff maneuvered Bridget on a stretcher to the elevator, Neil walked along side. He waited until Bridget was out of his sight before walking away.

At the registration desk, Neil asked the clerk to look up the number for Critter Control, explaining his wife's medical emergency and the need to trap the snake. She gave Neil the phone number.

He called. "Give me your number and someone will call you right back," the dispatcher said.

Within minutes, the responder called Neil and said, "I'm on my way to trap some skunks in a new development in South Charlotte. Give me your address and I'll stop at your place first."

"I'd appreciate that very much." He gave directions to his home.

"I'm about fifteen minutes from your house," the man replied. "See you soon."

*****

Neil waited outside his home until the Critter Control man arrived. Looking about sixteen, but probably in his late twenties, he stood about five feet eight inches tall, slim, with dirty blonde hair and brown eyes. His denim shirt had a Critter Control logo. He carried a long-handled stick with a straight piece of wood about five inches long attached at one end and a rectangular cage covered with a black cloth.

"I'm Adam," the man said.

"Thanks for coming. A big snake bit my wife. The doctor wants to know exactly what kind it is. It was in the kitchen when I left." Neil led the way.

"Holy shit," Adam blurted out at the sight of the snake. "That's a western diamondback!"

"So what. Is that good or bad?" Neil asked, unsure how to read Adam's obvious excitement.

"When armed, this rattlesnake is dangerous. Gosh, that pattern of diamonds is a work of art—just beautiful. He's a long way from home. I've only seen them in books, never in the Carolinas."

"Where's home?" Neil asked.

"A desert climate," Adam replied. "Like Arizona, maybe western Texas. He doesn't want to be in your kitchen. Snakes prefer to stay away from people. Unlike humans, they are not provocative. They're spectacular creatures and get a bad rap."

"Do you need much time to remove him?" Neil interrupted the discourse on the fabulous features of snakes. "My wife is in tough shape. I need to get back to the hospital."

"It shouldn't take long." Adam confidently put on thick gloves that were like fireproof mitts, pulling them over his shirtsleeves to his elbows.

"It would be easier if Mr. Diamondback decided to come out a little from under his domestic rock." Adam considered aloud his options for capture. "If we're lucky he'll slink out a bit."

"The only luck I've had lately is bad. Don't count on me," Neil said sadly.

"He's *so* stressed," Adam said with sincerity. "I'd like his exit to be smooth and simple."

"I'm happy to skip an Indiana Jones style wrestling match," Neil commented.

Waiting at a respectful distance, Adam removed the black cloth from the box and opened the top. The snake edged out slightly from its spot.

Adam slid the L-shaped stick under the middle of the snake, and with a skillful motion, he pulled it up from the floor, keeping the head farthest from his body. The snake curled back on the handle to assess its attacker. Adam swiftly placed the snake in the cage and flipped the top shut. Keeping a good space between himself and the cage, Adam used his long-handled stick to secure the latch on the trap. Then he replaced the cover.

"We need to call the doctor." Neil dialed the number. When he connected with Dr. Patel, he confirmed, "It's a rattler more than two inches in diameter and about five feet long. The guy that caught him tells me this kind of snake lives in the desert somewhere like western Texas or Arizona."

The doctor indicated that he would consult with physicians in Texas that dealt with that kind of snakebite more often.

"Before we leave, let me check around where others might hide," Adam said. "Here's how he got in." Adam pointed to the mail slot in the front door. "These scales scraped off during his slide into the house."

Looking at the traces of reddish brown skin on the light-colored tile, both men remained quiet.

"This was no accident," Adam said. "It would take a professional handler to transport this rattlesnake from the desert to here. Someone's out to get you."

Neil nodded his head in agreement. "I know."

"It's cruel to misuse this creature. And it's illegal. If you know who did this, you need to press charges," Adam insisted, clearly outraged.

Neil found it astonishing that most people thought of the legal system when wronged. "How can I be sure there are no more in the house?" Neil asked.

"It's hard to be certain. I'll look around." When Adam returned to the first floor he said, "I don't think there are any others in the house. Keep my phone number." He carried the container with the snake from the kitchen.

Chapter 58

Neil rushed back to the hospital, parked in the visitor garage, and at the main reception desk he asked for directions to the Intensive Care Unit. Exiting the elevator on the ICU floor, Neil saw a sign on the wall next to a phone indicating that it was the link to the nurses' station. He picked it up. A nurse instructed him to wait and she would escort him to Bridget.

As soon as the nurse appeared at the waiting room, Neil jumped up. "Is she going to live?" he asked.

"Hard to tell, just yet," the nurse said. As they walked, she talked in that detached, clinical fashion of years on the front line of life and death. "She had a bad reaction to the antivenin. She spiked a fever and was quite confused when she first arrived at ICU. I can only let you stay a few minutes."

He gazed at Bridget's pale face, picked up her hand, and kissed her forehead. "Talk to me," he whispered. "Please open your eyes." Pulsating machines and various beeps responded.

"Hang in there, baby. Don't leave me. Those bastards can take everything else from me but not *you*. My enemies meant that snake for me. I'm so sorry it got you. Hang in there. *Please!*" Still holding her hand, Neil collapsed in a chair next to Bridget's bed.

The nurse returned, checked the IV, and said, "The next eighteen hours are critical. She needs to rest and remain quiet."

"Can I check in periodically?" Neil asked.

"Certainly. Call from the waiting room if you need us. The cafeteria is located on the lower level," she said.

As Neil endured the agony of waiting, he functioned as if he was the one comatose. At regular intervals, he spent fifteen minutes at Bridget's bedside. In the waiting area, he barely glanced at the newspapers and magazines.

The waiting room phone rang, summoning Neil for Bridget's doctor to update him. As they stood together next to Bridget's bed, Dr. Patel rattled off medical facts. The night staff reported that Bridget had had brief moments of consciousness. The respirator was a precaution to minimize stress on her compromised system. He believed she would breathe on her own within thirty hours. Agreeing to speak with Neil the following morning, he left.

That afternoon Bridget opened her eyes. Neil stroked her hand, heartened that she was making progress.

After the respirator was disconnected the next morning, Bridget looked at Neil and said, "I'll fix dinner in a little while. Are you hungry?"

Neil laughed, "Don't worry about me. It's great to hear your voice. Do you know where you are?"

Bridget looked around. Neil brought her up to date on the hours she had missed. "Get well and you'll be home soon."

It took three more days before the doctor cleared Bridget for discharge. Neil rejoiced when the doctor said tomorrow. That evening he prepared for Bridget's homecoming by arranging flowers in their bedroom, bathroom, and dining room and shopping for basic food items so there would be no delay in getting Bridget home. The doctor said she could leave at eleven o'clock the next morning.

Arriving in her room ahead of schedule, Neil was surprised to see Bridget's friend Donna.

"Neil, we need to talk," Bridget said as Donna left the room.

"What's up, honey?" Neil hugged her. "You're crying. I thought you'd be happy to get out of here."

"I couldn't tell you on the phone. I'm not going home with you."

"Not going home?"

"I need some time to think. I'm going to Donna's."

"The house is safe." Neil reassured her. "I've sealed the front door letter slot."

"It's more than the snake. Our life has changed for the worse."

"What do you mean?"

"We've grown so far apart. You only talk legalese. I hate it."

"Please give me another chance."

"You're a different person. Resolving this issue with your former boss is all that matters. You can't help yourself. We don't go out. We've stopped entertaining. I don't want to live like this."

"Social life is too much effort for me. Everybody talks about their job."

"You're consumed with your case, reading legal books or becoming an expert on the NRC."

"I'm trying to defend myself. And I'm trying to get a job."

"There's no balance. When did you last look through your telescope or read a book for pleasure?" Bridget asked.

"I don't know."

"You use to have a lot of interests. You use to be fun. Now you do research and stare into space. I hate our life."

"I'm sorry. I'll make it up to you. Please come home."

"I can't right now," Bridget said with tears in her eyes.

Neil returned to an empty house and a message from Perry on the machine: *"The NRC referred the GB Polymers case to the Department of Justice. My superiors finally realized the benefit of charging a corporate officer. The problem with Connecticut plants drove that point home. They subpoenaed Richard."*

Only the day before, this news would have made Neil ecstatic. He did not return Perry's call.

Chapter 59

In his Manhattan office, attorney Olmsted pondered the particularly sensitive subject of Quality Assurance Manager Richard Grover. Richard's deposition with the Department of Justice required an attorney with white-collar crime experience and a flair for creative solutions. Washington DC lawyer Glen Fuller, personal attorney for the chief labor judge, assured Olmsted that his client assigned Neil's case to an ill, overworked New York judge, essentially burying Neil's labor department case. The civil case Neil initiated against GB Polymers amazed Olmsted and told him getting Neil to quit would not be easy.

Attorney Casper, the DC lawyer with contacts inside the NRC, disappointed Olmsted. Casper insisted he could prevent any real movement by the NRC against GB Polymers. The phone call informing Olmsted of a subpoena to depose Richard stunned him. NRC referrals to DOJ were rare. *How did the NRC convince the Department of Justice to pursue his client?*

Gordon had balked at Olmsted's suggestion of hiring a lawyer to represent all his employees until he understood that this attorney created an effective barrier between his workers and Neil and government agents. Questioning Richard under oath posed great risks for Gordon, so Olmsted persuaded him of the need for Richard to have his own attorney.

After searching throughout North Carolina, not just the Charlotte area, for an attorney to represent Richard, Olmsted spoke with five. All had won cases in recent years for business executives guilty of embezzlement, mail fraud, or sexual misconduct with subordinates in the workplace. They all suited Olmsted's criterion; however, Marvin Keating, of a Raleigh, North Carolina law firm, ended up in first place on his short list to represent Richard. Trusting his instincts, Olmsted skipped his usual face-to-face meeting and finalized the deal with a phone assessment. Keating accepted the assignment and agreed to Olmsted's terms of ongoing monitoring and commission payments on all billable hours. Promising to send Keating background material and a preliminary plan for Richard's defense, Olmsted set a time in two weeks for a phone call to discuss the details of handling Richard's deposition.

Two weeks later Olmsted called Keating regarding a strategy for the U.S. Department of Justice versus Richard Grover. They agreed on the deficits of their case that they needed to overcome, discussed possible scenarios, and reviewed Richard's responses.

"I'll prepare him for any questions the DOJ attorneys put to him," Keating assured Olmsted. Keating had considerable experience with white-collar crime, and in recent years he had successfully handled some high-profile cases. His three-year stint at the Department of Justice early in his career helped his understanding of that department.

"Did Richard get a suit?" Olmsted asked.

"Yes, last week I sent him to an upscale men's store on a shopping spree with no limits. He told the salesman he knew nothing about fashion and needed a suit to impress a new client."

"Resourceful, isn't he!"

"You'll love this," Keating continued. "Richard went for a total makeover. The salesman picked out the entire outfit including socks and shoes and then recommended a nearby salon for a haircut and manicure."

"You've got to love a man who works with you," Olmsted said. "How are you doing with the fishing trip?"

"Guide, accommodations, transportation, and equipment are all set," Keating answered.

"The outing is the weekend before our appointment, right?"

"Yes."

"Excellent. I'll be in Monday, and we can finalize details over dinner," Olmsted said. "We'll be ready for the feds on Tuesday."

"Piece of cake," Keating said. "Remember, most of the Department of Justice attorneys are very young and have only about ten months' post-bar experience. See you next week."

Chapter 60

On time, Richard reported to Keating's office. Olmsted noted the expert tailoring, high quality, all-season, lightweight wool, European lines and the expensive buttons on Richard's new suit. No wonder Chadwick hired him. Richard followed directions well.

"How was the fishing?" Olmsted thought Richard probably had tasteless tattoos under the fine clothing.

"Excellent," Richard said. "I had never been in the North Carolina mountains. The streams are amazing. I loved it. It's easy to catch fish with great gear. Thank you."

After the chitchat about Richard's weekend and the weather, they walked to the federal courthouse and located the conference room scheduled by the Department of Justice. Two young men in dark suits talked quietly as a court reporter set up equipment at the end of the table. Piles of folders indicated the DOJ attorneys' places at the table. Three chairs opposite were set for Richard, Keating, and Olmsted.

"Good morning, gentleman," Olmsted said in a breezy, casual tone. He then dominated the room as if he had called recalcitrant students into the office. "Do you mind if I move away from the glare? This lighting bothers my eyes." Without waiting for an answer, he rearranged the seating, put his briefcase on the table, and flipped it open, blocking the court reporter from his view. Olmsted motioned for Richard and Keating to sit down. "Shall we get started?" Olmsted said to the two men still standing.

"Thanks for agreeing to talk with us," stammered one of the men. "I'm attorney Arno and this is attorney Dosantes and, of course, we're with the Department of Justice."

Attorney Dosantes began, "This is a formal legal proceeding minus the judge, witness box, and furnishings associated with a courtroom. A copy of the transcript of this session will be available from the reporter. Mr. Grover, we have a few questions we would like you to answer. First, please raise your right hand."

Richard complied.

"Do you solemnly swear to tell the truth?" Dosantes asked.

"I do," Richard responded.

"For the record please state your full name," Dosantes said.

"Richard Mitchell Grover."

"My client needs a definitive answer on our request for immunity before he answers any more questions," Keating interrupted. "Please let the record show that in exchange for his cooperation he's granted complete immunity."

Olmsted had convinced the Justice Department to set priorities high and not waste time with Richard. In exchange for Richard's testimony, the Justice Department agreed not to prosecute Richard for lying, falsifying documents, and obstructing a federal investigation.

"We'll honor the request for immunity in exchange for Mr. Grover's cooperation," Dosantes replied.

"Thank you." Keating leaned back in his chair.

"What is your job title?" Dosantes asked without looking up.

"Manager of quality assurance," Richard replied.

"Where do you work?" Dosantes asked.

"GB Polymers."

"How long have you worked there?" Dosantes asked.

"Five years."

"Did you have prior experience with quality assurance?" Dosantes asked.

"No."

"Tell us about your background," Dosantes said.

"After high school I worked at various manufacturing jobs. I did shipping for a textile company. My first year at GB Polymers I worked in the manufacturing plant, then Chadwick Byrnes promoted me to manager of quality assurance."

"Did you go to college?" Dosantes asked.

"No."

"Who do you report to?" Dosantes asked.

"Chadwick Byrnes."

"Tell us what you know about ASTM International standards." Dosantes said.

"I have no knowledge of them."

"What does the phrase 10 CFR 50 mean?" Dosantes asked.

"I've no idea."

"Have you read any part of this Code of Federal Regulations?" Dosantes picked up two thick volumes.

"No."

"What guidelines do you follow for testing samples?" Dosantes asked.

"I'm not sure what you mean."

"How do you sample a production batch?" Dosantes asked.

"I take out a small amount and bring it in for testing."

"Tell us about this framed certificate." Dosantes pointed to a document the NRC had removed from Richard's office.

"It's from a course I took in quality assurance."

"A course you took after the NRC visited and asked about your qualifications, right?"

"I don't remember."

"At any rate, this training happened after years of managing quality assurance for GB Polymers," Dosantes said.

"Yes."

"What prompted you to take this course?" Dosantes asked.

"One of our customers told me about it. I mentioned it to Chadwick, and he thought it was a good idea." Richard looked directly at Dosantes.

"What customer?"

"I don't remember. We have had many visitors reviewing our policies and procedures. Probably someone who worked for a utility suggested the course."

"Isn't it true that customers expressed concern that GB Polymers lacked policies and procedures for monitoring quality?" Dosantes asked.

"I'm not sure."

"This two-day class is your only formal training?" Dosantes asked.

"That's right. I learned everything on the job."

Richard's composure impressed Olmsted. He had met innocent people who sounded guilty when interrogated by a lawyer. Rarely were individuals as cool as Richard was.

"About the visits to your company in the spring—were you involved in audits by utilities?" Dosantes asked.

"Yes." Richard sat motionless with his hands folded on the table.

"And were visitors from utilities given access to the lab?" Dosantes asked.

"No."

"Didn't the auditors ask to come in and look around?"

"Yes."

"How did you explain that?" Dosantes asked.

"We've confidential research projects that necessitate a no-visitor rule."

"Everyone accepted that reason?" Dosantes asked.

"Yes."

"Where did you meet?" Dosantes asked.

"Off-site."

"Do I have this correct? Auditors never came to your corporate office?" Dosantes sounded amazed.

"That's right."

"Did they visit the independent lab?" Dosantes asked.

"No."

"Did they visit your plant in Rockingham?"

"No."

"Let me summarize. Your company sold material to the nuclear industry and not one purchaser has been on site to conduct an audit. Is that right?" Dosantes asked.

"As best I know."

"All buyers have simply taken your word on compliance with a comprehensive quality assurance program?" Dosantes asked.

"I guess so."

"Are you familiar with a company named Spencer Chemical Research?" Dosantes asked.

"Yes."

"Did you ever work for Spencer Chemical Research?" Dosantes asked.

"No."

"Please identify the company named on this letterhead." Dosantes showed Richard a paper.

"GB Polymers."

"Can you tell us what this document is?" Dosantes asked

"An audit."

"What is the name of the company being audited?" Dosantes asked.

"Spencer Chemical Research."

"And is this your signature?" Dosantes placed the document in front of Richard.

"Yes."

"You audited Spencer Chemical Research in your role as manager of quality assurance. Is that correct?"

"Yes."

"Does Spencer Chemical Research have the capacity to test?" Dosantes asked.

"I don't know."

"Is it a dummy company?" Dosantes asked.

"I don't know."

"Explain the steps involved in testing a sample of a product designated for a nuclear power plant," Dosantes said.

"I, or a plant worker, took samples from batches of a product made at our manufacturing plant and then gave the sample to Ethan Porter who ran various tests and recorded the data. Larry Davis in the technical services department generated a document certifying the specific properties of the product," Richard said.

"Is this statement that material met specifications per standardized testing true?" Dosantes asked, showing a copy of a letter to a power plant.

"To the best of my knowledge."

"What is the date of this audit?" Dosantes placed a paper in front of Richard.

"June eighteenth of last year."

"Look at this calendar. Please tell me the day of the week for June eighteenth," Dosantes said.

Leaning forward to see the calendar Richard said, "Sunday."

"Do you have children, Richard?"

"Yes, I've two daughters."

"And on Father's Day you worked on a routine audit?"

"No, I was home with my family."

"Is this audit authentic?" Dosantes asked.

"No."

"You made it up."

"Yes."

"You neglected to check that the date you picked was a Sunday?"

"Yes."

"Did you give this audit to an NRC agent?" Dosantes asked.

"Yes."

"You submitted it as evidence that your company met NRC requirements?" Dosantes asked.

"Yes."

"Do you know that it's a criminal offense to submit fraudulent documents to a federal investigator?"

"Yes."

"How did this happen?"

"NRC agents asked me for an audit from our independent lab. I felt pressured to produce some paperwork."

"Pressured?"

"No audits existed."

"Who suggested you make up an audit?" Dosantes asked.

"It was my idea. I wanted the NRC to go away."

"Who suggested you give this audit to NRC agents during their visit?" Dosantes asked.

"It was my idea," Richard repeated.

"We know you handed it to Agent Perry. Who instructed you to do so?" Dosantes asked.

"No one."

"Were Gordon or Chadwick Byrnes behind this?" Dosantes asked.

"No. I did it myself."

"Who told you to make up the audit?" Dosantes asked.

Keating interrupted, "My client answered your question, Attorney Dosantes."

"Did a corporate officer at GB Polymers order you to produce this audit and give it to federal investigators?" Dosantes asked again, despite Keating's objection.

"No. I decided on my own."

"Let's take a break," attorney Arno suggested. "Please return with your client in fifteen minutes."

Olmsted smiled to himself. Arno and Dosantes sat dazed. Richard, Keating, and Olmsted exited the room.

*****

Twenty minutes later, Richard, Keating, and Olmsted returned with coffee cups in hand.

"It took us most of the time to locate the coffee. Do you mind?" Olmsted held up his grande.

"Not at all," Arno said. "I'd like to continue. Remember, Mr. Grover, you're still under oath."

"I understand."

"After you created the audit, did you receive a reprimand in your personnel file?" Arno asked.

"No."

"Were any changes made in your job responsibilities?" Arno asked.

"No."

"Were there any repercussions from your employer for what you allege you did on your own?" Arno asked.

"No."

"Are you still the manager of quality assurance?" Arno asked.

"Yes."

"What would you have to do to be fired?" Arno asked.

Keating interrupted, "I object. That question calls for speculation."

Dosantes and Arno looked befuddled.

After a pause Olmsted asked, "Anymore questions for our client?"

"No." The Department of Justice lawyers answered, looking like they had locked themselves out of a running car.

"Please send the transcript when it's available." Barely concealing his gloating, Olmsted closed his briefcase, nodded to Arno and Dosantes, and said, "Good day, gentlemen."

When they made their way out of the room, Olmsted slapped Keating's shoulder and beamed. "Where to for a celebratory lunch, compliments of Mr. Byrnes?"

"City Club," Keating responded.

"DOJ botched this one badly," Olmsted said.

"They never saw it coming."

Chapter 61

Neil woke up from a bad dream in a tangle of sheets, trembling and fraught with memories of chase scenes, masked attackers, and intruders. He struggled to focus on the illuminated numbers of his bedside clock; a blurry 10:17 emerged. *Impossible.* With effort, he extricated himself from the twisted linens and stumbled to the bathroom. A quick glimpse in the mirror disgusted him. *I'll shave today.* Lamenting missing all the signs of his wife's unhappiness, he regretted his single-mindedness and wondered how much longer he could endure Bridget's absence.

She did not respond to his latest flower delivery, which had included a note and a request to meet for lunch, dinner, tea, or a walk—whatever she wanted. Each day he e-mailed her that he missed her and loved her and left voice messages on her cell phone. They had two cordial phone conversations but no agreement to meet.

"What's the point? You're consumed with showing that Gordon's a criminal. Your chances of winning Powerball are better," Bridget said.

Neil went to his computer and e-mailed his attorney, "*Withdraw my complaint. Notify the Labor Department. I quit.*"

When I tell Bridget this, she'll come back. In the kitchen, Neil rinsed a cup, filled it with water and two teabags and put it in the microwave. As he waited for the water to boil he looked at the filthy sight of fast-food containers, empty liquor bottles, and pizza boxes covering the countertops and overflowing the trash.

I have to get a grip and shovel this crap out of here today. He took his tea and sat in front of a silent TV. CNN Breaking News flashed across the TV screen. As he clicked off mute, a newscaster said, "Twelve minutes ago, Maryland's governor declared a general emergency at the White Marsh Nuclear Power Plant, eighteen miles north of Baltimore, and ordered a mandatory evacuation of all residents within a ten-mile radius of the plant. People living in this area need to follow evacuation routes outlined in the White Marsh Nuclear Plant safety information brochure." A map in the center of the brochure illustrating each zone in the ten-mile radius of the plant, the exit route, and assigned shelter flashed on the screen. "Those living in the ten-to thirty-five-mile radiuses of the plant should stay indoors with the windows closed and air-conditioning off until the danger has passed. Seal any gaps around doors or windows with plastic or duct tape. People beyond thirty-five miles can continue normal activities. Viewers can follow developments and learn of any changes in instructions at www.MarylandEmergencyAlert.com."

Neil clicked the volume higher. The newscaster continued: "A spokesperson for the White Marsh Nuclear Power Plant said that early indications are that the main turbine shifted at the power plant, causing breaks in the pressurized water pipes. It is possible that the turbine blades separated at high speed, cutting electrical power lines, resulting in the fire and disabling the flow of electrical current from the backup diesel generators. With pumps unable to supply cooling water to the reactor core, it overheated and vented radioactive steam into the containment dome. For some reason, unknown at this time, the containment dome experienced a breach.

We have reports of nine plant employee fatalities in the turbine building. Ambulances transferred seventeen seriously burned individuals to Johns Hopkins Hospital. Other Baltimore hospitals are on alert. We'll update as soon as we have additional information."

The news continued with pictures of chaos. Clouds of black smoke and white steam filled the sky. Vehicles clogged all lanes of Interstate Highway 95 and backed up entrance ramps for miles. An aerial view of greater Baltimore showed traffic barely moving on alternate routes. People did not heed the recommendation to stay inside; instead, they jammed the highways, making routes impassable. Police reported numerous fender benders and long lines at gas stations. The bottom of the television screen ran a message from Homeland Security: "The NRC states that all other nuclear power plants are safe. The Maryland governor deployed the National Guard to assist in the evacuation around the White Marsh plant."

After declaring a state of emergency, the governor requested all citizens in the evacuation area to remain calm and follow the utilities' mass departure guidelines. Without noting the absurdity of the appeal, the governor pleaded with people to consult the White Marsh Nuclear Plant *Safety Information Booklet*. Seven months ago, the plant mailed revised emergency procedures to all residents in a ten-mile radius of the plant. According to the directives distributed to their homes, people should head directly to a designated shelter outside of the ten-mile area.

Ignoring instructions to rendezvous with their children at assigned centers, parents descended on area schools and demanded the release of their children. Neil watched in shock as his worse fear played out on national television.

Sitting rigid in his chair, he watched the drama, and a plethora of horrific scenarios flooded his mind. He did not hear the phone but did hear Bridget's voice on the answering machine and ran to intercept her message.

"Are you watching the news?"

"Yes, unbelievable. A radiation leak at a nuclear power plant in Maryland," he answered.

"Anyone hurt?"

"Yes, fatalities and serious injuries. The situation must be out of control because they ordered an evacuation," Neil said.

"Where can thousands of people go?"

"Nowhere. All roads are blocked."

"You tried to warn them. I'm really sorry."

"Me too," Neil said. "Listen, I told Walter to withdraw my complaint with the Labor Department."

"Don't quit now. We need to talk. I have more appointments. I'll call later."

"I'll be waiting."

The television reporter explained: "The reactor, in the process of powering up, had not reached full power. We'll have a live update from the chairman of the Nuclear Regulatory Commission later. His office at the NRC headquarters in Maryland is less than sixty miles from the plant. Just in are reports of power outages at area gas stations, preventing drivers from getting fuel."

The camera cut to an Exxon station on Joppa Road in the Towson area, where a reporter interviewed a woman attempting to fill her gas tank. Lines of cars blocked highway traffic. Bedlam ruled.

"There's no power. I was behind the last person to get gas," the woman said.

The reporter continued: "The Towson area is one of many electrical blackout areas around Baltimore. The utility company continues to receive reports of outages. Motorists are pushing cars involved in accidents to the side to keep traffic flowing. At intersections where lights are out, volunteers are directing traffic. Most people are unaware of the White Marsh emergency information booklet that they are instructed to consult and follow."

Chapter 62

After reading Neil's I quit e-mail, Walter called. "What's with you? The accident in Maryland strengthens your case. I am not notifying the Labor Department to withdraw your complaint."

"Then I will."

"Listen, I took your case on a contingency and I don't get paid unless you win a settlement."

"I can't take anymore," Neil said.

"Let's meet next week. I'm booked for the next couple of days."

"There's nothing to discuss. It's over."

"We have an agreement that I expect you to honor. We'll talk next week," Walter said.

"If you insist," Neil said.

*****

The next afternoon Neil answered the doorbell and found Bridget teetering on the top step tethered to a dog straining to run free.

With a wide grin, Neil said, "I'm so happy to see you." He attempted to hug her but the yelping dog pulled Bridget backward.

"Sorry. He's pretty hyper," Bridget said.

"It's wonderful to see you," Neil shouted as he looked with distain at the unruly dog.

"Let me get him inside."

"Are you taking care of that for one of your old folks?" Neil asked.

"No." Bridget shortened the leash, struggling to maneuver the dog inside.

The dog licked Neil's hand. "Uck. Stop, dog." Neil pulled away. The dog jumped and barked.

"He wants to be your friend," Bridget explained.

"Not likely. The feeling isn't mutual, mutt. Go away."

"I've been thinking about coming back," Bridget blurted and burst into tears, dropping the leash.

Neil put his arm around her. "I've missed you very much. Things will be different. I promise."

"I feel so guilty. I'm sorry I abandoned you when you needed me the most."

"I'm the one who needs to apologize."

The dog strutted up to Bridget with Neil's shoe in its mouth.

"I probably don't need that for a job interview anytime soon," Neil joked, hiding his intense dislike of the teeth marks on his dress shoes.

"Neil, I want us to work things out."

"Me too."

Bridget walked into the kitchen. "What's been going on? It looks like college guys live here. This place is gross."

"I'll take the trash out today."

"When did this start?" She picked up a vodka bottle.

"I'm sorry about the mess. I'll clean it, I promise."

"Is this what you've been eating?" Bridget looked at the empty take-out containers.

"These have not been my best weeks."

"I'm so sorry," Bridget choked back tears. "I've never seen you so miserable. It's frightening that this battle changed our relationship like this. I'm so ashamed I left you."

"Please stop. You're not to blame for anything. We'll get through this. We'll get our lives back."

"That's what I want."

"Good. Give me time to clean the house and myself. Only kidding … you can stay right now."

"I do have a condition for coming back and living here."

"Name it."

"He comes with me." Bridget attempted to remove the shoe from the dog's mouth.

Neil gulped. He saw the determination in her eyes. He had said to himself, *whatever it takes, I'll do anything to have her return.* Begging Bridget in phone messages to come home, he had told her about his lengthy discussions with Critter Control and that he followed their advice to snake-proof their home. He never considered a dog on that whatever list. Having had a life-long aversion to cats and dogs, he did not want to share his living space with a dog.

After a lengthy pause, Neil said, "Whatever it takes, dear, I want you back."

The dog ran under a table in the living room and knocked a picture to the floor. "Its okay, Einstein, calm down." Bridget stroked the dog affectionately. "Doesn't he remind you of Doc's dog in the movie *Back to the Future*?"

"I never got close to Doc's dog."

"I thought we'd call him Einstein. What'd you think?"

An insult.

"Einstein, meet your new master."

"Hi dog." Neil greeted the pooch without emotion. "Where did you get him?"

"It was Donna's idea. I told her I felt guilty leaving you and wanted to come back but I didn't feel safe in this house. Donna insisted that a dog is the best alarm system, and she offered to help me find one."

Neil thought of several things he did not like about Bridget's friend.

"We went to the Humane Society and asked about available dogs," Bridget explained. "The staff outlined the adoption process and wanted assurances that everyone in the household wanted a dog. It never occurred to me that the purpose of pet adoption is to meet the pet's needs. When I learned of the requirement to meet you and observe your interactions with the dog, I was discouraged from proceeding. I couldn't risk it."

"But that didn't stop you." Neil laughed, appreciating his wife's gumption.

"Donna suggested Animal Control and less honesty." Bridget petted the dog. "So we went there next. I proposed a high quality, loving environment for one of their death row dogs. When I saw Einstein, he won my heart. I didn't mention you and your dislike of pets."

"Not all pets. I'm a fish guy. Fish stay in their own space. They don't invade mine. They get plenty of exercise without my having to accompany them, and I don't adjust my schedule to meet their needs. They're also quiet. And most important, fish require no cleanup. They take care of themselves. I'm not into pet cleanup at all."

"You have no fish, remember?"

"So you're saying you're back if I agree to the dog?"

"Yes."

"Let me help you bring in your things."

"Mine are at Donna's. I only have Einstein's stuff in the car."

"The dog has things?"

"I shopped at the pet store before I picked him up. Animal Control had a list of essential items for new dog owners."

At the car, Neil saw three large plastic bags. "All of this is his?" Neil hauled the bags out of the car.

"I'm surprised too. There's considerable preparation involved in creating a pet's home. Where shall we put his bed?" Bridget pulled a cushion from one of the bags.

"Does it have to be in the house? When did doghouses go out of fashion? Dogs belong outside."

"We have an agreement, remember? The kitchen's the best spot. Do you like the fabric?"

Neil ruefully looked at the denim and said, "It's fine."

"Did I tell you that Einstein's housebroken?" Bridget tossed the dog bed near the back door. "A huge bonus, I'm told."

"What I'm grateful for is that you're back." He definitely did not want to think about how the dog relieved himself, but believed he could adjust to a dog in residence better than his wife's absence.

"I picked up some food and toys." Bridget continued to unpack. She pulled out boxes labeled as nutritionally superior canine treats, cans of dog food, various sized leather bones, and soft cuddly stuffed animals. "A flying squirrel!" Bridget held up a bright orange cloth. Einstein jumped and pulled the thing from Bridget. "It's supposed to be good for his gums."

Neil looked on with disbelief.

Chapter 63

Most of the weekend their new puppy, Einstein, yipped incessantly and required an inordinate amount of attention. When Neil sat, the dog put his head on Neil's knee. He licked Neil's hand when Neil was not swift enough to pull away. Bridget, however, appreciated the Animal Control staff's description of a dog's adjustment to a new environment as stressful for all involved. Lacking rudimentary skills in pet management increased their difficulties. After two exhausting days, the chaos of a new pet frazzled all three of them. Neil hoped Bridget would renege on her thirty-day commitment with the dog. He dreaded the next day when Bridget returned to work and he would have the dog alone.

The summer sun penetrated the drapes like a photographer's lamp, and light streamed into the room where Neil slept. Einstein jumped and barked with a less than gentle wake-up call. Neil rolled over and turned his back to the dog, but Einstein persisted, grabbing the bedcovers in his mouth and tugging them off Neil.

"All right! Stop, dog," Neil shouted. He got up, took two steps, and landed on a turd. "Great." He hopped into the bathroom while Einstein jumped playfully, happy for Neil's presence.

After he cleaned his foot in the bathroom, Neil put on rubber gloves and removed three paper towels from the roll. With sufficient layers between his skin and the offending dog poop, Neil picked it up and flushed it away. Then Neil fastidiously cleaned the carpet spot while Einstein tore around the room.

Neil opened his closet and reached for a hanger with a pair of pants. As he unclipped them, Einstein grabbed a leg and pulled. Neil tugged back. The dog spread on his belly, and with a haughty look hung on to the cloth.

"Great. You have a pile of toys and you want to chew on my pants." Neil released his hold. The excited dog dragged the pants around the room. Neil took another pair from the closet and slipped into the bathroom. *I can't put my pants on in peace in my own house.*

Dressed, Neil descended the stairs to the kitchen with Einstein following. He filled a mug with tea and microwaved it to a palatable temperature. Einstein jumped at the backdoor. Finally, Neil took the leash from a hook and with difficulty, attached it to Einstein's collar. The dog jumped with excitement, bumping against Neil's legs, running in circles, and bouncing up and down.

"Okay, okay. Walk normal, dog," Neil commanded, as if Einstein could comprehend such a direction.

Neil opened the door and Einstein charged after a chipmunk, jerking Neil off the back steps.

"Take it easy, dog."

Einstein stopped at the first shrub and relieved himself. Neil felt guilty; the poor dog had needed to go outside sooner. Squeamishly, Neil turned away to provide a modicum of privacy. "What am I doing?" he grumbled.

After preliminary explorations of the grassy area in the backyard, Einstein and Neil walked the short distance to the park as they had done over the weekend. Everything interested Einstein: a scent, a squirrel, and other walkers.

"Had enough, dog? I have." They returned home. Into Einstein's bowl, Neil poured the correct amount of dog food that Bridget had left in a plastic bag. He put water in a second bowl. "I hope that's it for a while, dog. I've got things to do."

Einstein perked up and moved closer to Neil.

"Great. You think I'm talking to you. Your needs are met. Play with something in your toy collection. You're on your own."

Neil put dishes in the dishwasher and turned to exit the kitchen. Einstein whimpered.

"Don't start, dog. We're not bonding."

Neil went upstairs to his study. Einstein followed. Neil shut the door, blocking the dog's entrance but not the sound of his wailing.

Carefully, Neil maneuvered through the piles of stacked boxes to his desk. He e-mailed Walter that he had changed his plan to drop the case and told him he would press on.

Bridget's return made it easier for Neil to resume his daily ritual of rereading the latest material related to his case, but today, concentration was a challenge with the dog's demand for attention. He got up and opened the door.

"Come in," Neil said.

Immediately Einstein nuzzled against him and stopped whimpering. After moving through the maze, Einstein curled under the desk.

Neil went back to his reading. When he got up to make tea or pour a glass of water or to use the bathroom, the dog followed him. "I'm not sure about this shadowing stuff, dog. As long as you're quiet, I guess its okay." Einstein jumped and licked his hand. "That's not okay, dog." Neil jerked away.

The day passed faster than usual. Bridget returned, and together they took Einstein for a walk.

"So how'd the day go?" Bridget asked.

"The dog's very needy. He never left me alone."

Chapter 64

A week later Agent Perry contacted Neil. "How are you doing?" "Not bad. Glad I don't live anywhere near White Marsh. How did you do in the evacuation?"

"I had an assignment out of state. I heard the news on my car radio," Perry said.

"Connecticut?" Neil asked.

"Yes."

"Susan told me in her last e-mail that you two have become good friends. Connecticut has bad memories for her, so I'm happy to hear that she'll move to the DC area soon."

"I'm working on it. Susan's ideal residence is far from a nuclear power plant."

"They're hard to avoid."

"Right. I promised her that we'd live more than thirty-five miles from any plant and we'll drink bottled water." Perry continued in his mission-oriented, no nonsense style that Neil liked about him. "I'm trying to understand what happened at the White Marsh plant."

"According to news I've seen, it was no big deal," Neil said.

"I'm certain the accident at White Marsh is related to shoddy material from GB Polymers. I have specific information that they supplied basic components to that plant."

"That one and ninety others," Neil quipped.

"Right."

"Did you finally retrieve the sales information from the evidence boxes?" Neil feigned ignorance about the source of Perry's proof.

"Some time ago I gave specific documents to my boss and suggested he look more closely at the White Marsh plant," Perry said. "Even with this recent accident, he is not very involved. He asked the resident inspector to submit his analysis. I've reviewed the resident inspector's preliminary report," Perry stated.

"Is it fiction or nonfiction?" Neil asked. "I'd love to read it."

"It's not a public document. Give me your take on what triggered the radioactive release."

"I thought it was a minor blip that the backup, safety system quickly controlled. The utility described the evacuation as overkill." Neil quoted from the news.

"That's not what happened. The report stated that at about 9:20 AM the main turbine shifted. This caused a blade to break off, and it cut through electrical lines and damaged pipes that carried coolant water to the reactor."

"The turbine shifted during the powering-up process, right?" Neil asked.

"Yes."

"And you're wondering why the turbine moved?" Neil asked.

"Yes."

"I'd say the grout under the turbine shrunk. Over time, hot and cold periods weakened the grout so that the base no longer fully supported the turbine."

"That's why it moved," Perry said.

"That's what I think. And why didn't your fail-safe system contain the radiation?" Neil goaded without joy. "Aren't layers of protection built into a power plant to make last week's emergency impossible?"

"We had a false sense of security. Our system relies on the integrity of all parts."

"So now what? You have materials used in critical areas of power plants that you know can't deliver on promises of strength and heat resistance."

"That concerns me," Perry said with his signature style of understatement.

"It should. If White Marsh had been at full power when the turbine shifted, the radiation release would have rivaled Chernobyl."

"I worry about similar situations at other power plants. The NRC doesn't want to take an unpopular stance of shutting down plants and increasing energy costs. Citizens suffer when plants are off-line. Brownouts are not fun. People here don't want to sound alarmist and further decrease the public's confidence in nuclear power."

"And the reason for your call?" Neil's impatience with the NRC's inability to regulate grew.

"It will take more public pressure for the NRC to assess and correct the problems at the nuclear power plants," Perry continued. "I don't know why Senator Armstrong never called for a committee meeting. I am frustrated that in spite of my efforts my own agency has done nothing. The media will compel action. I know someone at the

Washington Post I can trust. Anonymous leaks won't work. I'll identify myself to a reporter who will not use my name in his article."

"You're going to the *Post*? I'm stunned."

"Help me explain in layman's terms the complicated technical deterioration at our power plants."

"That's not a smart career move."

"Susan's a powerful motivator," Perry said.

"Good for her."

"Give me some simple language," Perry said.

"With substandard products no fail-safe system works. My staff tested the grout by repeating cycles of heating and cooling, as would occur at a plant. It lost compressive strength and shrank. That allowed the turbine to move and shake from its base. Severed electrical lines resulted in a fire.

The fireproofing product at the next level could not contain the intense temperature. The radiation penetration shielding on the containment dome lacked the strength at high temperatures to contain the steam pressure, and the final safety system failed. That's pretty much what happened," Neil said.

"We at the NRC have been too naïve and too complacent. Media pressure will wake up the agency."

"Where is the Department of Justice with Richard?" Neil asked.

"You were so right about Richard. They blew it," Perry said.

"Blew it? How's that possible?" Neil asked.

"Legal maneuvers," Perry said.

"Lies, fake audit, and even an admission from Richard—it couldn't be clearer," Neil said.

"Gordon has good lawyers. They insisted on immunity for Richard. The Department of Justice acquiesced, wanting Gordon and Chadwick not Richard."

"Bad move. Richard needed pressure," Neil said.

"Richard never served up Gordon and Chadwick. Insisting he acted solo, he took total responsibility."

"Cunning. I warned you about him. With nothing to fear, Richard played the fall guy and landed on his feet."

"For what it's worth I did suggest that DOJ consult with you before questioning Richard," Perry said.

"Basic war tactics: Know your enemy. Don't they teach that at the naval academy?"

"They do. They're not accustomed to doing so in nonmilitary situations."

"Costly error," Neil said.

"My superior told me the NRC made a referral to the Internal Revenue Service. If GB Polymers schemed to avoid taxes, his lawyers won't easily designate a fall guy to take responsibility for that crime," Perry said.

"That should take years and further divert the real focus," Neil complained.

"How's the civil case going?" Perry changed the subject.

"We're on schedule, about ten more depositions. We have statements from coworkers that support me. Anyone with any involvement with Material Safety Data Sheets verified that I never had responsibility for sending them to customers."

"Yet Gordon and Chadwick continued to cite that as the reason for firing you," Perry said.

"Yes. My lawyer has seen OSHA's response to Chadwick's letter. After he had already fired me, he inquired about the rules. Chadwick knew, in less than a month, that there was no requirement to update MSDS every two years."

"I'm glad that case is going well. One more thing: I've contacted a navy buddy who works for the Department of Energy. I asked him about job openings for a chemist. I described your skills, and he's very interested. If it's okay, I'll forward your resume."

"It can't hurt."

"I'll be in touch."

Chapter 65

In six weeks, Neil found it hard to remember life without Einstein. He enjoyed their routine and credited his new pet with numerous beneficial changes in his life. "For a dog, you're not too bad," Neil said daily. "Most important, you brought Bridget back, so I owe you." Einstein's ears perked, basking in Neil's praise.

To tease Bridget, Neil said, "I'm glad I thought about getting a dog." Einstein's energy provided enjoyable diversions, infusing Neil with vigor. Days no longer dragged. Both Neil and Bridget liked the new routine of eating breakfast together that developed after Einstein's arrival. While Neil lacked culinary skills, he could do breakfast.

Listening to the morning news on the radio, he heard that a front-page article in the *Washington Post* exposed the NRC as lax on safety. Neil turned up the volume. According to the *Washington Post*, the agency did not do its job in protecting the public. The radio announcer said, "The problem with the White Marsh plant in the Baltimore, Maryland, area could happen at other plants across the United States. There is a risk of even more dire outcomes, according to the newspaper's source. If a similar incident happened when a nuclear power plant was at full power, the radiation release could kill tens of thousand of people."

Wanting to check out the article online and give Bridget the news, Neil started to leave the kitchen for upstairs. Einstein objected with loud barking.

"I'll take you outside first." He opened the door and let Einstein run around the backyard briefly before he attached the leash. Leading the way down the driveway, Einstein made his usual stops to sniff, snort, and pee among the flowers. As they walked on the sidewalk, a motor suddenly roared from behind Neil and struck Einstein, sending him into the air. The pickup truck dashed off down the road.

"You bastard!" Neil shrieked. He crawled the short distance to his beloved dog. Blood spurted from everywhere. Neil scooped his dog into his arms, carried his pet home, and gently set him down on the grass. Einstein was dead.

"Neil!" Bridget screamed, "What happened?"

"Someone murdered Einstein," Neil wailed. "They didn't stop." He stroked his pet and wept.

Bridget grabbed a phone and dialed 911. "Dog killed on Berkeley. Hit and run." She snatched a blanket from the closet. Neil spread the cover and carefully placed Einstein on it.

A police car stopped. "You reported a hit and run?"

"Yes," Neil said.

"Your dog?"

Neil nodded.

"I'm sorry. Tell me what happened."

"I came out of my driveway as I do every morning around this time. I heard an engine roar. A black truck accelerated like a NASCAR green flag had just dropped. The right front tire ran over my dog. Still holding the leash, I fell, and the bastard raced out of sight."

"Notice anything—a license number, any markings on the truck?"

"Four by four on the side. Like a hundred others."

"You were on the sidewalk?"

"Yes."

"Bizarre accident."

"Intentional."

"What?" the police officer asked.

"That driver targeted me."

"Deliberate?" the police officer asked.

"Absolutely," Neil said.

Bridget hugged Neil.

"I can't believe Einstein is dead," Neil moaned.

"I guess you should be grateful they didn't get both of you," the police officer said.

"Right." Bridget wiped her eyes.

They completed the police report. "Maybe we'll get lucky and someone who saw the accident will call the department. A license plate would help. Again, I'm sorry for your loss."

"Thanks," Neil said.

The officer returned to his car. Neil and Bridget sat in silence.

"I can't take anymore."

"You can't quit. You've been through too much."

"It's clear that Gordon will continue to terrorize us unless I stop. I'm calling Walter to drop the civil case. This time he won't talk me out of it."

"No way. You can't give up because your former boss hired a thug to run over your dog. That's exactly what he wants."

"I've got no fight left."

"I do. Please don't call Walter. We'll figure something out. I have to dash but I'll stop back between appointments. We'll talk later about what to do next. For now, get cleaned up."

"I love you." Neil looked down at his bloodstained clothing.

"If I had a regular job I'd call in sick. The senior citizens in my appointment book are waiting for me. I'll stop by at lunchtime."

Neil patted Einstein through the blanket. "You were so much fun. You were a good dog."

Chapter 66

In his upper eastside Manhattan apartment, attorney Olmsted brooded over the package in his mail and Landers. Maybe he was right that Gordon's company shipped inferior products to power plants. Midori's elderly relatives in Baltimore had a terrible time with the evacuation that the White Marsh plant accident caused. They now lived in fear of another flight from their home and that a future problem at the plant might be more hazardous. When she mentioned her family members' anxiety about living near the plant and their inability to relocate because of lack of finances and poor health, he actually felt remorseful and for the first time regretted that he represented the party responsible for the plant malfunctioning. Olmsted's rationalizing skills failed with this near catastrophe.

He wanted to be rid of this case. *Nothing frightened Landers. He won't quit.* As Olmsted shaved, he had an idea. He hurriedly finished and called Harris Patterson's cell phone. "I know its early Harris, but I have to speak with you," Olmsted said.

"No problem. I'm in my office," Patterson replied.

"Harris, I received threatening mail at my office yesterday afternoon."

"Threatening?"

"Copies of my e-mails to Gordon prior to Landers termination."

"Not good," Patterson said.

"And the Charlotte detective's reports."

"Damn. Who'd have them?"

"I suspect Landers, of course, but I've no idea how he could have gotten them. They're postmarked Rockville, Maryland."

"We need to end this case," Patterson said.

"What's a lawyer's worst fear?" Olmsted asked.

"That's easy—going to jail with his client."

"And what would a lawyer fear if he had an innocent client?"

"Not getting paid."

"That's our message for Landers's attorney, Walter Butler. Let him know he'll never see a dime. Mr. Byrnes is restructuring his companies and will file for bankruptcy."

"Are my fees in jeopardy?" Patterson asked.

"No. Set a date to resolve this matter. Butler needs to manage his client. There can't be a trial. It's too risky for us."

Chapter 67

Bridget's insistence that Neil continue to fight amazed him. She said the Baltimore incident scared her into returning, and if he didn't see this battle to the end there would be more disasters.

A week after their dog died, Neil spotted an overlooked toy under a chair. Unable to get rid of Einstein's possessions permanently, they packed his bed and toys and stored them in the garage. *You loved this silly bone.* He stood for four or five minutes, remembering how much Einstein enjoyed chewing the wad of cloth. "I miss you," he said aloud, wiping a tear from his eye.

Moving to his desk to work on his civil case, Neil looked under the desk where Einstein had lain for hours attentively listening to a new fact or a strategy for his case. *This is harder alone.* He opened his file of deposition questions. The phone rang.

"I just got off the phone with Patterson," Walter said. "They want to settle. We're working out the details. I insisted on a neutral setting and a third-party mediator."

"Not so fast. We need to finish the depositions. The NRC will have no case without them."

"Are you crazy? Gordon's ready to settle."

"I don't trust him and his gangster lawyers. They don't like that we subpoenaed workers. Even if we settle the labor case, I still have the civil case. I want all the depositions."

"That's ridiculous. They're a needless expense."

"I'll force the NRC commissioner to act," Neil maintained. "Our evidence nails Gordon and Chadwick Byrnes. The NRC will cite them for violations."

"Not a chance. Give it up."

"Not before I hand over the convincing evidence in a neat package," Neil insisted.

"We need to finalize a labor case. It's not our responsibility to do the NRC's job. You've helped them enough. Look what it's done for you." Walter's annoyance with Neil's reluctance was evident in his voice.

"I want the public to know the truth," Neil said.

"No one cares."

"Public censure is an appreciable penalty for Gordon's big ego. The only punishment suitable for Chadwick is prison. Don't schedule any settlement discussion until after our last deposition."

"My advice, Neil: don't continue with these costly depositions."

"I can't stop now."

"Be reasonable. You need this over. Get on with your life. Find a job. Move on. Enough already."

"I'm blacklisted, remember? With my unresolved labor case, I'm not employable."

"You will be when you settle," Walter said.

Obstinately, Neil held his ground. "I know we can gather more evidence to compel the NRC to conclude that Gordon and Chadwick committed crimes. Gordon's lawyers have run out of stall tactics. That's the only reason they'll talk settlement."

"You're irrational. You've sacrificed a chunk of your life trying to get these clowns at the NRC to do their job. How much more abuse must you endure before you're convinced this crusade to convict Gordon and Chadwick is impossible?"

"I'll make the NRC reprimand Gordon Byrnes."

"A settlement will allow you to move on with your life. Resolving the nonlabor issue is beyond our control," Walter stressed.

"It's crucial that the NRC punish crooks like Gordon and Chadwick," Neil insisted. Executives risking people's lives for profit are criminals."

"They messed up the perfect case with Richard," Walter said.

"That's why our civil case is so important. We must move forward."

"It could take years," Walter said.

"I'll get the NRC to act soon."

"The NRC suspended their investigation. No one's even working on it."

"The new NRC chair will reopen the investigation. Resolving my case will help him establish much-needed credibility."

"You're nuts," Walter said.

"I'll draft the questions for our next depositions. Schedule them."

*****

Neil believed that questioning Gordon's secretary, Doris Kingston, would support his case. Walter and Doris's attorney agreed to a time and date for her deposition. Seeing her at the table in Walter's office, Neil felt badly. Her shoulders slumped, dark blotches circled her eyes, and she did not acknowledge Neil's greeting.

Walter asked Patterson's assistant, who sat next to Doris, "Will anyone else be joining us?"

"Attorney Patterson received a phone call as we arrived. He'll be in momentarily," the assistant said.

In characteristic style, Patterson arrived looking disheveled and preoccupied.

Walter began asking his usual questions to obtain identifying information, work history, and length of time at GB Polymers. He quickly moved into the specifics of her tasks as Gordon's secretary.

"Who cancels a terminated employee's building access?" Walter asked.

"I do." Doris answered.

"Did you cancel Neil Landers's access?" Walter asked.

"I don't remember. It was a long time ago," Doris answered.

"The security company provided a log of calls. Please read the date on the highlighted line," Walter asked.

"December 22," Doris answered.

"Who is the caller?"

"Me."

"Do you usually terminate a worker's building access while still employed?" Walter asked.

"No."

"Neil Landers was fired in January. Can you explain why weeks before his termination you cancelled his access?"

"I followed Mr. Byrnes directions."

"Thank you. No more questions." Butler turned to the attorney. "Do you need a break before we question Matt Hawkins?"

"I'd appreciate fifteen minutes," the attorney responded.

Chapter 68

Walter repeated his standard background questions with Matt Hawkins. For the record, he documented Matt's work history, length of time at GB Polymers, and that his wife was Mr. Byrnes' daughter.

"Do your responsibilities include payroll?" Walter asked.

"Yes."

"Please look at these documents that we obtained in the discovery process. For the record, please read raises given to the first ten employees," Walter instructed.

"They're all 2 percent," Matt responded.

"What percent did Neil Landers receive?"

"I don't remember."

"Let me help you." Walter pointed to a line on the payroll spreadsheet.

"Eight percent," Matt read.

"Is that a large increase?"

"Yes."

"Please review this list of employees. Does anyone else even come close to 8 percent?" Walter asked.

"No," Matt answered.

"Would you say that a large pay raise is typical prior to someone's termination?" Walter asked.

"No." Matt answered.

Neil smiled.

Walter continued questioning Matt, "Where do you live Mr. Hawkins?"

"In Ballantyne."

"What direction is that from GB Polymers?" Walter asked.

"South."

"Where does Neil Landers live?"

"Dilworth."

"What direction is that from GB Polymers?" Walter asked.

"North."

"Would you pass Dilworth on your way to Ballantyne?"

"No."

"Did you say to an NRC agent that you were on your way home the night you stopped at Neil's with Gordon's letter?" Walter asked.

"I don't remember."

"Had you ever been to Neil's home prior to that December twenty-second?" Walter asked.

"No."

"Who gave you that courier job?"

"Chadwick Byrnes," Matt answered.

"Why didn't Chadwick deliver the letter?"

"I don't know."

"Doesn't he live closer to Neil?"

"Maybe."

"He lives in Morrocroft, right?" Walter asked.

"Yes."

"Which is closer to Dillworth—Ballantyne or Morrocroft?" Walter asked.

"Morrocroft."

"So you drove out of your way to Neil's home?"

"Maybe."

"How did his wife respond to finding you at her door?"

"I don't remember."

"She screamed, didn't she?"

"I don't remember."

"Your presence upset her, correct?"

"She didn't seem distressed," Matt answered.

"She thought you were bringing her terrible news about her husband," Walter said.

"I don't remember," Matt stated.

"Did you ask Mrs. Landers if Neil was meeting with the NRC that afternoon?"

"I never said anything about the NRC," Matt answered.

"No further questions." Walter gathered up his papers and walked with Neil from the deposition room. Once outside he said, "I thought that Matt would have denied ever coming to your home."

*****

Neil returned home and tossed his jacket and tie over a chair. Although the depositions did not go badly, he had hoped Doris would have been more helpful. Walter succeeded in documenting that Gordon took steps to fire Neil within hours of learning that Neil had spoken with the NRC. Matt confirmed that he came to Neil's home and spoke with Bridget. Neil concluded these statements helped his case. *I have to motivate the new NRC Chair to reopen the investigation of my termination.*

With the hope of pressuring the new NRC Chairman to do something, Neil drafted a letter to convince him that ending his case would improve his ratings. He wrote a detailed account of his case to NRC Chairman, Anthony R. Kerr, stressing the chilling effect of an employer discriminating against an employee who raises serious safety concerns.

Chapter 69

Perusing his mail, Neil's attention went to a Department of Labor envelope with a San Francisco return address. All prior DOL communications came from New York or DC. He neatly slit the envelope and stared at the news as if it read, *your mortgage is paid in full, enclosed find a clean deed for your property.*

Neil had heard that Chief Law Judge Littleton quietly exited without disgrace or any real consequences for his crimes. His sweet deal kept his pension intact and required no reimbursement to U.S. taxpayers for the public funds he misused. There was no doubt that Littleton had nefarious motives for selecting the New York Judge with a staggering backlog and a reputation for writing lengthy arguments to handle Neil's case. *Good riddance to that corrupt SOB.*

Littleton's replacement assigned a San Francisco judge to resolve Neil's complaint. The judge seemed to grasp that a file represented a real person, someone without income, someone deserving a decision in a timely manner. As he read, Neil realized the new labor judge had set a trial date for Landers versus GB Polymers. He read the sentence a second time: a trial scheduled in Charlotte in two months. Neil called Walter.

"We finally have a trail date."

"I have better news," Walter said. "Patterson called me this morning about a settlement discussion."

"Not a good time," Neil responded flippantly.

"We need to consider it," Walter said.

"What happened at the Supreme Court? Didn't Patterson announce arrogantly that their DC lawyer filed with the Supreme Court?"

"It won't take the case," Walter said. "Patterson said that two of the Byrnes companies no longer exist. It's difficult to know how much longer the rest will remain solvent. You need to settle."

"I don't like aggressive scare tactics. If it's true that two Byrnes companies have disappeared, GB Polymers is definitely not one. He'll never eliminate that company. I'm calling Patterson's bluff," Neil said.

"That's a gamble I'm not willing to take," Walter protested. "I don't want to risk not being paid."

"Let 'em sweat. I know Gordon. He'll not dissolve GB Polymers."

"It's a waste of time and money to prepare for a trial if we plan to settle. We need to negotiate right now," Walter insisted.

"I don't agree. Our message is we welcome our day in court to present evidence that shows unequivocally that Gordon and Chadwick Byrnes are criminals. We want justice," Neil asserted.

"This is not about justice … it's about money," Walter said with exasperation. "Why can't you get it? No one cares about a corrupt business. It's a big joke to think the government with no business sense can prevail against Gordon Byrnes and his slick, high-power, legal firms."

"This is not ordinary greed. They messed with nuclear power plants. Defective material is in place under the reactor core. The NRC and the Department of Justice need to dispense consequences if they hope the public will have any confidence in their ability to regulate."

"Neil, let go of the idea of bringing them to justice. Get a job and move on."

"It's not that simple. How would you respond if a powerful, wealthy bully brutalized you? Wouldn't you want to take him on? How would you feel if a well-to-do thug kept you from practicing law? How would you cope with being blacklisted? I've been in a crucible for a long time and I want out, but I'm not intimidated by these threats of bankruptcy."

Without responding to Neil's series of questions, Walter repeated matter-of-factly, "You need to end this. I can't risk a trial."

"I can. I want the facts of this case released. If I do nothing, there will be more plants with problems similar to Connecticut and Maryland. I can't live with that."

"A favorable verdict will be meaningless. Gordon's lawyers will appeal for years. I'll never be paid," Walter said.

"I know we'll settle before that San Francisco judge adjusts her watch to Eastern Standard Time. Gordon, Chadwick, and their lawyers are not prepared for trial. They have spent all their time on motions in numerous courts. Let 'em worry. I won't give in today. We drive this process. We hang tough," Neil declared.

"It's dangerous," Walter repeated.

"Proceed with the civil case," Neil said.

"Please reconsider," Walter begged.

"Ask for the personal items left in my office," Neil insisted.

"Stop asking about your junk," Walter shouted. "Gordon Byrnes trashed your useless items."

"I doubt that. I know him. He has my stuff in a box somewhere just in case it might serve some purpose for him. He wants to settle.

Make him hand over my belongings. They have sentimental meaning to me. One item is particularly special, a drawing of the American Museum of Natural History in New York City. We took my niece to the Darwin exhibit when she was in eighth grade. She drew it as a thank you note. I want it back. I've a right to have my things returned."

"We stand to lose much more than your worthless trinkets," Walter contended.

"Before any further discussion of settlement, GB Polymers must return all my personal items."

"You're crazy."

"Don't blink. Keep them waiting. Ask for my things," Neil said. "Chadwick's deposition should prove interesting. Schedule it as soon as possible. I'll draft the questions. Schedule Gordon also. When we finish the last deposition you can set a date to discuss settlement."

A trial date pleased Neil. High stakes poker had nothing on this game he played with Gordon and his battalion of lawyers.

Chapter 70

Each day that passed with no response to his letter to the NRC chairman perturbed Neil. He thought about showing up in person to rant directly to the NRC chairman about the injustices his agency inflicted on him and to ask why it took longer to litigate this case than it did for the U.S. government to build the first atomic bomb. He followed his own advice and hung tough.

Cartons of documents filled his upstairs study. More boxes were in the bedroom and at the top of the stairs. Accustomed to the disorder, he walked around the excess clutter. Neil sorted the evidence, reduced it to a manageable pile, highlighted specifics with colored tabs, and drafted a simple overview with recommendations. The synopsis of his case read like a work of fiction.

Checking the NRC Website, Neil read the agency's new chair's speeches online, filled with phrases espousing a commitment to open communication and safeguards for individuals who raised safety concerns. The new chair's ambitious schedule of meetings over the next six months started with one at headquarters in Rockville, Maryland, next week. In following weeks, he listed one in each region of the country, eight near nuclear power plants with recent negative publicity, and with pleasure Neil noted that one meeting on hazardous waste in the Carolinas would be in Charlotte.

"I'll be there," Neil said aloud. *The NRC chairman must respond to my letter. He must go on record with his conclusions.*

*****

Unable to locate Chadwick, who had moved from North Carolina, Walter scheduled Gordon Byrnes's deposition.

"Driving to Davidson is inconvenient. You're interrupting my business," Gordon said as he and Patterson entered Walter's office on the agreed day. Neil enjoyed Walter's look of amazement.

"Good afternoon, Attorney Patterson. Mr. Byrnes, please have a seat," Walter said, motioning to chairs at the opposite end of the table from the court reporter.

"I don't have a lot of time," Gordon said as he sat down.

"I'm ready to start," Walter said.

"Proceed," Patterson instructed.

"State your full name and where you are employed," Walter began.

"Gordon N. Byrnes. I'm the President and CEO of GB Polymers," Gordon replied.

"Tell me about your education."

"I went to the best college in the United States, Yale. Same place as W."

"What degree do you have?" Walter asked.

"I'm a civil engineer," Gordon replied.

"Do you have any advanced degrees?"

"I know everything that's taught in graduate school," Gordon replied. "I didn't need another degree."

"Did your company supply basic components to power plants?" Walter asked.

"Landers is a no-good troublemaker."

"You haven't answered the question."

"He's hurt my business. He deserved to be fired."

"Your client is not being responsive." Walter looked at Patterson.

Patterson remained silent.

"Mr. Byrnes, did your company supply basic components to power plants?" Walter asked again.

"Landers cost me a lot of money," Gordon said.

"Please respond to the question."

For twenty-five minutes Walter persisted. Gordon continued to ignore the question and give speeches.

"That's all," Walter ended the deposition.

After they left his office, Walter said, "I never experienced anything quite like that. Gordon Byrnes's arrogance trumps Cheney's. I'd describe former Vice President Cheney as humble and likeable compared with him."

*****

With the depositions for the civil case over, Neil and Walter went to a settlement conference requested by Gordon's lawyers. The presiding judge introduced himself as semi-retired after a career with the Department of Labor. Attorney Harris Patterson explained that his client, Gordon Byrnes, was available by phone. Walter Butler introduced himself and Neil.

The judge outlined the procedure. "Mr. Landers, this process is informal. While I listen to the attorneys from both sides regarding your wrongful termination, I would like you to sit outside and wait. After I've heard the facts of the case I'll make a recommendation."

Neil liked his warm, old-fashion style. He exited to a bench in the hall. After about an hour, the Judge called Neil back into the meeting room.

"I've heard from attorney Butler and attorney Patterson," the judge explained. "I'm pleased that both sides want to resolve this matter. GB Polymers proposes a $100,000 settlement. Payments will be made over a two-year period."

"I'll not consider anything over time, your honor." Neil stated. "That pitiful amount is not acceptable."

"Do you have a counter offer?" the judge asked.

"Another zero," Neil replied. "For a million dollars, I'll withdraw my complaint. This matter obstructed my ability to work in my field. I've incurred considerable legal expense. I'll accept a million as fair compensation."

"May I phone Mr. Byrnes, your honor?" Patterson asked.

"Yes, please," the judge said.

Neil and Walter sat quietly waiting for Patterson to return. Neil thought Patterson looked relieved that he had not asked for more.

Ten minutes passed and Patterson had not returned. Butler exchanged some banter with the judge.

Patterson walked back into the room. Neil instantly knew that there was no deal. *A lousy poker player.*

"My client remains firm with his original offer," Patterson said.

"I withdraw mine," Neil said. "If this goes beyond today it will cost Mr. Byrnes more." He stood. "Let's go," he said to Walter.

"Thank you for your time," Walter said to the judge as they exited.

"Gordon is not rational," Neil said once they were outside.

"This is a disaster. You've made it worse with your ridiculous request for a million and then walking out like a hot head," Walter said.

"I'm sick of being pushed around. Did you think I should agree to payments over time?"

"No, that was outrageous," Walter said. "A better counter from us would have been less than a million. If you had let me speak I would have suggested something more realistic."

*****

Neil pulled into the driveway behind Bridget. She jumped from her car and came over to Neil. "How did it go?"

"A complete waste of time, total farce," Neil said. "Gordon's not serious. Walter's mad at me."

"Didn't you say he's scared he won't get paid?" Bridget asked.

"Yeah, he keeps mentioning that," Neil said.

"He's definitely no Atticus Finch," Bridget said.

"I'm worried he'll fold too fast," Neil said.

"He can't believe what he's up against," Bridget said.

"I can't either," he said.

"What's next?" Bridget asked.

"Tomorrow night I'm face-to-face with the NRC commissioner," Neil said.

*****

Neil showed his photo identification and signed in as a visitor at the Government Center in uptown. The receptionist directed him to a second floor room for the public meeting.

He selected a front row seat with an excellent view of the podium. Staff prepared the room and made final checks on the microphones. As they scrutinized attendees already in the room, Neil scribbled notes in a spiral-bound notebook, looking purposeful. Waiting for the meeting to begin, he scrawled illegible fragments of conversation, capturing, as best he could, the informal banter of those in the room. Drawing chaotic lines on the page, he sketched the room and succeeded in calming down.

Noticing people stopping at a table of handouts, Neil went over and gathered slick paper brochures with information on hazardous waste in the Carolinas. As he read, he thought the scientific information was weak.

The chairman entered, looking older than Neil expected. He wore a conservative well-tailored dark suit, the apparent uniform of government officials.

With most seats in the room occupied, the chairman began the meeting on time. Throughout the presentation, Neil took notes and frequently glanced at the sentences he hoped to utter. Neil reread his timeline of contacts with the NRC. Although the agency had prioritized his allegation as code red within a month of Neil's phone call, almost two years later, it languished.

On the chronology of his case, he highlighted in yellow the numerals for the anniversary of his first contact with the NRC. Next to the July eighteenth date, he inserted *no decision; case pending.*

When the meeting ended, the chair walked away from the speakers' platform. Neil approached him saying, "Congratulations on your new position with this important agency."

"Thank you." He slowed his step.

"I'm Neil Landers. I'd like to help you with your goal to protect workers on the front lines in the nuclear industry. I believe you said the NRC must create an open, honest environment for communication without fear of reprisal."

"Absolutely, we need many eyes and ears to carry out our mission," the chairman said.

"The NRC has an open case concerning my wrongful termination. It's mired in procedural confusion, legal stonewalling, and administrative indifference," Neil said in a non-threatening tone. "I recently wrote and asked for closure. Here's a copy of that letter and a timeline of my case."

The chairman tactfully listened and ignored his staff members preparing to create a barrier between himself and Neil.

"My case didn't occur on your watch." Neil continued, "I'd very much appreciate your reading my brief summary. I hope you'll act on my behalf."

"I'll read this," the chairman said, accepting Neil's papers.

"Thank you. I'll be at the public meeting on plutonium processing in South Carolina next month," Neil said. "I look forward to seeing you again."

Neil did not wait long for a response from the new chairman of the NRC. A week later, a letter arrived, informing Neil that the NRC would conclude his case as soon as possible.

"He doesn't want to see you at another meeting," Bridget joked when she read the letter.

The NRC chairman wrote, "I've assigned Mr. Doug Cole, a senior investigator in our Pennsylvania office. I've charged him to report his findings to me in a month's time."

"Another investigator from another region!" Bridget shouted.

"One with a deadline," Neil added. "You have to agree that's different."

"You've done this investigator's job," Bridget said. "It's very simple. It'll take minutes to assess and not much longer to write a report."

"I'll not give up until the government hits Gordon Byrnes where it matters—in the tender area of his psyche where he files his reputation, his strange version of being an upright citizen, and all the noble trappings he believes the Byrnes family name triggers," Neil proclaimed. "That's the real assignment for the new investigator."

Chapter 71

Neil juggled groceries onto the kitchen counter as the phone rang. "I'm Doug Cole from the NRC. I'm assigned to finish your case."

"Nice to hear from you," Neil said.

"It's embarrassing that your former employer's legal aggression stopped any NRC action," Cole said. "You got a bum deal."

"That's the truth," Neil said, surprised at the investigator's candor.

"How soon can we meet?" the investigator asked.

"Name a time and place. I'll be there."

They agreed to meet at the Centre City Marriott. Neil selected paperwork to bring with him. He stapled a summary. He inserted color-coded, Post-it tabs on the documents. He had a simple presentation of willful wrongdoing.

*****

Neil knew the drill. He showed up in the Marriott lobby and called Cole on a hotel phone to learn the location for their meeting. When he knocked at Cole's room, an average-looking guy about fifty years old opened the door.

"Agent Doug Cole," he said, extending his hand to Neil. "Come on in."

"Neil Landers. Pleased to meet you," Neil responded.

"What you got?" Cole asked, looking at Neil's folders.

"A scaled-down version of Landers versus GB Polymers," Neil answered.

"Good. I heard the NRC took hundreds of boxes of evidence in a raid," Cole said.

"That was months before I was fired. They have obtained very little since. But the worst is that no one at the NRC has put together the case," Neil said.

"Looks like you have," Cole said. "Let's have it."

Neil gave Cole a quick summary and handed him a written synopsis with an overview of GB Polymers's legal schemes and tactics.

"Were the lawyers on the scene before you were terminated?" Cole asked.

"Definitely—they helped Gordon and Chadwick fabricate a reason to fire me," Neil said.

"That's illegal," Cole said.

"Right. My civil case depositions have critical evidence. They show I was terminated for calling the NRC."

"I'll subpoena the CEO, Gordon Byrnes, for documents," Cole said.

"Please don't. Instead, subpoena me for the depositions in my civil case. That will give you everything you need."

"I guess that would work," Cole said.

"Any subpoena to Gordon would hinder finalizing this case. His lawyers will pick at every word and argue that Gordon does not have to comply."

"I have a deadline. I can't have a delay. I'll go with your strategy."

"Thank you," Neil said.

"Expect my subpoena, and thanks for coming by tonight."

Neil drove home confident that Cole would show that his former company and its corporate officers willfully discriminated against him and that his report to the chair of the Nuclear Regulatory Commission would trigger the necessary referral to the Office of Enforcement. At last, he thought, there would be an end to his open case and appropriate penalties.

Chapter 72

Attorney Patterson in Charlotte called Olmsted in New York to deliver an urgent message. "NRC agent Cole informed me this morning that he's the current investigator on the Landers case. He asked to speak with Gordon and Chadwick," Patterson said.

"Tell him they're not available," Olmsted responded instinctively. "Have him send something in writing requesting exactly what he wants from them. Give me his number. I'll call him myself."

"Before you do that we need to convince Mr. Byrnes to settle with Landers. He still balks at paying Landers anything. Investigator Cole could be trouble for us," Patterson said. "He mentioned that he reviewed documents indicating we participated in firing Landers."

"Oh, God we need to end this case now," Olmsted said. "The NRC may have our e-mails. Do you think Landers will take two hundred thousand?"

"Absolutely not," Patterson said. "He insisted on a million when we first talked settlement. His lawyer would go for less but Landers is in charge."

"Great, I'll figure out how to get Gordon to pay more. Meanwhile I'll call the NRC," Olmsted said. "I'll get back to you."

Agent Cole answered Olmsted's call to the NRC Pennsylvania office.

"I'm Jeremiah Olmsted, chief counsel for GB Polymers. Mr. Cole, please send in writing to my attention what you want from my client. I'll give you my address."

"I have your address but I don't need more papers," Cole said. "As a courtesy I called attorney Patterson to extend an invitation to your clients, Gordon and Chadwick Byrnes, to speak with me before I submit my written report. I know they discriminated against Neil Landers."

"How can you conclude that? You have no proof."

"I have twenty-seven depositions of GB Polymers's workers, including Gordon Byrnes," Cole replied.

"Where did you get employee depositions?" Olmsted asked, aware of sweat in his hands. "They were sealed."

"The NRC subpoenaed Neil Landers and ordered him to hand over his certified copies of the depositions. Mr. Landers complied promptly."

"My clients have no need to speak with you."

"One more thing, Mr. Olmsted," Cole said. "You know that it's illegal for an attorney to assist in the firing of a protected employee."

"Good-bye!" Olmsted said and hung up the phone. *I'll be damned if I'll go to jail for Gordon Byrnes.*

*****

Midori gave Olmsted the message that the NRC, via Agent Perry, requested Olmsted's preference for accepting delivery of the NRC decision in the matter of Mr. Landers's termination. Perry's call shocked Olmsted. *That investigator Cole acted fast.* Planning to meet at his Park Avenue office, he started to call back and realized he still had the unpleasant task of telling Gordon, so he decided on scheduling the appointment in Charlotte.

Damn those depositions.

"Agent Perry," Olmsted said. "Please deliver your communication to GB Polymers's corporate headquarters in Charlotte. Tell me the date and time and I'll be there with Mr. Byrnes."

Olmsted dreaded calling Gordon. The legal fees for the Landers's matter had already cost Gordon over two million dollars. Olmsted had no doubt that the NRC decision favored Landers.

He picked up the phone and dialed GB Polymers. "Hi Doris, may I speak with Mr. Byrnes?"

"Certainly."

"Jeremiah, how's the big city?" Gordon asked in a booming voice.

"Busy as usual. Mr. Byrnes, there is a serious risk of negative publicity if this situation with Landers does not end. It is in your best interest to settle. If we go to trial, it will be very public. I can't seal those court proceedings from the media."

"I don't want my good name trashed in the news by idiot reporters," Gordon said. "Make sure that doesn't happen."

"An NRC agent will be at your office next week. It would be better if you and Mr. Landers have come to an agreement."

"I want him gone," Gordon said. "The government's persistent meddling in my business is shameful."

"With your permission, I'll get rid of Landers," Olmsted said. "I'm advising you to send a check payable to attorney Walter Butler's firm for four hundred thousand dollars."

"I don't want to pay Landers anything," Gordon yelled.

"Trust me, he'll only receive a pittance," Olmsted said. "I'll get attorney Butler to agree to accept your check. That provides you with more privacy. There will be no paper trail of a payment to Landers from you."

"And Landers doesn't get all the money?" Gordon asked.

"He'll get very little," Olmsted said. "Better yet, he'll go away."

"If that's my only option, go with it," Gordon said.

"I plan to be in Charlotte for your appointment with the NRC next Wednesday at one thirty."

"Can you get here before noon?" Gordon asked. "We'll go to lunch first."

He's expecting something good. He wants to go out to lunch as if all is well. "My flight lands at ten-thirty. I'll take a cab to your office," Olmsted said.

Next, Olmsted called Walter. "I'm filing today to dissolve GB Polymers, Inc. As you well know this is an easy process that will not take long. Once complete, you forfeit any chance of receiving your fee in the Landers case. As a professional courtesy, I'm calling you with a final offer. Mr. Byrnes is prepared to issue a $400,000 check to your law firm. You can deduct your fees and expenses and pay Landers from your account. My client wants total confidentiality. He'll not issue any payment directly to Landers. The check can be in your office this afternoon."

"I need to speak with my client," Walter said.

"Yes or no, right now. This is our last proposal," Olmsted said. "You understand the risks, your client does not—a check to your law firm today."

"Neil has already said he won't accept less than one million," Walter said.

"$400,000 or nothing, make a decision," Olmsted insisted.

"Send the check."

*****

After rehearsing several lines, Walter decided on a direct approach. He called Neil.

"It's over. Gordon's issuing a check today."

"He agreed to a million?" Neil asked startled.

"No. Olmsted drew up the paperwork to dissolve GB Polymers. As a favor he agreed to issue a $400,000 check today while the company is still viable," Walter said.

"An act of kindness from Olmsted … in exchange for what?" Neil asked.

"Ending your labor complaint and civil suit," Walter said.

"No way. I might withdraw the labor complaint but I'm not ending the civil suit."

"We have to. There's no alternative."

"What's my net from this check?" Neil asked.

"Two-thirds is yours. I'll deduct expenses for phone, mailings, and all the direct costs for the depositions."

"Any tax liability?" Neil asked.

"State and federal taxes, of course. Count on about $150,000."

"That's not acceptable. Olmsted is desperate to avoid a trial. You wasted our leverage."

"We had no choice. Stop by Friday. Oh, and a box with your things arrived at my office this morning."

"Is the drawing of the American Museum of Natural History intact?" Neil asked.

"Yes."

Chapter 73

When Olmsted arrived at GB Polymers, Gordon said, "Doris made reservations at the Tavern, Jeremiah. Their special chowder is on the menu today. You'll like it."

Olmsted did not have food on his mind. He remembered his phone call with Cole implying that Olmsted broke the law when he advised Gordon on firing Neil.

While Gordon enjoyed his lunch, Olmsted avoided the chowder and hoped the queasiness in his stomach stopped soon.

Back at Gordon's office, Olmsted dreaded the NRC agent's arrival.

"You're sure I have to let the government into my building again?" Gordon asked.

"Yes." Olmsted sat stiffly across the desk from his client.

Gordon's phone rang. "Mr. Randolph Perry is in the waiting area," Doris announced.

"The government's impossible. It never quits," Gordon said. "Threaten them with a suit for defamation of character. Stop them from bothering me."

"Stay calm, Mr. Byrnes. Let me do the talking," Olmsted said. "Doris, we're ready."

Olmsted regretted that the short agent delivered the news. Gordon had many quirks, and his dislike of short people was huge, not to mention irrational. He evaluated all people as to how similar they were to him. Agent Perry epitomized Gordon's extreme opposite.

"Mr. Olmsted, Mr. Byrnes, I have a letter from the director of the Office of Nuclear Reactor Regulation," Perry said. "The NRC formally cited both Gordon Byrnes and Chadwick Byrnes personally for firing Neil Landers."

Cutting Perry off, Gordon yelled something unintelligible.

Robot-like, Perry continued, "You and all your various companies are banned from selling to the nuclear industry. The Nuclear Regulatory Commission determined that you failed to adhere to the requirements of 10 CFR 50.7, which prohibits discrimination against employees for engaging in protected activities. This violation has been categorized as the most severe under NRC enforcement guidelines."

Grabbing the paper, Gordon stopped Perry's recitation. Perry stepped back. Gordon trembled, swayed, and tumbled into his chair shouting, "This is an outrage."

"Stay calm, Mr. Byrnes," Olmsted approached him.

"This citation, Mr. Byrnes, will be posted on the NRC Website," Perry said as if he were conferring an award. "The NRC will send a press release to all news services today."

Gordon opened and closed his fingers and rocked in his chair, discharging rapid, noisy breaths. Still rocking, his face contorted and his eyes protruded. Olmsted moved to the doorway to get Doris's attention and assistance. Gordon Byrnes continued his bizarre movements and sounds, oblivious to his surroundings. Olmsted watched speechless and powerless. Doris came into the room, and seeing her boss's agitation grasped the seriousness and called 911.

"Mr. Byrnes, please calm down," Olmsted begged.

Three emergency medical service technicians and two Charlotte police officers arrived. At the sight of uniform-clad people, Gordon sprang at them, flailing his arms and shouting, "Leave me alone. I've done nothing wrong. The government conspired against me. I don't deserve to go to jail."

"Mr. Byrnes, please calm down," Olmsted pleaded again. "No one is taking you to jail."

"I've done nothing wrong," Gordon repeated. "I paid you hundreds of thousands of dollars. You're a lousy lawyer," Gordon said to Olmsted. Scattering the cruise brochures on his desk to the floor, he picked up a clock and threw it, barely missing Olmsted's left shoulder. Infuriated, Gordon grabbed his pen set with a marble base and heaved that into Olmsted's chest. Olmsted doubled over, grabbing a chair for balance.

An EMT took a step forward. "Get away from me," Gordon roared. He swung. The technician dodged. "Get out of my office. I'll have you arrested for trespassing." Gordon's next punch hit a technician. "Get out of here."

The lead EMT person nodded to the others, and like an ensemble dance troupe each moved into a predetermined position, prepared to act their part. One man caught Gordon's right wrist, pinned his arm, and with his body immobilized Gordon's right leg. Simultaneously, another technician secured Gordon's left arm and leg. "I'll kill you," Gordon screeched.

Continuing to protest vigorously, Gordon shouted at his lawyer, "I want my money back." To everyone in the room he again threatened, "I'll kill you."

He continued to fight as the EMT struggled to hold him. The EMT staff acted in accordance with their training and safely brought him to the floor. Restrained face down, he was eye to eye with the eagle on his carpet.

"I'll sue you," Gordon bellowed. "You'll pay for this."

"We're taking him to the psychiatric emergency room," the lead EMT said, looking at Olmsted.

Chapter 74

Bridget came home earlier than usual.

"Finished for the day?" Neil asked.

"Yes. I had a cancellation."

"Great. You're a welcome distraction from my ponderings of legal matters," he said, hugging her. "Walter settled. It's over."

"You don't sound pleased," Bridget said.

"He panicked and folded too soon. Walter sold out."

"Not without his fee, I'm sure."

"You said he's no Atticus Finch. You had that right."

"If it's really over and we can move on, that's marvelous," Bridget said.

"The amount's not fair."

"The money's irrelevant. We'll have a life again. Let's walk and talk."

"Lead the way."

They headed down the street to the park.

"Remember our introduction to Charlotte?" Bridget asked.

"We loved the first class flight, the comfortable hotel suite, and the lavish meals," Neil said. "Gordon treated us well that whirlwind weekend. By Sunday evening we had mentally migrated south."

"We found the city so clean and attractive," Bridget said.

"All the newness bugged me," Neil chuckled.

"I thought we'd be here for decades."

"It's been a learning experience," Neil said.

"You were so excited about playing with your new gadget, that expensive microscope."

"Yeah, that was almost as much fun as my first chemistry set," Neil said. "I've paid a high price for that adventure."

"How different things are now."

"Now that my case is finished, we're out of here," Neil said.

"I'm happy this nightmare is over."

"I wish I had a definite job offer," Neil said.

"You'll get something," Bridget said.

"This settlement improves my prospects. I'm anxious to get back to work."

"We'll start over wherever," Bridget said. "My work is portable."

"I'll go anywhere to work," Neil said. "That is, of course, if you'll go with me."

"You're stuck with me." She took his arm.

They returned home to a blinking light on their answering machine.

"Two messages." Neil hit play.

"Captain, major meltdown on Fairview Road this afternoon. Call me. Spock," Tom said on Neil's voice mail.

"Message two," the machine's robot voice announced, "Mr. Landers, I'm with the Department of Energy, please call me." He left his name, number, and extension.

"Tom sounds excited," Bridget said. "I wonder what's up."

"Department of Energy ... that's fascinating," Neil said.

"I'm more curious about Tom's message. Call him."

Neil called Tom's cell. "Spock, I don't like to bother you at work but you sounded anxious for me to call."

"Captain, there's not much work getting done. It's a challenge for me to keep up with the drama. Let me tell you about today, uh ... the last hour."

As soon as Tom began talking, Neil motioned to Bridget to pick up the extension. Together they listened to a complete report of Mr. Gordon Byrnes's psychotic break and humiliating exit from his corporate office.

"Medics tied him to a stretcher. He thrashed and screamed as they carried him out the front door. They took him to Charlotte Medical Center's psychiatric emergency room," Tom reported.

"God help the medical staff," Bridget said.

"Carted off to the psych ward ... unbelievable," Neil said.

"It was a sight, captain. Sorry you missed it."

"Thanks, Spock." Neil hung up the phone. He smiled at his grandparents' wedding photo, remembering that the war took his grandfather's life, leaving his grandmother with a young son, and she always said, "It had to be done—the Nazis had to be stopped."

"I'm calling that man at the Department of Energy."

Neil could not believe what he heard. "NRC Agent Perry recommended you for a job with our agency. We have an opening for a chemist to work with our design team on penetration closures for nuclear waste. I'd like to set up a time to discuss the project."

Neil dropped the phone. He bent to pick it up and fell over. Bridget retrieved the phone and put it to Neil's ear. "Sorry about that," Neil said. Sitting on the floor, he finished the call.

"Agent Perry spoke highly of your qualifications. We'd like to meet you as soon as possible to discuss the details."

"Can I call you tomorrow?" Neil asked.

"What's that about?" Bridget asked.

"The Department of Energy wants to talk about a job."

"And you said you'd call tomorrow," Bridget laughed.

"Yeah," Neil said with a wide grin."

The phone rang again. It was Perry.

"I heard you were in Charlotte," Neil said.

"You found out fast. I wished you could have been with me but it would have been against regulations to invite you."

"And we know you're a letter of the law man," Neil joked.

"It was unbelievable."

"I got a good description."

"Surprisingly, we've not been able to locate Chadwick Byrnes to officially serve him a notice. The NRC personally cited him also."

"That sounds like Chadwick. He's untouchable for the violent attacks on me but the posted memo that ordered co-workers not to talk with me nails him. And he knows it. Chadwick masterminded the marketing plan that targeted the nuclear industry and he let his father take all the blame. Nice guy."

"He's disappeared," Perry said.

"Thanks for the Department of Energy recommendation," Neil said. "They want to talk with me."

"Great. Susan Ridel will be very happy to learn you have a possible job offer. On a personal note, I hope that you and Bridget will save the day after Thanksgiving to celebrate our wedding."

"Great news! Congratulations!"

Neil called Walter. "Did you hear that the NRC finally acted?"

"What do you mean?"

"They cited Gordon personally in his office today."

"You're kidding."

"We gave up too soon. I told you the new chair would seize the opportunity to build credibility. Olmsted's sleaze tactics worked. He intimidated you. We had all the leverage and you didn't use it."

"Some money is better than no money. Byrnes's lawyers would have spun this out for years."

"I'll be by Friday to collect my box and the check."

Chapter 75

At six o'clock the next morning, Neil logged on to the *Washington Post* Website. He loved the headline: "CEO of Charlotte Company Guilty of Wrongful Termination." The article stated that the NRC concluded GB Polymers fired Neil Landers, director of research, for bringing safety concerns to the NRC. It summarized the legal shenanigans that delayed a decision in this matter until now. CEO Gordon Byrnes was not available for comment. The article stated that medics took him from his office to Charlotte Medical Center. According to the reporter, Mr. Byrnes' doctor admitted him to a psychiatric hospital yesterday for observation. Family members declined comment.

"Bridget, you've got to see this," Neil called. She looked over his shoulder at the computer screen and read along with him.

"How do we get a copy of this? I want the entire paper."

"I'll order one."

"Will it be in the *Charlotte Observer* also?" Bridget asked.

"Definitely. Let's go."

They headed out to purchase their local newspaper. They bought four.

Later that morning Neil received a phone call from Boston.

"Congratulations, Neil. I'm Bill Nevins, the executive vice president of the Union of Concerned Scientists. We're a nonprofit science advocacy group."

"I'm aware of UCS and its commitment to a healthy environment," Neil said.

"I just read the *Washington Post* article. I'm happy to see the NRC cited your former employer," Nevins said.

"Me too."

"We could use your help. Would you entertain working with us?"

"I'm very interested in your organization," Neil said.

"I hoped you'd say that," Nevins said. "The NRC has not properly addressed the questionable material in place at numerous nuclear power plants. The hot and cold cycling theory has merit."

"We know the utilities will not do anything without pressure," Neil said. "The Union of Concerned Scientists could help compel further inspections and analysis."

"When can you come to Boston?" Nevins asked.

"First, I'm interviewing with the Department of Energy. The possibility of working with the scientists on securing forty years of radioactive waste from a hundred nuclear reactors into safe geological repositories makes sense. Even if I accept a position with the Department of Energy, I will volunteer with the Union of Concerned Scientists. I'm finished making money for corporations that practice five-star greed."

Epilogue

GB Polymers, Inc. declared bankruptcy.

Gordon Byrnes was ruled mentally incompetent to stand trial. He resides in a skilled nursing facility. He spends his days mumbling, "bastards, lousy lawyers, the government did me wrong."

Chadwick Byrnes's whereabouts are unknown.

Richard Grover relocated to Grenada. It is not clear what he does for a living.

Chemist Tom Jameson is a research botanist at the University of North Carolina.

Randolph Perry and Susan Ridel are happily married and reside in Rockville, Maryland.

Attorney Walter Butler has a small law practice in Davidson, North Carolina.

Attorney Jeremiah Olmsted had a fatal heart attack while vacationing with Midori in South Beach, Florida.

Attorney Glen Fuller is still dreaming about having a case to argue before the U.S. Supreme Court. He writes articles on military buttons.

Attorney Harris Patterson practices law in Charlotte, North Carolina. His clients either are in jail or out on bail.

Neil and Bridget Landers are still together. Neil is employed by the U.S. Department of Energy. He splits his time between Washington DC and Boston, where he volunteers for the Union of Concerned Scientists.

Bridget Landers expanded her social work practice to include guest lecturing and training programs for healthcare professionals on the psychological impact of unemployment. She is also an active member of the Sierra Club.

Bio

Margaret teaches exceptional children in the Charlotte Mecklenburg School System. Her writing includes fiction and documenting life stories of family ancestors; particularly the colorful characters in the tree. She lives in Charlotte, North Carolina with her husband, Edward.

She is a member of the ASTM, an industry standard setting organization, the Union of Concerned Scientists, North Carolina Writers' Network, Charlotte Writers Club and The Sierra Club.

In her first novel, Cahill renders a unique twist to the classic story of bullying. An employer treats workers like fossil fuel to burn for the benefit of the bottom line. Her understanding of the workplace infuses her story with realism and humor.